SHADOW OF INNOCENCE

BOOK FOUR

SARAH HOAD

authorHOUSE®

AuthorHouse™
1663 Liberty Drive
Bloomington, IN 47403
www.authorhouse.com
Phone: 1-800-839-8640

Published by AuthorHouse   05/25/2012

ISBN: 978-1-4685-0469-9 (sc)
ISBN: 978-1-4685-0470-5 (e)

Despite My Family

The ever after

Days fade into memories,
as swift and painless as waves clashing upon a stream.
The life we hoped to have lived looks not but a distant dream.
The end seems close but not as near as desired.
Gone is a lasting breath within this moment,
seemingly raw and misleadingly irrelevant.
Each wish twists to nightmare and each fear surfaces as reality spins out
of control.
This is the final showdown, the tainted goodbye, the endgame.

By Steff Duncan

PROLOGUE

Strings of pain shot down her legs, causing her knees to become weak and forcing her to the ground. Her sickly thin, childlike frame fluttered to the ground, rolling over on the thick grass. Her large golden-brown eyes shut, trying to hide the flood of tears. She rolled over again, trying to force away the pain. She waited for her legs to feel alive, her soul to want to live. No hope.

Blonde wild hair fell over her pale face as she struggled. Her hands clutched at her stomach. She tried to call out but there was a dry lump in her throat, preventing any sound to escape her lips. Straightening her arms out, she arched her back, peering around the clearing in the woods.

The pounding of hunting boots echoed through the forest floor. The sound of tall strong bodies brushed through the shrubs, cutting their way to their prey. Men's voices were bouncing off the tall evergreen, while villagers ran through the woods, hunting . . . hunting her.

"Find her!" a hunter yelled. The man's voice caused the birds to shoot through the trees.

"Kill her!" another echoed.

Her blood ran cold, her heart raced with fear striking at her mind, her soul. She could not run, could not move, she was left for dead. What was happening? Her body screamed at her mind. The girl brought herself to tears, growing weaker with every passing second.

She gathered what strength she did have left to roll beneath the bushes, not far from her feet. Pulling the cover of the bushes over her head, she hid behind them. Inserting her fingers through the branches to created a hole which she could peer from waiting, watching.

She had never considered herself to have had a tragic life. It hadn't been all that bad until a few years ago when her mother remarried. She was still unsure what she did or said to have a hunting party after her. She was the only child from her beautiful mother whom every one had loved. But then she was locked away and left to get sick, slowly becoming a stranger to the small community.

She had always been a good girl, even when her stepfather moved in. She gave him no reason to hate her. But then he had turned everyone against her, a small child that he secretly desired for himself. He had done horrible things, unspeakable things and when she cried to her mother, she was punished. It was only so long before she was locked away for good and that was when she started to get sick. Strange things started to happen, unspoken things crowded her mind. The town's people started to talk and an up roar broke out.

"She is insane!"

"The child has been possessed by the devil!"

"She must be sacrificed so we can live in peace!"

These same cries had woken her last night. Using all the energy she had, she ran from her home. Overhearing the townspeople complain that the poison her mother had been giving her had not had the desired affect. Ever since that hour, she had been on the run to save her recently tortured life. Poison! Her mind screamed. That was what wrong with her. Why had she not understood earlier? She was poisoned! But deep down she already knew that, didn't she? She felt a sudden strange stir within her. Suddenly finding the recent events amusing, a small smirk spread across her lips.

Unconscious of her actions, she rose to her feet, heading back into the center of the clearing. Her body moving as her mind fell blank but she remained standing. Her legs apart in an attack posture, her white night gown was shredded and to her ankles. Her dark eyes were wild, staring at the path she had come down not that long ago. Her snow blonde hair was wildly flapping in the breeze, whipping around her small body.

"In the clearing!" a hunter directed. She smiled. Good, they had found her.

Several cries echoed as the pounding of hunting boots pressed down the path, weapons rattling in their strong hands. The blonde twisted her head to one side, running one hand down her small body. She flicked her tongue over her teeth. In seconds the hunters burst into the clearing, knives and spears gripped tightly in their hands. The group of men was at first taken aback by the sight of her, standing in the clearing with a crazed look about her.

"She has lost her spirit completely. The devil has taken over!" one man cried out.

A few other men started to back up, sliding back through the path in the woods.

"Kill her! But beware of the demon! Kill her!" her stepfather ordered. His spear raised in the air.

"Oh kill me?" she laughed. "Yes let's kill me." She shook her long hair, drawing the ribbons on her night gown and stepping out of it.

The men continued to stare at her, a few closer to the path turned to flee down it.

"Don't be afraid, it is still mortal, it can be killed!" her stepfather yelled, panic in his voice as he tried to convince himself more than his crowd.

"Can I?" she asked, watching as more of the hunting party disappeared.

The group cried out, rushing at her, their weapons held out in front of them. She remained were she was as the men drew closer. One man ran his spear past her, the blade clipping her arm. Another threw his knife embedding into her upper chest next to her shoulder blade, her body jolted with the impact. But she would not fall, they would not win. They were the enemy, not her.

The men smiled at the wounded child, blood trickling down her naked body. However she just grinned back, her head arching. She flicked her tongue, causing a clicking sound on the roof of her mouth. Some of the hunters stopped, fear ripped through their eyes at the unholy sight. More of the hunting party turned and ran back to the safety of their village.

Her stepfather threw his spear at her, the blade sliding past her head. The handle knocking her to the ground, her eyes starting to flicker back. The darkness that had settled in moments ago had now ceased. The events played in front of her, coming to sight. She stared down at her body in shock. She was naked, wounded and puzzled. How had this happened? Great amounts of pain flooded in, causing her to hunch to her side. She was already weakened by the poison but this was unbearable. She glanced over at the bushes, wondering how she had ended up in the clearing . . . the clearing that was holding the hunters.

She screamed, trying to cover her body with her hand. Where was her night gown? The men were now smiling; their weapons rose once more as they crept in on her. Her stepfather leading them, she glared at him. How could he? Why were they doing this? Questions rolled through her crazy mind as she tried to scramble to the bushes. She tried to escape her unfairly written fate.

"Here." Someone spoke behind her, ripping at her arm and pulling her into the bushes.

She turned to her rescuer, a handsome man. He stood over her, handing her his long black cloak. His skin was as pale as hers. His hair was as black as the cloak that had covered his toned frame. He stood tall over her wounded body, a thin smile on his lips as his dark eyes twinkled with wonder. Scooping her up in his arms, he ran from the clearing to a small stream, where he mopped the blood from her body. She watched his face as he cleaned her up. His strong hands were soft and caring against her burning skin. She could see by his reaction that she was going to die.

"Farewell until next time, my sweet," he whispered.

Closing her eyes for what seemed like a few minutes. She was shocked to find that when she reopened them, the stranger was gone and was replaced by the small group of hunters. Was it all a dream? What was going on in her head? All the voices and memories were driving her insane. The men were smiling as one by one they lent down by her small body. Each of the hunters took turns with having their way with her. She tried to scream, tried to fight but each time she moved, some part of her body was sliced.

She glared up as her stepfather moved on top of her, his green eyes laughing into hers. The child winked, she would show them. She would show them what the devil looked like. Snapping her arm up, she flexed her fingers snatching the knife beside her and swinging it across his neck. He fell from her body, dead.

One of the other men picked her up, slapping her to the ground once more. Although she could no longer feel any pain from her torn skin. She darted her hands up at them in rage and gasped when every weapon from the ground shuddered, then shot back into the bodies of their owners. Satisfied, she closed her golden-brown eyes once more. Falling deeper and deeper into what seemed like sleep . . . into the next life.

CHAPTER ONE

The piercing screams had woken her. The young girl found herself falling from her bed in fear again. She cowered on the carpet listening, waiting until the chilling scream sounded again, the screams from her mother. There was a loud thump and everything fell silent. The girl pulled herself to her feet.

She wound her long snow blonde hair around her finger tips. She was too afraid to go downstairs but too afraid of what would happen if she didn't. Her large golden-brown eyes glanced over at her still soundly sleeping twelve-year old sister. She turned back to the door, her small childlike frame slowly stepping forward. She could no longer hear anything downstairs.

Opening her bedroom door, she stood on the staircase directly outside. Taking in a deep breath and leaning over the old wooden railing, she looked down into the empty lounge-dining room. She could see no one. Where was her mother? She stepped further down the staircase, where she could peer into the kitchen through the arched doorway.

Their home was an old run down townhouse. The front door opened to a tiny kitchen then it led through to the dining and lounge room. The creaking old staircase sat to the right side, with two bedrooms and a small bathroom to separate them. She shared a room with her sister but that was the only good thing about the home. That she was close to comfort.

Looking down into the kitchen, she could see her mother draped across the bench. The woman was muttering something under her breath although her every word was slurred. Behind her stood a tall dark man who was pulling up his pants, swearing at her mother. He called her a slut and dirty bitch.

This was normal in her home, her mother was a prostitute and their home was constantly filled with strange men. There was no doubt her mother once was a beautiful woman, however now she looked years beyond her age. A consequence from the drugs she pumped into her body.

The girl sat at the top of the staircase, pulling her long white nighty over her knees. She wrapped her thin arms around her waist, watching the scene with disapproving eyes.

Most nights she would wake to this and most nights she would sit above the staircase, waiting for the men to leave. She didn't know what she would do the day one of them ventured up. Her mother spun around, her eyes drowsy and her shirt ripped open to reveal her beasts. She had a gash on the side of her mouth. The older woman moved over to the man, muttering something in his ear.

He laughed, pushing a few hundred dollars bills in her hand. Money herself and her sister would never benefit from. She had taken to sneaking into her mother's room when she was passed out and stealing half the money. Her mother never noticed, they could have given her five dollars and she would have been satisfied.

The man left, slamming the door behind him. Leaving her mother to grunt about the 'dud root' he was, before slumping over the sink once more. She pulled out her bottle of vodka, drinking it as if it were water. The woman swayed on her feet, hobbling over to the dining room table, where she fell flat on her face, passed out. The girl sneered at the disgusting woman who had never been a mother to her. She couldn't wait until she was old enough to get away from her, until she could escape the disturbing city of Adelaide.

"Heidi, is the man gone?" her sister asked, through the bedroom door.

"It is safe Mindy," she whispered.

Her sister quickly opened the door, coming to sit beside her on top of the stairs like she so often did. Mindy looked down at their mother. Shaking her head and bowing it to her knees. While Heidi glanced at the clock in the kitchen, she hadn't even noticed the time before now. It had felt so early but the clock read five-thirty. They had to be on a tram heading to school at seven, there was no use going back to bed now. She glanced to her sister, sighing and wrapping her arms around her.

Even though Mindy was only one year younger than herself, she was bigger than her. She had shoulder length dark brown hair and hazel eyes. Her face was covered in freckles where they only ran across Heidi's nose. Mindy was a little plump and her body already curving into her womanly form.

Sometimes Heidi felt so jealous of her. She still looked like she did when she was ten. She was not much bigger then five foot while Mindy was three inches over her. The two of them had different fathers but knew neither of them. They were results of one night stands.

Down on the floor, their mother started to snore. Both girls stood from the stairs going back to their room, where they had to dress for school. She hated school but she hated being at home even more. So her only choice was to pull on the burgundy and white uniform. She brushed back her hair, pushing a burgundy band over her forehead. Her hair still fell in tight curls at the ends no matter how hard she tried to brush them out.

Mindy put a lot more time and effort into her appearance. She was in the first few weeks at high school, so she wanted to make the best impression. Mindy sat at the mirror slowly twirling her hair and pinning it back with tiny butterfly clips then applying some lip-gloss. Something that she never did, neither of them had a mother who showed them how to look after themselves but her sister was lucky enough to have friends.

Heidi slipped out of the room, checking to see if they had enough milk for some breakfast, thankfully they did. She made herself some breakfast, leaning against the bench as she ate. Her eyes unmoving from her mother, she did not love the woman nor did she care for her. Her life had been like this since she could remember. She couldn't remember how she survived as a young child and to be honest she didn't want to know.

Once she finished her breakfast, she pulled her mother off the floor. She struggled to get the woman to the lounge room let alone up the stairs. She let her mother's body drop to the floor once more. She pried her mother's hand open, taking three fifty dollar notes out of three hundred that were there. It would buy them some lunch for school and some groceries after.

Heidi turned the small television on, watching, her body sitting in front of it but her mind elsewhere. Mindy had come down, had her breakfast and now sat beside her. Her sister watched the cartoons, giggling at every remark while she sat emotionless. As soon as the clock read six-thirty, the two girls headed out the door, waiting for the bus that would take them to the tram. The bus stop was directly outside their house which was a little easier due to the hurrying they already had to do.

A long black car pulled up at the house next door to them. The two girls watched curiously as two men directed a removal truck into the driveway. The house had been abandoned for ten years. No one wanted to live in a house that had been the center of a homicide. When Heidi was only three, a father ran through the home killing his wife and two children.

While she lay in bed, Heidi could hear the crying of the children and the screams of the mother even to this day. She sometimes confused them with the screams of her own mother. When she looked out of her bedroom window that stared directly into the dead children's, she swore she could see them. There was a six-year old girl and her four-year old brother. Both with faces white as snow and thick hair as black as a moonless night. They would stare back at her and wave, their hands transparent. She felt no fear looking upon them. When she would tell Mindy, her sister would look at her like she was lying or purposely trying to scare her but she could see them, she wasn't lying.

Who would move into a house like that? Their street sat on top of the hill with three old Victorian styled houses in a row, their home in the middle. 'The haunted house' as Mindy called it was on their right and on the left now a block of land. The house had burnt down four years ago and for some reason the past owners had never rebuilt. Heidi stood, staring at the men moving in all the plastic covered furniture. She felt afraid for the ghost children. What did they think of this? Her attention was snapped away when the bus pulled up and Mindy pulled her on.

On the tram it took them forty-five minutes to get to school, the lonely dark school reminded Heidi of a prison. It was Monday and it always seemed to be the slowest day of the week. All the bad classes where on Monday's—double math's. Mindy ran ahead to her crowd of friends, waiting at the front gates. Heidi slowly headed to her quiet spot on a stairwell. Another long day at school, another miserable day that chained onto the rest.

Her day had slowly slid by as it always did. Her classes were filled with students more interested in each other than their school work and her hidden in the back. She was almost relieved when the second last period ended. At the end of every day she had an hour with the school counselor. She had been seeing him since half way through last year for disruptive behavior. Disruptive behavior to them was her sitting alone and not talking to anyone, or not doing her homework.

Last year she had been caught stabbing the end of a compass into her leg. She hadn't even known she was doing it until she snapped back to reality, the teacher yelling at her. Most teachers couldn't believe Mindy was her sister, for she was popular and centered. Something she would never be but then did she really want to be like everyone else? No, there was something more about her; she could feel it in her soul.

Heidi walked down to the room on the side of the office, leaning on the door. Did she really want to go in? Drake Commack, her counselor, had been counseling her since she had started attending last year. He was twenty-seven and still looked at her with hope, not yet scarred by the disturbed students he was yet to receive. All last year she hadn't even spoken to him. It was only the start of this year when she had said her first few words, but still not much was said between them.

Drake was a smart man, who lived in her neighborhood. So he knew the gossip about her mother which she would never admit. For if she did, they would take her away and she may never be with her sister again. Who wants a thirteen year old girl? So she remained silent and the counselor couldn't do anything without her word. Heidi sighed, knocking on the blue door.

"You can come in Heidi!" Drake called from within.

Heidi stepped into his office, closing the door behind her. She flopped into the chair across from Drake. She had only an hour to kill before she could get some groceries and go home. She was so hungry and couldn't wait to have a house full of food. Drake sat across from her on his large leather chair. He had wanted the students to call him by his first name, hoping to break the difference between adult and adolescent. The fool, he should know it never worked like that.

Drake had blonde-brown hair, strings always falling across his brown eyes. He was quite a tall man, with a strong build, unlike what you would expect from someone who sat at a desk all day. There were faint freckles across his face and she could see tattoos hidden under his stiff white shirt. Drake confused her and interested her. She hated him trying to help her but was curious as to his reasons for trying so hard.

She slumped across from him, twisting her head to one side and staring at the man, watching him squirm in his chair. But today he did not squirm. He sat straight and tall, staring back at her, challenging her to speak first. He was a smart man, obviously paying a lot of attention to her. For he had figured her out, he had thought anyway.

Heidi grinned, twisting her head to the other side, her eyes drifting to the clock watching her minutes tick by. If he wanted to play his games then so would she. Drake sat still, his note pad to one side. He leant forward with his elbows sitting on the arm rests on his chair. His fingers clenched, wrapping around his thumb, he was crumbling.

"How are you today Heidi?" he asked sitting back. She had won.

"Someone is moving into the haunted house."

Drake raised his eyebrow, they very rarely spoke about her but she did speak about the children a lot. His face twisted in wonder and fear as she spoke. He tried not to believe her but because she believed it herself, it was hard for him to see through it. Besides he had heard the rumors since moving from Sydney two years ago. The neighbors had well informed him about the houses on the north hill.

Heidi had found out all she could about the man. He had a wife and three children. He had moved from Sydney to Adelaide where his wife's family was. His wife was a primary school teacher and worked at the catholic school not far from their neighborhood, his children consisted of a six year old boy and twins. The twins were a boy and a girl, who spent most of their day since they were born in childcare. Yes, she had studied him. She didn't like that he knew so much about her and she knew nothing about him, now it was her who knew more.

"I heard your mother was fired from her job in the café," he commented. Now that he had got her talking he tried to steer her away from the children. Although he was a bit slow for her mother had lost the job over two weeks ago.

"She quit." Heidi didn't know why she defended the woman.

Drake raised his eyebrow again, challenging her to look at him so he could see the truth. She did which confused his theory.

"Melinda told me she was worried about you. She said you weren't sleeping and you're waking up screaming," he pressured.

Heidi looked away, silent. How dare her sister speak about her and to her counselor! She remained turned from Drake for twenty minute's. The man watched the clock, realizing he had made the mistake he so often did. She would always stop talking when he pressured her about her life, when he yearned for information. How she hated Mindy right now, besides she never awoke screaming, it was their mother. It had to be their mother for who else could it be?

Drake took a deep breath, he was losing her and he knew it. "The children will not be happy with someone living in their home," he commented, coming down to her level.

"No, they won't."

"Maybe it could be good for them. It could bring them peace and you might not have to see them anymore."

She snapped her head to him. "They will not be happy if it's a man," she sneered.

Drake bit his lip, trying to read her thoughts but she was still angry over what Mindy had done. She moved from the chair placing herself in the corner, behind the door. Drake sighed, dropping the pad from his hand. When she hid in the corner she would not speak to him. Heidi stared into the corner suppressing her feelings, she could not cry, she would not cry in front of him. Drake had moved around his desk, fiddling with the drawers but she did not turn his way. Her large eyes darted back and forth over the lines in the wall paper, her head aching with the flood of thoughts, her pain.

The bell sounded, marking the end of the day. Heidi jumped to her feet, snatching her school bag. There was too much to do before night fall, especially a talk with her over-sharing sister. Drake didn't come to the door to let her out. She stood with her face against the wood, what did he want? She turned around slowly to see him lighting a candle on a single chocolate cup cake. He turned, holding it out for her. Confused, Heidi stepped back towards him.

"I am not supposed to get anything for students but I bought this at lunch. Happy birthday."

Heidi stood still, what did he mean happy birthday? It wasn't her birthday, was it? She drifted her eyes to the calendar, shocked to see that it was her birthday. She had never celebrated her birthday before nor had anyone else. Drake held out the small cup cake for her, Heidi smiled. She blew out the candle taking the cake. She looked back up in his eyes to see that he was equally as happy, she couldn't let him in. She snapped the smile from her face, throwing the cake in the bin.

She left the room, slamming the office door behind her, leaving the counselor shocked, leaning back against his desk. She couldn't let anyone get close to her, she wanted to be invisible but there was something different about her. She knew she was different. There was something that everyone else saw that she couldn't, they saw her as a freak and psycho but she saw herself as a child. The world was moving and everyone was changing but she remained the same. She was still the child without a shadow, without a soul.

* * *

After school Heidi had picked up some food on the way home, all the time thinking that it was her birthday. She was fourteen! Fourteen was still so young but she either felt so much older or younger. Mindy had got a lift home with a friend, leaving her to walk up the hill alone. She had missed the bus because she had to get their food. Leaning up the hill, she carried four bags in each hand. She was exhausted by the time she reached her house, her sister sat out the front waiting.

"Mums not home," she commented, gesturing to the locked door.

Heidi nodded. She didn't think her mother would be. She would be at the bar by now, buying all the drugs she could before nightfall when she would walk the streets. Heidi placed the bags at her feet, shifting through her school bag, searching for the keys as a shadow fell over her. Looking up to a tall man, she froze. The man had dark eyes with black hair, gelled in points, he was in his mid-twenties. He was lean, clothed in black pants and crimson red shirt. She raised her eyebrow, who was he? The enchanting man smiled, his deep eyes staring through her like he knew her.

"Hello my name is Zack Solveri, I'm your new neighbor. I tried to introduce myself to your mother but she left in a hurry." The man put out his hand, Heidi took a few steps back, throwing the keys to Mindy who quickly went inside. The man snapped back his hand. "Nice to meet you too," he muttered.

"Come on Heidi!" her sister called.

Heidi darted her eyes back to the man who rolled his head to one side smiling. There was something about him which was familiar. "Are you Heidi?" he asked, even though he already knew the answer.

"Why do you ask?"

"The children wish you a happy birthday," he whispered, handing her a bundle of old newspaper. Nineteen ninety-seven the paper read, the children were on the front. It was the day of their death, the day their neighborhood was turned upside down. Had their world ever turned back the right way?

Zack placed the bundle in her hand, walking away before she could do anything. She would have thought she imagined him it if it wasn't for the paper in her hand. Her body quivered. She ran inside slamming the door behind her. Who was that man? Did he mean the ghost children she also saw? She didn't know what to think. Heidi ran to her room, slamming the door, warning her sister away.

She threw herself on the bed, staring at the bundle of newspaper, slowly unwrapping it. Heidi gasped at the beautiful gift that fell out. It was a large amethyst stone in the center of a classic styled silver necklace. The necklace was beautiful but she couldn't shake the strange feeling as she brushed her fingers over the stone, like she was being watched.

Heidi looked out her window across to that of the children's room. They stood in the window screaming, shaking their heads, their small hands pressed against the glass. What were they saying? Heidi felt sick, her mind was screaming at her to run away but she could not tear her eyes from them. Without moving, the blind to her room was slammed shut and cold breeze shifted through the room.

She gasped, jumping from the bed. She reopened the window to look at the children. They had gone and standing in their place was the man from outside. He stared right through her, his body motionless but his eyes dancing with excitement. Heidi quickly drew the blind, leaning against the wall, her heart racing. First she found out it was her birthday and now someone had moved in next door, a strange man. She felt sick, she stepped back to her bed, falling as the house begun to shake. She fell to the floor, her large eyes darted back to the window as the blind was snapped open, no one there.

The shaking stopped, leaving her cuddled to the floor waiting for Mindy to run up the stairs, she heard nothing. Slowly rising to her feet, Heidi moved to her mirror staring at her pale thin reflection. She hated herself, hated the way she looked and the way she felt. She glanced down to her hand where she clutched the beautiful necklace. Why had the children given it to her? Was it because they cared or something else?

Heidi placed the necklace around her neck, hurrying downstairs to tell Mindy. She knew the look she would receive from her sister but she wasn't imagining it. The children were there, she could see them, she could feel them. Their voices followed her, their tortured spirits clinging to hers. She had to tell Mindy about the man next door, warn her to stay away. Something was very wrong and for the first time she could remember, she was afraid.

Heidi stopped at the end of the stairs when she saw the bags, her shopping. Sighing, she stepped over to the bags. She would talk to Mindy later, for now she had to do what her mother failed to do. She had to clean the house, so her mother could come home drunk, destroying it with whoever she partnered tonight and their routine would start again. School, counseling, disturbed nights, broken hearts and crushed dreams. Welcome to her tortured life!

CHAPTER TWO

The shuffling downstairs had kept her awake until the early hours of the morning. Her birthday was over before she even had the chance to celebrate or acknowledge it. She lay with her back to her sister, her eyes cast to the door, in hope that the people in the kitchen would leave. Her mother was, of course their attention but even she couldn't stay up much longer. It had been a long night. Her mother had arrived home after dinner, she stormed into the house, cursing at how the school counselor had rung her at the bar and embarrassed her in front of her companion.

Her mother had run about the kitchen, throwing what she could at her, cursing both her daughters. After her rage fuelled tantrum she had gone upstairs to shower then wait for her company. Heidi had heard her speaking softly with Mindy for a few minutes, saying that after tonight she planned to buy a way out of here. She was always saying things like that to them.

Heidi had started to wonder whether they were included in her thoughts or would she leave without them? Disgusted, she had run to her room not wishing to witness such betrayal. But once in her room, all she could think about were the children next door and the man.

The man next door had been so strange. It confused her that he would move into a haunted house and especially that he saw what she did. Since the window had slammed shut, she hadn't seen or heard anything next door. Although that didn't mean everything was okay, silence was more threatening than spoken words.

She had tried to tell Mindy but her sister was yet again predictable, by not hearing a word. All her sister cared was what movie she was seeing on the weekend. No one cared what she had to say, then again she didn't really want their attention. None of them cared for her, not her family, not school and definitely not Drake, although he did put on a good show.

The shuffling downstairs subsided but that only opened the night for their chatter. She could hear her mother's voice and the voices of two men.

Their talking quickly led to another argument. Heidi pulled her blanket over her head trying to block them out, nothing would cease them.

The argument grew louder and things started to smash, her mothers voice the loudest of them all. Heidi ground her teeth, waiting for it to end but it didn't and wouldn't. Fighting would only lead to more sex and more sex left her mother in a drunken slumber. That thought was the worst of them all.

Coming down the stairs to find her mother half naked on the floor with men's fluids and alcohol over her body, was not something she liked to see. She absolutely hated it. She hated that she had to see it and hated that she had to clean it up before Mindy came downstairs. She resented her mother more with every week that passed. Downstairs things fell silent, Heidi sneered, was her mother unconscious or in an act she didn't want to see?

Heidi threw off her blankets, snatching her robe from the door to wrap around her shaking body. Her paper thin nighty barely did a thing against the cold. Opening the door, she slipped from the room surprised that her sister was still sleeping. Well not really surprised, more frustrated that she was and that she could not herself. She cleared her head from her anger, walking out to the top of the stairs. To look down at her mother who was kissing one man, while the other had a needle in her arm, most likely heroin. Heidi screwed her face up in anger, this was pathetic. She would never let herself do that. She couldn't take this, not tonight. Leaning against the railing, her fingers turned white with her rage.

"Stop! Stop it now! You two need to leave now!" she screamed, from the top of the stairs.

The threesome froze, staring up at her. Her mother's eyes taking a few moments to adjust to who she was seeing, she sneered. The two men stepped back, one smiling and the other's face a mask of shock. It scared her the way that they were looking at her but she didn't move. Her mother moved to one of the men, whispering in his ear before walking beneath the railing, glaring up at her daughter. Heidi glared back; it was not her mother she was afraid of. It was the strangers with their eyes gleaming through her.

"Get back to bed girl. This is none of your business!" Her mother yelled.

"I'm not going to bed until they leave!" Heidi hissed.

"You don't dictate to me girl, get back to bed! Mama's working," she spat, turning to smile back at her company.

"My name is Heidi!" She was now shaking with anger. She hated her mother so much yet there was nothing she could do about it. She needed to relax, she needed some fresh air. "Fine. I'm going outside."

Her mother didn't hear her. She had gone back to one of the men, making out with him on the kitchen table. Heidi felt her stomach turn, she felt sick watching them. Especially since she and Mindy ate off that table, however her mother had probably done it on everything they touched. Her attention turned to the other man still standing beside the staircase, what did he want?

"Hi Heidi, I'm Greg. Do you wanna come down here for a while?" he asked, moving to the base of the staircase.

"Not near you!" she spat.

As quickly as she could, Heidi hurried past him and out the front door. The man only laughed at her, but he did not return to her mother. He walked over to the lounge slumping into it, watching her leave. With shaky hands, Heidi slammed the door behind her, stepping out into the cold night. The air numbed her face and hands, she shivered. Why had she come out here? It didn't really matter, as long as she was not watching or hearing them inside.

She walked down the driveway coming to sit in the gutter and folding her legs beneath her body. The street was quiet and dark, two of the street lights had been blown for several weeks now. It seemed even the council had forgotten them. Resting her head on her folded knees, she thought of how her body had reacted inside. Normally she would have remained quiet so why hadn't she tonight? Because it had been her birthday and her mother had never known. If she couldn't be happy then she would do her best to be sure her mother was also unhappy.

"It's a little late to be out here in the darkness, isn't it?" Someone spoke behind her.

Heidi looked over her shoulder to see Zack Solveri as he wandered down his driveway, dropping in the gutter next to her. She shifted away from him, glaring at the man. What did he want? He only smiled, a cigarette wedged between his lips. He pulled the collar up on his jacket, cupping his hands around the end of his cigarette to light it. Heidi turned away from him, looking down to her bare feet. They were so numb; she hadn't noticed she'd forgotten to put shoes on. When he moved she snapped her head back to him, he was offering her one of his cigarettes. She shook her head, smoking was for the weak and she was not weak.

"I needed some space," she whispered, without looking back to him.

"Understood. It's pretty crowded in there," he said, with a nod back to the house.

Heidi couldn't help but to smile at his remark but the yells inside quickly slapped it away. "You should get used to it. You're going to hear a lot of it if you live here," she muttered.

Zack looked over her head to the house, nodding then turning back to her. His dark eyes stared through her. "Women like that shouldn't have kids."

"No shit."

At her comment he laughed, giving her a playful nudge in the arm. He finished the cigarette throwing the butt into the gutter then climbed to his feet. "Well I'm off. Better get some sleep. You, young lady should do the same. You don't want those men to leave and find you out here alone."

Her eyes widened, he was right. She should get back inside before she was trapped out here. Zack lent down offering his hand. Heidi climbed to her own feet, glaring back at his offered hand. She turned, running up her driveway into the house looking within. There was only one man with her mother on the couch, where was the other? Really she didn't care. He was probably in the bathroom.

Running up the stairs, Heidi slipped into her room. She could still hear Mindy's soft snores, sighing she dropped into her bed. There was a strange feeling in her stomach while she was talking to Zack. There was something about him but she couldn't place it, although it wasn't fear.

No, he was kind and understanding but in her life nothing like that could last. Heidi closed her eyes, trying to force herself to sleep now that it had grown quiet downstairs. Just as she relaxed there was a footstep behind her.

"Hello sweetness."

Heidi gasped, snapping up in her bed to face the man from downstairs but before she could scream or move, something heavy hit her on the head. She fell backwards on the bed, first a bright light behind her eyelids then darkness. Heidi felt her mind fading. *Oh god, please don't let him hurt Mindy.*

*   *   *

The morning light streamed through the torn blinds, slices of it lying on her face, heating her. She felt a flush of pain but it wasn't the heat on her face that was painful, it was her body. She cringed at the pain in her stomach, rolling over on the bed; could it be puberty? She hadn't yet got her first period, although Mindy had started a few months ago. It embarrassed her that Mindy was developing and experiencing everything before she was. Another sharp pain in her stomach and between her legs sent her over again. Heidi snapped her eyes open. Her body felt like it was on fire. It was so painful.

She looked around her room, no one was in there. What was the time? Her eyes fell on the clock, a quarter past seven. Oh god! She was going to be late but when she went to move, she fell back to the bed in pain. It wasn't only her body that hurt, now it was her head too. What had happened last night?

She couldn't remember much, only that she had been upset after dinner and went to bed. Heidi tried to sit up again, fighting the pain. Once she was up, she threw back her covers, her lips quivered. She was naked! Why was she naked? She never slept naked and moreover, on the bedding and over her legs was blood, lots of blood. Puberty had really hit, a little late but here now in full force, as it seemed. She jumped from the bed, wrapping a sheet around her body and running to the bathroom. Her body screamed with every step but there was no time to dwell on it now. She was going to be late.

After her shower, Heidi ran about her room, dressing for school and finding Mindy's stash of sanity pads. She was still in pain but it no longer mattered to her. She had to find Mindy and go. But as she moved across the room, she spotted her bedding. Quickly, Heidi gathered up her bedding and her nighty that had been thrown on the floor. Running them into the washing machine that sat in the bathroom, she turned on the machine then grabbed her bag, hurrying downstairs to where her sister sat eating breakfast. Their mother was nowhere to be seen. Mindy smiled, running her hand through her groomed hair. Heidi hadn't even time to brush hers. She would never be as pretty as her sister.

"Quick! We have to go!" she called, packing a quick lunch for the two of them.

"What was wrong with you this morning?" Mindy asked, in no hurry.

"Time of the month. Now come we have to leave."

"Alright, alright keep ya plug in, I'm coming."

Heidi glared at her sister. That was one less thing she needed to hear. She pushed Mindy out the door, the pain only growing, burning, but she had to fight it. The two of them ran down the driveway to the bus stop. Heidi nearly collapsed with the spinning in her head. She dropped to the ground, waiting for the bus. She had decided as soon as she got to school, she would go see the school nurse.

She would have never thought hitting puberty would cause so much pain. In fact she barely knew what puberty was. Only what school had taught her, for her mother had never bothered. Her mothers idea of them learning about sex was to try and make them to do it, experiencing was the only way to learning she had said. She felt so sick but before she could find the time to rest, the bus pulled up in front of them. She hated school but it was always a relief to get there than stay home with her mother.

"I found three hundred dollars lying under our door this morning. Mamma must have forgotten which room was hers," her sister laughed at her wit. "You can go get us more food with it," she stated as they boarded the bus.

Her sister shoved the envelope filled with cash into her hand before hurrying to a group of her friends on the bus. Heidi crushed her hand around the envelope, quickly moving to the back of the bus where she could sit and count it all. Mindy was right, in her hand she had three hundred dollars yet as she looked at the money, her stomach turned. She felt sick, her head begun to ache again with the uncertainty with how the money came to be under their door. After a few minutes the pain passed and she decided it didn't matter. They had more than she had taken in a while and she would use it to look after her sister, she would use it to survive.

As they arrived at school, Mindy ran off with her friends, while she hurried to the office, hoping the nurse was already in. She wasn't. Consumed by anger and fear, Heidi walked to the dark north stairs, sitting to one side of them. Rocking her body, she waited for the bell. After she went to her first class, she would try the nurse again. The pain only seemed to be getting worse.

It wasn't long before the bell rung and a flood of students rushed up the stairs. Heidi got lost within them. Quickly hurrying to her first class, why? She didn't know. What could a teacher do for her? Even though she sat in class, she wouldn't learn anything. Just hide in the back, her mind drifting to last night. She never went to bed naked!

*　*　*

The nurse hadn't come all day. After her first four classes she had tried again and was turned away. The pain hadn't got any worse but no better either. She had finally finished her fifth class, though there was no point trying the nurse again. In forty minutes it would be home time. Besides she had to go to the counselor, if she missed it she was sure Drake would be pounding down her door. Heidi slowly drifted down the hall to the counselor's office, her hand gripping at her stomach. She had to be strong. She couldn't let him see how much pain she was in. He would ask too many questions and she still didn't have all the answers, especially regarding last night.

Leaning against the office door, she knocked. Drake Commack called for her to enter before her hand had left the wood. Heidi sighed, quickly standing tall before she opened the door. She hoped he didn't notice anything because if anyone did, it would be him. She didn't even look Drake's way. She walked straight to her corner like normal. Falling down with her back to him and her knees pulled to her chest. Her head rested against her knees, it hurt less curled in a ball.

Drake didn't say anything. She was fairly sure he wouldn't. Everything seemed normal so he would sit there and watch. Maybe he would attempt to talk to her in the next half hour but not now, not unless she gave him a reason too.

Why not shock him and speak first? She never spoke first, never spoke nicely to him but today she needed the distraction. The more she remained silent, the more she would feel the pain. After all, she really did need to talk to someone, didn't she? For one day she could let her silence abandon her, for one day she could be normal.

"I met the man that moved in next door. He gave me a gift for my birthday, said it was from the children and that they wanted me to have it," she whispered. Her voice muffled against her knees.

Drake was silent for a few minutes. "What did he give you?"

"The children gave me a necklace." She corrected him. Surprising herself and Drake, she stood from the corner moving over to his desk. She pulled out the seat on her side, flopping into it.

He raised his eyebrow, studying her for a moment then the necklace she pointed to around her neck. "Looks expensive, he probably found it in the house. Are you sure he said it was from 'the children'?" He didn't believe her. She should have never said anything. Heidi could feel herself growing frustrated, she hated them all.

"Yes, he said it was from them." She wasn't going to tell him what she saw afterwards. "I talked to him later in the night and he seemed quite nice even . . ."

She stopped. She hadn't talked to him last night, had she? No, after yelling at her mother, she had gone outside and yes, there she had seen him again. Then she had gone to bed and that man was in her room, he had hit her. It was all coming back! She had woken up naked, oh god! What had he done to her? She was bleeding and in so much pain. There had been money left at her door! What had he done? Had he raped her? She felt so sick, her eyes drifted up to Drake, he was leaning across the table, his face full of worry.

Her head was starting to spin but before she could try and make up some lie for her counselor, he was moving from behind the table. She wanted to scream at him to go away but nothing came out of her mouth. All she could think about was that man having her while she was unconscious. Someone taking her body and she didn't even know what had happened. She didn't want to remember anymore. She wanted to burst into tears but no, she could show no weakness.

"Heidi! Are you okay? You look flushed. Did he say anything to you? Do you want me to call the police?" Drake asked. He almost sounded angry or that he cared. It was all an act. He had to be acting, trying to catch her then destroy her family.

She shook her head but the movements made her feel like fainting. All she wanted to do was go home and lock herself in her room. She hated her mother. Her mother would pay for what she had cast upon her.

"I can call the school nurse."

"She's not in. I've been trying all day . . . I . . . I have to go home," she stammered.

Drake was staring at her. She could almost see what was going on in his head. He wanted to take her home; she could see it in his eyes. But should anyone see them, it would be the end of his job. He doubted she would let him help her, he was right. Without waiting for an answer, she stood from the chair leaving the office. Leaving Drake more puzzled then she had seen him. She felt suddenly sorry for him, she always gave him such a hard time and he was truly a nice guy. She couldn't help it, she didn't need him.

Heidi walked from the school grounds, her mind lost. What did she do? She didn't know for sure if something had happened but if it had, what did she do about it? She had only ever seen her mother fooling around with men, never watching long enough to see what sex was. How bad was that? A fourteen year old girl not knowing what happens in sex? And if someone had done that to her she would have no idea. Walking faster, Heidi wanted nothing more then to get home, to stop her body from shaking.

She needed a woman to talk too, she needed her mother but she had none. Tears forced themselves into her eyes but she would not allow herself to cry. There would be no one else to pick up the pieces, so she couldn't let herself crumble. She was a woman now. It was against her will but decided. She probably hadn't even hit puberty yet. All that pain and blood was from a man, it sickened and scared her. For he had probably been with her mother first and god knows who else.

She needed a doctor but they would ask too many questions, she was fourteen! They would call the police and the man would be put in jail but her mother would hate her. Mindy would be taken from her. She had to get away and find somewhere to hide, to think and maybe when no one was looking then she could cry.

Heidi hurried home as fast as she could but instead of going into her home. She jumped the back fence of the house next door. She wasn't really sure what she was doing. All she knew, was the haunted house next door was her safe place to think. Even though someone had moved in, it was more her house than his.

She dropped down on the other side of the fence and crossed the overgrown yard to the back door. Peering in, Heidi couldn't see anyone passing through the kitchen or lounge room. Boldly she stepped in, she knew she could get into so much trouble for trespassing but where else could she go? She had seen the screen door to her home was open which meant her mother was home. Her mother was the last person she wanted to see. Besides he would never know she was there.

She tried the doorknob, surprised it was unlocked. Heidi stepped into the dark room, everything still as she knew it. In the corner under the stairs was a wall of boxes but all the furniture was the same, not a thing out of place. Letting out the breath she had been holding, she climbed the stairs quietly, heading to the room that looked into hers. All the rooms were opened and Zack was nowhere in sight.

She was starting to feel guilty however she still continued on. In the room that once belonged to the children, Heidi dropped to the floor, staring out the window into her own room, at her bare bed. She felt sick again, last night the unthinkable had happened and she couldn't talk about it with anyone. How she hated her mother.

In the room she felt the presence of the children but today she would pay no attention to them. Her golden-brown eyes continued to stare out the window, watching her quiet room. If only her walls could speak of the horror they had seen, then it would be anything but quiet. When she adjusted her body, she was hit with a sharp pain. Heidi bent down cringing, a small cry escaping her lips. What was wrong with her? She closed her eyes, feeling the children disappear replaced with an unsettling feeling.

"I didn't know I would have visitors crying in my room." She heard the familiar male voice speak from the doorway. He was home! She felt so embarrassed, not for being in his house, but because someone had seen her weakened.

"I'm not crying," Heidi snapped, not turning around to him.

"No? Well why are there tears in your eyes? Why are you hiding here?"

She quickly climbed to her feet, her face flushed. It was a mistake to come here, she must seem like a silly little girl to him. "I'll go," she whispered, turning around, her eyes holding his for a moment. Zack smiled, not at all upset that she had visited his home. He slowly moved across the room, holding his hand up for her to stay then he placed himself in the chair she had been sitting beside.

"Do you attend the local high school? Isn't that where you should be?"

What was with all the questions? She wanted to leave, another part of her wanted to stay out of curiosity. "I got out early. Shouldn't you be at work?" she shot back. Her look of anger was quickly replaced with a small smile playing on her lips.

Zack laughed. "I'm holidaying. I bought this house and planned to stay a few weeks organizing what I want to have done then leave it in the hands of contractors. Once their job is done, I plan to go back to Melbourne and lease this place out but I can't do that with a young woman hanging out here, can I?"

"I like the way it looks now." She couldn't imagine this place ever changing. It would ruin it to make it modern. Its darkness and mystery was enchanting.

"Now that I'm here, so do I."

Heidi felt her cheeks heat up again, she wasn't sure if it was from him paying attention to her or another burst of pain. He treated her like an adult, not a stupid girl, he saw her but did she want to be seen? "I have to go home now. My sister will be home from school any minute," she whispered, looking down at her feet.

"Heidi!" Zack called, as she stepped past him and to the bedroom door, she slowly turned back to him. "You're more than welcome to make this room yours while I'm living here."

She paused, staring back at him, her chest pounding. Was he really going to let her come in whenever she pleased? She couldn't believe it. Heidi smiled, nodding in his direction. She stepped towards the door when the pain hit her again, this time harder. She gasped, wrapping her arms around her stomach, this wasn't right, it was getting worse. When the cramp subsided, she tried to focus her vision, turning to Zack hoping he hadn't seen. He had and he looked scared, she had to leave.

As she turned to leave there was a great wetness between her legs, she cringed again. What was going on? The room around her started to darken, she was scared. Heidi took a step towards Zack, she didn't know why but she did know she needed his help. Zack was already moving to her, she fell forward into his arms. The two of them falling to the floor, his strong arms wrapped around her body. She wanted to thank him but before she could speak, her world sealed in blackness, highlighted in pain.

*   *   *

Her eyes slowly fluttered open. She stared at a clean, bright white room. Crossing her brows, she tried to rise from the bed, where was she? Next to her she could hear the slow beep of a heart monitor. Heidi stared at it in fear for a few seconds then back around her room again. Oh god, she was in hospital!

The windows were open so the warm sunlight could stream in. Causing her to be in more shock, it was day time. How long had she been in here? And who had brought her here? She couldn't remember where she had been last. This always happened to her, her mind becoming vacant and blocking out half her life. She could never remember things until days or months after they had happened. What she did know was that she was in hospital and that was bad. It was day time and she was alone, always alone.

Heidi sighed, sitting up against the pillow, her eyes searching for something to call the doctor. She was sure there was nothing wrong with her. She was defiantly sure there were no bruises on her, no pain. All her limbs and mind were working, so why was she here? The blood . . . oh, she couldn't forget that forever. That man had hurt her and over the day she had got worse.

She remembered she had been at Zack's house. The children had been there also but disappeared the moment he stepped in. She had been leaving, hadn't she? Yes, leaving but fainting and the blood, he had caught her. It must have been Zack that brought her here. God knows her mother wouldn't. She didn't know whether to be grateful or angered, she hated hospitals.

Her chest felt so heavy with emotions she couldn't understand, she was so scared. What had happened to her sister? Did Mindy go looking for her? A whole night had passed and there was no one by her side. Why couldn't she have died? It would be so much easier than to live this life, especially now. If one of her mother's companions thought he could take her, then most likely all of them did now. How could she go back there? But then there was Mindy. If one of them laid a hand on her sister, she would kill her mother then the man that touched her. After, she would kill her mother again because that's what she had done to them, killed their spirits over and over again.

"Ah, you're awake, sweetheart."

Heidi snapped her eyes to the nurse standing at the door. She had been so consumed by anger; she hadn't seen the elderly woman come in. Pressing her lips together, she dropped her head to one side, studying the nurse moving to her bed, the woman's eyes on the charts. Heidi remained silent. She wouldn't speak to the nurse until the woman gave her an indication of what was wrong with her.

The nurse flashed her empty smile, before moving to the heart monitor filling out the charts. She then took without permission her blood pressure, temperature and even lifted the blankets to look in her underwear. Heidi hissed, bringing her knees to the nurse's face, knocking her backwards. How dare she! She didn't even ask. She was treating her like a child that didn't know her body. She wasn't stupid and that woman was not going to touch her again.

The nurse grabbed her nose, her grey-blue eyes watering as she read over the charts again. She was not angered. "Sorry sweetheart, it said on the chart to check. I should have warned you first. I just thought you would have already had a few and knew. Can you tell me your name or what you can remember?"

Heidi turned her head away from her, angered. She would not speak to her, not now.

"Okay then. I will inform your doctor that you're awake and then he can call the police about the situation. They will probably want to talk to you too."

Heidi glared at her, what did she mean the police? She couldn't talk to the police, for if they found out they would put her and Mindy in foster care. She might never see her sister again. It was always the same; couldn't talk to Drake, doctors, the police, she couldn't talk to anyone. The police would lock her mother up and all the men she owed would come after them. They would surely find her or Mindy, they always did. No, she couldn't tell the police, she wanted no one to know of this, no memory.

She hated her mother but wasn't going to let that bitch damn her children to this. This time she would lie to protect her and that night would be lost in silence. If it happened again her mother should think twice before closing her eyes at night. She saw no crime in the loss of that woman's life. The crime would be not to kill her.

CHAPTER THREE

The door slammed behind him as he entered the house, his brown eyes searching for his family. He could not see them but could hear them. His wife was in the bathroom bathing their children, of course she heard him but she would not acknowledge it. Not until he did or she needed something done, always the way. He felt like a stranger in his own home, the fly on the wall, watching his family's lives move around his. He stood in the middle waiting for them to see him, waiting for love.

He did love her and his children unconditionally however they didn't like one another. His wife and he got along for the children and sometimes so well themselves that it would confuse their hearts. Though it would never be the same between them, things would always go back to the distance and pain. They were heading in different directions. He was a goddamn counselor yet he couldn't save his own marriage. He struggled to find the peace he needed in his life.

With still no call from his wife, acknowledgement or an order, Drake moved to the table practically falling in the chair. His day had been a long one and his biggest problem was bringing his work home with him. Taking home all the frustrations and sadness of who he counseled. Everyday was different but today was bad. He had a horrible feeling in the pit of his stomach and it was weight he carried alone. His wife couldn't understand how he thought or what he felt. There had to something more out there for him. This couldn't be it. This couldn't be his life.

In his first period of the day, he had counseled a year seven boy who had been misbehaving in class and sent to him by the teacher. The kid wasn't that bad just a typical clown. A boy obsessed with the attention of his peers. He had spent twenty minutes talking about video games, days Drake wished he could go back to now. No responsibilities, no worries.

In second period he had a year nine girl who was caught skipping school. He had tried to talk to her but she was a plain bitch. Lecturing him on how she should be able to leave school when she wanted. No one could tell her what to do. She was a free person to do what she wanted and couldn't be stopped. A typical student that he counseled.

Third, he had another year nine student. She was fairly upset over her parent's divorce, at least this one he could help. She had been a pretty thing, talking in a voice barely above a whisper. She cried a few times but when the period was over she seemed somewhat happier. He had barely spoken to her, she didn't give him the chance. Though that's what she needed, to speak what was on her mind and believe someone was listening.

Fourth, he had another student with whom he could help. A year eight boy, who was at the lonely end of nasty bullying. With this one he had alerted the year adviser. Together, the boy pointed out the students and regained some control. The situation would be calmed and the bullies punished. At the end of the period he had another satisfied student, the best feeling to have lunch upon.

After lunch was fifth period which he was lucky enough to have no one in his office. But that just meant more time to go over his day and prepare for his last student, Adelheid Harrison. A year eight girl, who he had been seeing constantly for the past year. She was the one that left her presence building up within him. Heidi was a truly beautiful girl, disturbed, but breathtakingly beautiful. However she would never believe anyone who told her this. She was a loner and because of her mother, she was quite messed up.

She had large golden-brown eyes which he would see every time he closed his, her dark soul. Her hair was snow blonde though her eyebrows dark brown, it didn't look strange like the girls that bleached their hair. She had a cluster of freckles across her nose, her face a delicate heart shape which made her look even more innocent. She was a tiny girl. He was sure she was undersize for her age.

He cared for her and all he wanted to do was help but Heidi was a tough spirit to get along with. At the end of the day, he would spend their forty minutes together trying to get her to talk. Lately, he had been having some success though he never did speak about what he wanted. He knew her home was broken and was certain her mother was not looking after her, if not something worse. Heidi had a sister at the school, Melinda, who occasionally would talk to him but she seemed more together. Still Melinda would not speak about their home life or much on her sister.

Today his worst fear had happened. Heidi had not turned up sixth period. When he asked the school office, she hadn't turned up to school.

She was always at school, sick or not, probably because her home was worse. She was always at his appointments even though she hated them. Today she was not there at all and neither was Melinda which sent off more alarm bells. He had phoned their home and there was no answer. He had felt like going around there himself but there was no reason to panic, not yet anyway.

Yesterday Heidi had been more unlike herself. She had been in obvious discomfort and for a moment it seemed she would tell him everything then she hadn't. She had left early but he wasn't going to stop her, not with the look of pain in her eyes. Maybe that's all it had been, she was sick. She couldn't come to school, so why was Melinda also not there? Sick too? He was reading too much into it. Besides there was nothing he could do but wonder. Nothing, but come home with this weight on his body and soul.

He sat here, in the kitchen trying to clear his mind. When he had Heidi in the afternoon he always got lost in her emotions and when he didn't, well that was worse. Sometimes he wished he'd never come here, never met her, but there was something about her that kept him going back to work. He always needed time out before playing with the kids. Or he would carry this weight and he couldn't risk passing it onto them.

Drake sighed, dropping his head to the table, his bag falling from his shoulder. Something slid out of it. He cast his eyes to the floor where Heidi's necklace had fallen from his bag. She had left it in his office yesterday. Bending down, he scooped it into his hand, studying the captivating gothic design. Heidi had said her new neighbor had given it to her and that worried him.

Any man could destroy her if she opened herself. Especially a man who could play with her mind by speaking of the ghosts, giving her gifts in the ghosts' names. But how had the man known what his student obsessed about. Unless he saw them too; no, that was impossible. The children were Heidi's imagination, a way to express herself through them, weren't they? Nevertheless she had left the necklace from a man who could cause her harm. He had to find a way to get it back to her then gain her trust before someone else did.

Drake sighed, he was still doing it. Carrying the pain of others when he had more than enough of his own, but then again Heidi made him feel alive. If she would only let him help her, he might be able to. However there was something more then that, not sexual, although all he thought about was her. Every time they were in the same room, the world around them seemed to disappear. He would be left focused on her and that feeling. There was something more.

There had to be more to life than this. Drake placed the necklace back in his bag, lowering it beside the table. Tomorrow would be another day and if Heidi wasn't there, he would call child protection services. No matter what she said, he knew something was not right. He ran his hands through his hair. He had to stop thinking about her. Soon he would need counseling himself if he didn't leave his work at the front door.

"Drake!" His wife called from up the hallway. "Drake if you're sitting on your ass, get up and start dinner!"

Drake rolled his eyes, there had to be something more to this life, his soul desired so much more.

*   *   *

"Let go of me!" she screamed, pulling against her stepfather who only held her arm tighter.

"You'll hush when I tell ya to!" he yelled back.

She made no attempt to get away; why bother, he always won anyway. Beside the more she struggled, the more she would pay later. Her stepfather pulled her up the stairs of their small home. He moved to her room, undoing the lock on her door and throwing her in. She fell to the ground, her blonde hair flying in front of her face, veiling the tears she could no longer hide. She curled on her knees, her body heaving, though he had not left.

She cringed knowing what that meant. He would punish her now and for what? Going downstairs and asking her mother could they speak alone? He had probably guessed she would try to get her mother to leave him. The attempt had not done her any good. Her mother was so docile, she believed everything her stepfather said. But before she could say a thing, he had dragged her away. Even screaming and her mother hadn't turned to defend her only daughter.

Behind her, her stepfather pulled up the back of her dress exposing her back. She closed her eyes tightly, her body shaking while he took off his belt. She knew she was really going to get it this time. In her heart she still believed she hadn't done anything wrong. If he and her mother were kinder to her then she might have accepted him into her home. But he wasn't and all she wanted to do was run away. Why couldn't her mother see he was evil?

A shadow cast over her cowering body, she squeezed her eyes tighter, trying to loosen the muscles in her back. It hurt more when she was tense. He brought his belt down upon her back, causing her head to snap upright, the sharp pain flooding her body. Biting her lip, she tried to keep from screaming. Another whip and the tears burnt in her eyes, her body shook some more. After the third lash, she couldn't control herself anymore, she screamed. She screamed so hard the house around her seemed to shake. Her stepfather stopped, after all that's what he had been waiting for.

"If I hear another peep outa ya Olivia, you'll suffer more then that!" he spat back, then tying on his belt, he left her room. Olivia could hear the key turn in the lock on the other side, trapped again.

She hated him! He had ruined her life. Her real father had died five years ago when she was only six. It hadn't been a year before her mother started seeing other men. That was when things started to really go downhill. Her stepfather, Paul, had hated her from the start. She knew he did although he would never admit it to her mother.

He had locked her in her room. She didn't go to school like the other children nor did she have another in her company. She hadn't left the home since he had come into it. The only people she saw were those who entered the house but of late, she had been locked in her room the majority of the time. Now she only saw her mother, once a day when she brought up her dinner at night, her only meal of the day.

Crying and gasping for the air whipped out of her, Olivia dragged her body over to the window where she spent most of her days. She would stare out at the normal people, with their normal lives. At the beautiful women with their long garments and hats, hopping into their carriages to attend lunch with others. Then look to the men who were starting their day earnings, most of the men in town went into the woods to hunt for dinner or out to the farms where the harvest was in full swing.

Their town wasn't run on strong business, there were only seven stores in the whole town. They were surrounded by farms and woods which was the survival of their community. Most of the young men and their fathers who were strong enough had been called to the army, although no war had broken out in their country. There was talk of a war though she heard nothing more of it. Even if there was a war she probably wouldn't know until her home was blown apart. She knew nothing that happened on the outside of her walls.

The children ran on the streets in their uniforms and chalkboard under their arms. They had bags thrown over their shoulders with heavy books that weighed down one side of their bodies as they hurried to school. Why couldn't she be one of them? No stress, no fear, with her only care to go to school and remain in a safe home. She was only eleven but already she understood how cruel this world could be. She understood the darkness. She lived in the darkness.

*   *   *

She rode the bus home from the hospital, late Wednesday evening. Her mind spun over what had happened. Spinning over her birthday, then the next day at school when she had bled all day, to ending up in hospital today. She had been in hospital just over twenty-four hours and no one had come to see her. Not her mother, not her sister or anyone from school and by anyone she meant Drake.

She was sure Mindy would have gone to Drake for advice and then he would come find her. She wouldn't have spoken to him if he had come. Although the point would have been that he at least gave a damn, someone gave a damn. Mindy might not have gone to school, her sister might not know where she was if Zack hadn't told her. Then that was another problem of its own. Zack; how could she ever face him after what had happened? She felt so embarrassed.

She had been so scared all day. The doctor had come in after the nurse and demanded her home phone number but she did not speak with him. He had said she had been sexually assaulted and her vaginal area had been torn. Four stitches later they still wanted her to stay there. Of course she couldn't.

He had continued to tell her that she had been drugged, which explained her passing out. He wouldn't tell her what the drug was only that he needed to talk with her mother. He had treated her like a child! It was her body and she had a right to know what was wrong with it. When he had tried to speak with her it had felt patronizing and she was too overwhelmed to understand him. After trying to coax her to talk to him and failing, he left, allowing two police officers into the room, a female and a male.

The female officer had come to her side and tried to befriend her, while the male sat in the corner, listening. Heidi hadn't wanted to talk to them but she knew what would happen if she didn't—foster care. So she had created a lie, telling them that she hadn't been assaulted and willingly slept with an older man. The male officer was disgusted but they still wanted to know who it was because that was statutory rape. She had lied again, telling them that it was just some guy on the street. She didn't know who it was, the officer was more disgusted.

At least he believed her and they weren't going to stick their nose around her home. Although the female officer had looked less convinced but they couldn't get out of her what she wouldn't tell them. The female had promised to be back tomorrow, so they could have another talk when the drugs had worn off. For all they knew, she really could be a slut with a drug habit. Though she must have had fear dancing in her eyes because the female believed her less with every word.

They had left. The nurse had come back in to check her blood pressure and temperature before also leaving to report to the doctor. She had been alone at last. While they were distracted, she knew she had to get out. Heidi had ripped the drip from her arm. She found her school uniform wrapped in a plastic bag in the drawers beside the bed. She dressed herself, her underwear wasn't there but she hadn't cared. She slipped through the hall undetected before running on bare feet to the nearest bus stop.

Two buses later and she was on the right one home. An hour had passed since she had run from the hospital and the effects of their drugs had worn off. She was in pain again. She could feel the pulling of the stitches but she couldn't go back. They didn't know her name or where she lived yet, she wanted to keep it that way. Thank god, Zack hadn't said who she was; at least she could be grateful for that. She needed to get home. Mindy was probably very worried about her. Heidi whipped the tears from her eyes, she really was scared. She didn't know what to do or how to look after herself. How could she cope with what had happened?

The bus pulled up in front of Zack's house. Heidi climbed off it, warily looking at the haunted house. She never wanted to go in there again, never wanted to see him again. Hurrying along his yard, she ran up her own driveway. Her eyes caught two little shadows moving through the top rooms, following her.

Heidi ignored them, she ran inside, pausing at the front door when she saw the state of the house. It was trashed. There had been a party there. Her mother's doing obviously. The woman still lay unconscious near the back door, no one else was there. Heidi quickly hurried upstairs hoping Mindy was in there. Hoping her sister was okay, she stepped into her room.

To her relief, her sister lay on her bed scrolling through her homework. She glanced her way, a smile lighting her face. Mindy sat up quickly pulling Heidi into her arms. The sudden force of her body sending ripples of pain through her. She hid it, pulling back and dropping on the bed beside her sister. The two of them glanced out the open window of the room. Listening, but there was no reason to feel fear, their mother was alone.

Heidi wrapped her arm around her sister, her mind darting back over her day. Would they come looking for her when she wasn't in her room? If they found out where she lived, they would surely send the police. Then she and Mindy would be taken away, Mindy would find another home but no one would ever want her. She had to go clean up in case they turned up. She had to pull her mother to where she couldn't be seen. If only she could bury her in the yard. After all, she already looked after herself the best she could.

"Heidi, where were you today and last night? I stayed home today, one 'cause there was so much noise last night I couldn't sleep. Two, I wanted to wait for you. Why didn't you take me too?" she cried, surprising her. She had always thought Mindy wanted to stay here with their mother. That was one reason she hadn't left already, also that they had nowhere to go or money to survive on.

"I was in hospital, well ran away from hospital."

"In hospital! What happened? You should go back if you're not better yet. Why would you run away from hospital?"

"No, they were just observing me. You know what could happen if higher authorities got involved in our lives. I was hurt by one of mum's boy toys and found out yesterday afternoon, when I was next door. Zack took me to the hospital but they just wanted dirt on mum. I'm fine, really."

Mindy was silent for a few minutes before she whispered her voice quivering. "What did he do to you?"

"He drugged me. I don't know what else. The doctors wouldn't tell me." She couldn't tell her sister the whole truth, Mindy would be scared to death if she did. Besides she couldn't relive it herself, better to make it disappear.

Her sister stared at her in shock. Her eyes darkened, another thought passing her mind. "Why were you next door? There are no ghosts there. That's a game we play. You know that, don't you?"

"I just wanted to see inside then Zack came home. We talked a little bit and I headed home, that's when I fainted," she answered flatly.

"Don't go there again Heidi. We don't know him, he could be dangerous."

"No, he's nice and I felt comfortable there."

"We're just kids, he's a man. You shouldn't talk to him, I don't like him!" Mindy had raised her voice, Heidi grit her teeth before calming.

She sighed, shrugging. She didn't want to fight with Mindy even though she did not feel the same as her sister. Zack Solveri was a good man. There was nothing wrong with talking to him. After all, he had helped her when she needed it. Heidi waved the thought off. She had more important things to think about. Mindy had put something out there to think about. Did they stay in this life or run away? There was no guarantee that what they ran too would be any better but at least their mother wouldn't be there.

Although, if she took her mother out of the picture, she could hide their mother's body and they would still have a home. She would still get her payments from the government that they could live on, no one had to know. She dipped her head to one side, a smile creeping onto her lips. Yes, no one would know and she might be able to have a normal life, as normal as her soul would allow it.

*   *   *

"Where were you yesterday?"

Heidi stepped into the counselor's office, closing the door behind her. She dipped her head to one side, staring curiously at his worried and angry expression. She waited for a few minutes before leaning against the wall near the desk. It still hurt to sit down. She had been in pain all day but wouldn't let anyone see, not even Mindy. "Oh, are you upset I stood you up?" she remarked, clicking her tongue on the roof of her mouth. He hated it when she did that.

Drake's eyes narrowed. "We're not playing games today Heidi. Where were you?"

"Sick!" she spat.

"If you were sick, you should have called the office. You know the deal, Heidi. You're an inch away from being sent to an institution. Your sister will be taken to a new family. No one will take you in. Heidi, do you get that? You've set fire in two classrooms here, caused many problems, is that what you want? I have already contacted the police station and learnt you were in hospital yesterday. Don't bullshit me today, I'm not in the mood!"

Heidi screwed up her face, her body trembling in anger. How dare he say things that hurt her, he knew it did. He already knew where she was yesterday so why had he asked? To screw with her mind, to force the truth upon her. Now he had let the police know who she was and probably where she lived. A visit from them was not something she needed.

No, she wouldn't let him win. She would not give in. She was in too much pain and anger to let him take away the only thing that mattered to her, her sister. With her body shaking and her hands clenched by her side, Heidi turned to him, dropping her head to one side.

"What's up Drake? Your wife not putting out for you?" she spat.

To her surprise Drake did not yell at her, he dropped the pen he had been flicking around his fingers to the table. His face emotionless, she hadn't seen him so serious before, why the hell did he care about her? "Two more chances or I'm calling the hospital. They're not happy you left. The police are heading to your house tomorrow to finish speaking with you. If you just let me help and tell the truth, I can clear this up for you."

She was so angry now. This was not fun at all. "Go fuck yourself!" she yelled, he didn't move, not even a flinch.

"One more chance." Was all he said, his hand moved to his mobile phone on his desk.

Heidi turned from him, pursing her lips. Her greatest remark was always her silence. It had kept him working hard so far, why stop now? Drake was still looking at her, she couldn't see him but she could feel it. He waited to see if she would give in, she wouldn't. Her eyes glared into the corner she normally sat in, her body tense and arms crossed over her chest. Why was he being like this? Why was he acting so serious? He was ruining her fun. She wasn't going to come here anymore, not now.

He was her counselor but he had been so mean. That's what he wanted, wasn't it? He wanted to help her, he had looked so scared. She hated him. She glanced over her shoulder to Drake, he had his head bowed, his hand over the phone. Why was he doing this to her? She wanted to believe that he wouldn't really call but she knew this time he was pushed too far. He would call the hospital then the police if he had to. Her chest started heaving, oh god she was going to cry. She couldn't crumble now.

Behind her Drake lifted the phone calling the hospital, it was over. "I don't know what happened," she muttered, barely above a whisper. She bit her lower lip trying so hard not to cry. Slowly her body fell back against the wall where she had been standing.

Drake put the phone down, he moved from behind the desk, dragging the chair with him. Dropping it before her, he sat down. His big hands wrapped around hers. Heidi snapped her eyes to him. Never had he touched her before though she didn't pull away. Her body quivered, she was so scared. His face remained still but his dark eyes danced with curiosity and pride for he had won. For now anyway, and only because she was protecting Mindy.

"Tell me what you do know. Why were you in hospital?" he whispered, scared he might wake her from her trance and lose her.

She shook her head, afraid. How could she tell him when she wasn't sure herself? Her body trembled more but Drake lifted his hand resting it on the side of her face, his eyes pleading with her. "Please Heidi," he whispered.

"I went to bed Monday night when someone was in my room . . . a man . . . I don't know what happened. He hit me on the head and." She stopped, oh god she was weakening. Heidi closed her eyes trying to force the tears back. He couldn't win, she couldn't let him win! She looked into his eyes and saw not joy that she had finally done what he wanted but fear and compassion. Drake looked like he might start to cry himself, his hands tightened around her, his thumbs rolling over the back of them.

Heidi took a deep breath, she was too embarrassed to tell the rest, her hands felt sweaty and her head started feeling light. It was too much information that she wanted him to have but on the other hand, she had to relieve herself from it.

"I woke up the next morning and I was bleeding, you know where. I though I had my periods but the pain got worse, as you might have guessed. I was here and wanted to see the nurse but she wasn't in. Then as you know I went home early, not to my house, I went next door and Zack came home. He was there when I fainted and took me to the hospital," she cried. She couldn't control herself any longer, her whole body started to shake harder, she could barely talk anymore. This was already the most she had ever spoken to him.

"Mindy would be better off elsewhere, I want to die. I can't . . . I can't," she couldn't finish her thought.

"Shhh, Heidi, no you don't."

Drake reached out and pulled her into his arms. She knew he wasn't supposed to touch her but right now she didn't care. Her knees started to shake, she could barely stand anymore. As she started to slide down to the floor, Drake grabbed her shoulders, pulling her onto his lap. He folded her legs over his lap slightly and rocked in the chair.

Burying her head into his shoulder, Heidi cried. She wasn't thinking about what she was doing, only how scared she was. She really didn't understand anything that had happened to her. Not to her body or mind, she had never been able to cope with the world, especially not now. Heidi closed her eyes, she felt so sick, so angry. No one could move this darkness from her mind, not even Drake.

"Why didn't you tell me this on Tuesday, Heidi? And why did you go to the children's house?" he whispered in her ear.

"I always go to the children's house when I'm hurting," she replied, her body resting into his, her eyes closed. She felt so tired and in Drake's arms she felt strangely safe.

Drake's head rested against hers. "You can't do that now, someone lives there. You don't know this man."

"Zack said I can if I need somewhere to go. He saved me," she muttered, falling asleep.

His body tightened beneath hers. "I would have saved you."

*　*　*

He had wanted to say come to my house if you need to get away. He wanted to say that he'll look after her and her sister but he couldn't. He had already gone way over the regulations by touching her though how could he not? She was in distress and scared, she needed someone to hold her, to lift the pain.

He shouldn't be touching her, it was sparking too many feelings. He felt love for her, not the love of a woman but like she was his little sister. She needed his help, he was obsessing again. He couldn't control his love but more than love he felt anger for whoever had done this to her. The poor girl had been raped, she had been terribly abused and whoever had done it was still out there. Could it have been her new neighbor?

Drake adjusted his arm around Heidi's waist. Her body had become slightly heavier and he was sure she had fallen asleep, curled like a child on his lap. Her body looked even tinier, hugged on him. He slowly ran the back on his fingers down her arm. Why couldn't she see what he did? Why couldn't she let him help her so she could be happy? Without thinking about it, he placed a kiss on her head, she didn't move.

He knew what he really should be doing. By law he had to call the police and tell them what she told him. Even though it would mean she would hate him. He had to get out of this situation legally, the police needed to know what had happened. Heidi needed to be protected. She was only fourteen and someone had raped her in the middle of the night! Someone had knocked her out cold and raped her.

He felt sick thinking about it, he wanted to rip the guy apart. What kind of sicko snuck into a girl's room and did that? He needed to be caught and punished. Drake shuffled back on the chair to his phone on the desk. First he would call Melinda and let her know her sister was okay then he would call the police. Hopefully Heidi would go back to hospital, he was worried about her. He couldn't imagine what she must be feeling.

When he spoke to the police, he would explain Heidi's condition and they might be able to arrange for her to stay with her sister. But then what was her condition? There was really nothing wrong with her, only her depression and self destructive behavior, which were bad enough but not enough to have her locked away in some hospital and drugged for life.

Drake picked up the phone dialing the Harrison house. The phone was lifted on the other end. "Hello." A male's voice answered. A voice unlike the ones he was used too. Drake snapped himself out of it, he couldn't fall now. His free arm tightened around Heidi, her head falling back against his forearm. She was defiantly sleeping. He paused, staring into her calm face, angelic.

"Ah hello this is Drake Commack from Eden High, is Ms Harrison in?"

"No, she is not. Is there something I can help you with?"

"Maybe. Is Melinda home yet?" he asked, glancing at the clock. School had been let out half an hour ago.

"Melinda has gone upstairs to get changed. Look I'm their neighbor and I'm watching the girls tonight. I can let their mother know what you want me to."

Drake hesitated, so this was the neighbor. He was slightly worried that the guy had picked up the phone. But at the same time he was too concerned with Heidi to care. The man had a tone of wisdom in his voice. For all he knew, the neighbor could know what's going on and be trying to help. Why did he always expect the worse? Because normally his first instinct was right, he warned himself. But he needed to get Heidi home so he could call the police. He would lose his job if he was caught with her on his lap, especially after school hours.

"I'm Eden High's school counselor. With me I have Adelheid, she had fallen asleep in the office. I was calling to see if someone could pick her up?"

"Has something happened to her?"

"She was a little distressed earlier but once I calmed her, she fell asleep," he replied. He felt as though their roles had changed. At least he could hear the man cared for her, though that was not always a good thing.

"I'll be right there."

Drake sat staring at the phone for a few minutes before returning it to his desk. He could have drove Heidi home himself but that would mean more questions to answer. His wife would go ballistic if she knew his affections. He lifted Heidi's head on his arm, trying to stop it from dropping back. How could she be in such a deep sleep? Well, he was glad she was, she needed it. He couldn't believe how peaceful she looked, her body didn't even move with her silent breaths. Wait! She wasn't breathing! Drake grabbed her by the shoulders but with the sudden movements she let out a sigh, her color returned and breathing became normal. That was too scary for him.

He slowly stood from the chair, carrying Heidi's dead weight to the corner where she normally hid. He placed her on the floor afraid to let go but he had no other choice. There was no telling what would happen if he was caught with her in his arms. Soon her neighbor would come to take her home and he could judge the man in person. Drake stepped away, retuning to his desk but before he sat down there was a knock at the door. That was fast! It couldn't be the neighbor already, could it?

"Come in!" he called.

The door was opened with Melinda stepping in. She smiled at him, moving aside for a tall man to step in. The man had dark hair and unnaturally dark eyes. His skin was pale but that didn't distract one from the tone of his body. He was an elegant man though there was something different about him, something he couldn't place.

The man glanced straight to Heidi but didn't rush to her. He stalked across the room holding out his hand, Drake was impressed. Yes, this guy was a good man, with good intentions. He could trust him to look after the girls and felt comforted that someone would be with them.

"Zack Solveri. I know how often the girls are left alone and honestly that worries me. When their mother left the house this afternoon, I asked if I could stay with them until she got home. It surprised me when she said yes. She doesn't know me and she allowed me in her home to watch her girls." He was astonished, as was Drake.

Drake shook his hand, yes, a good guy. "That is a worry. Well, thank you for coming to get her." He didn't know what to say, he had expected trouble, not this.

Zack looked over his shoulder to Heidi again, he smiled. He moved across the room to scoop the blonde in his arms, pulling her body against his chest. Drake started to relax, he was happy, like himself he was also concerned and trying to help. As he had said, what kind of mother would let a strange man look after her kids? It was a terrible thought to think what could happen, but then it already had.

Drake drifted his eyes to Melinda who looked so excited. He had never seen her smile so bright. It was nice. He wished he could see that on her sister's face. He couldn't remember a time when Heidi smiled, only her fake evil grin, no smile, no joy in her eyes. He remembered the first time Heidi had spoke of her neighbor, she had been so scared and then the necklace . . . the necklace! It was still in his bag.

"Hold on Mr. Solveri. Heidi forgot this the other day." He fumbled through his bag pulling out the necklace, Zack's eyes lightened. Zack nodded to Melinda who skipped over to Drake, grabbing the necklace and putting it in her pocket.

"Thank you Mr. Commack. Come on Mindy, I remember promising to take you out for pizza if you directed me to the school."

Melinda's face lit up with excitement. "We get pizza!" She announced like someone who had never had pizza before, then again maybe she hadn't.

They left, leaving Drake standing behind his desk, trying to piece together his day before he went home and the weight suffocated him. Today was the first time he had seen the Harrison girls act their age. Heidi crying curled on his lap while she slept and Melinda excited about pizza. Heidi was fourteen and Melinda thirteen but he had never seen them express themselves like others their age. He felt strangely calm and satisfied. Today he had done something, he had helped Heidi and hopefully this was only the beginning.

CHAPTER FOUR

She lent over the toilet bowl throwing up. The pizza hadn't gone down to well and the pain of her body disagreed with anything she did. With her body shaking, Heidi collapsed into the wall, she felt lightheaded again. She had been in the bathroom for nearly an hour. Zack came to the doorway every few minutes to check on her but she wouldn't acknowledge him. She was far to embarrassed to face him.

After they had come home from getting the pizza, he had brought over some movies, where they sat on the lounges watching them. But she hadn't been able to control the pain in her stomach any longer, nor could she hide her tears. She had come in here to relieve herself and hide while her sister could watch some movies.

Heidi ran her hand through her sweaty hair, when would this pain end? She was going to pass out from it again. A shadow moved across the doorway; Zack again. She didn't have to turn around to know that. She remained against the wall, her back turned to him, still too embarrassed to see him. This time instead of leaving he came into the room, placing himself on the floor behind her. Heidi bowed her head, what did she say to him?

"Here kitten. I have brought you some pain relief. Please take some," he whispered. He had been calling her 'kitten' all night, she didn't mind it. Actually she really liked it. It was affectionate but not sickening like honey, sweetheart or baby.

Heidi turned around expecting him to look away but he didn't. He smiled, raising his hands. One held a glass of water and in the other was two tablets. She closed her eyes, it was thoughtful for him to bring them to her but could she trust him?

She closed her eyes but her body started to fall forward, trying to go to sleep again. Zack wrapped his arm around her shoulder pulling her against his body, he handed her the pills. She opened her eyes. She didn't care what happened to her. Heidi took the pills following them down with the water. Zack ran his hand through her hair, whispering to himself. He ordered the pain from her body, was he praying for her?

"You'll feel better soon," he whispered, kissing her head.

Heidi let her body rest into his. "I'm sorry you have to see this."

"Don't be. Let's go out and watch the end of the movie. I think your sisters nearly asleep."

They walked out into the lounge room. Heidi resumed her position in the middle of the couch. She rested Mindy's head on her lap and her head on Zack's shoulder who sat on the other side of her. He pulled the bucket of popcorn into his lap, slowly dipping his hand into it. She smiled, mindlessly stroking her amethyst necklace around her neck. Other than feeling so sick, tonight had been a pretty good night. The pain was starting to leave her body which helped her relax, making her forget about the other night. For a little while she was free.

That afternoon in Drake's office she had foolishly broken down, telling him everything about that night. She hadn't been able to control herself. She had found some comfort though, Drake hadn't yelled or called the police, he had just held her. Making all the shivers go away and the pain shift. She had accidentally been so relaxed, she had fallen asleep.

When she awoke, she was in a sleek car being driven by Zack and in the back with her was Mindy. Her sister had told her that Zack was looking after them for the night and taking them out for pizza. Drake had called them to come get her and had given back her necklace, she had previously forgotten all about it.

After getting pizza, Zack had taken them to pick out some movies, two things they had never done before. The pizza had been nice but it had made her sick or was it the day that had made her sick? Heidi rested her head on the other side. She could hear her sister's snoring which made her want to go to sleep herself.

The second movie had finished and Zack was now getting the disk to put it back in the case. His eyes scanned the room before coming back to land on her. Their eyes held for a few minutes before his darted away looking to Mindy, a smile resting on his lips.

"I should go put her in her bed. When do you think your mother will be home?"

"Not sure, you can go when you want. I will look after her," Heidi whispered, still watching him.

"I'm sure you will, but who will look after you?" he said, with a smile. She knew he meant it in a caring way but she hated it. She had always looked after herself. Just because he had been there for her twice, didn't mean she needed him. She was growing weak with him and Drake. She couldn't depend on anyone else. They would only let her down in the end anyway.

Heidi snapped her head to him, tilting it to one side. "I've looked after myself for years. I don't need anyone's help. You should go. I'll take my sister to bed." She didn't mean to say it so cruelly but that's of course how it came out. Zack looked a little shocked, his eyes became dull as he debated within himself whether to just leave or persuade her to let him carry Mindy to bed.

"Okay then, good night. You know where I am shall you . . ."

"I won't. Good night."

She was surprised that Zack didn't get offended. He let a small chuckle escape his lips before collecting the movies and leaving. She was always left unsatisfied talking to him. There were no arguments or games, he didn't humor or patronize her. She wanted to hate him but couldn't. She couldn't predict him and without prediction there was no control. She was helpless around him, a mere child. But then that was the fun of it, wasn't it? Because he was so unpredictable she didn't know where things would go with him, it excited her.

Heidi stared at the closed door, curious to see if he would return and try to help, but he didn't. She felt so confused, did she want him to? She smiled, defiantly unpredictable. Drake would have been back in a second, yelling at her for being so childish. She could really get to like Zack. Looking away from the door, she leant down trying to wake Mindy. Her sister woke drowsy but she was able to get upstairs and into bed. Easy, she had no trouble doing this by herself.

Her sister dropped straight onto the bed, falling fast asleep. Leaving Heidi to undress and redress her in her nightgown. She tucked Mindy in before falling backwards on her own bed, exhausted. She couldn't be happier that tomorrow was Friday. Only one more day and she would have a break from rising in the morning. Two days to sleep, two days to hide from this world and create a better one for herself.

Forcing herself to rise from her bed once more, she changed into her nighty. Shutting the door, she jammed her robe in the gap beneath the door to stop the cold air getting in and slowing anyone who might try.

Heidi jumped from the door to her bed, curling under her blankets. She rolled over to face the window.

Her hand ran down to her stomach, no pain. Come to think of it, she hadn't felt any pain since she was in the bathroom. Had it been the pills or Zack that had helped her? Her eyes darted out the open window, watching for Zack or the children but all she could see was darkness. A thick layer of blackness which had become her life.

*   *   *

She stirred, slowly becoming conscious to the screams downstairs, her mother again. Heidi closed her eyes tightly, rolling over to pull her pillow over her head. Tonight she did not care what they did to her mother, she wanted to sleep. Something downstairs smashed and everything fell silent. She didn't have to remove the pillow to hear the silence. She knew her mother would be on the floor unconscious. Still it was none of her concern. Hate was a powerful thing; it left you without a conscience.

Those men would go home and she would go back to a peaceful slumber. However the men had started talking in drunken voices that begun to drift upstairs. Things were smashing, their laughter louder, oh god! Were they destroying the house or possibly killing her mother?

Heidi felt the smile slide over her lips, that wouldn't be so bad would it? It would save her the trouble of doing it. Soon they would leave and she would wake up dealing with the same thing she did every morning. Hide the evidence of the night before and hope no one alerted the police, everything would be fine.

Things fell silent once again downstairs, Heidi sighed, rolling to stare at the roof. She would never be able to go to sleep now. Her heart was beating too fast and her mind had awoken too much for her to send herself back to sleep, back to her secret world. The slow footsteps up the stairs caught her attention, her body shivered with fear. They were coming upstairs and there was nothing good about that. What did she do?

Heidi leapt out of her bed, waking her sister. Mindy quickly woke up and when she opened her mouth to speak. Heidi slapped her finger to her lips, warning her to be quiet. Her sister snapped up in her bed, her eyes were wide with fear but she obeyed.

Slowly, they moved over to the windows where they opened it, peering down the two story drop. It was a risky jump and Heidi knew her sister wouldn't do it although she would. Better to break a leg then go through what she had earlier in the week. She glanced over her shoulder to Mindy who was no longer there. Her sister now hid under the bed and before Heidi could force her out the window; their bedroom door was thrown open.

The robe she had placed under it only holding it back for a second. Five men entered. Their shadowed faces smirking when they looked upon her. Heidi could feel her lip trembling, she knew what they wanted. It was written all over their faces and bodies. She had no escape. Her mother lay unconscious downstairs so there was no one to hear her scream. The only one in the room who would know was Mindy and she hoped her sister remained hidden. If they saw her, she would suffer the same. Heidi stepped away from the window; all she could do was protect Mindy.

"Greg you ain't wrong. She's a doll." One of the men commented stepping further into the room.

Heidi glanced to the one named Greg. Yes, she remembered him from Monday night. He was the one that had been in her room. He was the one that had caused her all that pain and drugged her. She wanted to kill him! The other four men stepped into the room, one closing the door and leaning upon it. She felt like she couldn't breathe. There was a huge lump in her throat, she felt flustered like she was about to faint.

"You shouldn't be here." All that came out was a whisper. Of course her voice was so childlike and sweet sounding all the men's smiles grew wider.

"Don't be like that doll, we only want to play." Another man piped in, placing himself on the bed. Heidi glanced under it to Mindy who was holding her own hands over her mouth. Her eyes were wide as she stared at the indent where the man sat.

"I don't want to play. I'm fourteen not a child. Now get out or I'll call the police!"

"How sweetheart? The phone's downstairs and you're not getting past us until you play nice." Greg had said in a more serious tone. "Don't you have a sister somewhere?"

"She's at a friend's house," Heidi quickly answered. Her body was still shaking but she was no longer sure if it was from fear or anger.

The men didn't look disappointed. "I guess we can share tonight, can't we boys?"

The four other men laughed, slowly approaching her. Heidi glanced out the window. She still had a chance to escape. If she did it, Mindy would be left under the bed and her sister had so much more to offer the world than her. Heidi lowered her arms by her side, not attempting to run nor fight.

She couldn't win against five grown men. One of the men grabbed her by the arms, throwing her down on Mindy's bed. Heidi turned her face away from the on looking, fearful eyes from beneath her bed.

The men wasted no time with tearing off her nighty. One man lent down pressing his mouth against hers. She closed her eyes, pressing her lips together. She wished the world would disappear, Wished she had another world to escape to. Hands moved over her body but she would not open her eyes, not look into their faces. She wouldn't hear their pants undo, wouldn't feel their body within hers. All she wanted to do was drift from her body with no pain to be felt. Her own private world . . .

*   *   *

She stood on the shore, the cold waves kissing her toes. While she stared out over the sea, there were two rock peaks standing from within the ocean. The sky was clear blue, so perfect. In the distance she could not see where the ocean and the sky met. It was one of the most beautiful things she had ever seen. She could smell the salty water and hear the distant cries of the sea birds.

Behind her were meadows of flowers in clusters of rainbow colors. Through the flowers jumped bunnies and she swore she could see a cat playing with them, not harming them. The full sun strung its rays to the ground, turning the sand beneath her feet to gold. Heidi closed her eyes, smiling. This was her perfect world, her escape.

She opened her mind and opened her soul. Heidi swung around herself before dropping to the sand, a smile resting on her lips. Waves hit the sand again drops of water sprinkling over her but she didn't mind. The long violet dress she wore would never get ruined here. Watching the sun start to go down, Heidi glanced around her surroundings again, no one else there. Of course she really hadn't expected anyone else, although sometimes when she escaped into her mind the children next door would follow.

It wasn't long before she stood from the sand again. Spinning around herself until she became dizzy and fell over. The waves dashed along the sand to meet her skin. She was happy here. She stood again, spinning around, more drops of water landed upon her. The world started to fade, no! She could not go yet! She had to stay and find some peace, save her happiness.

*   *   *

"Heidi! What have you done? Oh my god. Heidi!" Her sister's shrill screams snapped her eyes opened.

She looked around the room in shock. Everything was wet, a thick, dark wetness. She could feel it covering her naked body. She didn't have to look down to know it. Heidi darted her eyes to Mindy who now sat on the other bed shaking. Her eyes staring around them, Heidi followed her sister's gaze, she couldn't see anything. Why was Mindy so afraid? What was wrong with her? Where had the men gone?

Slowly, she moved to the light flicking it on, she screamed. The wetness over her body was blood. Dark, thick blood was throughout the whole room. Her hands ran over her body in fear, she was covered in it but it hadn't come from her. The only pain she felt was from between her legs and from her mind which was suffocated in confusion.

Heidi moved closer to a clot of blood on the wall only to shriek again. The blood had flesh with it, a thick piece of flesh. Oh god! Where were the men? Was it them spattered about her room? Or was she still dreaming, stuck in a twisted nightmare? She didn't understand how they could be torn apart, like they had exploded. She couldn't have done this, could she? Heidi released the breath she had been holding, glancing back to her sister who looked more afraid of her than their room. Whatever had happened here, she had unfortunately done it. Although it was unfortunate she hadn't been here when her body took vengeance. She had wanted them to die, they deserved to die.

"Quick Mindy, we have to clean this up before the morning," Heidi ordered, looking back down at her own body. First, she really should clean herself up and get dressed. She didn't want to know what they had done to her body before she had salvaged her dignity.

"What? You did this. You can clean it up. I didn't kill them, that was you! You screamed this horrible scream and they burst into pieces. You're a murderer!" her sister cried.

Heidi dropped her head to one side, thinking over Mindy's words. Her first thought was too bad she hadn't been there to see it. Then she forced her mind to logic, trying to understand what her sister meant when she said she had screamed and they burst. If that was so, she didn't kill them only cry out.

It was other forces that served them their justice. In a way, it made her happy to think that this could be her doing. It was funny that a tiny girl like her could kill five grown men without a weapon. Heidi smiled, yes, she did kill them and she enjoyed it.

"So what if I did kill them? You saw what they were doing to me and what one had already done. They deserved it!"

"They deserved to go to jail not to be torn apart. Their clothes burnt from their bodies, they felt everything Heidi. You had no right to play the executor and how did you do that?"

"I had every right!" Heidi screamed. Her sister jumped on the bed. She hugged her shaking body, her eyes large. Heidi took a deep breath to calm herself. She didn't want Mindy to be afraid of her. "We will try and piece together what happened later." She started to laugh at the joke.

"Not funny!"

Heidi swung her head to the other side, the smile still on her lips. "You're right it's too soon. Anyway, let's clean this up before someone finds it."

Heidi grabbed a towel and some clothes moving to the door before Mindy spoke again. "The necklace was glowing. It caused this if you didn't. The children must have done this and they have cursed us. They want everyone to die like them!" she cried.

Heidi rolled her eyes. "Or they were protecting me."

She looked past her sister to the open window; beyond their window was the children's. However the children were not there, they were becoming more and more vacant. On the window sat a black cat and from where she stood, she could have sworn the cat had black wings like a bat. The cat's eyes were glowing red; it was just sitting there and staring at her. It's almost snake like tail swung below the window sill. She had never seen a cat at the house before, it must be Zack's.

Heidi spun around leaving the room. She would look for the cat tomorrow. Right now she had to shower then clean. After, she would get Mindy to tell her everything then find a way to shut her up, so this may never be spoken of again.

Her sister always had a problem with telling other people their business. But now she held fear over her and maybe this time if she told her not to speak, Mindy wouldn't. She would lock this night away, along with her secret world. Lock it and savor it until she needed the pain again.

*   *   *

The school day had come and gone. She had forced Mindy to go to school but had stayed home. There was more cleaning to do then she had first thought. Her mother had regained consciousness but never came to see if her children were still home or even alive. The woman had gone to her own room then back downstairs, fussing there for an hour before leaving. Heidi had waited until she was gone. She then ran out of the room to get more hot water and wring out blood stained towels.

After washing away any evidence, she hurried back to her room. She had finished the roof and walls. All the bedding and clothes that had been left out were in the washing machine. All that was left to do were the floors and cupboards. She had thrown out almost everything that had filth on it which she couldn't remove. There wasn't much more to do now, soon she would be finished.

To her surprise she hadn't been in as much pain as she thought she would. Of course she could feel aching from within her but it wasn't pain. She had gone to the bathroom and seen that the stitches had been torn though there wasn't a lot of blood. She wondered why she wasn't in pain.

Had Zack really done something yesterday to help her? Or had she done something herself to block the pain? Whatever the reason was, it made it easier for her to get through the day. Easier for her to keep cleaning and not relive the horrifying events of the night.

It was near twelve. That meant she had two hours to finish the cleaning then get to the school in time for her session with Drake. She wanted to give him no reason to worry again. She was sure if she missed another day with what she had told him, he would send the police to her door. The last thing she needed was police sniffing around. Not until she had ditched everything first, even then she didn't want them.

Hopefully her conscious minded sister would keep her mouth shut and not go running to Drake. Mindy knew enough about Drake to know he wouldn't ignore this twice, if not once. For all they knew, he had already contacted the police after Zack had taken them home. Bastard, he would be next if he had.

Heidi laughed at that. To think she had all this power and could make anyone pay who wronged her. If she did have a list, her mother would be first then the whole school. Drake would be last or not at all. She didn't hate him really, just hated what he tried to do.

She hated that he had cracked her and she had let him. He was a good man with good morals. If he called the police, she would be angry but understand. After all it was his job. Then again, why was she so afraid of the police? Maybe what she thought would happen wouldn't and they could help her get her life back on track without her mother.

She drained the last towel of blood into the bucket. Stepping back, she stared at her clean floor and room. It looked as though nothing had happened, just a normal day where she had decided to clean the sheets, nothing at all. She hadn't even found that much of the men, only pieces of flesh, blood and clumps of hair still attached to the scalp.

She had expected to find pieces of clothing, eyeballs, fingers, bones and lots more severed flesh. She wished she had been able to see what happened. She was starting to wonder if maybe Mindy had been sure all the men were there. There just didn't seem to be enough remains. Aside from a swimming pool of blood there wasn't much evidence of five men. Oh god, she hoped it had been.

Lugging the heavy bucket down the stairs, Heidi washed the blood down the sink, cleaning it out afterwards. The place had a funny smell about it. Not like the normal musty damp smell but that of blood and human pollution. She shifted through the kitchen cupboards, finding the vanilla scented candles she had bought a few weeks ago. Heidi lit the candles with a lighter lying on the kitchen floor.

She was disgusted. Her mother would never care if they had hurt themselves with all the things she left lying about. Her eyes drifted up to the clock, it was nearly time to leave. She grabbed the candle and walked through the lower part of the house then the top. After she blew out the candle, she would finish the job when she got home.

As she was standing at the top of the stairs, the front door was opened. Her mother stumbled through it. Heidi silently lent against the railing, her white fingers clenching at the candle so hard hot wax ran onto them. She didn't notice. Her eyes remained on the woman pacing the lounge room. Her mother's hand pressed against her head, either from a hangover or the pain after being knocked unconscious last night.

She never glanced upstairs and if she knew her daughter was watching, she didn't acknowledge it. Her mother walked over to the lounge flopping upon it. Her dress lifted to her waist and straps falling off her shoulders. She snatched a packet of cigarettes, lighting one. Heidi felt the rage burning within her. Her mother had no idea what happened to her daughters last night. Heidi was sure if she had known, she would charge the men a price to abuse her daughters. Pimp her own daughter out just to make a quick buck. Her eyes narrowed at the thought and her lips pulled into a sneer.

"Why aren't ya at school? Ya want the cops 'round 'ere," her mother slurred. She didn't look her way as she spoke. She took another long draw of the cigarette.

"I was just about to leave. I have an appointment with the counselor." She didn't know why she bothered to answer, her mother never listened anyway.

"The counselor aye? The bastard that can't stop stickin' his nose in our business. Why are they still maken' you see him? A girl needs to be in class or hangin' out with her friends. Not spending her afternoons with a man, seems suss to me. What does he know anyway? When he gets kids, he'll see it's not easy. Kids are devils who ruin your life. What would he know?" she rambled. Her glassy eyes were staring at the blank television.

Heidi curiously walked down the stairs, stopping between the kitchen and lounge room. This is the longest she had spoken to her mother in a long time. She wondered if Drake had called her again. "He knows what he's doing Mama. And he has kids, three in fact."

Her mother snapped her head to her. Blood shot eyes running over her body. For the first time, it felt like her mother was really noticing her, really seeing her. Her mother smiled. "How do ya know that, love? Does he like to play little mummy with you? Are you his little whore?" she spat.

Heidi clenched her teeth in rage. It wasn't Drake that was hurting her, it was her mother and her little night visitors. That was the first thing she wanted to yell but she remained silent. Drake had touched her for the first time yesterday, when he held her she felt safe. It had made her feel happy; she liked his touch and comfort.

"Just like ya daddy. Good for nothing but a root. I should 'ave known climbing in bed with a German backpacker would create nothin' but a fuck up."

Heidi stared in shock at her hateful mother slumped into the lounge. She couldn't remember in her whole life when her mother had mentioned her father. All that she had known was the conception was the result of a one night stand. She never knew what nationality he had been or why he had jumped into to bed with her mother in the first place.

It was disgusting and it frustrated her more than relieved her mind. Her mother was nothing but a selfish bitch. She wished her mother had been in her room with the men last night. No, actually she wanted to see her mother burst into tiny pieces. She dropped her head to the side, smiling.

"Don't give me that look girl! Get used to this life 'cause this is gonna be you in a few years. You ain't nothin more."

"You don't know me! I'm nothing like you!" Heidi hissed. She bit her lip to keep her from screaming all her fury at the woman. Her mother grinned, slipping her second cigarette into her mouth.

"Ya think this man's gonna save you from this town? From whom you really are? Well go on, run away to him, isn't that's where ya got to be? As soon as a man burst's ya cherry you'll change your mind."

Heidi glared at her mother ready to explode but she quickly calmed. A sly smile consumed her face. The woman on the lounge raised her eyebrow. "Who told you my cherry hasn't been picked? Cause it has and the men who did it knocked you out first so they could have me. How do you like that? And I'm nothing like you because you want to know what I did to that man? I killed him mama. Killed him and his friends, but you know what the problem is, don't you? I have one more person to take care of. Do you know who that is mama?" She had spoken in a voice unlike her own, sweet but with an evil flick of her tongue to each word.

The cigarette fell from her mother's mouth. She darted her eyes around the house before pushing past her daughter, hurrying to the front door. "Help! Devil spawn! Somebody help me!" she started screaming, in a panic.

"Shut up! Nobody can hear you and if they can, they won't come. I know this from experience mama!" Heidi yelled back.

Her mother paused for a moment before screaming again. "Somebody help! She's evil. She's going to kill me, her and her evil charm!"

Heidi had felt the burning around her neck but she paid no attention to it. "Goodbye mama."

Her mother grew quiet, thinking she would leave but Heidi only smiled, edging towards the pitiful woman. The front door slammed shut, she could hear it lock on the other side. It shocked her but she wouldn't let her mother see it. Had it been because of her? Heidi stood in front of her mother. She wasn't sure what she had done last night to kill those men but she knew she wanted to do it now.

She closed her eyes and screamed. She screamed so hard that her body flooded with a strange heat. When she opened them nothing had happened. Her mother had run into the lounge room, cowering into the couch, tears sliding down her cheeks. Heidi closed her eyes again and relaxed. It was time to escape.

She drifted through her mind to her world. To the beautiful ocean and fields, a world of innocence. Most of all, her world where she could be all alone. Heidi opened her eyes, a small smile sliding over her lips, she was there. She stepped into the waves, darting her eyes past the peaks to where the ocean met the sky. Heidi crossed her eyebrows together. For the first time, she could see where they met, the sky was slightly darker. She shook her head, what did it matter if they weren't the same color?

She spun around to the fields, another surprise confronting her. Every rainbow flower was now blood red and the sun not as bright, or so it seemed. In the few times she had been here, her world had never changed. Heidi sighed, as much as it was strange she had to leave it. She had to return to her mother. She closed her eyes, her world disappearing around her, it was becoming easier to come and go.

Her vision adjusted, she glanced around the room as she had left it. No blood stained walls, no blown apart body. Everything was the same, other than her mother who lay sprawled across the lounge, naked. Her head was bent backwards and one arm dropped over the side, the other shielding her face. Her mother's eyes were wide with fear and her mouth open in a scream. Blood trickled from within it and down her cheek.

Her body had been stabbed too many times to count. On a closer look, Heidi could see her mother's breasts had been cut off, they lay on the floor. Between her legs had been pined together with corncob holder. Heidi cringed, pressing her hands to her mouth trying not to be sick, a steak knife dropping from her hand. Did she do this? She could never touch her mother like that. Yes, stab her but not cutting off her breasts and pinning her parts together, it was disgusting.

Glancing down at herself Heidi realized there was no doubt that she had done this. Her hands were covered in blood and on the floor by her foot was the knife she had dropped. What had she done? Why like this? It was sickening, something out of a horror film. Looking to the clock she saw that an hour had passed. Mindy would be home soon from school and she couldn't let her come home to this.

Another clean up was to be done. But at least this time it would only be herself and the lounge. Mindy had already seen too much. After all, she had seen more than herself. She would pretend that everything was fine and after a few weeks declare their mother had run away. It wouldn't be the first time weeks would go by without them seeing her, it could work.

"Looks like this time you could use my help." The smooth voice spoke from the doorway. Heidi glanced over her shoulder to Zack who had stepped into the house, closing the door behind him. There were two movies in his hand. He placed them on the table, striding across the room to her side. He stared down at her mother although he wasn't scared or disgusted. Oh god, what had he seen? Was he going to call the police?

"What do I do? I don't care she's dead but Mindy can't find her," Heidi whispered close to tears, and not meaning for the words through her mind to be spoken aloud. She cried not tears of sadness but of fear for herself and what Zack would think of her.

Zack's strong hand reached out, his fingers wrapping around hers, Heidi squeezed his finger. Somehow she felt he understood and didn't judge her, she felt bad about yelling at him last night and not accepting his help. Zack glanced down at her smiling, warming her heart and reassuring her that everything was going to be alright. She would never understand why he understood but was glad someone was by her side.

"Go upstairs and collect your own and Melinda's belongings, then take them to my house. Clean yourself up and wait there. I will hide the body, throw something over the lounge and when Melinda comes home, she'll see everything is normal. I'll come over and get her. Once you both are safe, I'll burn the house down."

"Gee, you've really thought about this, I might think you've done this before. But are you sure we should burn it?" she asked warily. This had been the only home she had known though if she didn't, her next home might be prison. Heidi rested her head on Zack's arm, he moved into her touch causing her to smile. She liked him and wanted to listen to him though she felt suddenly so tired.

"Burn away all the pain, the memories. There will be no evidence and you can be free. I can look after you and your sister. I will never hurt you Heidi."

Heidi felt the tears burning in her eyes. No one had ever cared for her. No one had understood and accepted her. "Do you promise?"

Zack turned to her, holding both her hands, his eyes staring into hers. "I promise."

Heidi nodded. "Burn it down."

As well as the instruction it was also her way of telling Zack that she trusted him. Zack smiled, planting a kiss on her head then moved to stand over her mother's body. Heidi stared at his face, was that admiration for the torture she had seen in his eyes? She shook her head, what did it matter? Her mother was dead now.

Turning, she ran up the stairs to collect her and her sister's things. It had taken fourteen years but she was finally free of her mother and free to be with her sister. Zack was right. Everything bad would burn with this house and everything good would come with her. A new beginning.

CHAPTER FIVE

It was cold. It always seemed cold even though the sun glared down on the earth outside. The sunlight never reached beyond the window sill. Her house faced the wrong way, not a slice of light warmed her room. She only felt coldness. She sat back on the bed, staring out at the life she had never been apart of. Her mother and stepfather had gone to church, leaving her locked in the room. Had her mother forgotten that she had a daughter?

Her stepfather had locked her in here nearly a week ago and she had yet to see the woman that had given birth to her. Her mother of all people should be trying to help her, not submitting to the man that had caused this. Her stepfather hadn't brought her up food in two days or let her bathe. All she could do was sleep to pass the time, silently wishing her body away.

The majority of the villagers were in church today. She knew they would ask her mother how she was or even where she was. Her mother would probably only smile, her eyes filled with sadness and say that her daughter was unwell, always unwell. Olivia was sure her stepfather was trying to make her sick. He would love it if something happened to her but she wasn't going anywhere. He hated her because she reminded him that his lover had previously been married. She was the result of her mothers love for another man.

She wouldn't let him take her mother away! He was a horrible man and she would stop at no end to make sure her mother saw that. Olivia wiped the tears from her eyes, sliding off her bed to sit in the corner. Clutching her stomach, she hugged her favorite teddy bear. All she could do was try to forget the hunger pains and pray. Pray the day that God watches the earth, pray that he shall strike her stepfather down and set her free.

Olivia pulled all the bears down from her bed, laying them before her, from smallest to largest. She loved them though sometimes there were days like today when she hated them. They had plain little faces and dull matted fur. How she would love a doll, that she could change its clothes and brush its hair. How wonderful to invent personalities, friends. However dolls were too expensive and her mother believed they turned little girls wicked, creating vanity. But she just wanted something to love.

Soon she would be too old for either bear or doll. Soon her childhood would abandon her and she knew nothing about becoming a woman. Her mother had taught her no sewing or cooking skills to make a good wife, nor had she been socialized like other girls her age. In five years she will have to leave home and marry, unsuited for that world.

Olivia sighed, it seemed she would never grow up or be noticed by the world. She would never to go to school or meet someone new. She might as well not be born. She kicked the bears away, pushing her body further into the corner when there was a tap on the window. Who could reach her window? She was on the second floor. Olivia slowly sat on her knees, peering over the bed to the window. There was no one there, of course there wouldn't be. No man could fly.

Curious, she walked around the bed, looking down to the side street where a boy stood. He was a little older than herself, maybe fifteen or so. She had never seen him before. A boy with wispy black hair, dark eyes and pale skin. He was strange but a handsome boy who would make girls heart melt in another year or two. When she didn't open the window, he threw a pebble that tapped upon the glass. Her eyes darted to him in confusion but smiled when she was greeted with his wide grin.

She opened the window. "Why are you throwing pebbles at my window? Who are you?" she quietly asked, though he seemed to have heard her.

"We have just arrived in town. My father had an accident in the cart just beyond the tree line. No one else is home but I saw a shadow in here, can you help?"

"I'm the only one home. There is not much I could do."

"Do you have a hammer I can borrow? Any tools?" he called back, darting his eyes around the base of the house.

Olivia looked at the shed beside the house, her stepfather kept tools in there. How would she get them for him, she couldn't. She didn't care if he borrowed them but that would mean telling him she was locked in. She felt her face heating up as she spoke. "There may be some in the shed but I can't get them. I'm locked in my room."

"Locked in your room?" he paused, looking around the open yard then back up the street where the church was. "Can I help myself to the shed? I promise I will bring them back."

"You're welcome to them if you can get in."

He dipped his head forward in thanks before jogging off into the yard and out of her vision. Olivia sat back into the rocking chair beside the bed. Darting her eyes back down to the church, still no activity, she was sure it was getting late. As she was about to move from the window, the boy reappeared with his arms full of tools. He gestured for her to move back, before he threw a long iron bar through her window. It fell to the floor next to her bed, Olivia gasped. She grabbed the bar quickly, looking down to say thank you but he had gone.

Olivia looked at the iron bar in her hands, hurrying to the door. She wedged it in the frame. Lunging her body against the bar, she pulled until the door creaked and snapped open. It opened easier then she thought it would. Olivia grabbed the iron bar hiding it beneath her bed. For the next time her stepfather trapped her within this room.

She rushed downstairs opening the front door to the boy, she nearly fell backwards. The boy laughed placing the tools at his feet, his hands diving into his pockets. He pulled out a small well crafted doll, it was beautiful. The doll was porcelain, with long black hair and violet eyes.

It was dressed in a white cotton dress with silk edging, something she herself did not possess. The boy handed her the doll. Olivia carefully clutched it in her hands, scared she might break it. Was he giving it to her? She couldn't accept a gift so precious, so spellbinding.

"This is for you, in return for your help. Don't hesitate in taking it, my mother makes them. We are carting her stall to set up in the markets here. This one is for you though. My name is Adrian. Who are you and why were you locked in your room?"

"My name is Olivia. Thank you for the doll and your help. My stepfather is not very fond of me," she answered, still staring at the doll.

Adrian nodded, a smile stuck to his lips. "It was nice to meet you Olivia. I will return the tools as soon as I can." With his words he jogged across the street, disappearing into the woods on the other side.

Olivia closed the door, trying not to let the smile on her lips slide away with her heart. Adrian had been so nice to her and he had given her three things she wished for within her heart. He had given her a beautiful doll, a friend and he had released her from her prison. She had never had a friend before or contact with another child her age. But then Adrian was new in town, he had yet to hear the rumors.

She ran through the kitchen, swinging open the doors to the pantry. She took two apples and some custard biscuits her mother had made the day before. Quickly running back upstairs, she locked herself in her room again.

Olivia hid the food under her bed, all but one biscuit which she ate hungrily. With the iron bar also hidden and no evidence of her being out of the room. Olivia huddled back into her corner with her bears, secretly placing the doll between them. Perhaps this life wouldn't be so cruel to her after all. Maybe Adrian was her knight and she the princess trapped in the castle.

*   *   *

His pen tapped against the desk while he stared at the clock. Every few minutes his eyes darted to the door, where was she? Heidi was ten minutes late. At first he gave her the benefit of the doubt, but after ringing administration to find out she hadn't been at school all day, he was worried. He had felt sick all day, waiting for this hour, waiting to talk to Heidi about yesterday. He hoped she didn't hate him.

Yesterday they had made so much progress, she trusted him and he had fallen in love with her in his arms. Not that of sexual love but a protective sincere love. What did he do now that his worst fear had happened? She hadn't come back after what she had told him. What if the men had come back and hurt her. He hadn't called the police yesterday but today he would. He had been so tired and Heidi was in safe hands, or so he had thought but he couldn't ignore this any longer.

Drake dropped his head to the table. It hadn't helped last night that he had got into a fight with his wife. Stupidly he had told her what happened during the day, she was angered. He had been trying to let her into his world, although it was against regulations to discuss students, he had. His wife had become jealous of his commitment to Heidi. It ended with him sleeping on the couch, lost in twisted memories of the day and now this.

This week had nearly destroyed him. He was going to drive himself insane with all this thinking. Drake looked back at the clock, half an hour had passed. It was time to take action, after all, what more could his wife do to him. Drake picked up the phone calling the office again to find out what class Melinda was in. At least the sister could tell him something and if she wouldn't, he would make her.

Melinda Harrison was in science class, block B, class 3, with Mr. McCollum.

Drake replaced the receiver, grabbed his coat and headed up into block B. hoping Melinda was still at school. Nervously he brushed back his hair, climbing the stairs, trying to decide what he would say to Melinda. He hoped when she saw him, she would spill. But if she was anything like her sister, it was not going to be easy.

Drake stepped up to the door of classroom three. He took a deep breath before knocking on the door and slightly opening it. Mr. McCollum stood in front of the blackboard, talking as he wrote. He nodded to the counselor, quickly finishing what was in his head before turning to him.

The year seven class was running a mess behind him. A group of girls sat in the back comparing mobile phones. On the other side at the back was a group of boys, the sporty group. Chatting and pushing each other around, egging on the girls with the phones. In the middle of the room were three boys, trying to make their school uniforms as black as it could be, Goths. They mumbled to each other, Drake was surprised if they actually understood each other, for he never did.

To the front were two girls who were willing to learn. Their pens rapidly running across the pages in their books, their eyes cast on the blackboard. At the last groups of tables Melinda sat, with another girl and two boys. The four were flicking spit balls at each other. Melinda and her friend were flirting with the two skinny boys.

Mr. McCollum finished what was on the board, glancing back to the class with a firm order for them to sit down and copy what was on the board. When they didn't quiet, he yelled that there would be a test on all the terms work tomorrow.

Slowly the kids obeyed. But instead of working, they pretended and their talk turned to whispers. Mr. McCollum sighed, walking over to the door, brushing his brow with the back of his hand. Drake was glad he only had two students at the most to deal with, not a class.

"How's it going Drake?" Mr. McCollum spoke, leaning against the wall next to him. The teacher's eyes focused on the class. "What can I do for you?"

"Looks like you've got your hands full."

"Yeah, year seven is like dealing with two year olds. Having them in the last period of Friday sends me straight to the pub afterwards."

"I can understand, one day I'll have to join you."

Mr. McCollum's face lightened. "Yeah, that'll be good."

Drake was watching Melinda the whole time he had been talking, she hadn't noticed him yet. All she was concentrating on were the two boys. He would have thought after what her sister had been through, neither would go near a boy for a while. However it didn't happen to Melinda, did it?

He could see Melinda would be the one to follow their mother's footsteps, he felt so angry. How could she not care what happened? He knew he was taking it too personally but he couldn't prevent the way he felt. Especially when he could see a boy taking advantage of Melinda and her being taken down that road, no chance for another choice.

"I was hopping to take Melinda Harrison off your hands for the remainder of the period," Drake muttered, getting to the point.

Mr. McCollum looked to Melinda, studying her for a moment. "She's all yours and Drake, see if you can get her eyes off the boys and in her books. The girl's already failing year seven," he commented.

Drake shook his head, appalled. "I'll try."

"Melinda can you pack up your things and go with Mr. Commack," Mr. McCollum called to the girl before turning around to him. "I'll be taking up your offer for the drink next week," he whispered, under his breath.

"I'm counting on it."

For the first time since he had been watching the class, Melinda turned from the boys looking at him. Her eyes brightened making her look her age again, although her face played a grim pout, for her company's sake. She packed her books into her school bag, leaving the class, giving her friends a quick wave before Drake shut the door. She walked silently behind him, heading to his office but he only stopped there to get his keys, phone and wallet then locked the door.

He glanced around them relieved to see no one around, then grabbing Melinda's wrist he briskly walked her to his car. He could feel her body pulling back against him. She knew he wasn't allowed to take her out of the school. She was too intrigued to speak out against him. Drake opened the back door of his car for her, waiting until she had hopped in before jumping into the driver's side. They quickly left the school property, driving towards the Harrison home.

"Where are we going? Why'd you take me out of class?" Melinda finally piped up, in the back.

"I'm taking you home and checking on your sister. If she is fine, well that is great but I'm still calling the police. Now is there anything you need to tell me?"

Melinda remained silent in the back. Drake shook his head driving through the streets. Heading to the top of the hill, he knew they lived there though he had never stepped into the premises. With every minute that passed, she did not speak, he grew angrier. Anger because he would have to call the police and afraid because he now felt there was undeniably something wrong. Why didn't Melinda want to help her sister?

"As soon as we stop I'm calling the police, Melinda. I'm sick of this. I can't ignore what is going on. This is destroying me, my family and most of all, yours. So talk to me, whether you do or not I'm still calling to police once we're at your house."

"No! No, Heidi will be mad. If you do call, she says they'll take us away and split us up!" Melinda cried.

"I know that's what Heidi thinks but that's not so. Please, I want to help. Why wasn't Heidi at school today? Is she still in pain?" he pressured. He was driving the long way home to make her nervous and tell him everything just so she could get home.

"She stayed at home to clean up. She was meant to come this afternoon to see you so you knew everything was fine. Are you sure this is part of your job? Do you kidnap all your students?" she spat. Drake smiled, that was something Heidi would have said.

"Only the ones I care about and know needs help. She didn't come this afternoon, why would cleaning hold her up?"

"Back off! One day she's not at school and you freak out! You're supposed to be the counselor. Take me home and leave us alone!" she suddenly shouted.

Her face turned red as he watched her through the rear view-mirror. He knew she was lying and he could see she was scared. Although in a way Melinda was right, he was becoming too paranoid, he needed to back off. Maybe throw his energy into the gym or something. Get his body, soul and marriage healthy again before tackling the world.

"Okay I'll take you home. I only care for you and your family and instinct tells me something is wrong. But if you won't accept my help . . ."

"Spare me the lecture and take me home."

He spun the car around in the next street, heading once more up the hill. He pulled up in front of Melinda's house staring out of the window. Two identical houses stood side by side. To one side was a bare block of land, where the third one had been burnt down years ago. Why hadn't anyone ever built on the land since? He would have if he'd known it was there when he moved to Adelaide. Who wouldn't want a large hill top home that looked down upon the suburbs of the city? It was a magical setting.

Drake switched off the engine, his eyes drifting back to the house next to the spare block of land, the Harrison home. The two story house was sadly run down with several weather boards falling from their place on the outer wall. The shutters were also falling down, rotten and probably infested with parasites. The lawns were over grown and it was in desperate need of a fresh coat of paint, actually a full makeover was more like it.

Drake glanced back at Melinda, surprised she hadn't run from the car. She too was staring out at her home, her eyes glazed with thoughts. What was running through her head? Was she scared to go home? He wished she would let him help her, he honestly thought she would have. But not today, no, she had something more to hide, something behind her terror filled eyes. He sighed, looking back to the house. All he had was good intentions, he never wanted to hurt her, never wanted to hurt Heidi.

"Heidi woke me up in the middle of the night. She tried to get me to jump out of the window. I thought she had really lost it until I heard the footsteps up the hall. I hid under her bed but she didn't hide in time, not before the men came in. I counted four but there could have been more, they grabbed her and tore off her nighty."

Tears were flooding from her eyes, her body heaving with memories she couldn't stop but to recall. Drake remained silent. Scared she might stop should he speak up. "They raped her, one after the other. The others held her down, laughing and cheering one another on. It was horrible, I watched it all. Heidi went blank as she always does. She looks like she is sleeping but with her eyes open. It's terrifying.

"Suddenly she started screaming very loud, her whole body was thrown about on the bed. At first the men thought it was funny until she sat up, forcing their weight off her. Her eyes were completely black and her head twisted to one side. She actually smiled at them. The men were afraid. I know what they did was wrong but it didn't have to end like that. The scream won't stop ringing in my ears."

Drake watched her through the rearview-mirror. His skin gave him shivers and all the hairs on his body stood on their ends. What had happened? Did he want to know? He already felt so sickened but he had to ask. Even if it risked snapping her from her recollection, he had to know. "How did it end?" he whispered. He didn't know what he would do if she said Heidi was dead.

"Heidi screamed a horrible scream. The men's faces filled with fluid and became red. Their hair started to fall out and the clothes burnt from their bodies. They were screaming and crying. They were so afraid as they clawed at their skin. They were burnt alive! From the inside! They burst open. Their boiling blood slapped against the walls, parts of their flesh sticking everywhere. Heidi woke up and had no idea what had happened. She had killed them! And you know what? That necklace was glowing around her neck. When the men burst, I swear it shot some of that light into them."

She fell silent, staring at the houses or more at the roof before snapping out of her memories. She grabbed her school bag, pushing open the car door. Her eyes caught his through the rearview-mirror. "Is that what you wanted to hear? That my sister has some evil power and killed people, did you want that Drake? I have to go help her finish cleaning. You had better go before she sees you. If she does see you she'll know I told and you could be next. See ya Monday."

With that she slammed the door, running up the front path to the ajar door. Drake stared after her, frozen. As much as he wanted to believe otherwise, he knew she wasn't lying. How something like that was possible, he wasn't sure. It sent tremors through him and sickened him to the core. He wasn't sure if his sickness was from Melinda description or what had happened to Heidi. Both, he guessed, both were too horrible to comprehend.

Once Melinda had disappeared inside, he pulled out his phone. Ringing child services with what he knew of the neglect and the rape, nothing more. They promised to send the police straight out to the house and asked him to wait. He was planning to anyway. He had barely put down the phone when Melinda came back out of the house. She was looking around the yard and street, something was wrong. Drake climbed out of his car, slowly walking down the driveway, the furthest he had been on the property.

"What's wrong?" He was actually afraid to ask.

Melinda looked worried. "No one's home, none of my things are in my bedroom," she cried.

"Okay, you wait out here and I'll go have a look around," he said. He was happy when Melinda nodded, sitting down in the middle of the driveway. Drake took in a deep breath, his mind still trying to register what the younger sister had told him.

He walked straight into the house without a further minute of hesitation. For if he did not, he may never go in. The kitchen and lounge room were spotless, something he found unusual. There was a strange familiar smell throughout the house, what was it? Drake headed up the stairs to the first bedroom. If it was the girls room Melinda was right, it was bare. Then maybe this one wasn't theirs. He moved past a tiny bathroom to the next, this one was dark. He felt along the wall finding a light to switch it on, gasping.

On the double bed lay the girl's mother, naked and dead. Long dead! Her breasts had been cut off and between her legs had been stitched up. She had been stabbed too many times to count. Her mouth was wide in a silent scream, blood spilling from her blue lips. Drake started to gag, stumbling backwards. Thank god Melinda hadn't seen this, hadn't found her dead mother. The sight was horrible and the smell, oh god that smell! God knows what it would do to the girl outside. But who had done it?

Looking around the rest of the room, Drake realized there was nothing in here for the girls. He had to get out. The smell was making him feel sicker and light headed. Besides if the police turned up, he didn't want to be found standing over a dead naked woman. Spinning around, Drake hurried down the stairs and out the front door, into the yard. He hoped Melinda hadn't decided to follow him back in. In fact Melinda was no longer in the front yard at all.

He turned around, searching for her but she was nowhere in sight. The earth felt like it was swaying beneath his feet. It felt like he was on a ship. Drake fell to the grass throwing up, the weight of Melinda's words suffocating his mind. Where was she? He would never forgive himself if something had happened to her. Also, where was Heidi? He couldn't explain the strange feeling nagging in his head, he knew things weren't as they seemed.

Drake ran to his car, running for his phone to call the police. They should have been there already, shouldn't they? They had better get here fast. There was a murdered woman upstairs and two missing girls, who so desperately needed help. He hurried down the overgrown pathway, slowing as his eyes caught his tyres. All his tyres were flat.

What had happened here? He couldn't have been inside the house for more than five minutes. How could someone take a child without a sound and slash all his tyres? Who would do that? He felt so sick, he opened the car door. Drake knew it was no time to worry about his tyres, he needed his phone. Just as he lent over the passengers seat to the drivers side, a police car pulled up behind him.

With some relief, Drake snatched his wallet and phone, jogging to the police car when something cracked within the house. Both he and the two officers paused, looking towards the house. They didn't even have a chance to speak, no chance to explain about the dead woman upstairs, no chance to cry about the girls. The house exploded.

Drake leaped to the ground behind the police car, bits of weather boards flying over the street. Something hit his legs, tearing them in fact. He winced in pain, peering under the police car. Small fires burnt on the lawn and in the rubble where the house had stood. That smell, he had smelt inside. It had been gasoline! He didn't want to think what would have happened should he still be inside. He'd be dead!

As dead as the officer sprawled on the road. The other officer hid under the police car beside him, he was young and afraid. Why not? He had just witnessed a house blow up. He should feel lucky he didn't have to see what was inside. Where was Melinda? Had she followed him back inside? Had Heidi been hiding somewhere inside? No, he couldn't think about it. Two girls were missing, their home had blown apart and all evidence of what had happened lost, all hope in flames.

*　　*　　*

Her large golden-brown eyes snapped open just in time to catch all the shadows darting from the walls. Only hers remained, illuminated by the moonlight. The shadows of the dead would always try to hide from her, yet they followed her wherever she went.

If she wasn't so afraid, it could make her laugh. However she was afraid of this night more than she was any other. For dark dreams had clouded her mind, dreams of a girl that looked like herself, who was consumed by pain and darkness. Things that now lay within her mind.

Heidi wiped the sweat from her forehead, dropping back onto the double bed. She rolled over to face her heavily sleeping sister. Heidi sighed, she should be exhausted after the day she had, but she wasn't. She was in a little pain from the previous night but her soul wouldn't let her mind concentrate on that night. All she could think about was the day between these two dark nights. Surprisingly, she wasn't angered about it but excited and most of all curious.

That afternoon she had packed all her own and Mindy's things as fast as she could, before she had ran out of the house with Zack not far behind her. He had sent her into this room, closing the blinds that looked upon her house. He had told her to wait while he burnt her house down and collected Mindy. While he was gone, Heidi had unpacked some of their things, curling up on the bed and waiting for her sister. It hadn't been long before Mindy was sent in, they had embraced one another. First out of love then fear, for outside their house exploded.

Zack's house shook. The earth shook. Zack had returned, running up the stairs to grab the girls in his arms. He stayed with them until the sirens had disappeared. They pretended not to be home when the police came to knock at the door. After all the commotion had dimmed outside, Zack ordered them chinese. He had said they could stay with him as long as they wanted. She had been happy but Mindy had cried, which made her feel like crying. She knew if she started crying now then she would never stop. No, she would not cry, not for her home, not for her mother and not for her innocence.

They had gone downstairs and watched television for a little while, then Zack had suggested for them to get some rest. She and Mindy had been put in the guest room while Zack had the children's room, his room now. Heidi had fallen straight to sleep but now found herself wide awake, listening to the hum of the wind outside.

The dream hadn't scared her as much as feeling alone when she snapped out of it. Of course her sister was by her side but she was asleep and Mindy didn't know what herself and Zack had done. Mindy didn't feel what she did. She sighed, she didn't want to go back to sleep, she wanted to feel safe and talk with someone. She wanted to walk through the rubble of her old home and savor it.

Heidi slipped from the bed, her feet landing on the cold timber floor. She wrapped her robe around her body, sneaking from the room. If she was going to go to sleep, it would be in the hot rubble, her dreams feeding on the memories there. She would not let herself fall into reality, not face the horror night, not fall into loneliness or become homeless, for thanks to Zack, she was neither. Zack was by her side and he had promised to protect her, she could feel his love for her.

Heidi slowly walked down the hallway. Standing at the top of the stairs, she glanced down through the lounge room window, seeing where her house once stood, now nothing but a pile of wood and dust, surrounded by bright orange police tape. She had thought if she looked hard enough maybe she could recognize something. She couldn't see a thing. She had expected to feel a little remorseful but she felt emotionless or even a little confusion, no guilt. Never would she take on the pain for this.

"Heidi, is that you?" Zack called, in a sleepy voice from his bedroom.

Heidi snapped out of her thoughts, glancing over her shoulder to see the slightly open door. For a moment she wanted to ignore that he had spoken and continue down the stairs. Go to the rubble, sleep within the ashes of the murdered but she didn't. Swinging her head back to the door, Heidi turned. Stepping one foot in front of the other, she approached his door, peering in.

The room was dark but the window that had faced hers was open, letting in a large stream of moonlight that landed on the half naked man. Zack lay on his stomach, the blankets were kicked to his feet and his head turned away from her. He wore long burgundy pants that almost made his legs disappear into the bedding. His naked back shone under the light, his form highlighted. Heidi looked away, waiting for him to yell at her for coming in but he didn't. Slowly, she walked over to the bed intrigued but afraid for disturbing him.

She liked him but hated to see him looking like that, lying over the bed. He was a man and she hated men. Although he was not one of them but still seeing him like that send shivers up her spine. Visions of the week drove their way through her head. She couldn't let them in, if she remembered everything she might never want to wake up. Heidi took in a deep breath, standing beside the bed. Would she come to hate him too?

"Where were you heading to this time of night?" he muttered, his head still turned from her. "You know there's danger out there."

"I can't sleep. I was just going to look at the house. I wouldn't have touched anything," she whispered. Zack rolled to his side, looking at her with his spellbinding dark eyes. He patted the bed beside him. Heidi glared back, not moving.

"I promised not to hurt you, did I not?"

"Just because you promise something to me does not mean I trust you."

Zack smiled. "And so you shouldn't. There are a lot of evil people out there who will lie to get what they want. Never trust anyone but yourself, Heidi," he whispered, lost in thought.

Heidi slowly nodded, twisting her head to one side. Her eyes drifted to the window again. "Where is your cat?"

He crossed his eyebrows together. "I don't have a cat."

"You must. I saw one in the window when I . . ."

"When what?"

"I'm tired. I should go back to bed," she said, bowing her head. She couldn't tell him what had happened, especially when she wasn't so sure herself. "I think I'm evil," she whispered, turning to the door.

"Evil or not you're still human. Still have emotions and need to be loved. Evil is a word created by people who were scared of something different. Someone like you and me," he spoke softly.

His words made her feel warm and calm, he understood her. Instead of trying to convince her she wasn't evil, he accepted what she thought. He was right. They were the same. He had blown up her house and taken care of her mother's body without a question. He saw no crime. Heidi turned back around, a smile on her lips. Zack returned her smile, his eyes dancing as he pat the bed again.

This time she hopped in, sliding over to Zack and pressing her back against his chest. Her robe still wrapped tightly around her. She was slightly scared but when she felt no movement in his body, she relaxed. After a few minutes Zack placed his fingers under her chin turning her face to his. Her heart was pounding, what was he going to do? Where would she go if he hurt her?

At first he didn't do anything then he leant forward kissing her upon her nose, before burying his head in her hair. Heidi smiled, pulling his arm over her body and closing her eyes. To her surprised she suddenly felt relaxed and safe in his arms. Heidi let her body drift into slumber, into her safe world. And should Zack try to hurt her while she slept, she would kill him too.

CHAPTER SIX

The police were there again. Two officers were interviewing Zack on the front lawn, while six others passed through the rubble. A digital camera attached to one officer's hands as he pulled things aside, taking photos of everything. His partner stood by the barricade speaking with the distressed neighbors. People she had never seen before in her life.

Sure they looked sad now but where were they when she was screaming for her life the night she was raped? Where were they when she and Mindy were left on the porch for a night while their mother was sleeping around the pub?

Heidi screwed up her nose, she hated them. She hated everyone. It had been a week since the explosion. Zack was helping hide them so authorities thought they were killed in the blaze, giving them freedom. Of course Mindy had been at school that day, the explosion had happened once she returned and Drake couldn't be sure that she hadn't followed him into the house. Heidi couldn't be more grateful to Zack or excited for she could get her life back. In a way she liked where it was now, she loved curling up beside Zack after a crazy dream. She loved having the father figure she had never grown up with.

Of course the police had never found her mother's body but they kept searching due to Drake Commack's statement. At the time, she hadn't even known he was there, why would he be? Drake had seen too much and when the house exploded, he was injured. He had surgery on his legs to remove fragments of tiles and burns on his back. Hearing about him in the news had made her sad.

Drake was a good man, he never deserved to meet her and care so much that it nearly killed him. Every time he was on the news Mindy would start crying, begging her to take them to his house. She wanted to accept his help but it was too late. Sometimes it sounded like a good idea then other days she hated Mindy for saying it. Drake was better off without them in his life anyway. He didn't need her to torment him again. Besides everyone thought they were dead.

They didn't need anyone to help them, sure Zack was there now. He was encouraging their independence so they could leave and start their own lives. After all, he had a life too. Heidi knew her sister hated him but what could she do about it? He had helped so much in the last week and all Mindy had done was whine and not listen. All she listened to was her own head and maybe when Zack gave her advice on how to survive in the world so young.

Sometimes she thought he would offer to take her in for good but he didn't, she respected that. He had told her he had many secrets and was different from other people. He had said there were others who would follow him and kill her. She didn't understand what he meant by that and really it was none of her business. But she did respect him and maybe even loved him a little.

Downstairs she heard the front door slam. Zack was back and obviously annoyed with the constant interruptions. Heidi glanced over her shoulder at Mindy lying on the bed, writing about the week. From what she had read it was mostly bitching about Zack and how he wouldn't let them go to school. All the letters seemed to be addressed to her friends, nothing really too important or containing any relevant information.

Heidi turned back to the window, where the police were packing up outside. Behind her she could hear Zack coming up the stairs. He passed their room with not even a glance before locking himself in his. Mindy looked up for a second, waiting, then continued with her sentence. Heidi understood he needed his space, she would too if police were at her throat everyday. Zack had taken a big risk for them. If he were caught he would serve jail time.

"We should go to Drake or the police, they will help us. I don't like Zack, he's insane!" Melinda spat.

"Insane. That's what people say about me," Heidi muttered, not looking from the window.

"Well if ya didn't act it, they wouldn't say it. Come on Heidi, if you don't come with me, I'll go alone."

Heidi spun around to her sister. "Go then. If you hate it here so much, leave. I'm doing all I can for you, don't you see?"

Melinda's eyes widened in rage but she shut her mouth.

Heidi sighed, hearing the harshness of her tongue. "Look, we'll pass another week then get out of here, okay?"

"How? With what money? Do you know what happens to girls on the streets?" her sister spat, rolling her eyes.

"One, I'll think of something and two, I'm no ordinary girl."

Her sister turned her head back to the paper, forcing anger into her face though Heidi could see the tears. She was losing patience with Mindy, their conversations over the week all ended the same. Ending in tears and arguments about their future. She could understand her sister's frustration but what could she do about it? All she knew was Zack made her feel safe. He was the first person who accepted her for her, she could learn so much from him. Heidi glanced down at the empty lot, another investigation over for the day, thank god.

"I have a gift for you two," Zack spoke from the door.

Both girls spun around to the tall man leaning against the door frame, two shoeboxes in his arms. She hadn't even heard him come out of his room. Seeing him, all she wanted to ask was what the detective had questioned him about this time. Though she knew by doing that, she would aggravate him and she would get no closer to some answers. She hated people trying to protect her and she hated that he was starting to become like them.

Her attention shifted to the shoeboxes under his arm. Her curiosity was starting to get the better of her. Slowly moving from the window, Heidi sat down on the bed next to her sister who quickly shut her book. She glanced at her sister then looked back to the man. Zack was watching them intently or was he watching her?

"What's in the boxes?" Mindy asked.

He smiled, approaching the bed, he handed each of them a box. "Why don't you find out?"

Mindy glanced first to her then the box. She lifted off the lid without further delay. Heidi's box remained on her lap as she nervously glanced into her sisters. In Mindy's box was a beautiful porcelain doll. The doll had tight red curls and was dressed in a cream cotton dress. Complete with a wide brimmed hat, shoes and gloves.

Her face had been delicately hand painted, soft pink lips, bright blue eyes and perfectly blushed cheeks. She was in perfect condition but obviously so old, she was precious. Heidi smiled, in a way it kind of looked like her sister. They had never possessed a beautiful doll like this before but Mindy face did not betray the same joy as her own.

"A doll? Why did you get me a doll? I'm thirteen not three. You know nothing about us!" Mindy slammed the shoebox lid back on, throwing it across the bed, so that it nearly fell off and smashed. Her sister didn't seem to care.

Zack did not look the slightest bit hurt. "Girls never get too old for dolls besides theses aren't to play with. Just old mementos of a better world. I thought you, Melinda would be grown up enough to appreciate that," he said with a smirk.

Mindy snapped her eyes to him with fear like he was about to hit her. Her eyes closed, tears rolling from them. Heidi smiled, Zack was good. He had turned her sister's insult into a witty remark shot right back at her, with no aggravation. She could learn a lot from him.

Mindy stood from the bed, snatching her book and leaving the room. She squeezed through the doorway trying to avoid touching Zack. The man only smiled, his eyes watching her move past him, showing no effort to make room for her. Heidi didn't worry about Mindy, her sister wouldn't go anywhere, just lie on the lounge and sulk.

"And what about you Heidi? Are you too old for dolls?"

"No. I think she's beautiful."

He smiled. "Open yours."

She had forgotten about the box on her lap, although she couldn't move her gaze from Zack. She watched his face dance with excitement as he stared at her. His dark eyes moving from the shoebox then back to her. Slowly, Heidi lifted the lid from the box, staring down at another doll, another beautiful doll. Her doll had long black wavy hair and white skin, ghostlike skin. It was unlike the color of Mindy's doll or the style. Its eyes were dark blue but as she moved closer, Heidi could see they were almost purple.

The doll was dressed in a pearl long dress with a black sash and necklace around her neck. On her feet were black slippers, which caused her skin to seem like it was glowing, she was beautiful. She gasped at the dark beauty of the doll. Her hands slid under it lifting the doll from the box as careful as if she were holding a newborn.

"Oh, she's beautiful, I love her. Is she mine?" Heidi exclaimed, bringing the doll to her chest, cradling it against her.

"She's all yours. I thought you may like her," he whispered.

Heidi felt her face heat up. She looked up to Zack smiling. Slowly he lifted his hand, running his fingers down the side of her face. When she didn't flinch, he lent forward kissing the tip of her nose, like he had done so many times that week. A kiss she valued, more than any other that could be given. It was comforting and non invasive but still full of love.

Something moved on the other side of the room, catching her attention. Heidi glanced past Zack to her sister, leaning against the door. Her arms were folded under her growing breasts in anger. Heidi chose to ignore her, looking back at the doll in her arms, it was perfect for her. So innocent but at the same time dark. Just a child, with a darkness in its soul and a power misunderstood, yes so much like her.

"Can I show you something?" Zack asked, his hand reaching for the doll.

She glared at him out of instinct then quickly calmed, looking back to the doll and trying to control her emotions. Zack didn't seem to notice her change in emotion. He carefully lifted the doll from her arms, standing it on his lap so that it faced her. He caught her eyes, the darkness in his own flicking as he waved his hand over the dolls face. At first nothing happened. Then tears started to fall from its crystal like eyes, blood tears. They stained the dolls face, sliding down its small neck to the dress. As soon as one drop of blood touched the white dress, the whole thing turned a deep red. The dolls innocent pursed lips had moved into a sly smile, even the eyes seemed to darken with shadows around them.

Heidi gasped, not in fear but captivated. It was amazing, it looked more beautiful to her now than it did before. She wanted it back, she wanted to be like it. To possess such power and to control her world. But all too soon Zack snapped his fingers and the doll returned to the way it had been before.

Heidi snapped her eyes to Zack in surprise. His eyes had become completely black and his ears were pointed. Within a second he turned back, a thin smile lighting his face. Heidi smiled back though her eyes betrayed her. There was something more to him, she had felt it but never seen. She wanted to know everything about him. His darkness only attracted her not dirtied her.

"Her name is Darla but you can call her what you want." He handed the doll back to her, Heidi cradling it once more in her arms. Her head twisted to one side and her eyes large in thought. Zack moved closer to her on the bed. "Are you afraid of me?"

"Darla, it's perfect."

"Heidi?" he placed his finger under her chin, forcing her eyes to his. "Are you afraid?"

"I want you to teach me," she whispered.

He jolted, had he expected her to say something else? His lips quivered between a smile and confusion. He was speechless though in a trance, he nodded. Before she could say anything he lent forward kissing her nose then brushed his hand through the dolls hair. "I love you Heidi," he whispered.

He turned leaving the room, pushing past Mindy who still leant against the door frame. Her sister had been so focused on getting to her diary, she hadn't seen a thing past Zack's back. As Zack moved Mindy glared at him, waiting until he had gone downstairs then she entered the room and shut the door.

"Can I see yours?" Mindy asked, climbing on the bed next to her, resting her head on her shoulder. Heidi turned her completely normal doll to her sister, who smiled grabbing her own from the end of the bed. "Have you seen the children since we've been here?" she asked, trying to catch a conversation she would get a reply to.

"I thought you didn't believe in the children," Heidi mocked. Mindy rolled her eyes, she wasn't reacting well to the challenge. No, Mindy just wanted her sister, so a sister she should be. "No, I think they're upset with what happened to our home."

Her sister nodded. "Mama never brought us a doll, did she? And these are really pretty. If we ever go back to school don't tell anyone I said that, hey."

"I don't gossip. My doll's name is Darla. What are you going to call yours," she asked, placing the dolls side by side.

"I don't know. Maybe, Hope because we could do with some right now. Darla is a beautiful name, she's perfect for you."

"Yes, Darla is perfect."

*   *   *

She couldn't stop laughing. Every bone in her body shook until it ached. But still she could not stop, even when she started to cry. Her teary eyes moved to the boy in front of her as she tried to control herself. Every time she attempted, he would do something to start it all over again. Taking in a deep breath, she did calm.

Sitting across from her was her friend, Adrian. He had a smile of mischief on his lips and a plan in his eyes. He put down the puppets he had brought over to show her, the puppets his mother had made. He had brought them there to perform a show he had made up. Gaining her approval, before he took it to the public at the Saturday morning markets. It had been a wonderful show, in fact the only and funniest she had ever seen.

Adrian had been her friend for three months. At first he had come over once a week as soon as her parents had left the house. Now he was coming over every second day, since her parents had been leaving her alone that often.

She didn't mind anymore, she had Adrian. He always brought things over that his mother had made for her market. Sometimes he even let her keep them. A porcelain doll like no other she had ever seen. It had long black hair, pale skin and dark blue eyes. The doll wore a white gown with black trimmings. Olivia thought she was beautiful but was too afraid to touch her.

"Your mother will be home soon. I had better take the puppets home before your stepfather catches me." Adrian had said, his eyes shifting to the window on the other side of the room.

Olivia smiled. "Thank you Adrian. Since I have been with you time is not so slow and I can tolerate being trapped in here."

Adrian's face darkened. "Just because you can tolerate it, does not mean its right."

She didn't need to answer. Her eyes gave away her agreement. Adrian pursed his lips, watching her for a moment before packing the puppets into his pouch. Hunting around for any evidence that he was there. She sat silently, shifting back into her corner beside the bed. She was surprised when Adrian placed a bag of food under it.

When he was finished packing, he came to her side taking her hand in his. The two of them listened to the horses and carriage pull up outside, hoping it wasn't holding her parents within. Though he didn't look as worried as she did, he never looked all that worried about being caught. She could see his thoughts flickering through his eyes, what was he thinking?

"Before I go, can I kiss you?"

Olivia darted her eyes to his. "You want to kiss me?"

"We are friends aren't we, yes? Friends kiss each other goodbye."

She nodded, leaning forward as he did their lips met, pressing together while his fingers moved through her hair. They stayed that way for a while before Adrian pulled back, a smile on his lips as it was on hers. Olivia could feel her face heating up but not in anger for she liked the soft kiss. It was much nicer then the way she had seen her stepfather kiss her mother, so much more innocent.

Adrian stood, grabbing his bag and moving to the door. He grabbed the iron bar unlocking it the way she had shown him. Paused in the open door and gazing around her room, strange looks crossed his face that were years beyond his age. He turned back to her.

"Eat only the food I left under your bed, not that from your parents. Throw their food out the window, understand?" he ordered.

"Yes, I understand."

He smiled, bending down to slide the iron bar back under the bed then he disappeared, leaving her in the corner. She glanced under the bed to see the bag of food, iron bar and boxes full of things Adrian had brought her. Soon there was going to be no more room under her bed. She sometimes wondered what her stepfather would do if he saw her collection. Of course he would be angered and she worried what he would do to her for defying his punishment. He would punish her for being her mother's daughter.

Olivia looked back to the mirror across from her and out of the slightly open door that Adrian hadn't shut properly. She listened to him leaving the house her heart sinking, she already missed him. Her eyes remained on the mirror reflecting the open door. What would it be like in that world through the glass? Would everything look different but be the same or would it be something better? She should really shut the door before her stepfather came home. But right now she couldn't find the strength, not yet, something new to look at was comforting.

She closed her eyes, letting her spirit drift from her body. Vacating her mind but unfortunately not her pain, her troubles were always attached. Her body slouched against the wall, not moving as she intended to do when she left. That had made her afraid. To see her body moving, doing things she didn't remember and couldn't control, her eyes pitch black. She had quickly gained her control but never forgot the lack of control she had felt.

Olivia opened her eyes after that reminder. She wasn't going to stray away too long, she couldn't risk it. She stared at the floor listening to the downstairs rooms, catching a shifting sound. It couldn't be her parents; they wouldn't be trying so hard to be silent. Whoever it was started up the stairs, slowly approaching her door then pausing. Olivia darted her eyes to the mirror.

She stared through the open door at a woman she had never seen before. A dark skinned woman like the native people who live further inland but somehow she was not one of them. No, her eyes were too round and wide, her lips full but not dominating her face and her nose narrow. Most of all she wore modern clothes. She was a pretty woman with long dark hair and colored silks complementing her womanly figure. Although it was hypnotizing to stare at her, Olivia wanted to call out to her. She wanted to know who the mysterious woman was and what she was doing in her home.

The woman's dark eyes caught the mirror. She first studied the room then caught sight of her, she heard the woman gasp. Was she surprised someone was in there? Wasn't it her she was looking for or something else? They stared at one another through their reflections for a few minutes before tears begun to slide down the woman face. Why was she crying?

Olivia was just about to leap through the door when the woman spun running from the house. The front door slammed, marking her exit. Olivia sat on her knees captivated, what was that all about?

She dropped back to the floor confused and intrigued. Who was that woman and why had she cried when she saw her? Did they know one another? She sighed, laying her head on the side of the bed, she would never find out. She had to face that she would never understand anything in this world.

$$* \quad * \quad *$$

She screamed, screamed to escape from the dreams and screamed to release her pain. She had to get out of this dream, get away from the men trying to put their bodies within hers. Heidi screamed harder as their hands tried to grab her. Strong hands held her upper arms and pulled at her. She kicked and fought back against them. They wouldn't hurt her again, no, they couldn't. She would kill them all.

The men fought back against her and someone was screaming, a girl. Was it Mindy? What was Mindy doing here? But she couldn't let her sister stop her from justice. Heidi screamed out pushing the arms away. There was only one now and he grabbed her so hard she was scared he'd break her arms. His dark face lent towards hers but instead of feeling lips pressed against her, she felt soft lips kiss her nose, Heidi gasped. She slowly calmed, watching the images of a nightmare disappear, replaced by the darkness of sleep. She opened her eyes.

Her room was as she had left it, no strange men trying to hurt her and no bodies. At the doorway stood her sister, who clutched her doll, shaking and crying. Heidi crossed her eyebrows together, why was Mindy upset? On the bed in front of her was Zack, his hands clutching her arms, a little too tightly. His dark hair was thrown over his eyes and chest marked red, had she been fighting him? Heidi gasped, her body still shaking, her heart aching. What had happened?

"But . . . a dream . . . I didn't . . ." she stammered, trying to catch her breath.

Zack grabbed her, pulling her body tightly against his chest, his hands running through her hair. She had never seen him afraid or worried before. "Shhh kitten, its okay now. Everything will be okay," he whispered, kissing the top of her head, practically smothering her body into his. Was he shaking too or was it still her?

"Everything will not be okay! You saw her eyes didn't you? You saw the things in the room float from the floor! What the hell is wrong with her! She's a freak!" Mindy screamed, not daring to come back into the room

"Shut up Melinda! Get the fuck out of here!" Zack yelled.

Mindy glared at him before turning and running from the hall. Heidi could hear her go down the stairs then the movement stopped at the lounge, the sound of the television suddenly turned on. Heidi pulled from Zack's arms, her stomach clenching. She pulled her knees to her chest.

Zack looked like he had calmed although he still rested one hand on her shoulder. What had she done? Was Mindy right? Did her eyes go black and things in the room start to move, she wouldn't be surprised if it had. After all, she had killed because of this strange gift. She felt so sick and scared; she didn't mean to scare Mindy. How could she ever be strong for her sister when she couldn't control her own mind?

"I'm sorry," she cried, her hands reaching for Zack's face.

He grabbed her hands, kissing each palm. Pulling her closer to him again and sitting her on his lap, holding her tight. "I'll tell you, you had me scared. Are you okay kitten?"

"What happened?"

"You just had a bad dream. You can get quite violent in the dreams. Are you feeling okay, Heidi? Look at me."

She looked up into his eyes and forced a smile. Really she was okay, her stomach was a little sore but okay. She moved closer to him, leaning her head against his shoulder. Zack smiled, finally. He wrapped his arm around her kissing the top of her head. Nothing had happened so why was she so scared? Why was he so worried? It was just a dream and he had run to her side to help her, he loved her.

"My stomach hurts, I need a girl to talk too," she whispered, suddenly feeling wetness between her legs.

"Do you want me to call up Melinda?"

"No, I need a woman. I can't talk to you about it," she said, blushing.

"You can tell me anything. I understand more about women than maybe you think."

"I think it's that time!" she cried. "And I don't want them! I don't want to be hurt or have someone hurt me and end up like my mother!"

Zack smiled, pulling her closer to him. "Well how about we make a spell, you want to do that?"

"Oh yes."

"Okay, close your eyes and rest your hands on your stomach," he instructed. Heidi did so and felt his hand rest over hers, his head resting against hers. "I will make a spell that you will never get your monthlies until you willingly have sex. Not through rape but you agreeing to be with a man. And should you never want to be with anyone, they will never come. What do you think?"

Heidi smiled, letting her body fall back into his. "Perfect," she whispered. She could fell a warm feeling surrounding her back and stomach but still she kept her eyes closed. Zack placed a kiss on her neck, slowly shifting them up on the bed. She let him lie her down, his body sliding into the bed beside her. His fingers ran through her hair and his other arm draped across her body.

She felt safe in his arms and even though she could feel his spell had finished, she didn't want to open her eyes. She wanted to savor the moment and the thought of magic surrounding them. Mindy would laugh at her if she told her what he had said but somehow she believed him or was it, believed in him?

Heidi moved back into his body comforted by his presence. He had said he loved her and she could feel it. She hoped he could feel that she loved him too. Nothing would draw her away from him. She would challenge his love but never leave him.

"Everything will be alright," he reminded her.

Heidi smiled. "As long as you're with me."

"I will always be with you, I promise," he said seriously. Heidi let her head rest into the pillow, her heart flutters easing. His words echoed through her mind as she let herself go to sleep, this time with no fear.

*　　*　　*

He sat at the bar alone, rolling the small note around his fingers, the few pleading words catching his eyes. *Help us! He is evil! He will kill us. Please, please call the police.* The note read. It was from Melinda Harrison, passed to him today from one of Melinda's friends at lunch time. She had said that Melinda had called her one night, speaking in a low tone. They arranged to meet where her house once stood. The note was passed with strict instructions for him to receive it straight away.

The girl was obviously a bit of an air head for this happened on Monday evening and today was Friday. He had wanted to yell at her and ask her why she hadn't gone to the police or given it to him straight away. Everyone believed the Harrison girls had been killed in the explosion because the police had found no other explanation for where they had gone. There had been a memorial at school. Didn't this air head think to say something, stupid girl! At first he was shocked, happy but now he was afraid. What had happened to the girls? He wasn't sure what to do next.

Now he sat with a note from a supposed dead girl, with a plea to save her from what? He had only one guess where she was. Next door to her old home, in Zack's house, he was sure of it, but why? What did a man in his late twenties want with them? Many things came to mind, most he did not want to think about. However now he was left with an option. Call the police and hand over the note so they could reopen the Harrison file or go there himself in case this was a cruel prank. After all it could be. That would explain why the girl thought nothing of it.

The police had closed the file a few days ago, sending out a report that Ms Harrison and her two daughters had been killed in a house explosion, due to a gas leak, old faulty equipment and Ms Harrison smoking in the house, convincible but all lies. He knew they were lies, he had been there.

He had seen the body upstairs and knew the girls weren't in the house at the time, yet no one believed him. His wife did and things had got better between them but he was still left with his memories and guilt, he knew he should have done something more.

The guilt had lead him to the bar every day after work. Where he stumbled home drunk, hoping not to face reality. The police knew this and no longer came to him for information. They no longer went anywhere for information, they had taken the easy way out. Closed the file and forget. It had saddened him at how easily the whole town had forgotten about the beautiful, yet disturbing Harrison girls. God knows he never could.

It had been weeks since the explosion and everyone had continued on with their lives like nothing had happened. He hated them for it. How could they all ignore this tragedy when two girls had supposedly been killed, no one grieved for them. Even Melinda's friends didn't seem affected that she wasn't there, but poor Heidi. Heidi had no one to remember her. The only person that would was him.

And every time he thought of the girls he was sick, especially knowing their life and their last few days. Heidi had never got to feel what happiness and safety was. There was no wonder she was the way she was, when all she had seen were the horrors of her life. Drake sighed, he wished he could have helped more, maybe forced them to the police but then they would have withdrawn further. He couldn't get Heidi out of his head and if the police never found a body, he probably never would.

After the explosion he had ended up in hospital for a week. There were cuts on his arms and legs. He had a broken leg and burns to most of his body. There was also one slash on his leg from the tile that had taken twenty-two stitches to fix. When he had returned to work, he had trouble focusing, his heart and body hurt too much.

He still couldn't understand why he was so affected by Heidi or felt the way he did. Everything seemed personal with her and no one at the school seemed to care. He thought he might explode himself.

He had thought he was drawn to Heidi so much because she reminded him of himself as a kid. He was from a broken home with distracted, drunk parents. There was violence and drugs everywhere he looked, he had been angry like her. He had been so much like her. But in time, he had opened up to the ones that wanted to sort his head out. He could never forget and get over his life but at least he had help. Heidi was alone.

There was no one but him who had wanted to help but he had been way over his head. Nothing to this extreme had ever happened to him, he didn't know what to do for her. A fourteen year old girl who had lost both her spirit and blood innocence, who had lost her home and any slice of reality that may have remained in that head. God knows what a man that age wants with them. Drake felt sick again.

The right thing to do was call the police and stick it in their faces at how lazy they had been. Although, on the other hand, he needed to see for himself. He needed to be sure they were there before he gave the police an excuse to send him away for good. He wanted to save the girls then go home to his family, redeemed as a man, instead of this coward he had become.

Drake pushed another empty can of bourbon away, his fingers flicking around the note once more. What should he do? He wanted to help but in this world that was not his job, it was the work of the police. He would probably never get over this if he didn't walk past that house and sneak a peek through the windows.

He needed to get over this, so he could become a good husband again, a good father and a better counselor. He would never let anything slide again. He would never put off calling the police when the situation needed it. It was all his fault. He was the adult in the situation and he hadn't followed the rules, he was being punished for his ignorance.

"Another bourbon mate?" the barkeep asked.

"No thanks, I should get my ass home," he muttered.

The man behind the bar nodded. "Want me to call a cab? You can't think about driving with how much you've drunk."

"I'll walk. The fresh air will sober me up some."

"Fair enough. You have a good evening Drake and say hi to Serena from the Mrs."

"Will do."

Shoving the note into his pocket, Drake snatched his jacket from the chair. Throwing it on as he stepped out into the cold air, he walked down the street. Letting the chilling breeze guide him on his forty minute walk home. But he didn't mind, by the time he did arrive home, he would have all this nonsense out of his head. He would be able to enjoy his family without a distracted mind, hopefully.

Serena most likely would smell the grog on his breath but knowing his wife, she properly wouldn't question it if he played with the kids and put them to bed. He still felt like he didn't know his own children. They wouldn't come to him when they cried and when they looked at him, their eyes were blank. Was it because of him or what his wife said behind his back? He loved them too much to grow old with regret in his heart and adult children he never saw.

He paused, looking around himself. It felt like he had been walking for hours though when he looked at his watch only twenty minutes had passed. More so, he had been walking in the wrong direction from his home. He had let the cold air guide him and it had taken him to Zack Solveri's house, he wasn't really all that surprised. It was his fate, wasn't it? But what did he do now that he was here? He couldn't walk straight up to the door and call for the girls or maybe he could.

After all, what else could he do but call the police and if they came he wouldn't be able to help Heidi. She would clam up or run and there would be no chance for her out there. On the other hand, he had to save her from this man who could be doing anything to her. He loved her! Drake froze, what had he thought? He loved her? Well he did. He loved her and she should have been his daughter or sister, something.

He walked up to the front door, taking a few low breaths before knocking. He wasn't sure what to say or do. All he hoped for was that the girls were there and alive. If the girls answered, he would grab them and run to his home, where they would call the police. But if Zack answered which was more likely, he hoped they could speak like men. Maybe he could even reason with the man and explain the girl's situation. Maybe Zack was looking after them because Heidi had asked him too. It all could be an innocent misunderstanding.

Drake knocked again, waiting. After a few minutes he knocked harder, nothing. Nothing at first anyway, but then there was the claw, his screams, the piercing screams of another, his blood. And then, oh god, he wished he had never come . . .

CHAPTER SEVEN

"Cry! Why won't you cry?" Heidi screamed. She was about to throw the doll across the room but thought twice, sliding it across the floor instead.

She pulled her knees to her chest, darting her eyes across the room to where Zack and Melinda sat, both staring at her. It was a cold day and Zack had built a fire for them in the old fireplace in his room. He had told them they could stay in there to keep warm. He and her sister were sitting on the twin seat sofa on the other side of the room. Mindy had been reading to him while he lay across the arm rest of the lounge, watching her. As she found him doing quite a lot, ever since the night she had awoken from that nightmare.

Mindy had been giving him a chance and was seeing as Heidi had said that Zack was not a bad man. He wanted to help them and really had given them no reason to hate him. Sure he and Mindy had had some fights and swore at one another but nothing that wasn't forgotten the next day. Her sister had found a new love for reading and did so to Zack everyday. They were mostly romance novel she had found about the home but Zack didn't seem to mind. Sometimes Mindy wouldn't know a word or understand what something meant but he was always by her side to help, listening and watching.

There were days when Heidi would also sit a listen but she was quickly angered by the act of love. She saw nothing pleasurable about being touched the way the book described, it sickened her. Today, she had no time for the nonsense in the story. She had brought her doll into Zack's room, sitting down in front of the fire with it. She had been waving her hand over Darla's face, trying to make her cry blood as Zack had shown her. It never worked for her. Heidi pulled her white nighty over her knees, staring into the flickering flames, enchanted by them.

The flames danced over the wood, forming small shapes before her eyes. But vanishing before she could distinguish any of them. She sighed, resting her head on her knees and wriggling her toes on the burgundy rug.

Mindy had started reading again, straightening the dark blue dress that was a little too tight for her.

Her sister always got dressed in the morning but she didn't, she was comfortable in her nighty beside what was the point in doing her hair and getting dressed when she stayed home. She felt comfortable and free in her nighty with her long hair loose to curl upon her hips. She looked back to the flames that were flickering higher. What would it be like to have them wrap around your arms, she wondered. Heidi lent forward, her arm outstretched to the welcoming warmth.

"Heidi, no! It will burn you!" Zack called, sitting up straight in the chair.

Mindy was also staring at her again, alarmed with what she was about to do. Heidi turned away glaring, she felt like a child but then she always felt like a child. Mindy started reading again frustration in her voice but Zack didn't relax. His eyes were sharp as he watched her hand outstretching for the flames again. She couldn't help it, they were calling to her.

Heidi watched him, her eyes holding his as she edged closer, her hand near the fire seeing what he would do. Challenging him to get mad and hit her, she wanted him to hit her. She could have a reason to hate him. It wasn't that she didn't like him, because she did but it wouldn't last. Happiness never lasted and it was better to destroy it now than let herself get hurt later.

"Heidi don't!" he yelled again.

Mindy had put the book down. She knew what Heidi was doing but still looked a little worried at the same time, for the flames were close. Her sister didn't think that she would do it. Heidi grinned forcing her hand into the flames. Mindy screamed but Heidi didn't feel anything, she watched the flames dance around her hand. It didn't look like it was touching her but it was, she was just numb.

Before she could pull her hand away, her body was thrown into the wall, she couldn't even comprehend what was happening. She hadn't seen Zack move but when she looked up, there he was standing over her, his body tense and full of rage but his eyes betrayed his love.

"What did you think you were doing? You've burnt your hand!" he yelled.

"Darla wouldn't cry!" she screamed back, not feeling a thing from her hand.

Zack's face softened. "Patience is a virtue."

She rolled her eyes away from him, catching Mindy running into the bathroom for a wet cloth. When her sister was gone Zack lent down next to her, placing his hand over her burnt one. "It will come for you, with control," he whispered.

Heidi opened her mouth to reply but stopped when his face changed, he was suddenly distracted. Mindy had run back into the room with ice and wet cloths but Zack didn't move to get them. Even when her sister came to her side wrapping up her hand, he was frozen. The two sisters stared at him.

Zack stood straight his head slightly to one side like he was listening to something beyond the house. His ears had also changed becoming more pointed, his jaw more defined and eyes sharper, darker.

His body convulsed wanting to change into who he really was, though he wouldn't in front of them. Heidi knew he was different. Of course he had said so himself but she knew he could change into another being, she was sure of it. Downstairs there was a knock on the door, obviously by the person who he had heard approaching for a few minutes. Heidi raised her eyebrow, what was he so worried about? It was probably just the police.

Zack looked down at them, his hand outreached to her, stroking her hair before pulling his hand away. He opened his mouth to say something. She could see jagged, sharpened teeth within, he closed his mouth. Before she could ask him what he wanted to say, Zack darted out of the room on the second knock. He moved so fast there was just a black blur behind him, the two sisters gasped.

"Did you see that?" Mindy asked, almost crying.

"Yes, but I'm glad you did too," Heidi replied.

"Who do you think is at the door? The police again?"

"No idea."

Mindy started talking again but Heidi was no longer listening. The moving fire had caught her attention. The flames were dancing higher and higher, jumping from the fireplace to the rug. She gripped her sister's hand but Mindy took it as though she was afraid of Zack. She couldn't see the flames like Heidi could and they were getting closer. The flames slowly became darker as they began to form the frame of a woman.

They started mimicking her body until a look alike stood in front of her. No, not her, but the girl from her dreams, the girl from years ago, the one trapped in her room. Her reoccurring nightmare. She screamed backing into Mindy who was now alarmed by her but still couldn't see why.

"*You must die before he kills you. I will save you, let me, help me pass,*" the fiery form hissed.

Heidi screamed. "Get away from me!"

"You're climbing on top of me Heidi," Mindy cried, confused.

"*Death is your freedom, save you from your pain.*"

"No! No! Go back to my dreams, you can't be here!"

Beyond her screaming, she could hear more downstairs, screams from a man. What was going on down there? The flamed girl wasted no time. She grabbed her by the shoulders dragging her back into the fireplace. Heidi screamed louder, her body was thrown to the floor. She clawed at the rug, at her sister's feet.

Mindy shook her head stepping backwards, watching as Heidi's nighty was consumed by flames. Heidi grabbed hold of whatever she could but the spirit clutching her legs was stronger. It pulled her into the fireplace, flames dancing around her. She screamed at first, not out of pain but fear then came the unbearable pain.

It was only a few seconds but those seconds felt like an eternity. Then something black flew into the room, Zack. But it was no longer Zack, it was a monster with large black wings and red eyes. With a body so abnormal but not disgusting, in fact it was alluring. The creature flew into the flames, grabbing her by the waist and threw her from the fire. Everything was disappearing around her, followed by her sister then the room. She fell through the darkness, hitting a cold surface, drowning.

Heidi swung her arms around her body, pulling herself to the surface. She dragged her body along the sand, gasping for air. She choked, rolling over on the dark abandoned beach, its only light was a slice of moonlight from behind the clouds. She was naked, naked but normal, not even her hand was injured. Where was she?

Heidi ran her fingers through her hair. It was still there, not singed from her scalp. Not a burn upon her, Zack had saved her. Pulling her hair over her face, she gasped when she didn't see the glowing blonde, she saw black. How had her hair changed? Slowly, Heidi stood wrapping her arms around her naked body. Long black hair blew in the breeze behind her, brushing against the small of her back. Where was she?

*   *   *

He coughed and gasped, stumbling along the road. His hands gripped at his stomach, his other hanging limp by his side. Something had attacked him and that something had not been human. Its clawed wings had torn through his skin like a hot knife through butter. The creature had thrown him out onto the road where it used its power to move a parked car, running him down.

He was bleeding battered and bruised, he could barely see but that didn't stop him from trying to get home and ring the police. His mobile was crushed beneath the car. The familiar screams from upstairs had given him enough determination to get off the road. Those screams over his own had given him a new drive to regain life. The creature had disappeared upstairs as the screams grew louder and more pain filled. He too wanted to run upstairs but he didn't.

Drake dragged his body down the street, hoping someone would see him and help. There was no one around. He was alone in his decision and alone in his pain. All he focused on was getting home. Wrap his arms around his wife, say he was sorry and hope to hear the same, then next week he would quit his job. It was destroying him, literary. He held too much to heart to be a good counselor. Work came home with him then made him distant from his family.

Drake stopped, leaning against a tree. He was starting to feel faint. If only his phone hadn't been run over then he could call an ambulance, taxi or more important things, like the police. Cracking his neck and rearranging his fingers on his wound, Drake forced himself on.

A walk that should have taken him fifteen minutes had taken him an hour. At one point he was sure he had passed out for a while. Probably had, but now he was home and pulling himself through the unlocked door, completely sober. He had been sober the minute he looked upon Zack's house. Perhaps having alcohol in his veins had helped him not feel the pain he had endured, helped him run on the adrenal.

He fell into the door, gasping for air, hoping his family would be in the dining room, but they weren't. Drake kicked closed the door, pulling himself to the kitchen bench, reaching for the land line, it was dead. Why was it dead? The lights were still on so it wasn't the power and he was always on time paying the bills, not even a dial tone.

He threw the phone back on the bench, letting out a roar of anger as he did so. Stumbling onto one arm after the other, Drake made his way down the back hall. There was an old mobile in his bedside drawer. He had brought a new phone coming to Adelaide but kept his old one charged in case anyone from Melbourne tried to contact him. New phone, new start—bad choices.

If he could get to that phone, he could call the police, an ambulance and maybe collapse onto the bed until they came. But first where were Serena and the kids? They should be running out to greet him, Serena at the stove with his late dinner. Sending him a disapproving look with where he had been but then it was later then he thought. Maybe his family was asleep. Why was he so afraid? The worst was over and he needed to say he loved them, maybe even say goodbye.

"Serena! Kids!" he called, down the hall. Where were they?

He was greeted by silence, for a moment anyway. For the next person that spoke was not one he ever wanted to hear.

"They're resting Drake."

Drake stood in the middle of the hallway, his hands pressed against each wall trying to get himself up. He spun around to Zack, his blood chilling and hairs standing on their ends. Zack stood before him as a man but he knew he was the creature that had attacked him. The man walked around his kitchen, looking at every object, even stirring the cold ham and pea soup on the stove. Drake hadn't noticed the soup earlier. That was a good sign, wasn't it? A sign that Serena and the kids were somewhere and they were fine.

He took a step backwards feeling more dizzy with every step took. He could see a trail of blood following him. He wasn't going to survive much longer. Where was his family? Zack had commented that they were resting. He hoped against hope that the monster hadn't done anything to them. Oh god, what would he do if he had? Of course his kids were still distant and his wife treated him like he was useless but he still loved them. They were his family, his flesh and blood. He couldn't lose them.

"You bastard, what do you want? What have you done to the girls? Where's my family?" he had wanted to yell but all his questions came in a string of gurgles.

Zack turned to face him, a smile on his lips and eyes dancing with joy. "I need to get rid of you. You're in my way and distracting my plans for those girls."

"Where are my family?!"

"Resting, all together in your bed. Quite sweet actually. They're wrapped in one another's arms, asleep for eternity, souls drifting through the skies together, beautiful."

His heart started to race, Drake spun around, pulling himself along the walls to his closed bedroom door. Behind him he could no longer feel the presence of Zack. All he could feel was silence, dead silence. With shaky hands he opened his bedroom door, pulling himself to stare at his family. They looked so peaceful lying in the bed, the quilt pulled to their necks.

His wife, two sons and daughter, all sleeping but he felt sick because in his heart he knew he would never see their eyes open again. Drake approached the bed sitting on the side, his hand resting on his daughter's cheek, so cold. Tears built in his eyes, his shaky hands moved down the bed, their bodies felt soft, he had expected them to feel stiff.

Forcing his blood drained body to stand, Drake pulled back the quilt crying and shaking his head. They had no bodies! Only their heads lay on the bed and under the quilt was blood soaked mattress but no bodies! Even the small bodies of his twins had been taken from their heads. He screamed. His body fell to the floor, he wanted to die with them.

As he hit the floor, he knocked something under the bed. He glanced over shuddering when he saw his samurai sword. The one that he had bought when he was eighteen and kept displayed on the wall. His heart clenched in his chest, not his prized sword! Why did the demon have to use his sword? It made him feel that this was his fault. His decision had brought the demon here and his weapon had killed his family.

Oh please, let them not have suffered, not have seen him. The monster had killed his family! His innocent family who had no choice in his decision, he had killed them. His scream was long and low, he struggled to pull himself upon the bed, facing reality, dead, dead, dead. It should have been him. The sick bastard was weak killing innocents. It should have been him to die but then he was dying, painfully and slowly, nevertheless dying. However he had seen the creature, he would never join his family again. Not with the blackness in his mind.

"You should have stayed away but now its personal," Zack spat, from against the opposite wall.

Drake glared at the monster in his true form. Large wings spread over his whole wall, the man in the middle of the beast resting his arms over his chest casually. He wanted to kill him but his body no longer held the strength to move, not even adrenaline could kick start him. The creature smirked almost daring him to move.

Drake glared back taking in every detail of the man. His pain alerting him that this was not his imagination, this was real. True, if he had stayed away this might not have happened but he couldn't stay away from her, couldn't stop thinking of her, he was cursed. Look at him, even beside his dead family and Heidi still consumed his thoughts, he was bound by some magical order to protect her.

"You're right," Drake said calmly. "Now it's personal."

Zack stood from the wall, a long grin lighting his face but didn't consume his eyes. Yes, now it was personal, he would not die. He would avenge his family and that soul of anyone else the monster touched. Maybe he was going insane but right now being insane was safer than looking back at the bed. The creature laughed disappearing, leaving him finally alone to mourn and to vow.

Without looking at the bed, Drake lent into the bedside table drawer searching for his spare phone. He called triple zero, his eyes coming to rest upon his family again. Before the operator had answered he fell to the floor, half unconscious but still screaming. Releasing his pain and harboring his rage. Now it was personal.

*   *   *

His strong hands grabbed her shoulders, a white towel flying around her, wrapping itself around her naked body. She looked curiously to the towel then twisted her head to one side, gazing to the creature before her. He morphed back into a man, holding her shaking body against his chest. She was not afraid of him but allured. She was more afraid of the spirit in the fire.

She had never seen anything like it, a man that could change into a beast. She had never seen so much darkness come from a misunderstood being. Some might call him evil and want him dead but he had saved her, he was as he said, just like her. Both misunderstood because they weren't like everyone else. If anything she liked him more, admired his power and thrived on his darkness.

"My hair," she whispered, pulling the black tangles in front of her face.

"Oh, I know kitten. Hush now. It will turn back in time," he sighed, kissing her nose, a strange look passed his eyes. "Shall we go home now?"

"Home," Heidi repeated, a word she never referenced with herself and sadly still didn't.

Zack pulled her closer against his chest, placing one hand around her back and the other over her eyes. Something began to spin past them, their bodies swayed like they were on a boat before it stopped. He pulled her back at arms length but Heidi didn't open her eyes, at first. She could feel that they were somewhere different. Her skin was warm and the ocean air no longer wrapped around her body.

Slowly she opened her eyes, gazing upon Zack's bedroom. There was no evidence of the fire on the rug or in the fireplace. Nothing in the room had been smashed or moved out of place. If she wasn't feeling a slight tingling through her body, she might have believed the fire attack never happened.

Heidi sighed, looking back to Zack who sat on the bed in his man form. He had his head bowed, sadness in his eyes as he ran his hand through his hair, brushing the loose strains from his eyes. He was truly a beautiful man. Even the being he had become was not unattractive.

"You should go have a shower. It will make you feel better. Are you in any pain? Burning?"

"No, not a thing. Not even from my hands," she whispered, glancing around the room for her sister. "Where's Mindy?"

"She's watching the television. She's a bit frazzled but I told her you were alright. She's confused but happy. You should go speak with her after your shower," he instructed. He didn't seem himself and he had yet to look at her. Had she scared him or angered him?

Heidi nodded, her eyes filling with tears. She ran from the room going to do as he said and have a shower. When she glanced back into the room, she saw Zack with his head bowed to his knees, his hair falling over his eyes. Was he crying? Oh god, what had she done? She was stupid to play with the fire after all he had done for her. Why did she have to test people like that? Why did she have to force away anyone that could truly care for her? First Drake, now Zack, which heart would she destroy next? Her sister?

Heidi hurried into the shower, falling to its floor. Her tears streaming down her face, she didn't understand why she couldn't let anyone love her. Not everyone in this world was going to hurt her, were they? However

Zack was right, the pounding pelts of water against her body felt good. After a while she became numb to them, her thoughts shifting to her hair. Black, long, straight strands. She had expected the water to wash it away, it didn't. Strange, she thought, slamming off the taps and stepping out onto the cold tiles.

She had felt better at first but now, she felt nothing. She needed to go talk with Mindy. Another crazy act on her behalf had probably disturbed her sister more. Heidi walked to her room, pulling on a black cotton dress and brushing her hair. Still the black did not come out. She sighed, placing the brush down and catching a shadow through the mirror, Zack.

She lowered her eyes to the floor as he stepped into the room. "I'm sorry," she whispered. "I didn't mean for anything to happen. I don't know why that spirit was trying to kill me."

"You scared me," he said, in a flat tone.

"I'm sorry," she cried.

Zack bowed his head, his arms crossed over his chest as he stared at the floor. "I don't know what I'm going to do with you," he hissed. Heidi spun around to him, what did he mean by that? Didn't he want her to live with him anymore? Was he planning to call the police? Tears streamed down her cheeks, now it was her turn to be scared. Zack suddenly looked back at her, his brows crossed. "What did you mean by a spirit trying to kill you? Was it the children?"

"No. Her name is Olivia . . . she tried to warn me of something but decided it was best to kill me. She was really strong, I couldn't fight against . . ."

"How can that be possible?"

Heidi almost laughed, twisted her head to one side, her tongue flicking on the roof of her mouth. "How could she be possible! How can you be possible? How can any of this be possible?" she laughed.

"You don't understand. Olivia is dead! It's not the same as the children, she shouldn't be here." Before she could question him any further, he stormed out of her room, slamming the door after him.

He was getting stranger. Heidi placed the brush back on the table, crossing her eyebrows together. She turned from the room to find her sister. She really needed to talk with her. Later she would try to talk to Zack and ask him questions about what he meant, about Olivia. Maybe even tonight when Zack isn't around, she would go up to his room, stand before the fire place and ask her questions. Some magic might still be lurking there and that magic might answer her. But Mindy was first. Heidi ran down the stairs into the lounge room.

Mindy sat on the lounge curled in front of the television. Her hands ripping apart a small piece of paper on her lap, she was nervous. Her sister turned smiling at her, gesturing for Heidi to join her. Heidi glanced back up the stairs to Zack who was walking down them. His eyes stared down at her but she quickly turned, jumping over the back of the lounge, falling beside Mindy. They looked at one another, over their shoulders to Zack then at the news program on the television. Mindy placed her finger on her lips, hoping she followed by keeping quiet.

"Are you okay? What happened to your hair? Zack said I was hallucinating but I didn't think so. Things are not right around here and I'm not willing to see it through," Mindy whispered.

"I'm fine. I really don't know what happened upstairs or to my hair."

"Did you see him up there? He was a monster, he took you and you both disappeared. Please tell me what happened. Where'd ya go? What was in the fire? Heidi, are you listening . . ."

She wasn't. She was afraid to remember what had happened upstairs, to picture him. She lent her body on her sister's shoulder, drifting through her mind to her safe world. To her fields and ocean with its two peaks, through the shimmering water.

Heidi opened her eyes, to the same world she had left, to a dark ocean meeting a dark sky. She crossed her brows together, spinning around to her flowered fields. The blood red flowers were now embedded in a field of thorns. Where had the lush grass and her bright sky gone? Looking beyond the thorn field was not purple mountains but dark caves. Her world was darkening just like her life back in the real world.

This was supposed to be her escape, nothing was meant to go wrong here. Heidi threw her arms and legs into the gravel that had replaced the sand, screaming. Her world was ruined. She had no escape, nowhere to be safe from reality. Why was this happening? She stood from the ground, with tears running down her face. She looked up into the storm brewing clouds, something hit her arm, then again. Heidi went back.

She opened her eyes to Mindy hitting her in the arm, Heidi snapped her gaze to her sister, glaring. Mindy ignored her anger, pointing her finger past her sister's face to the television. A breaking news story. They listened as the reporter told the sad story of a murder just a few blocks away. A woman and three children decapitated. The reporter was standing out the front of Drake Commack's house. She went on to say that a man was in hospital with life threatening injuries. Oh god, what had happened? She had her moments with Drake but never would wish this upon him, she liked him.

"That's Drake's house," Heidi whispered.

"Drake was at our door earlier. I . . . I wrote to him, begging him to save us and he came but he . . ." She looked over their shoulder to Zack in the kitchen. "He did these things and he has you doing it too."

Heidi raised her eyebrow, glancing over her shoulder at Zack making them dinner. He had taken off his shirt, leaning over the stove, his back flexing and arms incredible strong. Where did those wings come from? Heidi looked back to her sister, feeling her pain. "What do we do? We can't go to Drake, look what happened to him. Why didn't you tell me you had written to him?"

"Focus Heidi! Drake is practically dead. His family is dead. Our mother, then later that afternoon, the police officer was killed. Heidi don't you see, it's him. Things were bad before he came but not this bad."

She wanted to argue but couldn't find the words. Besides what was she going to say? Tell her sister that she had killed their mother? No. it was better left unsaid. "We're trapped."

"No, we have each other. We have to leave together. I know you said this so many times when we were at home but you're right, we have to go. We have no choice," Mindy hissed, her eyes wide with fear.

"No choice," Heidi repeated.

"Yes, no choice. Now, one by one we'll go upstairs and get what we need then run, okay? Nothing he has given you can come. Not the doll and especially not the necklace," her sister ordered.

Heidi looked back at Zack, who was still distracted, then back to her sister. She knew if she didn't do what Mindy wanted, she would definitely lose her. She knew there was something about Zack that didn't add up but wasn't confident that he had hurt Drake and his family, unless he did it to protect them. He had never done anything to hurt her. She was safe here but she couldn't live without her sister.

For the first time ever she felt guilt, not over killing but that Mindy had to see it. Guilt for Drake and his family. All he did was care about her and try to help, look at what had happened to him, she was to blame. Heidi took in another deep breath, nodding at her sister which produced the biggest smile on Mindy's face. Her sister ran up the stairs, putting her hand up for her to wait. Heidi sighed, turning back to the television.

"That's disappointing about your counselor."

Heidi jumped, snapping her eyes over her shoulder to Zack who was standing against the back of the lounge, his arms crossed over his chest. His eyes were darkened staring at the television. She didn't feel all that afraid, if anything she was more wary of him. She spun around on the lounge, twisting her head to one side. She listened to his breathing, nothing. What was he? And more, why did he want to help her?

She was nothing but a drug whore's daughter who did not stand out in a crowd unless her mind caused her to do something destructive. She thought different and acted different from those around her. She was violent and hated herself so why would anyone want to be around her if they didn't have to? She had tried to be normal but then she would always revert to herself, to this messed up life.

"Heidi, are you feeling okay?" Zack asked her, leaning on the back of the lounge.

"What is your name?" she asked, her eyes darting to the floor.

"What do you mean? You know my name," he questioned, he was becoming more alert of her resistance.

"I know the name you have told me but what is yours? You would have to change your name wherever you go or they'll find out your not human. So what is the name you were given at birth?"

He was silent for a few minutes before he spoke again, this time in a calm low voice. "My name is Xane." He didn't bother to ask how she knew what he was because he had shown her. He bowed his head.

"You promised never to hurt me," Heidi whispered, tears filling her eyes. She stood from the lounge, spinning around to glare at him, he looked shocked. He stood straight, his eyes wandering over her body, trying to predict what she would do, he couldn't. She knew how to keep him from her mind and he could no longer foresee her movements.

"I promised never to hurt you and I haven't. You put your own hand in the fire, not me. I still don't understand how you got yourself in there without dying. I've only helped you."

"You lied to me. I trusted you and you lied."

"About my name? That's for my protection, like you said."

"About the creature you are. You hurt my sister and that hurts me," she challenged, Zack rolled his eyes. Did he truly not care for Mindy? If not, why would he go to so much trouble to be nice so he could please her?

"Melinda's fine."

"You have destroyed Drake and his family."

This time he didn't stay calm. His face became red and his body shook with rage. She could feel the necklace around her neck burning though her skin. Was he doing that to her? "Stop! You're hurting me Zack! My neck!" she screamed clawing at the chain trying to pull it off but it burnt her fingers. He didn't hear her.

"I protected you from him! He was coming to take you away but you were fine. If I didn't do something he would come again. I've had them get in the way before. The innocent man they turn to who will turn them from me but not this time! I'm not playing cat and mouse with fools this time! You are mine!" he yelled.

Heidi stared at him shocked. She hadn't expected him to loose his cool or admit what he had done. But he had and now she had to leave him. She didn't understand who 'they' were or what the last few things he had said meant. But she did know she was fine before he came into her life and would be fine afterwards.

She couldn't stay here and look at him knowing what he had done to Drake. Poor Drake. He didn't ask for any of this and now he had lost everything, his family and surely his life. Oh, poor Drake.

Heidi took in a deep breath, looking him up and down, twisting her head as she had earlier. When he didn't try and defend what he had said or try to calm her, she turned. He had even looked shocked with himself but now he was angry, she had to get Mindy out now.

Heidi started up the stairs when Zack or whoever he was, grabbed her arm pulling her back to him. She tried to pull against his strength. Now she was afraid of him. Now she wanted to cry and run away. Oh god, what was he going to do to them?

"If you leave me you will pay Heidi. You may know my name and some of what I can do but you don't know me. So my dear kitten, the minute you walk out of my house you will become my enemy. What will you do?" he played with her and when she looked into his eyes, she saw that he was not lying.

She loved him but couldn't get caught in this web, couldn't become whatever he was, alone and self loathing. After all she was already half way there. But if she became his enemy she had no one to help her and she would definitely loose the only one who had helped her survive, Mindy.

"I love you," she whispered.

He smiled, releasing her arm and holding his arms out for her to run into them. "I love you too my kitten."

"But I love my sister more, goodbye Xane." When she spoke his name he had shivered. Before he could grab her she ran up the stairs, still afraid. For his body had snapped into a frozen fury.

"Beware Adelheid Harrison because I am now your worst nightmare."

Heidi didn't look back. She hurried up the stairs to the room she shared with her sister. When she walked into the room Mindy was sitting on the window sill with her suitcase at her feet. Heidi's was thrown open on her bed. Without hesitation she walked over to the suitcase, packing her clothes and her only pair of shoes. She managed to take off the necklace that had cooled, throwing it in along with the doll even though Mindy had asked her not too.

They were too beautiful and although she was leaving Xane and this house, she didn't want to forget. Once she was packed, Heidi joined her sister at the window. The first time she had wanted her sister to jump out of the window Mindy had hid under her bed and now she wouldn't be able to remove her from the edge. She was slightly angered over it but now wasn't the time to dwell on the past.

"Are you ready?" Mindy asked, throwing her suitcase out of the window before Heidi had answered her.

Heidi threw her bag down too with a smile on her lips but not in her eyes. All she could think about was the spellbinding man downstairs. Mindy stepped up onto the window ledge, moving to one side, grabbing hold of the drain pipe. Slowly, her sister shifted down the pipe, she didn't look where she was going. Heidi waited until Mindy had made it to the ground.

What was so hard about that?! She wanted to scream. Angered that Mindy was willing to leave them in harm's way when Heidi had decided to run but when it came to her decision to escape, she had no problems with heights. But this was no time to hold a grudge, their new life needed to start on a good foot. Heidi stepped out onto the window, gripping the same pipe Mindy had. She shimmied down it as she had so many times before as a child. Dropping to the ground, she sighed in relief. So far so good, Heidi grabbed her bag.

The two girls head for the street, hand in hand. Over their shoulders they carried their suitcases. First Heidi decided they would head to the city of Adelaide and hopefully have further plans by the time they got there. She glanced back over her shoulder, taking one last look at the house, at the window they had climbed from.

She gasped when her eyes caught sight of Xane, standing in the middle of the room. His arms were folded over his chest, his eyebrows lowered but face emotionless. When their eyes met, he smiled. He stepped aside so she could see the bodies hanging behind him. The ghost bodies of the children. The children's bodies hung from the roof, blood trailing down their chins and eyes.

Heidi shook her head, her heart pounding the fear through her body. He could kill the dead! He could kill them again and remove them from this world! Tears welled in her eyes. He had killed the only friends she had. He was destroying everything to guarantee that she remain alone. For what reason, she didn't know but she would find out. He didn't know as much as he thought about her and more, she couldn't be predicted. Her sister dragged her along the road unaware what lay behind or before them.

CHAPTER EIGHT

She rolled over clutching her stomach and grinding her teeth in pain. She had fallen from the kitchen table a few seconds ago and no one seemed to notice. Her mother and stepfather sat on the lounge, listening to the radio report updates on the war. Neither had noticed her lying on the floor, she hadn't even finished her dinner when the pain hit.

It was her fourteenth birthday and her stepfather had allowed her to come out of her room and eat with them, although her parents had eaten earlier, so she was left alone to ingest a cold meal. But a fool she was, eating her stepfather's food and ending up ill afterwards. Adrian had warned her so many times never to trust him.

Poisoned! Always poisoned but what choice did she have but to eat? She barely had any food other than what Adrian brought her and the poisoned filth she received. She had been so hungry but now she was paying for it. She had to eat to grow stronger even if it meant poisoned food. For Adrian had promised her that when his family moved to the next town, she could join them. Running away requires strength, something she greatly lacked.

Her mother didn't seem to care or notice. There were times when the woman would add her own sleeping mixtures to her daughter's meals. Silently wishing for her to disappear through sleep. The feelings were mutual, she wanted them to disappear. Dreamt of feeding them the poisoned food, dreamt of them suffering.

The pain in her stomach started to pass, causing all the muscles in her body to tighten. Contract and then release as she fought to survive. Slowly, Olivia climbed to her feet. She glanced over to her mother, who sipped her wine, leaning against the heartless man that had turned their world upside down. Her stepfather slurped his home made brew, huffing his comments to the radio, the same thing everyday. All criticism about the war yet she didn't see him out there fighting for their country.

Olivia supported her body against the table, glaring at the two low souls she had to live with. Using the help of the walls and the furniture, she guided herself back to her room. At the moment she would rather be locked away than have to look at them. Some birthday this had turned out to be. Her birthdays were more a curse than a wondrous event.

Finally, making it up to her room, Olivia slammed her door, letting her body fall to the bed, in anger and exhaustion. She wanted to grab her stepfather's hunting knife and tear them apart. But that kind of talk was what Adrian said would lead her to the hunters, crazy talk.

The hunters of their town were known for trekking and killing any person who they didn't believe to be like everyone else. Like herself, should they ever meet her, she would be their prey. Olivia let her tired body fall off the bed. She curled into the corner rocking back and forth, a smile settling on her lips. She would never let them hunt her, she would be the hunter.

*   *   *

A business man walked passed, briefly stopping at a newspaper stand to get the morning paper. He pulled out a five dollar note when a few coins fell from his wallet. The man only glanced at them before grabbing his paper, the rest of his change and walked down the street. She watched and waited until no one was around, or that the man from the newspaper didn't come around to collect the coins. He didn't.

Slowly, she stepped out of the boxed alley, walking to where the money fell. She innocently lent down to adjust her shoe, slipping the change into her hand, standing then walking off. She shoved the hand full of coins into her pouch bag, glancing in at the collection she had already found today. She had made nearly fifteen dollars, not bad for a Monday morning.

Heidi turned into the next alley, dropping to the ground, exhausted. Mindy and herself had been on the streets for twenty days, twenty days that felt more like months. They had managed to survive in the city for a week before the police had stalked them out, so they had run. Not far, just to the next small town, hiring a caravan to shelter in.

Mindy stayed in the caravan all day and all night sulking in self-pity. Something she couldn't do. She had to get money somehow to pay for the caravan and buy food. She collected whatever money she found even if it sometimes led to pick pocketing, she didn't care, they had to survive. Of course she missed Xane but her thoughts couldn't revolve around him, she had their future to concentrate on.

Glancing back on to the street, she waited to see if someone else would be so arrogant to miss some change, nothing yet. She pulled her long white, dirty skirt over her knees, rolling her hands into the sleeves of her black sweater. She dropped her head to her knees. She was so exhausted and sick. If they did get any food for the day, Mindy ate it through the night while she hid in the streets, fascinated with the night crowd. Wishing she was strong enough to be one of them.

To be older, stronger and wiser. To have contacts and be able to get anything she wanted but she was just a child to them. If they saw her, she would be used for their sick desires and leave her where she had started. Planning to run away again. Why did she ever leave Xane? She had been safe and comfortable there.

Because Mindy had wanted her to run away, she told herself. She had been led away believing things between her and her sister would get better and that as long as they had one another, everything would be fine. What a fool she had been. Mindy had used her to get away from Xane when she had never wanted to. But she had, due to false hope and now she was her sister's criminal slave. She wished she had never left Xane.

Looking across the road she spied the police, under cover, but she knew what they were and they were looking for her. Heidi sighed, it was time to move again. Confidently, acting as though she hadn't seen them, she stepped out onto the street. Weaving through the crowd, trying the lose them. While they searched for her, Heidi ducked from the crowd, running to the caravan park.

Mindy was not going to be happy but since she had got them into this mess she would leave. Heidi decided to get them far away from Adelaide or even get them out of South Australia. She ran down the less populated street, looking over her shoulder every few steps to see if the police had spotted her. So far so good. A few minutes had passed before she arrived in the caravan park. She had to sneak to their van, hoping no one saw them and became suspicious of two young girls living there. Although it wouldn't matter now.

Heidi tapped on the door five times in the secret code before stepping in, quickly closing it behind her. Mindy sat in front of the small portable television, eating their last loaf of bread as she watched and obsessed about the day time soap. She hadn't even notice her sister come into the room.

Heidi glared at her, throwing their half packed suitcases on the single bed and waiting to see if Mindy had noticed her. She didn't.

This frustrated her more, she could have been anyone and Mindy wouldn't know until she was dragged away or worse. Angrily, she packed both their bags making sure to keep her necklace and doll hidden. She took off her black baby doll shoes, slipping on her sandals. With a quick brush of her black hair, she threw on another black jacket then threw their bags to the front door. Mindy was still unaware and in her flannelette pajamas.

"Come on we're leaving!" she spat, standing beside their bags.

Mindy looked over her shoulders, darting her eyes up and down before turning back to the television, making no effort to move. "Where are ya going? I like it here, why do we have to leave?"

"More police are hanging around, probably notified by the ones in Adelaide." Heidi said.

"Why are we afraid of the police anyway? We ain't done anything wrong."

"Mindy I am stealing out there. If they catch us they might find out about the men. We're supposed to be dead remember, you have no idea what could happen should they find us. We will be blamed for everything."

"Oh don't get your knickers in a knot. That house has lost any evidence of those men. Can I at least wait till after the show?" her sister replied, like they were discussing going to the mall.

Heidi could feel her blood boiling. "No! We are leaving now and we're getting as far as we can from here. We'll go to Sydney or Melbourne, it will be easier to disappear in those cities!" she yelled.

Mindy switched off the television, spinning around on the floor equally as mad. "How do you expect us to do that? We can't drive and it would take months to walk there, if we do get there."

"We'll hitch hike, now come on!"

"Heidi do you know what happens to hitch hikers? They are never seen again. They'll want payment, how do you suppose we'll pay them?"

"Easy," she whispered, spinning her head to one side, a cold smile sliding across her lips. "We'll let them live once we get there."

She had said it so coldly but with a twinkle in her eye which made her sister shiver on the floor but she didn't object again. Heidi grabbed her bag, surprised as Mindy ran to the bed, quickly changing. Shoving her pajamas in the bag and standing tall by her side. Heidi smiled, if that was all it took to make her sister jump when she said so, she should do it more often.

Grabbing their bags and their free hands clutching each others, they slipped from the caravan park, heading out onto the highway. Heidi wasn't sure how this was going to work but she had seen plenty of times in movies with people walking along the highway, their thumbs stuck out. It couldn't be that hard, could it? But what if the police found them first? Oh god, she hoped this worked.

*   *   *

They had been walking for two days. Well, really for a quarter of these two days with how much Mindy whined and stopped. Heidi pressed on, practically pulling her sister along side of her. So far they had only a few cars that stopped but the people inside were to unsettling and she made some excuse about waiting for the police. They had quickly left.

At this point she thought they might end up walking all the way to the east coast which was half way across the country. Everyone that stopped or looked their way was not someone she was going to hop in the car with. Nevertheless they had to keep going, there was no backing out now. There was sure to be someone good out there even if they would only take them half way.

Heidi glanced around their orange lit surroundings, it was dusk and soon they would have to find some form of cover to hide in for the night. They had to try a few more cars for the night, to be satisfied with their efforts for the day. Of course that was impossible with the sulking big baby hanging off her arm. With another burst of traffic flying by, Heidi stuck out her thumb walking backwards with the traffic. A few cars beeped their horns but nobody stopped. Sighing, she dropped her suitcase flopping upon it, Mindy wasted no time in mimicking her.

"Heidi I'm tired. Let's stop for the night. This was such a big mistake," she mattered, glancing at the lowering sun.

"We'll wait for another traffic flow and if no one stops then we will stop for the night, deal?"

"Whatever."

She chose to ignore her sister's arrogance by quickly standing again, her hand out to the highway. Mindy remained on the ground by her feet. More cars and trucks flew by. Not one of the drivers looked her way. She dropped to the ground again, tired and hungry. Maybe Mindy was right and it was time to turn in for the night but just as she was about to admit it, a white old dirty truck honked and pulled up behind them.

The two girls spun around studying the vehicle. They had said they wouldn't hop in with a trucker because most truckers were dirty old bastards. Heidi stood, pulling Mindy to her feet and heading in the opposite direction from where they had already come from, not daring to look over her shoulder.

"Hey! Where are ya goin'? I thought you two wanted a ride?!" A woman's husky voice called.

She stopped. She hadn't expected to hear a woman's voice. It didn't mean that a woman was safer but it was unexpected. Heidi turned around, looking the mid-thirties woman up and down. She had on a pair of worn jeans and black belt. Her shirt was a black see through waist length shirt with a purple and gold sparkling one beneath. She had rusty blonde hair and minimal make-up on but was quite pretty without it.

The woman slammed the truck door, tracking over to them, her tall boots covering the bottom of her jeans. Melinda clutched her hand but Heidi could tell her sister was hopeful. At this rate Mindy would jump in with anyone to get out of walking, Heidi thought to herself.

"Hi, I'm Layla. Did you girls need a lift? I'm heading for Ballarat for a few days to pick up some things then to Melbourne's north," she said. Extending her hand, Heidi looked up Layla's arm at all her tattoos, a sleeve of skulls and roses, she took a step back. Not that she had a problem with tattoos, or thought someone with them was more dangerous than someone without. It was the extended hand which concerned her; she didn't like anyone to touch her, not now, not ever.

"I'm Melinda and this is my sister Heidi. We wanted to go to Melbourne, right Heidi?" Mindy keenly said, hitting her arm as she did.

Heidi wasn't sure about the woman but she was better than anyone else they had met and there was something about her she liked. "We have no money," she replied bleakly.

"That's alright, I can use some company. You can pay me by unpacking my truck when we get there. Besides you never know, I could help you out. Are you two runaways?"

"Yes."

"No," Heidi corrected her sister.

"Too bad. I'm a bit of a runaway myself, back when I was your age and now. So do you need that ride or not? I plan to be in Victoria by this time tomorrow. You do know it's illegal to hitch hike, don't you? Cops slime all over this highway."

"Please Heidi," Mindy begged, pulling on her arms, like an excited child pleading for a lollypop in the supermarket.

Heidi rolled her eyes. "Fine."

"Alright then, come on girls. I'll throw your bags in the back. I haven't eaten yet so we'll stop at a truck shop in a few just down the road."

They followed Layla up to the back of the truck where she opened it to a cargo container full of furniture. Heidi raised her eyebrow at Mindy but her sister couldn't wipe the smile from her face. She turned away as the door was slammed shut and locked. Layla ran around to the driver's side unlocking the cabin, calling for them to jump in.

Heidi opened the door but gestured for Mindy to get in first. Her sister had no objections, climbing straight in. Slowly, she followed slamming the door behind them and strapping on her seatbelt. Mindy was practically jumping up and down with excitement, she slapped on her belt leaning over the front. Neither of them had been in a truck before or really any sort of vehicle other than a bus or tram.

"So are you two friends or sisters?"

"Sister's," Mindy answered.

"And are you the eldest?" Layla asked Mindy.

"Oh no, I'm younger. Heidi is eleven months older."

Heidi could see Layla's eyes widen, she could practically read her thoughts. She was probably thinking 'but she's so much smaller.' Anything would be no surprise. Heidi crossed her arms over her chest, staring at the road as they pulled onto the highway. She had to admit it was better than walking. Mindy started telling Layla that they had barely any takeaway and had been living on the streets then in a caravan for nearly a month. Layla had listened, she asked no questions but Heidi could feel her eyes moving over her in curiosity. All she wanted was for her sister to shut up.

"Why have you got a truck full of furniture?" Heidi asked, interrupting Mindy's mindless chatter.

"I got home from work and found my boyfriend of seven years in bed with another woman. I don't put up with shit like that. I've been played before and swore it would never happen again, so I left. I have a cabin in the outskirts of Melbourne where I used to live, I'm going back there. I have a job waiting there too, a job I have neglected for too long."

"Wouldn't you already have furniture there?" Mindy asked, intrigued with the story.

"Of course. But no one pulls that bullshit on me, so while he was out I took everything," she said with a smile.

Heidi wanted to smile too but she sealed her lips focusing on the road. She liked Layla, she was independent and free, something she hoped to be one day. "What if he takes you to court?"

"Always so glum my dear. No worries there. He won't. One, he is too lazy and two, I told him if he called the police I would come back and cut of his dick." This time the two girls giggled which caused Layla's smile to widen. "So who wants something to eat?"

Mindy shouted out her approval but Heidi remained silent, she did feel hungry although at the same time she felt sick. She rested her head against the truck door, feeling Layla's hazel eyes upon her again, but she didn't mind. She could feel that the woman didn't mean them any harm. Actually it was perfect that she had found them. Smiling, she thought of what Layla had said about her boyfriend and chopping of his dick.

That's what she should have done to those men. She should have taken away their weapon. Heidi yawned, suddenly feeling so tired. They were safe now, how long it lasted she didn't know but tonight they would be safe. She let her mind drift into slumber while her body listened and waited for her enemy to come and he would come.

* * *

"This is my brother's house. He has been looking after my cabin and has the only set of keys. What do you girls want to do? We've been in the truck for two day and I know he'll welcome you for the night. Unless you wanted to look around Ballarat yourselves," Layla said, pulling up the truck.

Heidi and Mindy looked out to the lowest brick home with its well kept garden and laced curtains through the windows. The street they pulled up in was beautiful, with its well kept homes and lawns. Children played with a sprinkler on the front lawn and on the other side of the road some kids their age were coming back from a bike ride. Then there was more kids a year older than them sitting in a gutter, listening to an ipod.

Why couldn't they have been raised in a street like this? With its safety and friendly neighbors, a street full of support and love. How different life would have been for them had they grown up in a street like this, with their families.

She glanced at her sister who was buzzing with excitement. Heidi already knew Mindy wanted to stay the night but she didn't. Not that she didn't believe Layla, she just wanted some space and wasn't about to spend the night in a strange man's house. It was safer on the street.

"I'll stay. It will be wonderful, won't it Heidi?" Mindy asked, undoing her seat belt as Layla had done.

"Heidi what do you want to do?" Layla asked. The woman wasn't stupid, she could see her hesitation. "My brother's a good man and there is no one else in the house. It will be just us."

"I'll pass," Heidi whispered.

"Oh come on loosen up. What could happen?" Mindy cried.

Layla climbed out of the truck with Mindy following her. They went around the back to get her suitcase and a box. Heidi watched from the window as the two of them approached the front door, it swung open before they reached it. A man in his forties embraced Layla then was introduced to Mindy; he shook her sister's hand. He then looked past her to the truck, smiling then to his sister again.

The three of them stood talking for a few minutes before Mindy carried her suitcase inside, followed by Layla's brother with the box. Layla headed back to the truck opening her door, Heidi sat still, hoping she wouldn't try to force her to do anything she didn't want to. The woman pulled herself into the truck beside Heidi, resting her hand on her knee. Heidi glared at the hand, shifting her leg. Layla sighed, folding them in her own lap.

"You can stay in the truck for the night if you want or I know a really cool park where no police drive by at night. However you might get a few underage drinkers there when it gets dark," she said.

"Thanks, I might get changed then go for a walk," Heidi muttered.

"I'm here if you want to talk you know?"

Heidi swung her head to the woman looking her up and down. "I know."

"I've been where you are. Having to steal for money, hiding out in parks. I know what you're going through."

"I doubt you do," she sneered, shocking Layla.

Heidi climbed from the truck, walking around to the back and lifting the door just enough for her to squeeze through. She unzipped her suitcase, pulling out a long pair of black loose pants and a purple jumper. She brushed back her hair, tying it in a white ribbon. Every time she saw her reflection she was shocked, she looked so different, so ghost like. Searching for her shoes, Heidi found her necklace, carefully lifting it from the bag. She placed it around her neck, hiding it under her jumper. The knock on the door startled her, Heidi tripped over her suitcase moving to the door.

"Wear something warm, it's going to be a cold night and the door is always opened if you want to come in. Heidi, I can help you if you'd just let me," Layla called, from outside.

"Thanks. I don't mean to be so horrible, it's just . . ."

"I know sweetheart. Life's a shit hole, just remember what I said." She heard Layla walk away.

Heidi sighed, why did she have to push everyone away? Why was she so hateful to Layla . . . to Drake? That was why. Keep them away or they'll die just like Drake had. Although they didn't know for sure if he had died, she didn't believe he would survive the attack. Especially if he woke up and found out his family had been murdered, no one would want to survive it. It was easier to believe he was dead than suffering because of her. She wiped the tears from her eyes. She should have left when Mindy wanted too, she should have gone to him and maybe he and his family would be alive today.

Heidi glanced down at her scattered suitcase, spying her doll thrown to one side. She gasped hoping it hadn't smashed. She spun the doll over happy to see it wasn't broken. Grabbing one of her jackets, she wrapped it around the doll when she stopped.

Slowly, Heidi ran her hands over the dolls face watching it, at first there was nothing but then the dolls eyes changed. Long blood tears trickled down her face although unlike with Xane, the clothes did not change. She didn't mind too much, she had done it, well at least half of it. Heidi kissed the doll, wrapping her up and hiding her back in the suitcase where she was safe from the world and her sister.

After all her things had been packed up and her bag locked, Heidi slipped from the truck, slamming the roller door closed behind her. Throwing a pouch bag over her shoulder, she strolled away from the house and towards where she had seen some shops as they had driven in.

Hugging herself in her jumper, Heidi stumbled across the park near the small strip of shops. She would get something to eat and drink later; right now she needed to relax. Maybe even disappear for a while. She stepped off the path, moving for the empty park, her eyes fixed on the swing. It had been so long since she had been in a park.

She sat on the swing, slowly rocking in the breeze, her head leaning against the chains and eyes fixed on the ground. It was getting dark but she didn't even flinch, the swing drifted over the dark shadowed ground. Heidi got higher and higher until the world around her seemed to disappear.

Of course one might find it odd to see a fourteen year old playing in the park but she didn't care. This was when looking younger came in handy. As she flew backwards her black hair covered her face but once she swung forward, it disappeared leaving her to see the world. Through the darkness into the light or was it through the light into the darkness?

The night rolled in and she settled to sleep in the top of the house climbing frame with the slide. The night wasn't as cold as she had expected it to be. She had swung for hours before strolling over to the convenience store, buying herself a bottle of water and snack pack which contained ham, cheese, crackers and chocolate, perfect. After her quick dinner, she had climbed up there. Curiously watching the night life, her thoughts drifted to her sister.

She hoped Mindy was okay and that she was having a hot dinner then offered a warm bed to sleep in. Even as she thought all of this, she did not regret her decision. She could look after herself, no one needed to be her savior. Heidi dropped her head to her knees in the corner of the cubby house, like she did everywhere.

Hidden in the corner becoming a part of the furniture, alone but not afraid. So different from everyone else around her. No one loved her and she didn't know how to love or care for anyone else, except for Drake . . . poor Drake; it was all her fault.

*   *   *

They traveled to the northern outskirts of Melbourne, through bush land pulling up in front of a lovely and quiet large cabin. It was so peaceful and quiet out here, Heidi already loved it. It was what she was looking for, what she needed. Layla pulled the truck up jumping out and jogging up to the front door, she looked happy to be home.

They had left for Melbourne that morning, after she had arrived back at the truck from her night out. Mindy had eaten a large breakfast and had a hot shower, she was babbling with excitement. Chatting constantly to Layla though the woman seemed more focused on her. Heidi thought she had seen surprise in her face, maybe she hadn't expected her to stay out all night.

After they had unloaded some of the truck at Layla's brother's house, she had climbed into the truck with not a word to Layla's brother who was waiting for them to say their goodbyes. She had caught the challenging looks of her sister and still gained her disapproval. Who cared? When they were ready to leave Mindy and Layla had climbed into the truck, slamming the doors and leaving Ballarat for Melbourne.

Two hours later they had arrived with the only words that had been spoken coming from her over excited sister. She hadn't minded too much, it was rather relaxing for it meant that she didn't have to talk. She lent her head against the door. Every now and then Layla would ask her something but for all they knew she was asleep. However now they had arrived and it meant herself and her sister could have their own space and leave, although this place was very beautiful.

"Wow, its so pretty here," Mindy commented, leaping from the truck and walking around the back. Heidi followed, her large eyes running over the enchanting privacy of the cabin. "What is it you do Layla?" Mindy asked. Curiously, Heidi turned to Layla also. This answer was something she had wondered herself.

"I manage a club in town but only go there four nights a week and with the remainder of my time I open my house to runaways."

"Is that a joke?" Heidi hissed.

Layla turned to her smiling though it didn't reach her eyes. "No joke. I provide a safe place for them to stay. Like a shelter but I don't call their parents or force counselors on them, if they need me I'm here. Its peaceful here and surprisingly a big help. I don't tolerate drugs or any abuse. This is an escape and they are free to come and go, no questions asked. Ah, I've missed it here and my work. It's a wonderful feeling to watch someone heal themselves and gain back their lives. I created what I needed when I was your age," she said proudly.

"Runaways, does that mean your home is open to us?"

"Mindy no! We are fine on our own. No one can be with us, you know what can happen." But her sister ignored her, stepping between her and Layla. The woman still hadn't lost her smile however this time her eyes were shining too.

"Of course. There are eleven rooms and since you are first, feel free to choose your own room. If that's what you want."

"So what happened when you went with your boyfriend to Adelaide? Did you just kick everyone out?" Heidi pressured.

"Oh no, I have full times and empty times. When I went to Adelaide there were two boys here and they came with me. They found jobs and girlfriends in Adelaide and decided to stay, happy ending," Layla replied, happy Heidi was challenging her so she could prove she was what she said.

Heidi pursed her lips, glaring at the woman but her sister seemed only more impressed. Really they didn't have anywhere else to go and it was so isolated out here. "And we can leave any time we want? No deals attached, no payments?"

Her smile grew wider. "The only thing I want from the teens that stay here, is to help keep the house clean and help with dinners. I have rules about treating everyone with respect and no fighting. You can go whenever you want just as long as you are safe. I'm not about to let a runaway run off with a pimp or drug lord."

"Fair enough," Heidi muttered. She opened the back of the truck, pulling out her bag then her sister's. Mindy was still smiling stupidly.

Layla hurried past them into the cabin, she swung the door open then ran around opening all the windows. Mindy grabbed Heidi's free arm, pulling her to the door. "Oh thank you Heidi. I didn't think you would stay but you did something I couldn't predict. This is great, I love you," her sister squealed.

The two sisters walked out into the cabin, both placing their bags at the door and gazing in at the welcoming beauty. The front room was large and joining the kitchen on the left side. The lounge was on the right and between them was a large empty space. All the furnishing was thick dark pine and the fabrics were dark green. The floor was ember floorboards and in the lounge room there was a fireplace with a large oval rug before it.

All the windows had wooden shutters covered by lace curtains and there were no lights on the roof or fans. It probably wouldn't get hot enough out here for fans and there was the fireplace for warmth. The cabin was lit by scattered lamps, causing a soft warm glow throughout the room. It truly was magical.

There was an open doorway in the kitchen which she could look through and see a laundry and bathroom. In the center of the lounge room there were two halls extending from it where she assumed the eleven bedrooms to be and maybe a few more bathrooms. She could see herself really liking it here though she wouldn't let on to Mindy that she did.

Mindy had stepped further into the room, shifting around the windows where Layla had just pulled back the shutters. Heidi glanced over to the lounge when she spotted a young man sitting, a guitar in his hand. It looked like he was singing a melody although she could not hear anything from his lips. He turned to her, winked, then disappeared. Heidi gulped, the dead were here too. They did not scare her but reminded her of her friend ghosts Xane had destroyed.

There could be an advantage to the lingering dead, for as long as they were here Xane wasn't. His energy feed on theirs not allowing them to be seen. She had figured that out all those nights alone on the streets. She had remembered the way the ghost children were scared of him and could never appear to her when he was around. Heidi stepped into the room, closing the front door behind her. Layla came back into the main area after opening all the windows down the hall.

"Has anyone died here?" Heidi asked, glancing back to the empty lounge.

"Heidi! What kinda question is that?!" Mindy exclaimed.

"No that's okay. I have nothing to hide. Yes someone has died here, a seventeen year old boy named Boyd. He hung himself in his room nine years ago. He was finally getting better when his parents found him and tried to get him to go with them, he left. Two weeks later he was back but so far from the happy musician we all knew, he killed himself after three days. It was horrible, such a waste of a beautiful life. He was the first and hopefully the last I would have in my care that I couldn't save," Layla said, looking around as she spoke, tears in here eyes. She took in a deep breath, glancing back to the girls. "Why do you ask?"

Heidi looked from the lounge back to the weakened woman. There was no reason to freak her out. "No reason, just curious. Which room was his?"

Layla crossed her eyebrows together, trying to work out if she wanted to stay away from the room or burn it down out of fear. She wanted neither. "The fourth room in the first hall."

"I want that room."

Her sister and Layla looked at one another. Layla was clearly confused and shocked but Mindy had a look of no surprise. Heidi grabbed her bag, dragging it up the first hall to the fourth room. With no one around her, she knocked on the door, it opened. She stepped in, closing it behind her and placed her bag to one side.

The room was comfortable with a small window with dark blue, almost black curtains. The bedspread was the same and the rug under the large single bed also black. The bed sat in the middle of the room. There was a bedside table on either side of the bed with modern black lamps on them. Beside the door was a classic wooden chest of drawers. In the other corner was a single seat blue couch.

Heidi sat down on it, glancing around the room, her new home. Though she still had no true feeling of home, not even in the house she had grown up in. Where did she belong? But then to find a home could take time and it was so peaceful here. Peaceful was what she needed to keep sane.

CHAPTER NINE

She sat in the corner stroking the guitar strings even though she didn't know how to play. She had found it under the bed and since the dead boy no longer needed it, for he had a guitar of his own, she had claimed it. Mindy and she had been in Layla's cabin for two weeks. In that time Layla had gone to shelters with pamphlets and now their isolated cabin was filled with runaways.

Mindy loved it. She got along with the eight other boys and girls always bringing the attention to herself. But Heidi hated it. She hated everyone around trying to talk to her. She didn't know how to get along with people or be comfortable around so many of them. Layla worked three days and two nights a week. When she was at home, she didn't pressure anyone to talk, just joined them watching movies, like she was one of them.

Heidi would have rather been going to work with Layla than staying here watching the fifteen years old boys getting cozy with her sister. She hated them all, maybe even her sister sometimes.

Grabbing the pick again, she strummed the guitar, facing the wall, and this time the sound that came out actually sounded like music. She looked back over her shoulder to see if anyone had heard but no one was listening to her. They were all watching a horror movie, screaming and laughing at the old film. The runaways ranged from thirteen to sixteen. The youngest was Mindy and the sixteen year old, was a girl named Alicia. Who had runaway because her dad wouldn't buy her a car when she got her learner license.

Her sister was playing footsy with a boy she liked, he was two years older than her. Heidi was sickened by it. She turned away, glancing at the door as she did often when she was waiting for Layla, only an hour to go. Mindy was so happy which made her feel guilty to want to leave but she was an outsider yet again. Why didn't anyone ever like her?

She tried the guitar again making it sound like it was screaming, it sounded horrible. Why did she want to play the guitar anyway? Heidi threw down the instrument, looking back to the group who were no longer paying any attention to the movie. They all sat on the lounge, some in each others laps as they discussed their stories. And of course it was her sister who was talking again.

She was describing their drug abused mother and all the men that came through their house. The group seemed intrigued when Mindy started to tell them of the night the men came into their room. Heidi hoped she would stop but with every eye on her, Mindy continued. Speaking selfishly at how she had hid under the bed as the men moved in on her. Heidi couldn't hear anymore.

Mindy had no right to use their pain as a popularity contest, especially not at her expense, describing her naked with five men over her. She felt sick. After all she didn't remember any of this herself. Oh god, what if she kept talking and told them what happened next? Heidi stood from the corner, throwing down the chair behind her. Causing the group to look around shocked by her presence, she glared at them.

Without another moment she stormed down the hall, slamming her door behind her. In the lounge room she could hear the group silenced but it only lasted for a few moments before there was a roar of laughter, her sister's voice bellowing the loudest. How dare Mindy! She hated her right now, maybe she should just leave. Heidi fell backwards on her bed trying to escape to her safe world but then not even it was safe anymore, was it?

She couldn't escape, her ears still listened to the group outside, her mind too active for her to release. Heidi sighed rolling to the side, watching the shadows dance on the walls. That's funny, she thought. There was no breeze outside and nothing was moving within the room. Curiously, she watched the shadows, her eyes large with wonder as the shadows grew bigger and bigger, some flickering like flames.

Heidi thought if she could touch them they would be solid for that's how they started to look, like dark objects. Above her more shadows danced on the roof, slowly joining together and swinging down towards her from the light.

She sat on her bed, her heart beating faster as the long shadows from the light shade swung at her. She gasped rolling off the bed. The shadows had created a noose and it was diving after her! Heidi darted around the room, jumping over all the little shadows that were reaching for her, like wild veins in a horror movie.

Something moved within the mirror which caught her attention, it was another person, Olivia. The spirit from her nightmares pressed her hands to the glass, her face lit with shadows, her smile cracked and crazy. She was controlling them! She was the one directing the shadows after her. Trying to kill her again! Why?

Heidi hissed, tumbling over the bed. She looked over her back, nothing had caught her yet, then back at the mirror. Olivia was laughing behind the glass, moving her arms faster. The shadows mimicked her movements. Heidi's heart beat faster. She wasn't going to get away from them.

With one quick movement, she leapt to the door but not before something grabbed her around the neck swinging her into the air. She tried to scream but no sound came out, she was being choked, no, hung. The shadows were trying to hang her just like the lone boy ghost years ago. How did Olivia know that? Unless she was always there with her, watching and listening. Now she was afraid.

She tried to scream again, this time the only thing that came out were gurgles. Her hands clutched and scratched at the solid shadows around her neck. It pulled her higher and higher. Her eyes drifted to the mirror where Olivia had fallen to the base in hysterics of laughter. Oh god, she was going to die! She would be found dead with signs of strangulation but there would be no rope, no evidence.

She could feel the heat rising into her face, her eyes bulging and head aching then feeling like it was without a body. She was going to pass out, her body stopped struggling. Just as she was about to close her eyes and give in, the door to her room was thrown open. She was dropped.

"Heidi!" Layla screamed, running into the room. "What do you think you were doing?!"

Heidi had fallen to her knees coughing and choking, her head spinning. The shadows around the room had disappeared as soon as the door had been opened. Olivia had stomped her foot then also disappeared. Only the faint glowing image of her eyes twinkled in the mirror before they were gone too. Heidi gasped for air, slumping further into the floor.

She had nearly died again because of that spirit. No ghost had ever tried to kill her before. It was normally the opposite, it was she who hurt others whether she wanted to or not. What was this ghost's problem? Did Layla see any of this or just her trying to hang herself? How it must have scared her, reminding her of Boyd. She didn't want to hurt Layla. She didn't want her to think this was personal. She wouldn't hang herself, never like that.

"Heidi I have certain rules here. I offer help and shelter but if you're going to try to kill yourself under my roof, I'm going to have to send you to someone who can help. You knew what happened in here, why would you do that to me?" Layla cried. Shutting the door behind her and sitting beside the shaking girl.

"I didn't try to kill myself!" Heidi protested but all that came out was a hiss that stung her throat.

"Oh Heidi I saw you. What do you think happened? You were hanging from the roof to clean it? I'm not stupid. I heard about what your sister said out there and I know that must have hurt but killing yourself . . ."

"I wasn't trying to kill myself!" Heidi yelled, her head spinning again.

"I can't help you here," Layla whispered, bowing her head.

Tears fell from her eyes. "I wasn't trying to kill myself. Kick me out if you want but at least listen to me first. There were shadows flickering around the room and they came after me and tried to hang me. There was a spirit in the mirror controlling them. She wants to kill me! This is the second time she has tried. The first time was in the fire . . ."

"Heidi stop! No nonsense, pack your things and I'll drive you to the hospital."

"I'm not crazy! Look don't you see there is no ropes or chair to get me that high. Believe me or not but don't patronize me. I'll leave within the hour."

Layla sighed, looking past Heidi to the roof then around the room, her eyes widened. She darted them back to stare at the breathless girl. Heidi stared back, trying to portray the truth in her eyes, she never lied. She hoped if she was kicked out that Mindy would be able to remain here. Her sister couldn't be punished for what she had done but then she wanted her to be punished, didn't she?

She listened beyond the door to hear her sister yelling over someone else yet again. She was so angry with Mindy and now they had told Layla too. Everyone knew about her being raped, knew in detail about her shame but not her defense. No, Mindy would never speak about that but to Heidi half the story sounded worse than the truth. If they found out she had killed, her next home would be prison. After all the police thought she was dead, so whatever she did, she looked guilty.

"When you first arrived you asked had anyone died here, why?" Layla asked no more than a whisper. Heidi snapped her attention back to Layla, she looked so sad but in a way she couldn't blame her. She was just upset that she had caused the woman's sadness.

"Because I saw him sitting on the lounge, playing his guitar. I have always seen spirits, among other things. I don't expect you to believe me."

Layla grabbed her hand, helping her to her feet then leading her over to the bed where they sat beside one another. She placed her hand on the girl's knee, her face stern but kind. "Strangely I believe you. I know this is hard but please tell me everything you have seen and what Melinda blurted out. Please tell me about the spirits and the one in the mirror. I can't see them but I can feel, in this room especially, please" Layla begged.

"I have done things that . . ."

"I don't care. Nothing will pass through my lips. Please tell me, we won't leave the room until you are finished. It will help you get it out of your mind and me to understand."

Heidi crossed her eyebrows together, for a few moments she studied the woman's sincerity. Layla was right, someone had to hear her story and not the attention seeking version Mindy was telling. Yes, Layla had earned her right to know. If anything happened to her there would be at least one person who knew everything. Who knew of Drake and his family, knew of Xane and who he was, someone who knew about her mother. Yes, it was right to tell Layla. "Okay, I will tell you everything." She begun.

*   *   *

After three hours, she had told Layla all about her life, about how she felt and her disappointment in her sister. She hadn't spared a detail even down to the men's deaths, her mother's death and her imaginary world, that she couldn't control from the darkness. Layla had listened, not once interrupting or showing any signs of alarm. Only sadness crossed her eyes and fear when she spoke of Xane.

When she was completely finished there were people calling for Layla beyond the door but she didn't hurry away. She took her time making sure Heidi knew her story was safe with her and that she would do anything to help. Layla of course had been right and after she had left to prepare dinner, Heidi felt better. Felt as though a weight had been lifted from her shoulders.

An hour later she had returned with a plate of lamb, potatoes, vegetables and Boyd's guitar. Layla gave her a long hug before going back out to make sure everyone settled for the night. Heidi ate half the dinner then grabbed the guitar. She sat on the floor and leant back against the bed, slowly strumming the strings. Even though she wasn't making any music, it was still peaceful to try and to hum along with an imaginary tune. She had been quietly playing for half an hour when she felt a strong breeze behind her. It was eleven pm and most of the house would be just about asleep.

Heidi looked over her shoulder to the spirit boy who sat cross legged on her bed, he smiled. She smiled back, turning her attention again to the guitar. In all the years she had seen spirits she had never heard them speak. Other than Olivia but Olivia was no ordinary spirit.

She tried playing again when two cold hands sat over hers, placing her fingers on the right frets and then moving her other hand along the strings. He adjusted her right hand on the frets then strummed her other again, adjust, then strum. She was playing music! He was mimicking the tune she had been humming all day, it sounded good. His hand lifted from hers and she continued to play, a soft smile falling over her lips.

"Thank you Boyd," she whispered, glancing over her shoulder.

Boyd smiled, nodding his head, his gray eyes looking down to his guitar.

"Thanks for letting me use your guitar and room," she said. Heidi placed down the guitar sliding it under the bed. She sat on the bed cross legged in front of him. "I wish you could speak to me."

Boyd smiled again, placing his hand over his heart then moving it to her heart. He touched his eye, running a pretend tear down his cheek. Sadness, though he wasn't mocking her, he was trying to tell her he had been listening to her story and was sorry. Heidi smiled nodding, with a sigh she lent forward placing a kiss on his cold cheek and almost swore that he blushed. Why was it she was more comfortable around the dead than the living?

He turned his head in the direction of the hall, focusing on the approaching footsteps, quickly he patted her head, pointed to the window holding his arm up in a fighting pose then disappeared as the door was opened, Heidi laughed. Layla stood in the doorway curiously looking around the room then studying her.

"Its time for lights out, you need some sleep. It's so cold in here, has he . . ." she didn't know how to say it.

Heidi grinned. "Boyd was just teaching me how to play."

Layla looked intrigued. Heidi could see that the woman truly believed her. "I wish he could speak to you and tell you why he did it. I had a talk with your sister and she promised to come apologize in the morning. But I was thinking maybe next week you can come to work with me, sometimes. Would you like that?"

"Yes, thank you."

"Okay, good. Sweet dreams," Layla said, starting to shut the door.

"Layla?"

"Yes sweetheart?"

"Did Mindy realize she had upset me? I mean did she know what she did was wrong?"

Layla froze in the doorway the hall light casting shadows on her face as she frowned. "I don't think so. She said you're the one with the problem by running off. Don't worry about her. Mindy has some growing up to do, she'll realize it soon."

The smile snapped off her face. "Good night Layla." The woman left and Heidi dropped herself down on the bed. "Good night Boyd." She closed her eyes, snuggling down under the blankets. She threw her clothes to the floor, resting in her underwear. Her mind floated past her world searching for a new one, a safe one. She left her body, with the amethyst necklace burning around her neck.

*   *   *

She silently approached the closed door in the second hallway, darting her eyes down to the lounge room to see if anyone else was coming up the hall, no one. Heidi grinned, turning back to the closed door, of the fifteen year old boy who had been sleeping with her sister for two weeks.

How dare her sister have sex with him and more, how dare the pervert do it? It disgusted her, Mindy was just a kid. What was she thinking? And after all she had seen, you would have thought that she would stay clear away from boys.

Stepping up to the door, Heidi lent against it listening to the hum of the radio inside. He was alone and relaxed, even better. Stroking the amethyst around her neck, she knocked on the door calling upon Xane's power. She was not his enemy, only his student who disapproved with who he hurt. She loved him and knew he loved her. After all, she still had powers like him and this time she would use them willingly.

"Come in!" the boy called. Heidi grinned, looking down to the shimmering stone, she stepped into the room.

The boy, Alex looked up from his motorbike magazine watching as she entered. First surprise crossed his face then a force of anger. Heidi didn't care. She wanted him to hate her. It would only make this easier. She confidently strolled around the room, running her fingers over his things. Her head twisted to one side watching him. He glared back though she could see he was afraid of her. She wondered how much Mindy had told him.

Swinging her head to the other side, Heidi studied the boy trying to find some reason her sister was attracted to him, nothing. He was like every other pimple faced, skinny, raging hormone boy. And beyond all the things he would grow out of, he really didn't look that cute. But she would always remember him, always the first life she took consciously.

"What do you want freak?" he spat.

Heidi smiled. He had just given her a reason for no remorse. "I just wanted to meet the boy who was screwing my sister."

"That's none of your business."

"Ah you're right. What you two do together is none of my business but you see, I know my sister and know that what is said to you is somewhat about me. So that makes it my business, does it not?" she played, keeping her face emotionless. He was confused. Stupid boy, any man would have got the hint and got the hell out of there.

"Ah, um I guess."

"Hmm, and do you know what the biggest problem is?" she continued, twisting her head to the other side, a smile on her face and fingers twisting around one another.

"What?" he asked, squirming upon the far side of the bed.

"I don't remember giving her permission to tell you about me. So I guess you know what happens next? No? I'll help you. I have been left yet again with the job of cleaning up our problems and at the moment, you are the problem." Heidi moved to the center of the room, watching the fear roll across his face. Oh yes, he knew everything, her sister had told him what she feared. Never mind, she would fix it. He was twice the size of her but that wouldn't matter, she didn't physically need to touch him.

"No! Please don't hurt me. Listen, yes she told me everythin' but I aint gonna tell no one else, promise," he begged.

"I hate promises," she whispered to herself, twisting her head again, her eyes glazed. Alex moved for the door while she was distracted but her eyes darted to him and she stepped in his way. "That was not playing fair Alex. Now I have an offer for you. Jump out of the window and run back home. Never contact my sister again or, well you know, don't you?"

Alex nodded, frantically he ran around the room grabbing a few things before opening the window and jumping out. Heidi curiously walked to the open window, watching him dash across the back clearing in front of the woods, she smiled. He didn't think he was going to get away that easy did he? No. She glared angrily at him, focusing on all her energy. Collecting and gathering her darkness then shooting her fury at the perve. Alex stopped just before the woods edge, turning back to her, his face a mask of shock, he screamed.

His body started to shake, his skin burning, his face started to melt, being attacked by a swarm of acid. Heidi stared at him, did she do this or was something else doing this for her? She could feel the necklace burning again and catch the glowing in the corner of her eye. No, no time for it, focus. Focus on the boy, watch him burn, turn to dust as he died. Heidi glared back through the window, wrinkling her nose. She felt no remorse, he deserved it. They all did.

Alex's body disintegrated before her eyes, his bones exploding in a puff of dust. His skin fed the fire and his screams disappearing within the winds. He was dead. Nothing but a pile of dust. She took in a deep calming breath. She had done this, all on her own. Consciously, she had killed. She didn't really know what to think. It felt as though she wasn't quite here, like it was a movie or something. But no, this was real.

When she had killed before she hadn't been present, her world had protected her from the pain. This time she had set out to do it, she had wanted the darkness, Xane's darkness. No fear, no pain, no remorse. Heidi twisted her head to the other side, curiously watching to see if the dust rose and came after her. Of course no such thing happened but it would be fun if it had. All the more to test her powers, her complete dark powers! The glow of the necklace disappeared.

"Heidi, are you ready? I have to be at work in an hour! Come on let's move!" Layla called from the kitchen. She turned to the door, walking out and leaving it opened and undisturbed behind her.

"Coming!" she called, in the sweetest voice.

Grinning, Heidi skipped down the hall, humming to her favorite tune. She moved into the living area, catching Layla throwing her bag at the front door. She looked up smiling then she nodded to the running car sitting out the front. Heidi grabbed the bag, walking out to the car and slipping in the front. Her attention was caught by the group of teens in the trees. Girls in bikinis and boys in their board shorts, they were all running through the trees with water bombs, it looked like fun.

Why couldn't she be one of them? Playing and oblivious to the cruel world she was in? What was wrong with her? On the other hand, she loved her powers because they were her protection and would she give them up to be one of them? If she was one of them, she wouldn't need the powers.

Mindy was playing with them, wearing a daring pink bikini for her body. Where had she got it from? They didn't have any clothes like that, especially brand swim wear. Hell, she didn't even think she owned swimmers. Heidi turned away, angrily crossing her arms over her chest, was she a freak? All she wanted was a friend, one that was living and to relax, be carefree like them but she had been her mother's daughter.

Layla hopped into the car beside her, glancing at her but knowing better than to disturb her thoughts. Heidi smiled. It felt strange that someone actually understood her. That would mean that Layla was her friend, wouldn't it? Yes, she had a friend, one who listened to her and took her to work everyday for the past two weeks. It was actually what she needed, distraction, or they'll all be dead.

An hour later they arrived in St Kilda where Layla's club was. Heidi had been surprised when she first went to the club, for it was a strip club although Layla was not a stripper. She had said she used to be when she was nineteen to get off the streets but now managed the club and took pride in looking after the women there. Heidi admired her for it and she loved helping out there, surrounded by the beautiful women, with their perfect full bodies. So unlike the childlike body she had.

It was illegal for her to be there, so she mostly hid out the back. Collecting all the money when the dancers came off stage. She counted it and wrote down the earnings then placed it into a pencil case for herself and Layla to divide for the girls later. If the police happened to come in, the club backed onto a kebab shop. She would jump the fence and hide behind the shop, until someone would give her the signal that they were gone.

"There's a bucks party tonight, so I have decorations in the bag but of course that would mean you have to stay out the back all night. Those men can get a little rowdy and I don't want anyone to get confused and make a move on you." Layla instructed as they pulled up in the car park across the road from the club.

"Enough said. I don't go out there anyway."

"I know but sometimes you watch from off stage and if they become uncontrollable they may see you. Besides the girls don't want you watching when their requirements are a little full on. If I end up calling the police, I definitely don't want one of them seeing you."

"I understand Layla. Is there anything I can do out back to help?" she asked, hoping there was.

"Not unless the girls need it, although you can help me with the decorations before we open."

Heidi nodded, grabbing the bag and stepping out of the car. They walked across the road unlocking the club and slipping in, hidden by the afternoon glow. She hurried in, tearing open the bag of decorations. Following Layla's instructions by running around the club and putting them up as best she could.

It was an hour before they opened. Half an hour before the dancers arrived and due to her height, doing it all by herself was a struggle to get it finished in time. Layla was on the phone out the back organizing more parties. To her surprise when the dancers arrived they helped her, instead of going out the back. They spoke kindly to her, accepting who she was and for the first time she was a part of something.

Once all the decoration were finished, Heidi hurried out the back hiding in the dressing room while the dancers got ready. She watched them change then do their hair. They glittered their skin and painted one another's faces as they always did. They talked about men, their lives at home and their families, all things she didn't have. Heidi sat on the beanbag next to the closest, listening and observing their behavior. She was so quiet, that they had forgotten she was there.

The men arrived and Layla came in organizing the girls, hurrying them out into the hall. Once Heidi was alone, she bowed her head, tears streaming down her face. She was always left alone. She liked the women but they were older than her and saw her as a child, standing beside them she looked like a child. She wanted to be one of them, beautiful, enchanting and womanly but most of all, she wanted to be powerful. Would anyone ever love her or want her? Would she ever be happy?

CHAPTER TEN

"I don't understand how twelve kids disappeared in two months officer. You know the caring establishment I run here and seven years ago I only had the one problem. This time, they're disappearing as fast as they're coming and not even packing their things when they go. There are some things a runaway never leaves behind. I wish I knew what I was doing wrong. I'm sorry I'm no help to you. Yes, they were all here at one stage over the last two months but all disappeared in the night, not so much as a goodbye." Layla cried, sitting at the kitchen table, her long nails nervously tapping on the surface.

"That's fine Miss Phillips, just write down whatever you can remember about these kids. I doubt it is anything you have done. These kids probably planned this to annoy their parents. You know how they are. Would it be alright if we talk to the remaining ones?" the older officer asked.

"Of course but I have some rules, no personal information or trying to get them to go back home. Some of the new kids don't know half on that list, as I said they go as fast as they come. Also if they don't want to talk they have that right officers," Layla said sternly.

"We understand Miss Phillips. Now where can we start?"

"First hall, the first room is mine so go to the second. It is late, they should all be in their rooms. Please be patient with them."

"Thank you Miss Phillips," the second one replied. The two officers grabbed their pens and note books, walking up the first hall. Layla bowed her head to the table, running her hands through her hair, her eyes darkened with stress and sadness.

Heidi gasped, dropping down from the outside window, her heart falling with Layla's sadness. She had never wanted to hurt her. She crawled along the ground, heading around the back of the cabin to her room. There, she could climb through the window before the police reached her room. This was all her fault! She should control her rage and vengeance but she couldn't. They all had to pay though it was at Layla's cost. At least the bodies had disappeared. Her friend hadn't been tortured with seeing that at least, only the confusion to their running away.

Jumping through the window, Heidi flopped to the bed, darting her eyes to her tangled bush hair. She pulled out as much of the twigs as she could, straightening her favorite white cotton dress that she had on over her jeans. She tried to brush the dirt from the dress as best as she could until she was satisfied. No matter what she did she still looked a mess, like a little kid who had spent her whole day in a tree.

She dropped beside the bed, pulling the guitar from beneath it and occupying herself with pretending to know the notes. Actually she did know a few of them now, thanks to Boyd. In the hall she could hear the officers enter the bedroom next to hers, Mindy's room. Of course her sister was barely ever in there. She spent most of her time in the second hall where most of the boys were.

Tonight however her sister was in her room. Heidi could hear her loud voice crying out to the officers at how much of a victim she was. All of her friends had disappeared without saying goodbye, Heidi smiled to herself. Mindy was such a drama queen. She was sure her sister wouldn't say too much because she no longer knew all that much. It seemed all that had happened before these last two month Mindy had forgotten, much to her delight.

A sudden presence in her room alerted her. Heidi looked over her shoulder to Boyd standing on her bed, looking out of the window. He was confused as to where the voices were coming from. He could hear sounds all around him, not from any particular direction, unless he was watching someone's lips move or through music due to the vibrations.

She clicked her fingers, the movement catching his attention. She pointed to the wall she faced. He nodded, glaring at the wall. He disappeared then reappeared beside her. Heidi smiled at him, leaning against his solid cold form. She still didn't understand why she could touch spirits. Whenever she saw a spirit in the street they could walk right through people but not her, no, to her they were another being.

She tilted her head listening to her loud mouthed sister through the wall. Trying to hear if Mindy actually knew anything or was wasting their time. Of course it was a waste of time to talk to Mindy, for she defiantly didn't know what had happened around here. Heidi had been very careful to be sure of that. Besides Mindy wouldn't dare speak of their home life for her sister seemed afraid of what would happen if she did. And she was very right to be afraid, Heidi told herself.

"They only know of twelve disappearances," Heidi whispered to Boyd.

Boyd held up his two hands then put them down holding up one again, a smile sliding across his lips, a wink and a twinkle in his eyes. Heidi grinned, he understood and never judged her. He had even offered a few times to haunt some of the kids that were making trouble for her. He wanted to hurt the ones that called her a freak.

She appreciated it but this was her fight, not his, and she didn't want his conscience dammed anymore then it already was, especially on her account. He had helped her more than enough by alerting her when they were going to play a horrible trick on her. Really she couldn't thank him more.

"That's right, there have been fifteen but don't worry, I can handle two simple cops. I'm not afraid."

Boyd threw his hands back in laughter that she couldn't hear but she smiled anyway. Her attention shifted back to the conversation next door. Her sister finally shut up and the door was closed, next was her turn. She hated people she didn't know trying to talk to her, she wanted them to disappear.

Boyd turned her face to his, shaking his head. She knew what he was trying to tell her and she wouldn't hurt them. They would be missed, then more would come around. But that didn't stop her from wanting to. Her ghost friend vanished, emerging on the other side of the room. He sat by the mirror, leaving the chair free for the police. Heidi adjusted her body on the floor, pulling the guitar into her lap and waited for that knock on the door, waiting for the invasion.

Within seconds there was a knock on the door and one of the police officers announced who they were before they entered, uninvited. Heidi placed the guitar on the floor, watching them enter. One came to sit on the lounge chair and the younger one remained against the doorframe. The one in the chair pulled out twelve photos of her victims, laying them along the floor, his eyes unmoving from her.

She could tell he was curious for he didn't know her. He knew most of the kids here because they had caused trouble on the streets. But he hadn't seen her before and he wanted to know where she had come from. No parents were calling with her description unless he had heard from the police in Adelaide. No, no that wasn't possible. Cops don't talk across states unless absolutely necessary, like they were hunting for a killer. Besides according to the records in Adelaide, she was dead.

"Hello, I'm sergeant Adams and this is officer Ryan. We are looking into a few disappearances involving adolescents lodging here. So if you could help us with anything you know it will be appreciated. I don't think I know you, what is your name and age? And can you tell us anything about these people I have before you?" he spoke, his eyes still not moving from her cold gaze.

She would have lied about her name but her bigmouthed sister had probably told them so she told the truth. "My name is Adelheid Harrison and I'm fourteen. These kids all lived here over the last couple of months. Didn't they go home? Most of us are here for a while but really want to go home. I wasn't close to any of them so I thought they'd gone home or to another shelter."

They were both staring at her now, her innocent voice confusing them. Maybe they had thought she was younger. "True, but their parents are still searching for them. Normally we keep track of the kids and try to convince them to return home if they don't, there's not much we can do but watch. We know what shelter they are at or what corner they hang around, these twelve have completely disappeared. How long have you been here?"

"Three months."

"And where are you from? I don't recognize your name, where are your parents? They must be worried about you and your sister. Melinda is your sister, is she not?" he said breaking eye contact to look over his shoulder at the other officer, who had been writing everything down.

Heidi tried not to show her hatred. She closed her eyes for a few moments calming, before opening them again. "Yes, Melinda is my sister. Our mother is friends with Layla, we were clashing so when she found out Layla was starting this place up again she asked if we could come with her."

"You see our mother was just recently married and her new husband has three young kids. It has been a little hard so we came here to cool off, to have a break and let them settle in our home," she lied, her eyes holding theirs. She could feel Boyd moving closer though she didn't dare look his way. She was going to give them no reason not to believe her. After all, she was getting good at this, lying that is.

"Oh I see. As long as your mother knows where you are. So you and your sister don't know any of these kids left?"

"Nope."

"Will then Miss Harrison thank you for your time. Be sure to contact us should you find out anything from the others," he said, gathering up the photos. The officers nodded at one another before heading out the door, the younger one pausing.

"Can you play?" he asked, nodding towards the guitar.

"I'm learning. I'm not very good though. Do you play?" she questioned. Holding all her strength to act calm and normal, so far she was convincing.

"I'm in a band. We play at the local youth centers. You should gather up some of the kids and come down to watch at an open night sometime."

"Yeah cool. I'll ask about."

"Yeah cool," he repeated. "Sorry to bother you tonight, have a good night." He left, following the older officer into the next room.

Heidi pressed her hand to her racing heart. She swung around cracking her neck before pushing the guitar under the bed. Thank god they were gone. She knew she had done well to convince them, she was who she pretended to be. She hated talking to them but being quiet and hiding in the corner would have caused them to call someone.

No, she wasn't so simple. She knew what they thought and she knew how to manipulate it in her favor. She was an innocent sweet young girl to this world but in her mind she was unstable, evil and a murderer. And they hadn't questioned anything that Mindy had already told them so she was to be thankful for her sister's stupidity. Mindy had raved on about nothing, not even where she had come from, they probably couldn't get a word in. Nevertheless it had worked for her, no one questioned she had anything to do with the disappearance's. And really why would they?

"So, how'd I do?" she asked, looking back at her ghost friend.

Boyd smiled wickedly, putting two thumbs up. Heidi grinned, perfect.

*   *   *

She waited in the lounge room, her bag resting beside her and her head leaning against the window she stared out. Soon Layla would be home from grocery shopping and take her to the club. She was already forty minutes late. Tonight she was so excited to go with Layla for her friend had promised that she would get to help her behind the desk. Since the cops checked in last night and probably wouldn't for another few weeks.

It had been the same cops that had come to the cabin four days ago. They had come to the club to inform Layla that the missing kid's cases were in the hands of the missing persons unit and nothing more would be done about it unless they were handed new information. They had left and everything had been fine, everything was fine.

In the kitchen were three other kids trying to prepare dinner. They weren't very creative when it came to cooking a meal. There were two boys watching television and a seventeen year old girl lying on the lounge reading a novel. Mindy and the recent boy she had been interested in had snuck away to his room, probably to have sex. Most likely anyway because the boy's bedroom was the first in the second hall and the bed was banging against the lounge room wall.

No one seemed to notice or maybe it was that they didn't care like she did. Heidi felt disgusted, her sister was becoming their mother and they had barely said a sentence to one another in the last months. It was sad but if she did have a conversation with her sister, she might likely kill her. Not because that was what she wanted but because Mindy was everything she hated.

It suddenly felt cold. Heidi wrapped her arms around her body, her eyes searching the darkness outside. Where was Layla? Maybe she was so excited that she was watching the clock. How couldn't she watch the hour tick away? She really should go to her room and do something else other than waiting. Time always was slower when you waited with it.

With that thought, Heidi snatched her bag hurrying down the first hall. Six heads from the lounge room turned and followed her in curiosity. Slipping in her room, she slammed her door and threw the bag on the chair before flopping on the bed. It felt strange in her room. She liked the feeling although it still was different.

She let her arm fall down the side of the bed, strumming the strings of the guitar with her nails, secretly calling Boyd. He was always around somewhere but when she pulled the strings, he would appear to her. He would stay with her until she went to sleep or changed, then he would respect her privacy and leave. Although she couldn't hear him, they had their ways of communicating and she knew he wasn't around. They kept each other company, he was her only friend in here. She knew something was not right. Heidi glanced around the room, definitely no Boyd. She strummed the guitar again, waiting, still no sign of him, strange, he always came to her.

Moving her arms up on the bed, Heidi sat up looking around her room then to her opened cupboard. She always closed her cupboard and drawers but today the doors were slightly opened. Black hair fell through the door, swinging in an invisible breeze. Heidi knitted her eyebrows together, she lent forward from the bed, opening the door completely. Her doll sat in the middle, her violet eyes crying blood and her clothes had changed. Something she hadn't yet mastered to do by herself. Twisting her head to one side, she studied the doll. Her tongue flicked against the roof of her mouth.

Heidi stood from the bed, her hand waving over Darla's face, it didn't change back. Screwing her face up in frustration, she snatched the doll from the shelf. Why had the doll changed and why couldn't she make her change back? Nevertheless Darla was beautiful and she was long overdue for a cuddle.

She pulled the doll to her chest, pressing her there for a few minutes. Her fingers running through the dolls hair, the same black as her own, she wondered if the doll looked like her slightly. With its black hair, pale skin and tiny body. She couldn't touch her for to long, someone might enter her room and if they saw her, she would be called a freak again. Heidi placed Darla in the back of her cupboard where she normally hid, closing the door.

She quickly moved to her chest of drawers, opening the bottom one where she hid her amethyst necklace. It was glowing. Heidi grabbed it, fear starting to rise within her. The chain was so hot in her hand that it started to burn her, she dropped it back in. That was strange, she thought to herself, or was it? Didn't she know what this meant? Of course she did—Xane.

He was close, she didn't know whether to be excited or angered over his sudden appearance, maybe even terrified. No fear, no, she wouldn't be afraid of him. Last time she had seen him, he had killed the children. She hated him for it but shouldn't be fearful of him. She knew about her own power and in a way he was to thank for it. Really, she couldn't contain her slight excitement, to fight him or to love him she didn't mind, both were exhilarating.

She shut the bottom drawer, walking out of her room and running her hand through her long hair then along her white dress. She wanted to look good when she met him, she wanted to look strong. Now, where would he be? She walked back out into the lounge room, no one else in there but the six who had been in there when she left. The three in the kitchen now sat in front of the television, eating toast and the two boys sitting at their feet. The girl reading her book had moved to the other lounge still reading. No one in there but mortals.

Heidi turned walking up the second hall, screwing her nose up when she past the room her sister was in. No one up the second hall either. She headed back into the main room, back to the window. She peered out through the rain, trying to see any headlights. No lights but in the middle of the clearing her nightmare stood. The man she was allured by, the man she hated but the demon she loved, Heidi grinned. She felt no anger as she looked upon him, not yet anyway, only longing for him. She left the cabin, stepping out into the rain.

Heidi stood in the middle of the clearing, meters away from him, her hair flat on her head. Her white dress soaked, sticking to her body although it didn't bother her. All she saw was him, all she was interested in, was him. Why was he here? What did he want with her? Surely it couldn't be to make her pay for leaving. He could have anyone else should he choose to.

Xane stood still and emotionless, his fiery eyes staring at her, she didn't move. She couldn't understand if he was angry or intrigued. When she looked closer at his expression, she thought she saw a hint of surprise. Had he expected her to be afraid and run away? Did he know what she had done here? Did he want to kill her or love her?

"It's so nice to see you again," she said with a flick of her tongue at the end. Finally his face changed, with a small lift to his eyebrow but a movement nevertheless. She placed her hands on her hips rolling her head to one side, watching him as he was her. He expected her to talk again, threatened by his silence but she wasn't uncomfortable. It was his turn.

"Enjoying your life I see," he whispered, screwing his face up and glancing around the surroundings, several minutes had past before he had spoken.

Heidi shrugged still grinning. "Can't complain."

"Made any allies yet?" he said, his eyes twinkling suddenly.

"You know me, always the loner."

"Yeah I know you. I also know for some reason there is always an adult enchanted by you. Too bad they can't stick around to watch the games really begin," He said. His face lit with his evil grin, Heidi crossed her brows, dropping her arms by her side.

"Don't taunt me over Drake. He was a fool getting into something that wasn't his business." She hissed, although she didn't mean in. Drake was a hero to her.

Xane's smile grew wider. "I wasn't talking about the over protective counselor."

Heidi twisted her head to the other side, if not Drake then who? She had never got along with anyone else older than her other then Layla . . . oh god, not Layla. She snapped her body straight, her eyes widened. Xane laughed.

He started to walk around the clearing, circling her. Heidi took in a deep breath, hoping he hadn't done anything to her friend. Layla deserved it even less then her counselor did, Drake had crossed the line but Layla hadn't. He had hunted her then killed her, that wasn't fair. She could feel the anger rising through her body, that bastard.

"What have you done?" she whispered, panicked.

"Go see for yourself," he said, stepping behind her. His arm pointed over her shoulder, down the road into the woods and his other sliding down her arms. It felt so weird having his body so close to her, her heart fluttered as her chest tightened in anger. Why did he send her soul into confusion?

Heidi didn't wait for him to try and torment her again, she ran off before he could grab her shoulders. She ran down the gravel road, rocks stabbing her feet but she couldn't stop, she ran on. Lifting her wet-see-through-dress off her body, it felt like it was slowing her which of course it was not. All the while she ran. She wished he was only tormenting her and he had only scared Layla, not killed her. What would happen to all the runaways if she was killed? The world wouldn't be as bright without Layla in it.

Please don't let her feel pain, please don't let her feel fear, Heidi silently begged. Oh, where was she? She kept running down the hard road, her wide eyes darting around the woods, what had he done with her? As she rounded the corner she saw it. Heidi froze, her body shaking, her breath being sucked away by the fear for her friend.

In front of her, against the tree was Layla's blue car. The heads lights had been smashed but were still on. Otherwise she might have run right into the car with only the darkness around her. The whole front of the car had been crushed. The doors were buckled, clearly jammed. Heidi ran up to the smashed car, running around to the driver's side. Her friend was there, her body twisted against the steering wheel, her head was crushed in and her long ash blonde hair was covered in blood. Heidi leant into the smashed window, shreds of glass cut her arm as she felt Layla's neck for a pulse, nothing.

She knew Layla was dead before she had touched her. All she could hope for was she had died instantly and hadn't seen anything that would keep her spirit trapped here. With her body shaking, Heidi took a step back from the car, still staring at her dead friend. It was all her fault.

"I warned you that if you left you became my enemy Heidi. This is what happens to my enemies, everyone dies. Did you think nothing would happen? Did you think you could run away and I would never find you?" Xane growled, appearing behind her. Heidi remained still, trying to control her breathing so she wouldn't cry. She couldn't let him leave her defeated.

"I am your enemy, not her. You're a coward, you should kill me," she hissed, over her shoulder.

Xane grabbed her shoulder, spinning her around to face him but his sudden force was surprising even to him. For as he turned her, he knocked her into the back of the car. Heidi gasped, her head slamming on the ridged metal behind her. She shook off the pain, climbing to her feet. Her eyes snapped to the demon. He looked alarmed though that first expression was quickly replaced with his safe smirk. She hated him right now.

How dare he take Layla away from her! This just didn't affect her, it affected everyone. He was a coward. He hadn't been around for months then found her in Melbourne's north and the first thing he did was kill her friend. Big mistake on his behalf, she would make him pay for this even if it meant not finding out what he wanted.

"It's not your time to die Heidi and I'm no coward. You're the one that ran," he spat.

"I left so I could help my sister not because I wanted to. Being with you was the only time I felt like I could be myself and accepted!" she cried. The back of her head was stinging which made her dizzy and the grief was rising in her throat, soon it would be uncontrollable.

His face changed, becoming calm again. He moved forward, his arms extended but she stepped back, pressing her back against the car. No, she was no fool. He had just killed Layla and hurt her. She might be able to be herself around him but she wasn't safe. Xane closed his hands, drawing his arm back to his body, he was puzzled.

"Are you happy with your decision now? You have sacrificed your life for Melinda and look at how she has repaid you. She never acknowledges your presence and laughs along behind your back. I helped you so you could gain life and strength," he replied calmly.

Heidi looked over her shoulder at her dead friend, the anger shaking her body once more. "Mindy has equally helped me and she wouldn't laugh at me." Though she doubted what she said.

"Wouldn't she? Look, I'm in a good mood as you can tell because your friend's body is still attached to her head. So I'm giving you one more chance. Join me. I can nurture your power. We could accomplish so much together, what do you say?"

Her head hurt more, Heidi twisted it to the side but with her movement, she felt weak. The rain pounding the crushed vehicle seemed to grow louder. Her dress felt heavier as did her body. She forced her eyes to focus on Xane, what had he been saying? Did he want her to go with him? He was talking about powers, why would he want her? She shook her head, trying to shake the feeling of sickness away.

She couldn't go with him. He had killed Drake and Layla. She couldn't leave Mindy no matter what he said. Her sister needed her and needed her to be sane. Yes, Xane was right that Mindy hardly acknowledged her but that was because her sister was trying to live her life not that she hated her, wasn't it? Besides at least she knew how Mindy felt about her, he was a secret and she hated secrets.

Heidi took in a deep breath, running one hand through her wet hair and over something sticky, blood. Her blood! That was probably the reason she felt so faint, she had split her head open. Did he know?

"Heidi!" he called, forcing back her attention from her fingers tapping the back of her head.

"What would you do if I refused again?"

His smile faded. "Then I wouldn't be in such a good mood."

"How do you even expect me to look at you again after what you have done? Layla was my friend! She was no threat to you. Tell me Xane, why do you waste your time with me, waste you power? You could control so much yet you hang out in Australia following a fourteen year old girl."

"Don't flatter yourself so much, you're not the only one I have an eye on. And Australia is so multi cultural, bringing all hidden spiritual powers from all nationalities here. To a place of birth for the supernatural and a way to my world through its assorted magic."

Heidi tried not to cry. She had hoped he truly cared for her and that he was following her. In one way it would have made her happy if he had said yes, but now no one cared for her. Not even a sick demon wanted her. She was just convenient, convenient to torture and convenient for those men back in Adelaide to rape. Her teary eyes looked back to Xane. He had bowed his head, his saddened eyes moving from her. He couldn't even look at her! Was she that horrible! Was she that different from the rest of the world?"

"I'm not leaving with you."

He snapped his head back to her, his eyes flashing in flames but he had expected it. "You are prepared to throw away your last chance?"

"Last chance for what? Joining you is nothing of value to me. You have killed two people close to me, how could I go with you if you destroy everyone that could help me?"

She had expected him to get angry but he remained calm, he smiled once more. "You're not a very quick learner are you? If that's your final decision then prepare to live with it, foe," he said, with a laugh.

This time Heidi also smiled. "I'm as prepared as I ever will be, I relish it."

Just to piss him off, she blew him a kiss as he started to disappear. She caught his surprised expression again. He couldn't predict her and she was beginning to love that he couldn't. He disappeared, leaving her feeling suddenly alone.

A destroyed car holding her dead friend was behind her. Her body shivered in the cold rain. She still felt dizzy but she couldn't let herself pass out here. No, she had to get home and call someone. She had to give Layla some dignity and have her body taken care of. Her poor friend had died far too soon. Heidi turned down the dark road, slowly moving in the direction of the cabin. Her steps were off balance but she should get there.

The trees around her seemed so much taller than when she had first ran through them, they seemed darker. The rain was falling harder or so it seemed, she might as well have been naked with how see-through her dress had become. Heidi left the side of the car forcing herself further down the road. She wasn't more than a few meters from Layla's car when headlights came down the road. She spun around in the rain, staring through the mist at the slowly approaching lights. No car normally came down this road other than Layla's or the police.

Oh god, she felt so lightheaded. Heidi watched the car pull up beside Layla's, someone stepped out flicking on a flash light. The light scanned the car and Layla, the person leaning in checking to see if her friend was alive. She couldn't see the person holding the light, only the glare from their car headlights.

Heidi took a few steps backwards when the flashlight darted to her, she couldn't see anything but three blinding lights. Who was it? Not a policeman for there would be a light on the top of the car and they would have called out to her. She took another few dizzy steps back but her body buckled beneath her.

"Hey is someone there? Are you okay young lady?!" a male's voice called. She wanted to tell him she was fine and to go away but no words would come out. She felt even more lightheaded and sick. She felt like she was being strangled all over again. The man started running to her, yelling. Heidi fell to the wet surface, her mind suffocated by darkness.

*   *   *

Why did her world grow darker and darker every time she came to it? Heidi stood on the graveled shore, staring out over the black ocean into the hovering storm above. Behind her was the field of thorns, not even one flower remained. Beyond the field were the caves and more storm clouds shadowing them, soon the darkened sky would join. She took in a deep breath. Her world was no longer beautiful, even the darkness was unsettling to her.

She wanted to go home but there was no way out of here and besides, she had no home. This had been the closest thing she had to a home and it had changed so much, she didn't even want to be here. Why had it changed? Had she done this? She was becoming sane in the outside world so was this where all her depressed anger and dark thoughts went?

Heidi crossed her brows, slowly spinning around herself, her golden-brown eyes rolling over her world. Every time she was here, she had never ventured from the sand, only once to sit on the edge of the field. But that field was no more and the sand had become hard gravel. She couldn't go out into the field of thorns or stare too long at the new caves. What was hiding in those caves?

Maybe all her answers hid there, she was so curious yet there was no way to cross the field of thorns without being torn to pieces. Heidi stared into the mysterious darkness trying to guess what could be in there, calling it out telepathically. Could it be where Olivia hid? She hadn't seen the spirit since she had tried to kill her a few months ago, not even in her dreams had she appeared. Or could it be something else, something better left in the dark?

As she wondered something moved in the shadows of the cave entrance, a human form. Heidi stepped as close as she could to the edge of the thorns, squinting her eyes trying to make out the figure, yes a human figure, a female. The woman stepped from the cave, standing in the dim light of her world, how had someone else got in here? The woman had flowing black hair and a beautiful corset pearl dress, Heidi gasped. It was her doll, Darla.

Her doll was standing across the thorn field but mortal and older than herself. She wouldn't have been more than her mid-twenties though. She had blood red lips and violet eyes that were glowing from where she stood. They only difference about the woman from the doll was that the woman had no shoes and gloves. And the woman's body was full and curved. She was more beautiful as a human, enchanting.

Heidi closed her eyes shaking her head. Make it go away she begged within her mind. She opened her eyes. No living doll standing by the caves! But that wasn't good, for Darla stood in the middle of the thorns. Her eyes deep and lips pulled into a tight smile, oh god it was real! Heidi closed her eyes again. How did she go back home?

Opening her eyes again, Heidi gasped when the woman stood right in front of her, not much taller than she was now. Darla's eyes shone, her pale skin seemed to shine and there seemed to be a silver energy radiating from her. Although she was afraid, she couldn't help but admire her. Darla dipped her head towards Heidi, her long blood painted nails reaching for her face, Heidi took a step back.

"Who are you?" she cried.

"You know who I am Ella. I'm EnDarla." Her voice was unlike any other she had heard. The woman lips moved though her voice spun around them, a sound so soothing yet so deadly.

"I thought your name was Darla and I'm not Ella."

"Darla is what you call me, my Ella."

"I don't know who you are. I don't know any Ella's. You're my doll!" Heidi cried, still walking backwards. EnDarla came closer, a wicked smile crossing her lips.

"Not quite yet, Ella."

Before Heidi could make another move, the living doll charged at her. Long sharp nails dug into her skin, shoving her backwards. Back towards the black ocean, she tried to push the woman away but her strength wouldn't win over that which wasn't real. What was EnDarla going to do to her? Could she die in her own world?

EnDarla threw her into the ocean still smiling, her violet eyes became darker almost black. Heidi started to scream but before the sound lifted from her body, the woman shoved her head under the water which had become more like oil. She kicked and hit, trying to fight off the body above her own but nothing she did would move her, oil began to fill her mouth.

Her head grew lighter and a pounding echoed around her, she was going to drown. The gorgeous woman above her was laughing, a long chilling laugh that consumed the pounding of the ocean. Heidi struggled harder, colored spots flashing behind her eyes. Her body felt so heavy, she was afraid that if EnDarla dropped her, she would sink but then she was only in knee height water, wasn't she?

She stopped moving, her mind blackened and body exhausted, the arms holding her disappeared, her living doll nightmare had gone. Heidi threw her head up, spattering out all the oil from her lungs. She dragged her body to the gravel, snow blonde hair covering her face. Snow blonde hair? Heidi grabbed hold of her now normal hair, it was blonde again and she was alive.

She darted her eyes to the caves, spying EnDarla laughing there though she couldn't hear her. The woman was crying blood as she laughed; the tears stained her face and her clothing changed. Just like the doll, the evil doll. Then she disappeared in a burst of lightning. She had to be her doll, or was her doll based on this being? Heidi shuddered, she felt so weak. She closed her eyes.

Reopening them seconds later, where was she? In her world? No, a bedroom, her bedroom in Layla's cabin with the dark haired man from the car. He was leaning over her fixing her head. A doctor? A dead doctor if he touched her again. Heidi collapsed into the darkness of her mind but this time however it was different, for she would never see any light again.

CHAPTER ELEVEN

She waited at her window, waited for Adrian to return. He had left a few hours ago to help his mother in the market but had promised to return tonight. When he did, they would run away together. She would go with his family and she couldn't wait. Her bag was already packed and hiding under her bed in case her parents returned early. They were out all the time, Olivia was starting to think that they had completely forgotten her but Adrian hadn't. She loved Adrian and one day, she would be his wife.

Downstairs the front door was unlocked, Olivia sighed. Adrian was too late, her parents had returned and it was going to be a struggle to get her out of the house. But that wouldn't stop her, not tonight. Olivia walked back to her door, peering through the cracks to see her mother coming up the stairs. Her stepfather remained downstairs, preaching about the war again. What did he know of war?

She knew more than he. She knew of death, of fear and the fighting within ones soul to take a life, to take his life. She felt it every time she looked into his eyes, two voices in her head arguing over how to take his life. Should she poison him like he was her or have him hunted and brutally killed like he had the children who were not right, according to the villagers anyway.

But it wouldn't matter now, she was leaving with Adrian and once they were far away from her family, everything would be wonderful. She was looking forward to finding some happiness in her life, to be able to smile and laugh. To see something else other than these four walls. It would be wonderful to have a life of her own. If Adrian had never come into her life, she doubted that she would have one. Either the poisoned food or by her own hand, she would be dead now.

Olivia moved away from the door, lying down on her bed and listening to her stepfather call after her mother. Ordering her to make him his lunch, her mother excitedly did so. Why? She would never understand how her mother could love him? She closed her eyes, it would be best to sleep like she spent most of her time doing, dreaming of imaginary worlds.

Of wonderful lives while she waited for them to leave again, waited for Adrian. Curling into a ball, she let her mind drift from her family to a place where she could imagine how it would be to be carefree and happy. A place where there was no war killing their men and no sadness destroying peoples homes.

Something smashed downstairs, Olivia snapped her eyes open. She didn't know how long she had been asleep but the shadows in her room had moved. It was now dusk. She sat up in her bed listening, where had the smash come from? Downstairs she heard laughter, her mothers, and more laughter from her stepfather. What were they doing? Another glass smashed then the sound of heavy footfall, of dancing. Were they drinking down there? At this time of day! She shouldn't really be so surprised, this behavior was sadly becoming more than normal.

Olivia climbed from the bed, moving over to the window. She glanced at the lowering sun. Adrian should be coming for her soon. If she knew where his mother's market was, she would have climbed from the window and gone to find him. For if she climbed out now someone would find her and she would become hunted. She no longer looked like their idea of normal. Her skin was too pale, her hair too long, white and dull then her body was too thin. The whites of her brown eyes had become red and her lips were the same shade as her skin. They would surely kill her if they saw her.

The life in the town had dwindled, all the children home washing up for dinner and their parents discussing their long days. The streets were bare and the shutters on most of the homes closing for the night. Had Adrian's mother finished at the markets? She hoped Adrian would still come for her. Maybe he was watching and waiting for her parents to leave. After all they weren't normally home this long.

Olivia stared down into her yard, searching for Adrian. He could be waiting in the bushes of her yard. She scanned the shrubs, no Adrian but someone else was hiding in there. A dark woman, who was looking through her dining room window, watching her parents.

Olivia looked harder, she knew that woman. She had seen her almost nine months ago. She had been the stranger in her home, the one watching her through the mirror, the one who seemed alarmed to see her. What was she doing here again? Had she been watching her all this time?

She ducked to the other side of the window, curiously watching the woman. Olivia tuned out from what her drunken parents were doing, all her focus on the woman. She wasn't afraid but greatly intrigued. Was the woman following her or after her parents? Although she wasn't sure, she had a feeling that the woman was there for her.

Olivia glanced back at her door, listening to downstairs. Her parents were playing music and still dancing, she was safe from being noticed for now. She turned back to the dark woman in her yard, the woman who was now staring at her, she looked alarmed. She had to get down there. She had to speak to her, first to see what she wanted and second, to see if she was real. She hoped she was real for what would that mean for her if she wasn't? Olivia climbed up on the window sill, her unsteady legs swaying as she moved to the side of the house.

The woman quickly spun striding across the lawn, why was she leaving? She had to hurry and get down there before she disappeared. Olivia looked around herself, there was nothing around for her to climb down. She should jump, she wasn't that far from the ground and if swift, she might not get hurt. She sat on the window sill pulling her legs up and closing her eyes, she dropped to the ground. Her heart skipped a beat as she plunged into the ground, her ankles clicking and jolts going up her legs but she was fine.

She brushed off her beige dress, sprinting across the lawn after the woman. She moved faster than she expected considering she had been trapped in her room. Why hadn't she tried to escape through the window before? Her legs stung a little but she wasn't about to let that stop her. She would deal with what damage the jump had cost her later. She hoped it didn't effect her running away with Adrian. Right now, she had to catch the woman who had slowed, assuming she wasn't following. Olivia ran up behind her.

"Why are you following me?"

The dark woman spun around, her face wide with surprise, hadn't she seen her jump from the window? She dropped her head to the side, studying the strange eastern fashions the woman was dressed in. Where was she from? Something told her that she wasn't Australian. She flicked her tongue on her teeth waiting for her to reply but the woman was no longer looking at her. She had darted her eyes back to her house. Olivia didn't let it worry her, her parents were too drunk to notice anything.

She could tell the woman was distracted but she wanted to know so much about her. Olivia glanced at the woman's hand where she ran her thumb over an enchanting purple necklace. It was stunning. It looked like the foreign jewelry Adrian's mother made. Maybe it was from Adrian. Maybe he had a message for her with it. Olivia looked back to the eastern woman who was again staring at her. Why hadn't she answered her yet? Didn't she speak her language?

"Is that for me?" Olivia asked. She knew it was bold but why else would she have it, it didn't look like it belonged to her. She already had one on, similar but a dark blue.

"Take it with warning of destruction and death. I'm sorry for inconveniencing you and promise you will never see me again. I pray for ones stronger than us who will break this curse. I pray for your soul." She spoke perfect English with a slight accent. Her voice was soft and beautiful like her.

Olivia crossed her eyebrow together but before she could ask anymore questions, the woman disappeared right before her eyes. She gasped. Her hand waved through the air before her. The woman had really gone, not a trace of her. Maybe she was imagining it but as she looked down in her hand, there was the necklace. Yet how did a being disappear? She was going crazy.

Behind her, in the house her stepfather started yelling to her mother, ordering her to change her clothes so they could go out to the tavern for a good meal. Olivia glared at the house over her shoulder. She was out of her room now. She could run away but not without Adrian and now she was slightly curious to stay. To see if the woman would return and explain about the necklace. Who was it from? The woman or was she the deliverer?

Inside the house her mother and stepfather were ready to leave, they opened the door just as she ducked into the bushes. They left and once she waited for a while, Olivia ran in the front door of her home. She hurried up to her room where she would wait for Adrian.

She couldn't wait to see him because for the first time, she actually had something to tell of her own and with this new found excitement she could do anything. Was the excitement of them leaving together? This spellbinding day was the beginning of happiness for the rest of her life and she couldn't wait for it to truly start.

*　　*　　*

"Heidi, Heidi please wake up!" She could hear Mindy calling, quite close to her ear. Her golden-brown eyes fluttered open, staring at the ceiling of her room in Layla's cabin. What had happened?

She was lying frozen on the bed like a plank of wood, with something wrapped around her head. Her focus stopped shaking and she was able to look to her worried sister. Mindy lay over her so that she could see nothing else but her and the ceiling. Her sister was crying and shaking, most likely trying to draw the attention to her. Heidi rolled her eyes. She was in no mood for Mindy's antics. She needed to know how she got here and what happened to Layla.

Oh Layla, she would never see her friend again, would she? She wanted to hate Xane, wanted to set out to kill him but even with Drake and Layla's blood on his hands, she couldn't. Heidi sighed, turning her attention back to her sister then glancing to her cupboard. The doors were open again and the doll sat in the middle of the shelf, normal, no blood, no presence.

She glanced at the empty wall, ignoring the doll. Her mind moving faster then she could control. She could feel Mindy hovering over her back, trying to catch her eyes, but she would have no success. She couldn't look at her sister, not after she had abandoned her so willingly over the last few months. Somewhat she did believe Xane when he had told her how her sister behaved behind her back, she had always known. However she didn't want to be angry at Mindy forever, she needed her. Without her sister she had no one. Xane would surely kill anyone else she became close to.

Anger, yes maybe she did hate him and rage was such a part of her, she didn't know how it felt to be calm and happy. Her life had never been good but Xane had made her think it could have been better but then he had destroyed that. She hated him but wanted to toy with him like he had her.

"You won't get her to talk. She's always like this, nothin' but a loner. Ya might as well call the police then leave. I'll call an ambulance for Layla," Mindy stated, emotionless. Heidi crossed her brow, who was her sister talking too? She hadn't looked any further than the wall to see if anyone else was in the room.

Heidi rolled off her back, trying to sit up. Her head was spinning but she wasn't going to let the pain stop her. She glared past her sister to a man standing beside the door. The man from the car, what was he doing in here? His dark hair fell into his curious hazel eyes, he wasn't that tall but definitely strong if his toned arms were anything to go by. His eyes widened as she stared at him. What was he thinking? What had he seen?

The look on his face told her he had seen something he couldn't explain, he was hoping she could. She knew nothing, only Layla's death and her dream in her world, the world she was nearly murdered in. What had he seen on this side? Mindy stepped into her gaze, placing her hands on her hips and her lips pursed in frustration.

"Where do ya think ya get off scarin' me like that! What am I supposed to do if you die! Huh, didn't think of that, did ya sis?" Mindy spat. The man against the wall looked angry at how her sister was speaking to her although he made no movement to stop the verbal attack.

Heidi snapped her head to her sister glaring. "What happened and who is he?" she ordered, no compassion in her voice.

Mindy glanced over her shoulder as if she had forgotten about the man at the door. "You were in a car accident with Layla, Layla was killed. What are we gonna do now that Layla's dead? We can't stay here on our own, not with everyone disappearing all the time." Her voice had started to crack, Mindy lowered her head, taking a deep breath. Her sister's movements seemed very planned for their company.

However she was more angered with Mindy's words. It seemed her sister cared nothing for Layla after the woman had done so much for them. She hated her right now. Layla had been everything to her, her friend, her family and mentor and she had died because of her. Mindy could never appreciate that type of love. Never understand how she felt about her dead friend. Heidi gulped back her tears. She would never have Layla with her again. But now wasn't the time to cry, not when there was this stranger in her room.

Mindy moved beside her on the bed, turning to the man. "Who are you?" she asked. Heidi glared at her sister again, hadn't she already asked the man this? Stupid girl!

"I'm Dr Dylan Emmett. I live on the next property. A tree had fallen over my road so I used Layla's. I found her car crushed into a tree and you must have been thrown out of it. I carried you here after you passed out and luckily someone knew you. I stitched and bandaged your head, other than that wound and several bruises you should be fine," he replied formally.

"A little young to be a doctor aren't you?" Heidi hissed. She hadn't meant to snap, it was just her automatic reaction to the thought of being touched by a stranger.

"Maybe. I left school early and applied for a job in the high security prison on the other side of the city as a guard. They trained me as a doctor quickly, due to all the previous doctors quitting. I've been there for five years now. How about you? How long have you been here with Layla?" he asked curiously, no offence taken to her remark. He stepped into the room, his guard slowly lowering.

"Since she returned," Mindy answered. Heidi rolled her eyes, she could tell her sister liked the man but she probably liked anyone that paid attention to her. "I should call the police about the car accident so Layla can be looked after."

"I have already taken care of it, services should be arriving soon," Dr Dylan said with a quick look to his watch.

"What?!" Heidi cried.

"People had to be notified," her sister spat.

Heidi began to panic. "We have to leave! With Layla dead, they'll take everyone to another shelter or to their homes. We can't go back to Adelaide."

"You can't leave. They will look after you, besides you need some rest."

Heidi glared at the doctor, his warning not stopping her from moving off the bed and searching for her bag. He didn't know them. He had no idea who they were or what she had done. If she went back, she would surely be caught for her crimes. This time she didn't care if Mindy came with her, she would still leave. It was probably for the best anyway. This house would never be the same without Layla and Xane had found her.

She couldn't let him find her again, his warnings were not lies. She understood that now. He wanted to destroy her and the least she could do was keep him challenged and run. With her head spinning and her body aching, Heidi threw whatever she could into the bag, making sure to hide the doll and necklace between her clothes.

"We have nowhere to go," Mindy whined.

"Unless you want to live where the doctor works you'll deal with what we have," Heidi growled. She glanced again to where Dr Dylan stood, waiting for a reaction but received nothing. There was something not quite right about him.

"Well I'm not going," her sister huffed.

"I wasn't ordering you to, only suggesting. Nevertheless, I'm leaving whether you come or not."

She zipped up her suitcase throwing it to the floor. Her eyes scanning the room for anything else she may have missed, nothing. Only saying goodbye to Boyd, where was he? Xane had long ago left so Boyd should be able to reappear soon. She couldn't leave without saying goodbye to the only friend she had made here. Mindy huffed behind her. At first she thought this would really be the end of the sisterhood between them.

Then Mindy turned around, storming out of the room. She swung the door into the doctor as she passed him. She was coming! Heidi smiled, she had the feeling that Mindy might follow, which meant they weren't completely torn apart, yet. Dr Dylan threw the door back staring at her, why did he stare like that? Like he already knew her, how could he when she didn't know herself?

"The police will want to talk to you, you can't just leave. Whatever you've done I'm sure it's not that bad."

"You know nothing." It was all she could say as she opened the window and threw her bag out, not glancing back at him. "Tell the police what you want and tell my sister to catch up." She pulled her body up on the window sill, pushing her legs over the edge before she looked back to him, a smile on her face. "See ya," she said, getting ready to jump out.

Dr Dylan smiled. "Yes, see you soon."

Heidi jumped out crossing her eyebrows together, what did he mean by that? She had only been playing but he was so serious and his words so sure. Of course they would never meet again so why would he say a comment like that? She decided it wasn't important, she had to get her bag and run. Not down the road where Layla's car was, she had to run through the bush land.

There was a track she had seen several meters from the road, running parallel through the woods. She would take that one. Throwing her bag over her shoulder, Heidi ran from the house not waiting or looking back for her sister. If Mindy truly wanted to come, she would catch up and if she wasn't smart enough to go down the same path then they weren't supposed to walk down the same road together.

She ran around the side of the house, peering into the clearing at the front path on the other side of the first line of trees. She paused, glancing out at the front of the cabin where two police cars and one medical assistance van had pulled up. They were already there! If Mindy didn't hurry up she probably wouldn't get out of there.

The police knocked on the front door, she could feel their eyes wandering the woods but so far they hadn't seen her. Heidi pulled back against the wall, what would she do if they circled the cabin? Where did she go next? With her eyes scanning the clearing, she focused on an old rusted trailer several meters away. Then a few meters past the trailer was a large green water tank, an easy jump away from the woods, perfect.

She could do it, she was sure she could. Stroking the amethyst necklace she had snuck around her neck, Heidi peered into the clearing again. Two officers were at the door, two in the second car on the radio. There was one medical officer peering through the front window and the other was unloading supplies from the van. Good, they were all distracted.

She glanced over her shoulder to see if Mindy had followed her out the window, not yet. Holding her breath, she dashed into the clearing, practically falling behind the trailer. She curled behind the wheel, would Mindy be small enough to fit there also? She released the breath she had been holding. Her heart was pounding so fast and her hands shaking but she was confident they hadn't seen her. Heidi glanced back around to be sure. No one had moved, nothing had changed. With a second flight of energy, she ran to the water tank, much bigger and much safer to be hidden behind.

So far so good but then something rustled beside the house, her eyes darted to where she had been standing seconds ago. Mindy stood pressed against the wall, one bag on her back and two at her feet. Why did she need so much stuff? Heidi shook her head, quickly glancing back out into the clearing, hoping the officers hadn't heard what she had. The two officers in the car were now standing beside it. The officers at the front door were climbing through the window. The medical team were throwing in their equipment then climbing through themselves.

She looked back to her sister who put her hand up for her to wait. Heidi twisted her head to the side, pursing her lips before turning and walking into the woods. She didn't stop when she got there. Her walk moved into a run as she hurried down the narrow path only coming to a stop when she saw the flashing lights.

Flashing lights from police cars and an ambulance illuminated the woods where Layla's car was. Further down the road Heidi could see an approaching tow truck, everything was being cleaned up. Layla's body was already in the ambulance, her eyes filled with tears, her friend was truly gone. She slowly continued down the path, careful not to move too fast and draw attention to herself. She doubted they would notice if she had.

They stood against the vehicles discussing how bad this was, that someone who had helped so many was dead. And it was all because of her. Xane had killed Layla to get to her and for as long as he was entertained by this, it would never end. He was killing to keep her alert and alert she had become, alert her body and her emotions were. This was all because of her.

Grinding her teeth, Heidi slowly continued down the path, her eyes fixed on the crash scene. They were sure to go looking for her when she was missing from the cabin and she would be a suspect until her name was cleared. Let it be, she told herself, she was already a suspect. Besides if they found out her and Mindy were alive, there would be a tornado of questions.

Better to hide and not be seen, better to listen and not be heard. Heidi hurried past the scene looking at the road before her. The path split in two different directions from the road. Did she follow it, or stick to the road where she knew it would lead? This day was full of change so she would follow the path she didn't know. It seemed taking the different road was necessary. Although she would have to slow so Mindy could see which way she went. Heidi walked to the fork in the path where she stopped, spinning around and waiting for her sister.

"Heidi! Heidi what are you doing out here? You're supposed to be waiting in the cabin for me." A familiar voice called from behind her, Heidi gulped; it was Layla.

Heidi turned to her friend, who was hurrying towards her. Layla's body was dull and slipping through the trees but she didn't seem to notice. Layla stopped in front of her, placing her hands on her hips in a playful angered manner. Layla smiled but all Heidi could do was stare in surprise. Not surprise that she was faced with this but surprised because she had heard Layla. She had heard the dead speak! Or was it, she had just heard someone who had only been dead for a short while speak? Every other ghost she had met had been dead for a while but Layla, Layla was fresh.

"Who knows what could happen out here, come on let's get you back home. You know the strangest thing? I can't seem to find my car," Layla whispered, puzzled.

"Layla, how do you feel? You were supposed to be here hours ago," Heidi replied, biting her lower lip. She felt like adding that it was yesterday which they were supposed to meet but for now she chose to humor her friend. How did she tell someone that they were dead? That they would never go home again. Her friend dropped her hands from her hips, glancing around the afternoon sky, confusion crossing her face.

"I feel fine, why? I guess it is a bit late. I was hurrying home to get you on time but then . . . then the sky went black. I hit something, a cat but as I got out of the car the cat turned into a man. I jumped back into the car to get away but my car took off, I had no control over it. I guess I fell asleep and had that strange dream then crashed. When I came to, I must have started walking home. It doesn't feel like it really happened but here I am without my car. I feel light, I feel . . ."

"Dead," Heidi whispered, tears filling her eyes. This was so painful to tell her friend she was dead. To hear that Xane had done this but at least Layla thought it was a dream.

"Dead! No, though I should call a doctor to see if I'm okay. I know this doctor who lives next door, I should see if he is home."

"Dr Dylan," Heidi interrupted again. Layla looked back at her, studying her this time.

"Yes, have I told you about him? Heidi why do you have your bag with you? Are you leaving?"

Now she was starting to think, Heidi thought to herself. She shook her head trying to find the right words to say when Layla gasped, speaking again.

"Your hair it's . . ."

"Blonde, I know, this is my natural color. Layla I don't know how to say this but you didn't have a dream. There really was a cat then a man but he was no man. You met Xane, the demon I told you about. He caused your car to crash and in that crash you were . . . you were killed Layla. You're dead! He attacked me but Dr Dylan helped us in your home and called the police. I'm running away from them, with you no longer here I'm leaving," Heidi said. Layla was shaking her head, slowly backing away from her. Heidi had to gulp back another burst of tears, if her friend didn't believe her she would get stuck here.

"No! I can't be dead! Not yet, not now!"

Heidi sighed, she really should take Layla to the crash site before the tow truck removed the car. But she couldn't bare seeing it again and hurting her friend. Down the path she could hear heavy footfall running towards them. She didn't need to turn around to know it was her sister. Layla caught sight of Mindy, calming down. Layla smiled, hoping Mindy would tell her what she wanted to hear but of course that wouldn't happen. Her sister ran to her side, stepping between her and the ghost. She was panting and leaning over to catch her breath. Behind Mindy, Layla gasped, her hand rising to her mouth, she started shaking her head again. Her eyes searching Heidi's for some clue to if she was lying but she would find no relief.

"Thanks for waiting!" Mindy hissed angrily before standing up and looking around them, staring through Layla. "So which way do we go?"

Heidi hadn't taken her eyes of Layla. Her dead friend sighed, pointing down the path opposite the road. Heidi nodded. "Down that path," she said, pointing where Layla did.

"Okay, let's go then," Mindy ordered, picking up her two bags and starting down the path.

"You go ahead, I'll catch up," she whispered, her sister shrugged, continuing down the path. Heidi turned back to Layla. "I'm so sorry Layla. I would have never come here if I knew this would happen. This is why I didn't want to befriend you, I'm sorry." She cried, once Mindy was out of hearing range.

Layla wiped her eyes though no tears fell from them. "It wasn't your fault. He killed me not you. There must be a reason he wants you, you are destined for greater things Heidi, I felt it when I met you. So promise me you'll follow whatever fate has planned for you and destroy him. Immortals have no place in a mortal world. Promise me you'll stop him from doing this again," she cried, lifting her head.

Heidi cried, letting the tears fall. "I can't make promises, I can't keep Layla. I'm not the girl you think I am. I have done horrible things . . ."

"So you keep saying yet you draw the attention of good people. I know it's hard to believe me but please try. Remember me and my work. Please make my death worth something."

"I'll do whatever I can. What are you going to do now?"

Layla smiled. "Discover my new world and find an old friend. Maybe we can move on together."

Heidi returned her smile. "Boyd would love that. Goodbye Layla, I love you."

"Goodbye my precious little one, keep strong and safe . . ." she continued saying something else but her voice slowly disappeared, like every other ghost, she couldn't hear her. But Layla didn't seem to notice at first and when she did, she smiled, nodding her understanding.

Heidi lent forward embracing her friend for the last time. She was careful not to fall through her while she wasn't solid yet and alarm her. Pulling away, she blew a kiss at Layla before turning to run down the path where she could see Mindy walking. Kicking a stone along the road, Heidi ran to Mindy.

Heidi didn't have to look over her shoulder to know that Layla had left. The sudden warmness in the air told her so. Mindy looked back at her smiling as her sister came to her side. She surprised Heidi by linking their arms together.

Heidi smiled, although she resented her sister for some things she had done, she couldn't help but to love her and it only made sense that they restart their journey together. After all, they only had one another and maybe because they saw two different versions of this world, they could combined them and find the perfect solution for survival.

* * *

Four fingers, one thumb. Stretch them out until they felt like they could pop from their sockets before pulling them into a fist, one finger at a time. Roll them out one by one, stretch, than pull them back into a fist. Out and in, twisting her wrist around itself. So alluring, so hypnotizing at how the body worked. A small body like hers yet it held so much strength. In and out, in and out, her mind focused and settled. Large golden-brown eyes searching her pale palm as she curled against the wall.

She had to focus so she would not hear. She couldn't listen to the scene behind her. She had to hide in the darkness and focus on her own strength and mind. She had to explore her power and her charmed gifts. Do not listen. For a long time she had been hiding, hours, days, weeks, now months. Two and a half months, hiding and drifting to her world, no change, neither safe nor threatening.

In and out, twisting her hand around and around, her wrist clicking with the movements. Listen, she told herself, listen to the click, feel the joints. No! Don't listen, don't look, hide and focus. She rolled her head to the side, crouching into a smaller ball beside the wall. Still watching her hand, drifting through this life. No, she couldn't drift, don't listen. Don't think of the ones already lost in the past.

Her eyes were tired, her hand moving slower and fingers cramped. She couldn't lose her focus, she couldn't come out of hiding but she had to listen, just once. She ignored her inner orders and dropped her hand. Her head snapped upright, listen to the world, she told herself. Listen to the water under the bridge; listen to the few cars above, to the trees rustling in the breeze. Then listen to her newly fourteen year old sister having sex on the other side of the stream, no, she couldn't bare it.

Heidi dropped her head to the other side, her eyes darting back and forth along the clay bricks. Her hand slid around the mud she was sitting upon. Don't hear them, she ordered herself. But she could. Her sister was moaning and the stranger was panting over her, it was the third person she had tonight and what for? The most she ever got paid was fifty dollars. Sex, money and then survive but they weren't surviving.

Mindy spent the money on more products to make her look older and sexy, to attract more men. Heidi had started to think her sister enjoyed this. There were times when Mindy tried convincing her to follow, saying the men would give her more money. But she would never allow a man over her. Never become a mother to a bastard child. She played her part by hiding in the streets and stealing what money she could. Then she would buy food with it. Maybe if her sister was more sensible they could afford a roof over their heads too, instead of hiding under this bridge.

She couldn't listen any longer. There was sure to be another one after this one and she couldn't let herself listen to all of them. It was sickening. The man over her sister finished himself off. He pulled up his pants then left. Heidi spun around glaring at her sister on the other side of the stream. Mindy didn't care. She pulled down her skirt and pulled her panties up from her ankles.

She flashed Heidi a twenty dollar bill grinning, nothing was worth sacrificing her dignity for. Heidi glared harder, her face screwing up, twenty dollars for that! It was pitiful, especially when Mindy was risking so much. She used no protection unless the man wanted to and they couldn't afford the pill. Mindy could contract any disease or fall pregnant. Heidi couldn't decide what would be worse.

Her sister flopped to the ground, lightning a cigarette and when she finished, she would surely go hunting for a new man. Alluring them with her young body, her pretty smile but somehow she was still getting bigger. They mistook her fat for large breasts. Just wait until she really got them, then she would sag, it was disgusting.

Heidi stood, brushing what dirt she could off her jeans and black sweater, she was too disgusted with Mindy, she had to go for a walk. Maybe find someone with a heavy wallet and release them from their excess weight. She smiled at her silent joke, yes, take their money and survive. She was hungry, tired, angry, maybe she should find another place to sleep tonight. She couldn't watch anymore of this.

"Did ya see what I got?" Mindy called, sitting in the mud, dabbing out her cigarette.

"Twenty dollars was all your dignity cost you!" Heidi spat.

"Ha ha very funny, don't be a bitch Heidi. I got the twenty bucks and a few grams of speed, ya want some?"

Heidi screwed up her nose, she would never take drugs. It dulls all senses and takes life away from its true form, no, she was not stupid. She wanted to experience life in every form, good or bad. Her sister had started doing drugs a few weeks ago and she had started getting them often. If Mindy wanted to kill herself then that was her choice, she had better things to do. In a few weeks, she would be fifteen so she would be able to get a real job and survive better. This time she would not take her sister with her.

She would grow stronger, then find Xane and make him answer for what he had done. She would trick him into teaching her his powers then kill him. No one fucked with her. After she was free, the world would have to look brighter and maybe then she could find somewhere that felt like home. Oh, to be free and find a home.

"Where are ya goin'? Streets are bare Heidi, why don't ya stay here and chill out?!" her sister called.

"No thanks but you go ahead and kill yourself. I have better things to do."

She spun on her heel before Mindy could reply. This was meant to be their new start! A new beginning to a happier time but her sister would always be her mother's daughter. However she should have learnt. This wasn't the first time Mindy had screwed up their fresh start. It was hard to admit but she was beginning to hate her sister and if they hadn't once been close or she had needed another presence, she would have killed her.

Heidi ran up the steep muddy hill to the narrow street that linked the country with the outer suburbs of the city. Normally she would catch a train into Melbourne city and rob whatever man she could but not tonight. Tonight, she wanted to go into the woods, half an hour through them and she would be at Layla's cabin. She would walk far enough that way just to distract herself, to focus and out there, she would be able to listen to her thoughts.

Wrapping her arms around her body, she hurried down the dark road into the woods. In there she would find somewhere to hide and think mostly about her sister. She couldn't bear who Mindy was becoming. Mindy was a dug addict and a slut, it was disgusting that they were related. She did somewhat want to save her, everything she had done so far was for her sister. If not for Mindy, what did she have to live for?

Heidi stopped by a tall thick tree, dropping down beneath it and hugging her knees to her chest. She missed Layla, she hoped her friend had found some peace and a little more than Layla, she missed Drake. Oh, she could never forget Drake, how she missed him also. Soon she would be fifteen and it would be a year since she met Xane. A year since she had lost her innocence in more ways than one and nearly a year since Drake had been killed. It wasn't fair, maybe she should fall into her dreams and this time not return, fall into Olivia's world like she had hers.

She was so alone. Heidi rested her head back against the tree, watching the insects flying around in the glow of the moonlight, she felt so cold. As the thought crossed her mind, something warm wrapped around her body, something furry. She gasped, looking down at the large panther curling around her back. The panther looked up at her with fiery eyes, Xane.

She felt torn between screaming and running or just sitting here being herself. No fear, no intimidation, control of her soul. How could she possibly love him after all he had done? She looked back to the moon, waiting to see if Xane wanted anything more than coming to her cry. The cat continued to stare at her. When he made no movements, Heidi grinned, lifting her hand to stroke his head, her body relaxing.

"I'm cold, I'm alone and most of all I'm lost. Who am I? Why do I have this gift but no purpose?" she whispered, her throat tight with her oncoming tears.

The panther roared, nudging her back with it head as it circled her again. Pushing itself between her and the tree. Heidi started to cry, she was so confused. The panther lay down placing a big paw on her leg, Heidi knocked it off. The panther nudged her back again, placing his paw back on her leg, this time she left it there.

A small smile crept over her lips, her eyes gleaming. Such power he held, she wanted it. She dropped her body into the panther, feeling the warmth of its fur. Her head rested on its neck, her hand stroking its fur, she felt so safe in his arms. Why did he make her feel like this? How come she couldn't hate him? Closing her eyes, Heidi let her body relax into his. Maybe tonight she could get a decent nights sleep.

"I hate you," she whispered.

The panther made a funny noise that almost sounded like a laugh, its paw tightened against her leg. His head turned so that it could nudge his nose against hers. He loved her, so why did he hurt her?

CHAPTER TWELVE

Night had finally fallen on what seemed like the longest day ever, her fifteenth birthday. She walked through the woods coming back from Layla's cabin. It had been the third time she had been there in the last few weeks and still no one had taken ownership of the cabin. Therefore, she had decided it was hers and if Layla returned to tell her she should leave, she would go. But for now, she couldn't sleep under the bridge any more, nor in the woods where the panther waited. She needed to be rid of any bad distractions.

Mindy needed to get out from beneath the bridge also. Her sister had become ill and had rashes appearing all over her body. Heidi was worried Mindy had caught something from one of her men. Lately, Mindy had been sleeping with men and not even asking for any money afterwards. That is why they needed to get to the cabin. She hoped by hiding there she could settle her sister down. She would give her one more chance and if her sister couldn't change then they had to go their separate ways. And on top of everything, she really needed to get away from Xane.

Heidi hurried to the bridge where she could hear her sister swearing and splashing in the stream, what was she up too? She walked down the hill, peering under the bridge to Mindy, who was crying and flustered. She crossed her eyebrows together, pausing to wait for her sister to notice her, silently wishing that her sister would have some birthday surprise. Mindy glared up at her, throwing rocks into the stream where she sat. Heidi sighed, she had no birthday surprise.

Disappointed, Heidi walked down into the stream, looking her sister up and down. Trust Mindy to make her birthday about herself but never mind, soon they would be in the cabin where they would be safe, with no distractions and no audience. Heidi twisted her head to one side, waiting for her sister to volunteer what was wrong. Mindy remained silent, she threw the rocks harder, swearing every time she did.

"I think we should go back to the cabin. No one else is living there or has been to visit. We will be safe and you won't have to do this anymore. I can get a job to pay for food, otherwise all will be good there," Heidi explained.

"Don't you even care what's wrong with me?!" Mindy screamed.

Her sister threw one of the rocks at her, not meaning to actually let go but she had. The sharp rock flew through the air towards her, Heidi glared at it. Her hand wrapping around the warmth of the necklace, the rock froze in midair before her. She gasped as did her sister then the rock fell to the ground, causing no harm to anyone. Was it in her imagination or had she really stopped the rock? When she looked back at her sister, she knew she wasn't dreaming. She could see the fear within Mindy's eyes.

"What is wrong with you dear sister?" Heidi hissed. The rock was spinning in the dirt at her feet, she couldn't look away. How had she done that? How had she stopped it and could she do it again?

"I think I got an STD and I'm two months late!" Mindy screamed.

Heidi snapped her eyes back to her sister, angered. "What do you mean two months late?!"

"What do you think ya idiot! I'm pregga's and sick and you don't care!"

"Of course I do but you dug this grave yourself. Are you sure you're pregnant? We can't look after a baby Melinda. Maybe it's the STD's you've got that messes with your cycle," Heidi babbled pacing back and forth in the dirt. She had to be right. They couldn't look after themselves let alone a baby. And if Melinda really had an STD then that would harm the baby, wouldn't it? No, this couldn't be happening to them. Not on her birthday.

"You called me Melinda," her sister gasped.

Heidi looked to her again, had she? She hadn't noticed but there was really no reason to call her the name of the sister she loved. This girl before her was her mother's child, a traitor and a bitch. Her name was Melinda and she would never refer to her in the loving manner of Mindy. No, her sister had disappointed her for the last time, she had ruined everything and Melinda had to face that.

"I can't have a baby Heidi! Do something!" her sister screamed, when she did not answer.

Heidi glared at her sister. "I'm trying to help you. Now we have all the more reason to get to that cabin," she whispered, twisting her blonde hair around her fingers.

"Did ya hear me? I'm fucking pregnant! Ain't no cabin gonna change that."

She started pacing back and forth again, her fingers winding around one another. "We don't know that for sure. We will go to the cabin and go see that doctor on the next property. With him we will know for sure. Then we will decide what has to be done." She paused, dropping her head to one side and focusing on her disgusting sister. She thought over what she had said. Yes perfect, everything would be fine. She spun back to Melinda smiling, her sister raised her eyebrow but at least she was now calm.

"Ya promise it will be okay?" her sister whined.

"I can't promise but we will try."

Melinda nodded. "Ya would kill it wouldn't ya?"

"We have to do what is right for us. Melinda, you're fourteen and it would be selfish to bring a baby into our world. It will turn out like us. Sometimes you have to be cruel to be kind. But we don't know for sure yet. Let's go to the cabin, have a warm shower and a comfortable bed to sleep in. I will get the doctor."

"Sounds wonderful," Melinda whispered. She stood from the stream, walking up to Heidi and embracing her. Heidi grabbed their bags and helped her sister up the hill to the woods. "By the way, happy birthday."

Heidi smiled, her sister had remembered and she did somewhat care. Maybe there was still hope for them yet. She could still save her sister and hopefully keep the men away. Of course pregnancy was a big issue though if they talked to the doctor it might not be that bad. Whatever the challenge, they could find a way to work through it.

She was looking forward to getting into the cabin, to feel a hot shower on her back. To lie in a bed and refuse the temptations of the panther. Hopefully the police had left the cabin alone, so her and her sister could have their privacy. Their first step was to get there and convince the doctor to help them. Then, with the verdict, they would decide their fate.

Grabbing her sister's hand, Heidi led her down the narrow path back to where she had just come from. Melinda moved along willingly, dragging her bag, her face a mask of both fear and relief. Yes, her sister still needed her.

Heidi grinned. When she and Melinda got along, she felt more sane than when she did without her. And her sister seemed more grounded in her presence. They needed each other and she couldn't wait to get to the cabin and settle down, for them to be completely alone. It would take nearly forty minutes to walk Melinda there, for her sister looked dreadfully pale and tired. The complete opposite of herself.

"What job will ya get? What will we do if I'm . . . ?"

"Don't think about it," Heidi replied, pulling Melinda's arm along harder. "I know my way around the city so I'm sure I can find something honest."

"What's honest?"

"You know, work in retail or as a waitress. I'll find something."

"What do ya know about work anyway?" Mindy questioned again.

She raised her eyebrow at her sister. "I worked for a while with Layla, remember? Anyway let's focus on getting ourselves organized first, then we'll think of particular things later."

Melinda nodded her agreement and with a new burst of energy, she hurried. Her hands pressed against her stomach, trying to keep in step with Heidi. The two sisters walked the distance back to Layla's cabin, stopping when they stepped into the clearing. It looked so much smaller in the dark, lonely and mysterious. Like it was set in a cloud of smoke, like it was from her world. Nevertheless it was beautiful and welcoming in her eyes, Heidi pulled Melinda out into the clearing desperate to get inside.

They ran to the front door, surprised to see that it had been broken open and wouldn't clasp shut. However she wasn't too worried, it was easily fixed. Together they entered the familiar cabin, strangely things seemed darker now. There was no electricity and the furniture was covered in dust. The gloomy cabin only reminded her about the lose of Layla, the lose of the soul light that lit this cabin.

Melinda dropped her bag at the front door, forcing the door shut then falling onto the dusty lounge. She tried to turn on the television but it was obvious it wouldn't work. Heidi remained at the front door, her bag slowly sliding from her hand. She guessed there would be no hot shower tonight. She wondered how they would turn on the electricity. Sighing, she walked to the lounge, falling beside Melinda. She ignored the cloud of dust that flew around her as she hit the lounge's surface.

Her eyes darted around the cabin, she felt safe and relaxed here but first she had promised to get her sister some help. Every time she looked at Melinda, she looked more and more ill. Hopefully, it was the course of her body's defiance, not pregnancy. She couldn't think about it. Not now, not until she knew for sure. She had to go get the doctor. Heidi stood from the lounge heading back to the door. She had to get him before it was completely dark. She still didn't know what to say but she was sure it would come when she faced him.

"Where are ya goin'?" Melinda called.

"To the doctor's house, you need help."

"You don't know where you're going. Heidi it can wait, please don't leave me alone," her sister begged.

"No, it can't wait. Don't worry you'll be fine here. Just relax I'll be back soon."

She left before Melinda could cry out in rejection again. As soon as she stepped out into the clearing, she broke into a run, trying to reach the doctors house quickly. She could understand Melinda's fear for not waiting to be alone, she felt the same. It only took her ten minutes before she was running up the path of the doctor's cabin, a lot smaller than Layla's.

The cabin only looked like it had one bedroom and looked as if it could be abandoned. Although there was smoke coming out of the chimney, so that meant someone was home. Parked in front of the cabin was a black Commodore, the one she had seen the night Layla had been killed. Around the back were several old rusted cars, all probably didn't work. Taking in a deep breath, she knocked on the front door, unsure of the reaction but she couldn't leave. Not without knowing what was wrong with her sister.

The door opened almost immediately, to a man that was not Dr Dylan. The man was a lot taller and muscular with a thick scar through his left eye. He had a shaven head and dark curious eyes. His right arm was in a sling and deep purple bruises covered his body. Could this man be Dr Dylan's partner? She wouldn't have picked the doctor to be gay and even as she looked at this man, he didn't appear gay.

Heidi gulped, she hadn't expected someone else to open the door now she was lost for words. She took a few steps backwards, shaking her head. This wasn't right, it was a bad idea. She had to leave. The man before her was in his thirties, his eyes brightened when he looked upon her, she hated him already and she didn't know him.

"Can I help you sweetheart?" he asked, opening the door wider.

"No. I must have the wrong place."

"Are you sure, there's no other houses around here," he said with a smirk. She glared back at him, hating the way he was looking at her, like he knew her or could see straight into her soul.

Heidi glared again, spinning around. She would have to take Melinda into the city tomorrow, this was wrong. Just as she was about to step into a run, someone called her name, causing her to spin back around to see the doctor standing beside the other man. Some part of her still wanted to run back to the cabin but the other part wanted to stay, curious about how Dr Dylan remembered her name.

Heidi slowly turned around, dropping her head to one side. She glanced to the young doctor. He nodded for the man to go back into the cabin while he stepped outside shutting the door behind him, a suppressed smile on his lips.

"I can't forget someone like you," he said, answering her unspoken question. "That's my mate James. He got released from prison today and I'm helping him get on his feet. What can I do for you? You weren't at Layla's funeral. I lied to the police for you, you know? Thought you'd be on the other side of the country by now, considering how fast you ran away."

Heidi tried to swallow back the knot in her throat. She hadn't thought about Layla's funeral, people had died in her life but she had never been to a funeral, she had forgotten they existed. She wanted to snap back at him, tell him not to be so smug but that wouldn't earn her his help. No, she had to suppress her ego and allow him to help her sister.

"I've been living on the street with my sister but she's run into some trouble and with Layla's cabin vacant, we have come back. Melinda is sick and I was hoping you again, could help and again remain silent regarding us," she asked, her body shaking. Why was she so nervous?

Dr Dylan smiled. "Of course I'll help. Let me get my bag and I'll be on my way. Oh wait, can James come with me? I don't really want to leave him alone."

"Whatever."

She didn't wait for them to start following her. As soon as Dr Dylan moved from the door, she turned, running back to the cabin. Hopefully the doctor would be quick then leave with the other man, so she could have the remainder of her birthday to herself. To sleep in a warm bed, maybe search for Layla's and Boyd's spirits. Although she couldn't feel their presence earlier, it would be wonderful if they had found peace together.

In time she could get her sister off the drugs, bringing her to become full of mind. A mind that doesn't miss a thing, like herself. To take drugs was weakness, it was to hide from life not thrive on its every moment good or bad. Each led to stronger feelings and fuller experiences, she would thrive. Learn from the bad and excel in the good, no, she was not weak. Running out into the clearing, Heidi hurried inside, making it just in time before the clouds disappeared behinds the night's veil of darkness.

Melinda sat curled on the lounge, watching the television that had strangely turned on. As she looked in, she realized the lights were also on, how had the electricity turned back on? Her sister had found a washer and now had it over her head, she didn't remember Melinda being so reserved and quiet. Stepping into the room, Heidi walked to the lounge sitting on the adjacent chair, watching her sister. Melinda was fourteen! She couldn't be pregnant. It sickened her but she couldn't show it.

It wouldn't be long until the doctor arrived and they would know for sure. She presumed that when they saw she had gone they would take the car. She just hoped Xane allowed them to make it. Just as she relaxed into the chair, there was a knock on the door. The two men stood next to the open door, she crossed her eyebrows together, had they walked? She hadn't heard a car pull up.

"Come in," she said, in a manner that made them feel stupid for remaining at the door.

Dr Dylan came in first, hurrying to her sister. "Melinda what's wrong? Can you tell me how you're feeling?" Her sister loved the sudden attention.

Melinda started talking to him but Heidi didn't listen to them, she turned to the other man who remained at the door focused on her. What was his problem? His gaze made her feel uncomfortable but she wouldn't show it. She swung her head to the other side, staring back at him.

She could guess what he was thinking, after all Dr Dylan had said he had just been released from prison. He probably hadn't seen a woman in a while but they weren't women they were girls, unless he liked that. It was disgusting. She would have to kill him soon if he didn't move his eyes from her.

"Can Melinda and I use a room, so I can check her out with some privacy?" asked Dr Dylan.

"Of course, take anything you need."

Melinda and the doctor left the room, his brown leather bag clutched in his hand. Heidi was certain her sister would be safe with him but not so sure about herself. She looked back to the older man who had walked into the room, making himself comfortable on the other lounge. What did he want? If he tried speaking to her she would leave, go and have a shower, since somehow the power was working.

"I'm James. I didn't catch your name."

"That's because you don't need to know it."

"Fair enough. I just want you to know I'm here to help, you see I know. I know everything, probably more than you," he said with little emotion.

"What the hell are you talking about? I don't know you or know what you're talking about," she spat.

"I think you know exactly what I'm talking about. I've been there before, for two of them. Apparently I've missed the third but here I am for you, the youngest. I can be your guide until you have empowered the monster and the hunters . . ."

"What the hell are you on about?! I really don't know what you're talking about. You've got me confused so back off. I want nothing to do with you."

"People have died and will always die until you're in our hands and we can prevent it. We're wiser and our numbers have grown."

"Who are we? Talk to me again and you'll be sorry."

"You can't let them die, the ones who have already paid because of Xane"

She froze. Oh God, she did know what he was talking about. He knew about Xane, he knew more than she did. What had Xane done? Who had he already done this to? Why her? She wanted to run into her room and cry. How dare he come here and change everything. And what had he said, the hunters, who were the hunters? She would never go with him, never depend on others. Although he was right about one thing, people were dying because of her and somehow he knew what would happen next. But maybe she didn't want to find out.

"Drake and Layla have died," she whispered, bowing her head. "And many others."

"You see. I can help, come with me."

She looked back at him, smiling an evil smile. James sat back his eyes wide, no, he didn't know everything. "The many others didn't die at Xane's hand . . . they were killed by mine." Of course Drake's family hadn't died at her hand but he wouldn't know about that, he may, however, know of all the missing children.

She smiled, darting her dark eyes to him and flicking her tongue on the roof of her mouth. This time it was his turn to freeze, his eyes ticking over with questions. Heidi shook her head, looking past him, finally she had silenced him. While he sat there in silence, something in the window caught her attention, a black cat, Xane. What was he doing here? Did he know this man? Was he curious to know how much he told her or was he there to kill him? Heidi glared at the cat, he couldn't follow her all the time, couldn't ruin her life. She could handle herself just fine.

"I'm pregnant!" Melinda cried, stepping back into the room.

Both she and James snapped their heads to Melinda and Dr Dylan coming back into the room. Heidi's eyes narrowed at Dr Dylan. Did he know what James did? Would that explain his comment the first time they had met. Her sister cried, running out of the room, loving every eye that followed her. Heidi sneered, rolling her head back to the window, glaring at the cat. Dr Dylan ran after Melinda but James remained in the chair studying her, she defiantly hated him. If he was a so called hunter then she wanted nothing to do with them, she was fine.

"You have no idea," she hissed, pointing at the cat in rage.

She was so angry, about him, about Melinda, about their new start being sabotaged again. What were they going to do with a baby? She hated that Xane thought he owned her and followed her, she would be better alone. Flicking her finger up, a burst of light flooded from it, hitting the alarmed cat. Knocking him straight from the window sill in a ball of flames.

James gasped, his knuckles turning white on the arms rests. She was alarmed too but didn't betray it. Did not betray the burning feeling her finger felt or the pulses of fear her body was sending through her. She used the power to her advantage. Sneering at James, she hurried out of the lounge room to her own. Leaving the older man shaking in the chair, she heard him pressing the buttons on his mobile but she didn't care. She had to get away from him, away from her slut sister and away from Xane. Oh god, Xane was going to be pissed.

*   *   *

Fire! A ball of fire had shot from her finger, she had power. Heidi grinned, she had been so angry. Her whole body had shaken with the rage. Then the power, her power and her released fury. With her finger caressing the burning necklace upon her neck, she slipped back into her room from the bathroom. Alone again. Melinda was resting and the two intruders had left, now she was safe.

Heidi dropped down onto her bed, watching the shadows of the trees outside dance across her wall. Shooting her arm at them she tried to make fire come again, nothing. How had she done it before? Heidi sighed, laying back, her eyes focused on the shadows. Her mind on the night of her fifteenth birthday, a day that had barely been in celebration of her.

Everything was always about Melinda, what was she going to do with her sister? Everything had changed. Even with this cabin safer than under the bridge people still knew they were there. The doctor and the criminal knew.

The shadows in the room moved faster, all joined together to bring forth the haunting spirit from her dreams. The spirit that had tried to kill her twice already. Heidi snapped up on her bed, was the spirit going to try to kill her again? Olivia smiled at her, slowly floating across the room to sit beside her, what did she want? Olivia remained silent as did Heidi. Both were waiting for the other to speak first, both challenging one another.

Olivia suddenly sighed, lying back on the bed. Heidi watched her with curiosity and impatience. All she wanted to know was why the spirit was here. And why wasn't she trying to kill her? She would not cave first. The spirit had come to her so it was her who should break the silence. She felt no threat from her at the moment. Pity, she was looking forward to a fight with her new found power, she was looking forward to winning.

"Killing you does not work. Befriending you sickens me. So all I can think of is calling a truce," Olivia finally whispered.

"What if I don't want a truce? I kind of liked the relationship we had," Heidi purred, flicking her tongue on the roof of her mouth.

"What would you do? Kill me, I'm already dead. Xane killed me years before you were born as he will kill you. I thought I'd save you the pain since I know what your life will become but I see we are different, you don't have my weaknesses. I have also heard of this life and maybe you actually have a chance at surviving."

"I don't remember asking for a conscience," Heidi spat.

Olivia disappeared from beside her, reappearing seconds later directly in front of her face. "You're not listening to me! You don't understand. Heidi its simple, kill Xane or be killed by Xane."

"I will not, go away and leave me alone. As you said we are different, so let me live my life. Get out of my head!"

Olivia smiled dipping her head to one side. "You must and you will. Hmm, out of your head you say." Her smiled grew wider before she grabbed Heidi by the shoulders lifting her from the bed. "That's a good idea. If you won't stop the pain, then I will."

"Let go of me!" Heidi cried, pushing herself from the arms of the spirit. Where was her power?

Olivia's grip tightened, the spirits eyes started glowing before with one big jump she threw Heidi across the room. Her body hit the wall, causing it and the others down the hall to shake. Her hands rose to her head, trying to tap the pain away, she snapped her eyes open ready for another attack. The spirit had gone. Standing to her feet, Heidi slowly walked around the room, her body tingling, she was raging for the fight.

Nothing changed, she was disappointed. Heidi moved back to her bed lying back down and trying to control the aching in her head. Her thoughts drifted back to her fire ball at the cat. What did Xane think of it? Would he proud of her or angered? She really didn't want to find out. All she wanted to do was rest from her exhausting day then spend tomorrow trying to decide what would be done about her sister and the baby. She hadn't a chance to really think about it yet.

Heidi's eyes moved to the shadows, the shadows that were disappearing. She smiled. She wasn't sure why Olivia had left but was grateful. The spirit had probably become frustrated because she wasn't listening to her but who did she think she was to come tell her how to live her life? Seeing Olivia in her dreams and nearly being killed by her had made things worse. Why was Olivia interested in her anyway?

"I'm not trying to change you, just guide you. Yes, I have made mistakes with trying to prevent the problem, with taking your life but he will always be there to stop me and should he be pushed, you will be killed before twenty. Listen to me Heidi, please just hear when I speak.

"Every time our soul walks it grows stronger, each group of four, one possesses power. When I saw the gypsy, she had the power and this time it's you. All of us are mortals with abilities but some are stronger than others, some can

be played easier. This time you have the power but you are playing into his hands.

"Take a step back and take a closer look before you run into his arms on a cold night again. Heidi without you he will not pay and for all the ones that have sacrificed so much already, their sacrifices will be empty. Don't let their deaths be without cause."

Heidi snapped up on the bed again, where was Olivia? She had listened to her lecture but couldn't see her. Of course she didn't understand what the spirit had said but let her go on, hoping to find some true reason to tolerate her, she found nothing. All this talk of killing Xane was tiring when she already planned on doing it. And all the warnings were pointless for she had nothing to loose, not anymore.

She looked to the mirror next to the bed, gazing into it to see Olivia. She gasped, she did see Olivia but not within the frame of the mirror, she was in her. Heidi screamed, this couldn't be happening, how did she get inside of her? Olivia's spirit within her body was a few seconds later in her movements than her but she could still see her or more the shadow of her around her own body. How did she get rid of her?

How dare she try and take over her body with no permission. She growled slamming her fist into the mirror, the shreds of glass flinging through the air, slipping through her skin but she didn't care. She was so angry and more, she could do nothing about it. Heidi ran from her room, every mirror she saw, she smashed. Every glass in the windows she smashed because through them she could see her reflection, she could see Olivia.

She had run around the house screaming for nearly fifteen minutes before she fell to the floor in the middle of the first hall exhausted. Melinda had come out of her room, watched her for a few minutes before becoming afraid and hiding. However that hadn't slowed her down. She sat curled in the corner, tears running down her face. Everything was falling apart and she couldn't keep it together. But then had she ever been able to keep it together?

She had been rocking in the corner for nearly an hour. She had been imitating Olivia or was it Olivia controlling her? She would never know. She hoped she could only hear the spirit, not be controlled by her. It was hard to accept that she would never have her body or soul to herself again. With every thought that ran through her head she would second guess it, wondering if it had been truly her own. She couldn't live like this but now she hadn't the energy to dispose of it.

Heidi closed her eyes, leaning against the wall. Tomorrow she would talk to Melinda. Tomorrow she would sort this entire confusion out. And if all else fails, tomorrow she might settle, listen and maybe learn something. Something told her she should listen to Olivia but with what Olivia had done, she hadn't the patience. No more thinking, no, she had to rest and re-gather herself and then tomorrow attack the world.

CHAPTER THIRTEEN

They were having a baby! How could they have a baby when they couldn't even look after her? She wanted to scream, she wanted to reveal that she could unlock that door and run downstairs to hit them. And they were so proud, her mother presenting herself through the town. Acting as if this were her first child and her stepfather, of course he was happy. It meant that they could get rid of her without anyone being wiser, besides she had already been forgotten within the town.

But she was still stuck in this tiny room. Still being feed poisoned food and still without Adrian. He had never returned after promising to three months ago, had he run away without her? She had cried for weeks before she realized he was not coming back and then there was the gypsy. She caught her watching from a distance often but was unable to get to her without being seen. Nevertheless, now even she had disappeared. All she wanted was happiness but something that seemed so simple, slipped further and further away.

It was best to sleep her time away. To close her eyes and drift, leaving this world where it was. However right now, she wasn't able to do that, she was too angry. Downstairs she could hear her mother laughing as she readied herself for bed and her stepfather opening another wine. He normally wouldn't go to bed until he passed out. Olivia curled in her bed trying to shut out the noise downstairs.

She heard her mother go to bed and waited until her stepfather would a few minutes later, but she heard nothing. Better to go to sleep than think about them, she couldn't hate them anymore than she already did. Olivia closed her eyes, rolling over and pulling the blanket over her head. In the next few days when her mother left with her stepfather to see the midwife, she would run away. If it was by herself she didn't care, as long as she had enough time to go before the hunters went searching.

Something moved within her room, Olivia snapped her eyes open, having not realized she had fallen asleep. She sat up looking around her room, she couldn't see anything. After a few minutes went by and nothing moved again, she lay back on the bed. It was probably all in her head but as her body hit the bed, something moved again. She remained hidden in the bed, her eyes darting around the room, who was there?

"Settle down love, I've just come to tuck you in," someone whispered in her ear.

Olivia gasped, it was her stepfather. What was he doing in her room? She could feel his breaths on her neck, his drunken breaths. His hand slowly reached out, moving beneath her nightgown. She wanted to scream but her lips had sealed so tightly she was afraid she wouldn't breathe. His fingers moved around her nipples then down to her panties, what was he going to do?

She quivered under his touch, tears falling from her eyes and streaming down her cheeks. Surprisingly the thing that crossed her mind was that she wanted to run to her mother and cry against her bosom. Of course that wasn't an option, he would never allow it. Her stepfather moved over her body, one hand in his pants and the other running over her chest. She had an idea what he wanted but what could she do? Only escape to another world, leave her body here, which is what she did. She closed her eyes, relaxing and drifting away, leaving him to do the unthinkable while she vacated.

*   *   *

The darkness surrounded him, not the darkness of his home but of his mind. He closed his eyes sighing again, trying to find the strength to get out of his small flat. Despite the fact that he wouldn't, he never could. It had been nearly a year since his family had been killed and nearly a year since he was put in hospital fighting for his life. He had been in hospital for five months before being released back into the world, alone.

He couldn't go home, not after what he had seen in his bedroom. He would have surely seen his family everywhere he looked, surely heard them. No, he had gone to the only other place he had felt comfortable, to the pub. And that was where he stayed, drinking all day and then stumbling to the flat above when he was ready to pass out. The pub owner had been very generous, letting him the room at a price he could afford. Since he no longer had a job, hell, he didn't even leave the premises.

A few times he had thought about selling his home but every time it went on the market, no one would buy. Locals were too skeptical, especially since what had happened to the houses on the hill. First, the murder of those poor children and their mother, then the house two doors down had burnt in a fire. Second, the Harrison's house fire leading to the deaths of the girls and their mother. Then his attack there and three months later the third house, Zack Solveri's house was destroyed in a freak storm. It was all too terrible and he couldn't let himself think about it, couldn't face the pain. Why hadn't he done more?

What could he have done? He was a mortal dealing with a demon. There was no way he was ever going to win that fight. Besides why did he care so much? Heidi was not his family, Serena and the kids had been, they were the one's who had paid for his choices. But Heidi and Melinda were innocents in this. They needed someone to love and care for them too.

No! He had to stop thinking about what could have been. Let bygones be bygones and live this life. But then why did he want to live? There was nothing left for him here. He was thinking too much, he needed a drink. Drake stood from the bed, slowly shifting his heavy body over to the small sink in the bathroom. He splashed his face with water, trying to rid himself of the dark bags around his eyes. He looked horrible. He was overweight, unshaven and his mousy brown hair was messy and greasy. But he didn't care.

He walked down the narrow hall of stairs to the pub, the bartender nodded his way but Drake didn't acknowledge it. He stomped over to the bar, slumping into his usual stool by the wall. Out of sight—out of mind. He couldn't stand their looks, couldn't bare their comments. All of them wondered what he was doing with himself, all of them thought he should be dead. Well why not make them happy and finish himself off? Because he had promised revenge, hadn't he?

One day the pain in his side would stop hurting and he would find the strength to walk out of here. Some day he would find the demon bastard and kill him for what he had done. How? He wasn't sure but he believed Zack would return to the hill to gloat and when he did, he would be there. Dropping his head to the table, Drake tried to force the thoughts away. Every day the same questions and every day he could only find the same answers, this world was a curse for mankind.

"Hello there Drake, I'm happy to see you out today," the barkeep called across the bottle rack.

Drake huffed, refusing to raise his head from the bar but the bartender expected no more. The burly man went on to serve other drunks, after all, who else would be in a bar at eleven in the morning? Hopefully, everyone else would also be trying to hide from their pain so he didn't have to deal with their questions, their pity. He hated everyone and sometimes he thought that this is what Heidi had felt, such anger and rage with no one to understand it. Well he understood it now and he felt bad he hadn't before.

What was the harm with not being able to help one student? But the truth be told, he would have probably done it all the same again, he couldn't pull away from Heidi. He couldn't forget her. It was like they were bound somehow. As much as he had completely loved Serena and the kids, he didn't think about them as much as Heidi. He would always grieve for them but not the way he was for Heidi. Why was it like that? Why was he so fascinated with a dead fourteen year old girl? Drake smiled, she would have been fifteen now.

The bartender moved in front of him, since there were no more demands from the bar. He lent across the bar trying to catch Drake's gaze but he wouldn't look up. He wouldn't talk first. He had nothing to say to the man, he couldn't even manage a thank you. Although he was thankful, very thankful he just couldn't betray it.

"There was a well dressed man in here half an hour ago looking for you. He had been searching all over Adelaide for you. In his hand was every paper of the attack, displayed in a folder, Drake. Someone at the school had said that he could find you here but I sent him away. Thought he was a reporter but now I'm not so sure.

"He was suited up and had a European accent. He didn't believe me when I said you weren't here, he said someone would be here soon and left." The bartender was obviously rattled with the visitor. He had always been good with turning the reporters away but like he said, this didn't sound like a reporter.

Drake raised his head as the man passed him a bourbon and coke. His voice had been lowered and his eyes were darting around the room as if he were going mad. "Are you sure he wasn't a reporter? Did he leave you a card?"

The barkeep shook his head. "That's another thing. He didn't say anything about if you wanted to contact him, no cards. It seemed like he was just here to find you then send another one. Drake I think you should get out of here, something didn't feel right about him."

"What did he look like?" he asked. His mind was running over his memories of Zack, was he back to finish the job? However the guy had said someone else was coming, could he be working for Zack? It was possible. If it was Zack he would not run, he would face the demon and he would die trying to defeat him.

"Blonde hair tied behind his head, gray-blue eyes. He was lean and tall, very tall. His skin was very pale and he was in a black suit as I said, with a large black folder. Said his name was Lachlan, you think you know him?"

"No, I don't know him. I'll stay and see what his friend wants." It didn't sound like Zack but sure sounded like someone who could work with him, Drake thought to himself.

"Okay but watch your back. I didn't like the feeling I got from him and get this, when I made a comment to everyone else in the bar about the man, they all claimed they hadn't seen anyone."

Drake snapped his eyes to the bartender, trying to see if he was bluffing him but the look of fear in the burly mans eyes told him what he wanted to know. It was real, the strange man had been here and it was very possible no one else had seen him. Oh god, what was he going to do if it was Zack? Kill him but what if it wasn't? What did the strange man want with him?

"Thanks Daniel. I don't know who he is but come get me if he returns. I'm going to go back up to bed. Thanks for the bourbon."

Drake turned, hurrying back up to his room. His mind needed to be clear so he could think. He couldn't have a drop of alcohol tonight, not even to make him sleep. While the imaginary picture of the strange man was in his head, he needed to draw it. So that the next day he would know this wasn't a dream, he would know that someone was searching for him. But why? To kill him or something more? Whatever happened, he would face it, he would not be afraid.

*　　*　　*

She sat in the corner shivering, the moon had long disappeared behind the clouds and the darkness sent a cold breeze throughout the cabin. She was so cold but was still unsure if it was from the night or how scared and alone she felt. Her sister had gone to sleep long ago and she didn't want to wake her. After all, in her current state she needed the rest. Still, she couldn't sleep, not with the spirit inside of her head. Oh god, would she ever think normally again, would she ever be able to relax.

Olivia hadn't spoken to her again but she knew she was in there, she knew that really she wasn't alone and she hated it. Her body was begging her for rest but she wouldn't give in. She hadn't slept for two days, since her head had been invaded. Melinda hadn't even noticed anything was wrong. Her sister spent the day playing on her pregnancy. Ordering Heidi about like she was a queen, well no more. She was no ones slave especially that of her tramp, drug addict sister.

She slid down further into the corner, listening to the trees rustle outside. What were they going to do now? Her sister was pregnant and for some reason wanted the baby but they couldn't have a baby here. There wasn't enough food in the cupboard for them let alone a child. Besides neither of them knew how to take care of a baby and then there was the birth . . . what the hell were they going to do then?

The only thing she could think of was to send Melinda to an outback abortion clinic although her sister wouldn't hear of it. Her sister had to think practically. She was so caught up in her drugs, she had probably already hurt the baby. It was best if it wasn't there. And then what were they going to do for themselves? Melinda was too young to get a job and she would struggle herself. All they really needed was enough money to buy food.

She could keep stealing but this was supposed to be a fresh start. Why keep bothering trying to have a new start, Melinda found a way to poison it every time. But the more she thought of getting a job, the more she realized it would be impossible. She had no identification, no contacts, she hadn't finished school and really she didn't exist, did she? This was stupid, nothing ever worked out the way she wanted it to.

Heidi moved from the corner of her room, slowly crawling to the bed where she pulled herself upon it exhausted. She hated her sister. Hated her for all she had done and said, hated her for telling Dr Dylan and James too much. Hated her for becoming their mother and falling pregnant but in the end, Melinda was her sister and she had to deal with it. After all, she couldn't just kill her the way she had their mother, could she? No, Melinda needed her help, she needed to be changed, so she had to deal with it.

The shadows danced across the roof but this time she had no reason to fear them, Olivia was inside her now, she wasn't going to kill her. There were times when she wished she would, so all this could end. Watching the shadows, her eyes grew tired and hesitantly, she let them close. She let her body relax and her mind drift into slumber, maybe with Olivia in her body she could find a better world through her.

She stood on the gravel beach, the dark clouds above her thickened with the anger of the storm. Heidi glanced up then around, over the thorns to the caves, lightning seemed to be flashing from within them. Why couldn't she go elsewhere, this world was no longer safe or peaceful. She ran her hands down her long black dress, she glanced at herself, since when did she own a beautiful long black gown?

The only clothing she had in her cupboard were white nighties. For nothing else fit her. Her hips had become more curved and her breasts had grown. She wasn't able to buy anything else, so she had to deal with what she had. But this dress was beautiful, it was classic with all the bodice trimmings, even her hair was wound up upon her head, finished with black ribbons. How she would love to have a mirror and see how pretty she could be. All she ever saw was a crazy looking girl with messy snow blonde hair, large eyes and dressed in childish nighties. Hell, she didn't even own a bra, she didn't even know how to look after herself.

"Are you going to stand there and stare or join me?"

Heidi spun around to the voice, gasping as her eyes landed on her doll again. EnDarla sat at a glass table set upon the gravel. She waited in a chair, her hands cupping a classy wine glass. Slowly she stepped towards her doll, what did she want? Last time they had met she had tried to drown her and now she wanted her to join her for a drink. She wasn't that stupid, the drink was probably poisoned.

EnDarla sat upon the chair, one leg crossed over the other. She was wearing the same long dress, with her hair tied up too. On her hands were long black gloves and her face was beautifully painted, she envied her for her beauty. If she had more beauty and confidence she wondered where her life could have taken her.

What the hell, Heidi thought, she was probably going to die anyway, might as well get some answers before she did. She approached the table, dropping herself in the chair opposite EnDarla. Her hands held down her puffy dress, keeping them distracted so they did not reach for the drink.

"Why do you always assume me to be your doll?" EnDarla asked, filling both hers and Heidi's glass to the top.

"Because you are my doll, you look exactly like her."

"So why couldn't your doll be a mimic of me?" she asked again.

"Because this is an imaginary world, in the real world you're a doll."

"I see. But what if I was to say that this world wasn't imaginary, that you were actually traveling to my world where the doll is based on me and somehow slipped through to your world."

"There are no other worlds."

"That's not true."

"Then what is the truth? That two worlds live side by side, one filled with immortals the other with mortals and we are all here to entertain your world? You come through and play with our lives like we are dolls as you are to me." Heidi said, pushing the wine away. What was her doll thinking? She was only fifteen. She would never drink alcohol, no, she wanted to remember this.

"Precisely," EnDarla said, with a sly smile.

Heidi shook her head. She had had enough of theses games. "Who is Xane and what are you to him? He was the one that gave me the doll, obviously he knows you. Was it all a game for you to help drive me mad?"

"True, I know Xane however we are not allies. Xane possesses a doll that looks like me and he gave it to you because that is what he perceives as beautiful and he wanted you to have a beautiful doll. In no way is it attached to me, the reason I am here is because I was fascinated in what he was doing. I decided to play my own games. He doesn't know I'm here."

"How many of you are there?"

"As you said, a whole world."

Heidi sneered, shaking her head, how could they just play with her like this? Were there not any rules to prevent them from coming here? If only she could find a way to send them all back. It wasn't fair that they were superior and could play with lives the way they did. She was bored of this conversation. All it was doing was going around in circles. She wanted to go back to her world and sleep so that she could speak with her sister tomorrow. Then again could she be one of them? She had power also and as EnDarla had said, she had traveled through to their world.

"I'm going back to bed and I leave you one warning. Don't come to me again because every immortal has their Achilles heal and I'll find yours."

EnDarla face darkened, she put down the glass, standing from the table as Heidi had. "Your death is already underway, don't underestimate my power child."

"I'm not, but you're underestimating mine."

"You have no power, you are a mortal!"

Heidi smiled letting the rage fill her body, she pulled her hand back letting the fire emerge from her soul, skipping around on her hand. EnDarla's eyes widened, she really had no idea. Heidi reached back and threw the fire into the sky, into the storm. The fire sent a crash of thunder through the sky. Her hand was burnt and stung but she would not show her doll that. She hid her hand behind her back, mimicking a bow and grinning. EnDarla smiled, crossing her arms over her chest.

"You will pay for that. No mortal can posses our power without consequences. Xane is a fool allowing you this gift!"

"So you do know him well," Heidi grinned.

EnDarla growled, thrusting her hands forward and shooting lightning at her. Heidi leapt out of the way, thinking of her nice bed, thinking about the cabin, she disappeared. Reopening her eyes in her bedroom. The doors to her cupboard were wide open and the doll stood on the middle shelf, its hair flowing in the breeze. Outside a storm had hit, Heidi climbed out of her bed. Standing in the center of the room, her eyes darting around catching a shadow in the corner, Xane.

"What do you want? I've already dealt with one to many immortals today. Fuck off Xane! I'm not in the mood for your games."

Xane rushed at her without his feet walking upon the ground and as his body flew out into the light, she saw that he was in his demon form. Heidi gasped as his hand flew out grabbing her around the neck, his face leaning towards hers. Uneven teeth sneering but she would not be intimated, she was too mad. She spat in his face causing him to growl, but he couldn't do anything that would harm her, death would be a blessing.

"You fool. Why did you speak with her?!"

"You gave me the doll, what did you expect?"

"I warned you and now you have proven to be my enemy!" he yelled, letting go of her. Heidi grabbed the doll in the cupboard slamming it into the ground, smashing it into tiny pieces. Xane glared at her.

"Is it beautiful to you now Xane? Is that who she is, your wife, you lover? And I will gladly be your enemy. You have done nothing but make everything worse."

"Your life was already bad, don't blame this on me."

"You're right, it was bad but you made it hell."

Xane growled striking her face. Heidi was flung to the floor and when she looked up he was gone. Where had he gone? As a matter of fact where had the room gone? She was surrounded by darkness but for some reason she could see. There was no room, no furniture, no cabin or outside. Where was she? Heidi stood, slowly walking around herself when she heard something shuffling through the darkness, then she saw him. He was a few meters from her, walking away.

Heidi clenched her teeth; he was not going to get away that easy. She wanted answers and she was going to get them. She started walking towards him, he didn't look over his shoulder. She didn't care; she was going to fight him. She had power didn't she? Xane moved faster and so did she, running to keep up with him. Something shining upon the ground caught her eyes.

Heidi stopped, first looking to him then back to the long jaggered hunting knife on the ground, she grabbed it. Flicking it around her burnt hand then clenching it in the other hand, she continued after him, holding it in front of her. She wanted to kill him, to kill an immoral for all they had done to her, for all their games others had probably suffered.

"Don't be a fool Heidi, he is tricking you. Don't follow him." She heard Olivia cry within her head. Heidi growled, no one would tell her what to do. Xane was going to die.

Xane darted to the side and she followed, keeping the same distance behind him. Suddenly he stopped, turning around to look at her. When he saw she was so close he grinned. His wings disappeared into his back and his glowing eyes ceased. He was in his mortal form again, Heidi took a few steps forward, waiting for him to fight her but he didn't. He lay down on the floor, closing his eyes and crossing his arms over his chest. He reminded her of a vampire. A vampire! Could they also exist?

She crept closer, not removing her eyes from him, watching to see if he made any sudden movements but he didn't, didn't even breath. Heidi walked right up to his still body, she was standing over him, her body shaking in rage, what was he playing at? She could stab him right here, is that what he wanted? Maybe not, maybe it wouldn't do anything to him but it would sure make her feel better. Standing over him, she lent down and kissed his lips. His eyes snapped opened, confusion.

She smiled, lifting the blade and slamming it into his chest. He gasped, then smiled which angered her more. She stabbed and stabbed him, tearing the knife through his chest and stomach, stabbing him until he closed his eyes, until the rage exhausted her. Then when she was about to collapse onto the ground, he started laughing. A high pitched laughter before he disappeared, leaving her alone in the darkness. What was the point of letting her stab him if he had nothing to say, no come back, just amusement.

Heidi sat on the floor, glancing around herself. Watching the colors of the objects around her slowly reform, the darkness sinking. She started to feel sick, looking around her sister's room, how had she got in here? Slowly, she climbed to her feet going to wake her sister up to tell her about her dream but when she stood, everything came to her. She screamed, looking at her sister's torn up body, staring at her sister's fearful shocked expression. What had she done?

Oh god, Xane had tricked her! Why hadn't she listened to Olivia? She had known, she had seen. Oh god, she had killed Melinda. Heidi screamed harder, throwing her body to the ground and throwing up. She couldn't look at it, couldn't let herself feel the warm blood on her hands or covering her nighty. Her poor sister! She must have been so scared, must have been afraid as she watched her kill her and kill her baby.

Heidi threw up again, she had killed the baby! How could she do it? Why hadn't she known he would do this? But he was right, he had said she would pay after he had killed Layla, he promised he would make her pay. And oh god, she was paying now. He had said she was his enemy but now he was hers, she couldn't forgive him for this. She was angered with Melinda but she would never kill her sister.

Quickly Heidi rose to her feet and closed her eyes. She ran out the door, slamming it behind her. Running down the second hall into the first, she threw herself into the shower. She scrubbed her skin, ripping it apart but she didn't feel it. She had to get her sister's blood from her body. She couldn't stop until she was done. She couldn't stop the heaving or the crying. With her body feeling weak and her mind pushed to emotional exhaustion, she fainted, falling to the shower floor in the base of blood, falling . . .

CHAPTER FOURTEEN

"I told you so didn't I? Why didn't you listen to me? I told you."

"Shut up!"

"Look what happened, he made you kill your sister! There's no going back from that."

"I said shut up!" Heidi screamed.

She was going crazy. She was hearing all sorts of things in her head and had killed her sister. Oh her poor sister, twenty-four hours later she still lay where she had been murdered. Heidi had pushed one of the lounges up against the second hall door. She would never go down there again. So she hid in the first hall, waking up in the shower then running out into the hall where she sat. Her hair a mess, her white nighty blood stained and her body shaking.

Every shadow that moved she jumped at, every whisper, she screamed. Her body shook and her eyes darted along the walls, images of her sister's body flashing past her eyes. Heidi pulled her knees to her chest, what was she going to do? Now she was truly alone and of course now that Xane was satisfied, he had left. Well good, she hated him anyway. She knew soon she would have to go down the second hall and move Melinda's body, it would start to smell, but she couldn't face it right now. She was scared that if she looked at her, she might see the fetus inside. After all, she had really torn her apart. But she had thought it was Xane, it wasn't Melinda she was after.

What if the doctor came back to check on them? Oh god, what would she say? She clutched her stomach, she felt sick again but if she throw up anymore she would surely faint again, she was so weak. She really should get into her room and lie down but how could she when all she would do was think about the previous day and EnDarla. Oh she hated that witch! She knew she played a part in all the chaos yesterday.

"Next time listen to me and maybe no one else will get harmed."

"There is no one else to harm Olivia!" Heidi cried. "I've lost everything, home, family and any friends I could have had. This game isn't fun anymore. And why is he doing this? Because I left his house a year ago? It doesn't make sense," she whined.

"He would have done it anyway. He was waiting for an excuse."

Dropping her head to one side, she traced her fingers through the carpet, drawing circles. She wanted to scream, wanted to throw her fist through the wall or fire balls. She had thrown some fire balls out of rage earlier but every time she did, she collapsed in pain. What good was a power when it hurt? The fire burnt her hand to the point where they were now blistered and she couldn't move it. With the other hand she traced insanely through the carpet and with her injured, she cradled in her lap.

Olivia hadn't given her any proper answers and probably wouldn't, she could feel her retreating. Heidi laughed to herself, she was finally truly alone but now that she was, she didn't want to be. Tears started to slide down her cheeks, she had no idea what to do. She was just a stupid fifteen year old girl, a naive killer. The only future for her was in death or prison.

Slowly Heidi climbed to her feet, wandering further down the hall where she collapsed on Layla's old bed. Where was her friend? Why couldn't her spirit come to her, she needed guidance. She needed love and protection but more then that, she needed vengeance on Xane for what he had made her do. For everything he had made her do or feel, like extreme hatred, loneliness, confusion, excitement and love. She closed her eyes, silently hoping that they would never open again

*   *   *

They had left early this morning, she had heard the screams, the panic and then the door had slammed. She was glad they were gone but soon they would be back and with the baby. She didn't want a baby to come, for when it did, she would be sent to the hunters. She had heard her stepfather talking to the hunters outside her window, she had heard his lies. He had told them she was wired wrong, that the hunters needed to take care of her.

Her mother had also heard him and they ended the night in a fight. Why had her mother chose now to finally care? Her stepfather had hit her mother and then there came more cries because she was afraid of what he would do to the baby should it be a girl. But Olivia had no sympathy. She knew her world would turn to dust. She knew the day would come when her stepfather would show his true colors to her mother. Too bad it hadn't come before she was nearly dying and her mother was giving birth to his child.

Nevertheless, she had a few hours to decide what she was going to do. Whether to run or stay and plead with her mother. She was sure this time that her mother would come with her, after all her mother knew everything. Well most things, she knew about the punishments, she knew about the food and she still sat back and let it happen. But she didn't know about the rape and that might be the last straw to make her listen.

Olivia sighed, she moved around to her door unlocking it with the iron bar. She hurried downstairs where she could get herself her first safe meal. If she could eat enough food and gain enough strength then she could run away. She was still torn between two minds whether she wanted to take her mother and the new baby? Right now, her main priority was to get well enough to make the decision.

She climbed the cupboards to find all the baked food she could before something outside distracted her. People were talking against the wall next door. Olivia placed down the food, slowly walking over to the kitchen shutters, opening them just enough to peer out. It was her neighbor, a hunter and one of the midwives leaving her night shift from the doctor's room at the end of the street. The three were locked in an intense chatter, their voices hushed. What were they talking about?

"Oh the poor thing, she had been so excited to have the baby," her neighbor said, pressing her hand to her mouth and shaking her head.

"It will be a tough few months for Paul, especially being left with Madeline's eldest daughter who is so poorly," the midwife stated.

The hunter grunted. "That child needs to be sent to the woods."

"Mathew, hold your tongue. The dear girl does not need that talk with the loss of her mother," the neighbor cried.

Olivia froze, what had she said? The loss of her mother? What had happened to her mother? She started to panic, her mother couldn't be dead. No, she would definitely be sent into the woods if her mother had left her. She loved her, of course the last few years she couldn't understand how much she had changed. But she would always remember their lives together before her stepfather invaded them. Olivia moved back from the window, she felt like she was going to be sick.

"Paul does not need the distractions of a sick girl when mourning his wife."

"I think that is Paul's decision, don't you? He loves poor Olivia so," the midwife spat back.

"Hush, hush, he is on his way home."

The group fell silent as heavy footsteps pounded past them, Olivia gasped. Her stepfather was back, she had to get back to her room. But the food, he would know she could get out if he found the food. Leaning across the table, she threw what food she could into the cupboard before rushing to the stairs. She was half way up them when the front door opened. She looked over her shoulder to her stepfather, who had a sly smile upon his face.

"Well, well, well somebody's got a secret," he hissed, shutting the door behind him and locking it.

"What happened to mama?" Olivia cried.

"Your mother is dead, that damned baby girl she gave birth to killed her," he said emotionless.

The tears rolled down her cheek, how could he not care? She couldn't believe her mother was really dead and also a baby girl, her sister. It all sounded a little too convenient to her. Did he kill her mother and the child because it wasn't a boy? No, he couldn't because that baby was still his flesh and blood, she wasn't. Olivia started walking backwards upstairs, she had to get away from him. She was probably the next to be killed. After all, it was an easy lie to say she died with grief for her mother, very believable.

"Now I have no wife but you can be my wife, can't you love? You can cook for me and keep my bed warm. If you do I'll make sure you're free to roam the house. You can eat when you want and when you're a little older you can give me my son." He said moving towards her.

Olivia shook her head, he was disgusting. "I'd rather die than willingly bed with you, you monster!"

"I can arrange that if that's your choice."

"I hate you, you probably killed mama. You are the one who deserves to be hunted!"

He laughed, reaching up the stairs and grabbing hold of her ankle, he pulled her leg from beneath her, pulling her body down the stairs. Olivia screamed but he was quick to hold his hand over her mouth. He pulled her over to the lounge where he bent her over it, lifting up her dress. She gasped then screamed again when he let go, her cries would do nothing only anger him more which it did. Her stepfather brought the lamp post down on her head to silence her until he finished what he wanted. Before the pain hit her body, Olivia vacated to her imagination, where she still had a mother, still felt happiness.

*　　*　　*

He slumped down in the bar stool, staring at his empty mug, trying to fight the temptation to ask for another. It was five o'clock on a Friday afternoon so the bar was full, although he hid in the corner. Some would look his way but Daniel, the barkeep, would inform them that it was at their own risk for he would hit them. Drake hated who he had become but he had fallen so far, he didn't know how to pick himself up.

Today no one glanced his way; the locals were used to him and let him be in his corner. No more comments about how he looked. No more pity and thankfully no more questions about his family or the Harrison girls. He glanced over his shoulder at the company in the bar, no longer recognizing their faces. The offers for him to go back to work had stopped coming, after all who wanted a counselor who couldn't help himself? He was pathetic, he silently hoped that this drink would kill him and he wouldn't have to wake up the next day.

Giving in, Drake shoved the mug across the bar, Daniel filled it immediately. He pulled the mug back against his lips, gulping it all down at once. Then he threw the mug back down on the bar. No more. If he had another drop tonight he would pass out and be humiliated yet again, he couldn't bare that again. He hated being known as the crazy drunk man, the one who yelled about demons and murder but in a way it was his fault, he should have remained silent.

Someone took the stool beside him, Drake sneered not looking their way but hoping they left. He hated it when people came too close to him, the man called for a beer for himself and Drake. When Daniel threw two beers their way, Drake didn't accept it. He grunted, grabbing hold of his empty mug again and hitting the beer away with it. The nerve of the guy, if he was a little more sober he would have smacked him down by now.

The man's hand reached into his vision catching the beer and placing it between them. Drake grunted again, lowering his head onto the table, he would wait for Daniel to fill his mug one more time then leave before he passed out. Daniel was bound to request that he go upstairs soon anyway, especially if he caused any trouble.

"Horrible weather we're having," the man commented beside him. Drake didn't answer so the man continued. "I had a work associate come here a few months ago and he couldn't stop raving about the weather. Suppose I should have come with him."

"Fuck off," Drake growled, lifting his head and tapping his mug. Daniel filled it again but before he could raise it to his lips, the man's hand rested on his arm lowering it. That was it! He was going to hit the guy now but when he finally looked at the man, he paused.

The man was obviously not from around here, although he had an Australian accent, he wasn't from these parts. The man had a shaven head and a thick scar running through his left eye. He was a big muscular guy with a serious dead stare. His arms were covered with tattoos as was his neck. The man pushed a card with a single phone number into his hand. Drake left it on the bar, he barely glanced at it, all he could do was stare at the man.

"Am I to assume you met my associate Lachlan?"

"No, the guy left without a word," Drake answered. He had forgotten all about the ghost man months ago, a vague picture entered his mind. He had thought the man was a minion of Zack and had expected to be killed but when nothing happened, he forgot. Then who was this guy?

"I see, I was told otherwise. My name is James and I work for an underground organization that hunts demons. Reports have shown that you were mixed up in an attack and lost your family so I am here to offer vengeance. Come and join my hunters in our war, we will train, house and feed you. All you have to do is abide by our laws and offer any information you might have," he said under his breath.

"What is this? Have I been set up on some joke? Fuck off or I'll be forced to knock you out."

"No joke. I can prove it."

"I'm listening."

"You once counseled a girl named Adelheid Harrison but by all the records we could find she was killed in a house explosion. Well she wasn't, she lives in a cabin north of Melbourne with her sister."

"Get out of here. How dare you come here looking through photos, creating lies, can't the Harrison girls rest in peace!"

He stopped, watching as the man's face reddened, glancing around the bar Drake saw that everyone was staring at them. Some looked scared and some amused but everyone was watching. He hadn't even realized he was standing, with his fist raised in the air. Quietly Drake sat down, taking a long sip from his bourbon, after a few moments the bar started echoing with chatter and laughter again.

"Is everything alright here?" Daniel asked, leaning across the bar.

"Fine. I'll head upstairs in a minute," Drake slurred.

"Probably a good idea," replied the barkeep stepping away.

The man pushed a piece of paper in front him, Drake sighed, running his hands through his hair. James was really starting to upset him and now thanks to him there was going to be new rumors floating around town. It was the last thing he needed. When Drake didn't take the card with the number or the blank piece of paper, James stood, starting for the door. When he left, Drake slowly reached out turning over the paper to see it was a picture of Heidi. He froze.

James hadn't been lying. The picture was recent. She didn't look like he remembered. She was stunning. Of course she had always been beautiful but now she was gorgeous. Her eyes were still large and full, her long dark eyelashes framing them. Her lips were full and her skin pale and delicate, child's skin, perfect skin. She looked to have grown a little taller though not much and her hips had filled out a little as her breasts had. She was still tiny, delicate as a doll and absolutely beautiful.

For a few minutes all he could do was stare at the picture, his finger stroking it. Why did he suddenly feel like he wanted to kiss her, to love her? Maybe it was because she was familiar to him or because in a way he did love her. Or because she was the only thing left, she was proof he wasn't crazy. In the picture Heidi was sitting in front of a cabin, leaning against the wall and looking up at some trees.

Drake placed the picture in his pocket, climbing from the bar stool. Some people had turned to look at him but he didn't take any notice of them, something bigger was at hand. Something he had always known but they had tried to make him forget. He started running on unsteady feet to the door.

"Drake are you sure you should go out there?" Daniel called, watching out for his wellbeing. Drake smiled, good old Daniel.

"I have too Daniel. Thanks for everything but I've got to go to Melbourne."

"Melbourne?"

Drake hurried out the pub door, when he hit the night air he felt dizzy but nothing would stop him. He had to find James, the man was there to help him and he would accept it. He felt foolish for not listening to him earlier, for it to take a picture to convince him that Heidi was alive. Didn't he already know it in his heart? His dark eyes darted around the streets. Finally he caught James up ahead, stepping into a limousine. Drake ran towards him, suddenly un-normally sober.

"James wait! James!" he called.

James stopped, spinning around to him and Drake stopped, leaning against the limousine catching his breath, he was so unfit. But if James would keep his promise then he would be fit soon enough, he had found a reason to live. One, Heidi, two, to regain his life and three, maybe the most important, he had a real shot at vengeance.

"If the offer is still on the table, I'll come with you. I'll train, I'll do anything you want, just let me see her. Let me help and have my revenge," he begged.

"Of course the offer still stands, hop in. I'll go over the conditions on the way to the airport but you have to wait before you can see Heidi, for a while anyway. She's not ready for you, not ready for any of us right now. You need to train and be guided, we will give you all the knowledge on Xane and the other women we have, once we're in Melbourne."

"Who is Xane and the other women?"

"Xane is Zack Solveri's real name and Heidi is not the first he has done this to, she is the fourth. The other three are dead, or so I am told. Come, I'll explain on the way. You don't need go grab anything first do you?"

"No," Drake said, hopping into the limousine.

He shuffled along so James could slide in after him, the door slammed behind him. James called out for the driver to go and the car started to move, Drake glanced over his shoulder looking at the pub. This would hopefully be the last time he was here, the last time he was ever this low. He was heading to a new, stronger life. He was heading along the path of his destiny.

*   *   *

She fell from the bed exhausted and weak. Every time she was awake she saw people from her life that she had lost. She saw Drake many times. He was wild and bloody like she had seen him on the news. He would talk with her, trying to get her to open up but when she opened her mouth to speak, he would walk away. Walking to his family and playing with them, laughing with his wife about her. When she would run to him crying that she needed his help, he would disappear.

Other times Layla would be there talking with her, trying to make everything okay. When she would move to hug her friend she would fall straight through her. And then there was Boyd who would surf around the cabin on his guitar, he would never hear her when she called, he would never look her way. There were others things she saw too, like shadows chasing her and Olivia speaking but all this was in her head. When she would focus, they wouldn't be there.

The worse one was Melinda, who stood with their mother, the two of them spitting down at her when she pleaded for forgiveness. They would only laugh in her face, then grow angry and start abusing her. They weren't real but that didn't mean that it didn't hurt or scare her less. She knew she was going insane, but how was she supposed to stop it when she had no support?

"You killed me! I would have never thought you would kill me. After all I had done for you sister."

Heidi took a deep breath, slowly looking up through her hair at her sister, standing by her bedroom door. She sighed; it was all in her head. This couldn't be real. Her sister had been dead for weeks now. Slowly and with much effort, she managed to pull her lethargic body up against the bed, glaring at her sister. She wanted to tell her to go away but her heart wouldn't allow it. It felt like her body was falling apart just like her mind.

"I'm sorry Melinda, I thought . . ." she stopped. There was no real point in talking to something that wasn't there. No point in trying to say she was sorry, when the person she wanted to know it would never hear it.

"You thought what? That I was Xane? Did you want to kill him, make him pay for the wonderful powerful life he has shown you?"

Heidi crossed her brows together, why would her sister say that? Melinda hadn't known how she felt towards Xane and in no way would she refer to it as wonderful. It wasn't Melinda, she reminded herself. It was all in her head, she was torturing herself. Refusing to reply, Heidi moved to the door, standing beside the invisible memory before pushing herself out into the hall. She needed to eat. Her body was already giving up on her. She needed to find some energy.

"Don't walk away from me!" Melinda called after her.

"Why? You're not really there," Heidi spat, moving into the kitchen, holding herself up on the cupboards.

"Aren't I?"

Heidi stopped, glancing back at her sister who stepped into the kitchen, she didn't believe her. Her sister was dead and she didn't see the dead anymore, she had closed her mind to them. The face of her sister smirked, one eyebrow rising, Heidi glared. No, this time she was not imagining, this being was here but it wasn't her sister, it was Xane. She turned leaning against the bench, why was he here? Hadn't he done everything he could to her? Oh, she wanted to kill him but she hadn't the energy to even make herself some food.

"Xane, what do you want?" she hissed.

Xane laughed, morphing into his mortal form, this was one big game to him. "How did you know? No one else can do that," he said with a smile.

"No one else is pathetic enough to waste their time with me."

"Now, now Heidi, my time is not wasted here. Besides I like hanging out with friends."

"Friends?"

"Yes friends, you have paid for betraying me so now were friends."

"Get out of here Xane! We are not friends. I have no time for you. You killed my sister!"

"No, you killed your sister!"

"Forced by your magic so therefore, it was you. Go away and let me die in peace."

Xane stepped forward, his face now serious but she held her hand up for him to stop. If he came any closer, she would stab him with the knife near the sink, just out of spite. She spun around, to get herself some food when he didn't move towards her again. But she moved too fast, she fell. Her body slumping into the floor, she was okay but couldn't get up in a hurry. Xane moved forward but she glared at him and he took a few steps back, disappearing.

He had looked saddened. He was guilty for trying to torment her when she was already destroying herself. She didn't care. She didn't care how guilty he felt, he should feel guilt. He had caused all of this. Heidi sighed, glancing up into the cupboard. She couldn't even reach the food. Dropping her arm, she closed her eyes, leaning into the counter. She had to sleep, gain more energy then get the food to survive. She had slept so much lately as she had seen Olivia do through her dreams. It was easier to sleep your life away than face it. It came easier and easier, close your eyes and drift away, her mind faded.

* * *

Her eyes fluttered open, she was in her bed all tucked in, how had she got there? The last thing she remembered was letting her body fall to silence in the kitchen. She needed to go back there and get some food. But who had taken her to the bed? Heidi tried to sit up, pulling her back up against the pillows. She glanced down at herself, her nighty had been taken off and she now wore a white cotton dress and her hair had been brushed.

The door to her room opened with Xane walking in. Figures, she thought to herself. She should have known Xane wouldn't have left. He moved in carrying a bowl of soup and some bread, smiling when he saw she was awake, she glared back. What did he think, that because he had looked after her everything was fine between them? No, he had killed her sister. He would never be forgiven for that.

Xane walked over to the bed, placing the bowl in front of her and some bread beside it. He then moved to the chair, pulling it up to the bed and sitting beside her, watching. Heidi glared into the soup, not wishing to speak with him or acknowledge him. He didn't like that. He moved forward on the chair, his hand brushing down her arm. Why did he look so worried? He couldn't care for her not after what he had done, could he?

"Eat up, you need to put more meat on those bones," he whispered.

She sneered, crossing her arms over her chest and still staring down at the soup. Why was he here? She hated him! She could do fine on her own.

"Still upset with me, hey? Look Heidi, you played with fire and got burnt, what can I say? I did warn you what would happen if you were my enemy."

"Aren't I still your enemy now?" she growled, still refusing to look at him.

Xane looked hurt. "No, you tried me and I killed Layla then you defied me again and it was your sister, now I come with another offer."

Heidi glared at him and before he could react, she threw the soup bowl in his face. He gasped, letting the bowl smash over his head and the hot soup drip down his face. His eyes flickered with anger, the flames consuming his eyes before he calmed, laughing and vanished the soup. Why was he so calm? She hated him! She would never leave with him. She turned back to stare at the blanket, her stomach growled as the scent of the soup disappeared.

"Do you want to hear my new offer?"

"Fuck off and let me die in peace."

"Heidi you don't have to die, listen please. I won't tell you until you listen with an open mind."

She turned away from him, glaring at the other side of the room. Her stomach was hurting so much as was her head. She didn't know what to do. She didn't want to give into him but she was so hungry. Tears rolled down her checks, she was so scared, what did she do? Give into him and forget or at least listen to his offer, she could betray him later should his offer lead her where she needed to go.

She pulled her knees up to her chest, dropping her head to them and crying. She could feel his body move behind her. She could feel his head resting on her back and his hands running down her arms. Why did he have to love her? Why did he have to be like this? He made it so easy to believe him but in the end she needed his help, she needed to survive. She could at least listen to his offer and make her decision after she knew what he wanted. Heidi rested her head back. Xane moved back, letting her head rest against his chest. He bent down kissing the tip of her nose and brushing his fingers through her hair.

"*Don't listen to him, more lies, more tricks, you will die!*" Olivia screamed in her head, but she chose to ignore the spirit again.

"I'm listening," she whispered, her throat dry.

"Thank you. I have come from my world to kill a certain few mortals, mortals who are capable to possess powers, people like you. I have destroyed all I have been sent here to, other than you."

"So you do want to kill me."

"I did. That was my plan but I'm tired, I have been doing this for thousands of years and there is something I desire more than the power your soul will give me. I love you more than I thought I could, so at a risk

I ask of you a child. I want a child to love and raise in my world. I want to love someone and I want to be loved in return. You understand that don't you?

"I want you to be its mother and in return, I will retreat from your life and let you live it. With finances to survive comfortably, of course. But there's one other thing, by laws of my world, I can't actually have sex with you but I can possess the body of one who is. If you do this, I will always protect you and give you whatever you want from this world."

Heidi took in a deep breath, was he telling the truth? Would he really just leave her forever if she gave him a baby, but then that was it, could she have a child and give it away knowing she would never see it again? And what had he said about not being able to have sex with her? That would mean she would have to find someone else to have her so he could do what he wanted. She couldn't do that. And what did she want from this world? Nothing came to mind, nothing but wanting what he did, to be loved.

"I'm fifteen!"

"A fifteen year olds body is not incapable of having a child, just frowned upon by those around them. Besides you won't have to raise a baby just birth it."

"Why can't anyone from your world give you a child?"

"Because there are too many immortals, immortal and immortal can not breed unless blessed by the gods, something I am not. Besides I want your blood within it."

"I'm fifteen!" she cried again, truly scared. Was she really thinking about doing this?

"I know kitten although it might take a few years for a man to come here."

She thought for a moment. He was right, he was asking her to one day have his child, not now. And she knew he had killed her sister but having a baby would bring the lost family back and really she could think of no one else she would ever want to give her a child. Imagine the power it could have but then he was taking it away wasn't he? No, if she was to have a child, she would be a mother. And as long as she promised this, he would protect her, no more fear, she would always have him.

"No Heidi! Don't do it, don't bear a demon spawn."

Shut up! Maybe Olivia's mistake was she didn't cooperate with him. Well she had made that mistake twice and wasn't going to lose anyone else. She would agree.

"There's not enough in it for me," she whispered, trying her luck and his patience.

"What do you want?"

"I don't want to have a child then never see it again and I also want to be loved. I want to belong with someone, I don't belong here. I will do all you have asked but after the child is born, instead of letting you take it, I will go too. We will live together in your world. I as your queen, you know I'm capable of it."

"I know you are. Only if you're sure, my world is full of things never seen in this world."

"I can handle it," she looked back over her shoulder, he smiled.

"Perfect, agreed, once you bare my child, you will be my queen."

"Agreed."

His smile grew wider. He pulled her upper arms, spinning her around so that she faced him. Heidi grinned back, yes this was right. This was what she wanted. This was how she had to survive. Xane lent forward to kiss her nose but instead of kissing her nose, he pressed his lips against hers, her eyes widened. Her first real kiss! He was kissing her! His hand ran behind her head, pulling her closer against his body, she kissed him back. Her body hot and her heart fluttering, her soul melted into his. Oh god, she did love him.

"*Fool.*"

CHAPTER FIFTEEN

"Xane!" she screamed. She fell to the floor, her body aching and shadows danced through her head. Why was she being tormented by Olivia? But she already knew the answer. Olivia was trying to punish her for letting Xane back into her life. Well whatever she had to dish out, she could take. However at the moment she didn't have time for it and the only thing that stopped the insanity was her king. "Xane!"

Where was he? That was the fifth time she had called, normally he wasn't that far away. Heidi spun around herself, trying to grip onto something, trying to stop the room from swaying, Olivia's doing again. Three months had passed since she had committed herself to Xane's way, three months of hidden torment from Olivia. She wouldn't be able to take in much longer, she was going insane. Olivia created so many visions. She really couldn't tell which ones were real anymore.

She would see all the people she once knew coming to her and trying to speak with her but they were all Olivia. Olivia knew everything she did but she had very different opinions on her life. The most painful ones were Drake, she couldn't bear having his fake presence around her. She hated the spirit for it.

Olivia also attacked her in other ways. Xane would feed her and try to make her strong but the spirit would destroy it. She would make her sick after she ate. She would play her tricks and make her faint out of nothing. Just because that was her way of escaping things from her life didn't mean she choose the same distraction. Heidi liked to make the things worrying her come alive then make them pay, not fall asleep.

Olivia had admitted to being raped by her stepfather and every time he did it, she had passed out but she wasn't the same. The men that had raped her over a year ago had been scattered around her room, people die when they hurt her. Yes, she and Olivia were very different. And she was doing things her own way, she needed Xane and now she knew why he needed her. Olivia wasn't going to stop but when Xane was around, the spirit was blocked out and when they went to Xane's world, she wouldn't exist.

Heidi fell to the floor, exhausted from fighting Olivia, the spirit laughed within her head. She had thought she had won. The plate from the table fell down with her smashing on the floor, shards of ceramic cutting her face. Heidi cried out again as one hit the side of her face, slicing open her check. She snapped her hand to her face, feeling her hot blood roll through her fingers.

"Here give me your hand, I can help you."

Heidi looked over her shoulder to see a blurry vision of Drake Commack, she cringed. No, not now, she didn't want to deal with this anymore. But as she stared into Drake's warm brown eyes, how could she be mean to him, even a vision of him? After all he had died because of her, hadn't he? Slowly she stood up, facing the tall man, he smiled, his eyes lighting with his smile. Without thinking about it she put her hand in his, leaving her cheek exposed.

"Oh, that's a bad one, come into the kitchen. I'll wash your face," he said, taking her into the kitchen. All she could do was stare at him, he looked like she had remembered.

"You're not real," she whispered.

He smiled, "Of course I am. Are the children telling you stories again?" he said with a laugh.

As he washed her face, she reached out to stroke his face. He was as perfect as she remembered, even down to the way his eyes crinkled when he laughed. Oh god, she wished he was real, she wished he hadn't died the way he had. To watch his family die, by a creature and then to feel the pain as his life was also taken. She could hear Olivia faintly chuckling but she didn't care. She couldn't think of anything else but Drake.

"Drake, the children are also dead. I'm far away from home and your not really here."

He paused, looking into her eyes. "If I'm not here where am I?"

"Dead!"

As she cried out the word his face started decaying before her eyes. He was trying to say more to her but she couldn't hear his words. All the skin on his body darkened then peeled away from his bones. She started to cry, her hand snapping to the side of her face. Oh, it hurt. She collapsed back to the floor, listening to Olivia laugh harder as Drake disappeared. Why wouldn't she stop doing this to her? Heidi took in a deep breath, trying to control her anger, this wasn't fair. She had chosen what she had to survive, to stop anyone else from getting hurt.

"Xane!" she screamed louder.

After a few minutes Xane jumped through the window as a cat, slowly morphing into his human form. He glanced up the second hall which he had cleaned up then down the first before looking to her. His face shocked, he hurried to her side. Sitting her on the bench and wiping down her face with some tissues, her face felt better with his touch. She stared into his worried eyes. He really could pass for a mortal with the compassion he held. She would never have believed that the supernatural were more moral than maybe the mortals.

"What happened?" he asked, after he had cleaned her face and placed a few butterfly clips from the first aid kit over her cheek.

"*Tell him about me and you won't live to be his queen.*"

"Nothing," she whispered. "I guess I fainted again at the table and the plate broke," she lied.

Xane looked to the broken plate then back at her, sighing. "You have to be careful. I can't understand why you keep passing out but I do my best to try. Listen, I have been called back to my world for a little while. You will be safe here, you have all the food you need and you're safe. The best way I can hear you, is through the necklace and I'll come to you, okay?"

"Who has called you? EnDarla?" she questioned, he looked shocked which meant she was right but it only left her with bigger questions. Who was EnDarla?

"It's a long story, I have to go there to reenergize and so I'm not caught in this world but I'll be back once I sort out a few problems."

"Are you and EnDarla . . . ?"

"No. EnDarla and I knew each other as mortals, it's complicated. I'll explain it all to you when you are my queen. I love you Heidi, I'll be back soon."

He kissed the tip of her nose then softly on the lips before taking a few steps away. "You will tell me everything, won't you?"

"Of course."

"I didn't know you were once a mortal," she whispered, thinking about what he had said.

Xane smiled. "I'll tell you everything Heidi, when I get back."

She smiled back at him and he nodded before disappearing. Heidi sighed looking around the large empty and lonely cabin. She hated it when he wasn't there, hopefully because he had said he would be gone a while, Olivia wouldn't torture her. The spirit would have plenty of time to convince her otherwise of Xane. Heidi pulled her knees to her chest sitting on the bench, tears forming in her eyes . . . all alone.

*   *   *

Something rattled at the front door. Heidi's eyes snapped open in her bed. She sat up listening to the front entry, something rattled again. Was someone trying to get into the house? Well it wouldn't be hard, there was no glass in the windows and the place did look vacant. Heidi climbed out of bed adjusting her long black satin pajama pants and white singlet top. She threw her long hair over her shoulder, slowly approaching the door, careful not to make the floor creak.

Another sound but now out in the lounge room, yes someone was definitely out there but who? Xane wasn't back yet and if he was, he would have come to her. Could it be the police? She had actually been surprised that they hadn't been around yet but maybe tonight was the night she was caught. Or could it be something simple like the doctor next door, coming to check that her sister was alright.

After all should her sister still be alive in a few months she would be giving birth. Heidi took a deep breath. She didn't need to think about Melinda or the baby now. Although the person sneaking into the house could be James, god, she didn't want to see him again. Really, what was she panicking about? Whoever was breaking into the house she would just kill them, no problem.

Her big question was did she go out there to kill them or wait for them to find her? She opened the door a fraction to peer through it. In the hall and lounge room were dark, not even a flash light moved around. Nevertheless she could still hear the whispering, they hadn't left. But their whispers were too quiet for her to understand. She was too curious to wait, she wanted to know who was in the house.

Keeping her body strong and alert, she opened the door wider, slowly stepping out into the first hall. Her hand wrapped around the amethyst necklace around her neck, she wouldn't need Xane but it calmed her to know he was listening. "Olivia I know you're angry but someone is in the house."

"*Don't run, it could be help, we need help.*"

"I don't need any help, I can sort them out."

"*I know you can Heidi. Just don't go in to hastily. Everyone deserves a plea, check who it is.*"

"Do you know who it is?"

"*No.*"

Heidi shook her head, she knew Olivia never lied. She had no reason not to trust her. She pressed her body up against the wall, slowly descending down the hall, her eyes sharpened and adjusted to the darkness. She hoped there was only one person, two at the most. She didn't want anyone seeing something and running away before she could get to them.

She took another few steps down the hall, her eyes staring straight ahead. She hadn't heard anything in the last few minutes and couldn't see anything moving. Maybe it was all in her head but then she had heard the way Olivia replied to her, the spirit was scared. Should she be afraid also? No, you are different from her remember, she told herself. Heidi nodded, yes different, she was stronger.

She stood in the hall for a few minutes while nothing else had made a sound. She should go back to bed, she was driving herself crazy. Heidi let out the breath she had been holding, yes, go back to bed. Keeping her eyes on the lounge room, she took a few steps backwards, slowly edging back to her room when her back pressed against something. She froze, it wasn't something, it was someone. How had they got behind her?

Spinning around, she turned to her invader, a man. Obviously a man, he was tall and muscular but she couldn't see his face or much else, for the veil of darkness hid him well. She bit her lip trying not to shriek, quickly taking a few steps backwards. Who was he? Another trick from Olivia? No, he was real, she had felt his body, completely solid and there was no coldness to the air to imply he was a spirit.

"Who are you?" she whispered, still backing away.

"Aren't you just the sweetest little thing," he whispered, his voice deep and with an accent she could not place. "Just like a little doll, what's your name girl?" she glared back at him, was he going to rape her?

"This is my house, I'll ask the questions," she hissed.

He smiled, she could see that through the dark. His lips pressed tight and lifting on either side. But he didn't answer her. While he remained silent, she gathered what anger she could ready to kill him. He would pay for entering her home. The man took a step back trying to scare her into answering him but that only made her angrier, feeding her power.

She ground her teeth then stepped back and with one big thrust through the air, she formed a fire ball and threw it past him. He gasped, ducking but something behind him caught the ball lighting the whole hall. The man snapped his head back to her, still shocked and she gasped. He was not a man! His eyes were silver and checks drawn, with his lips pulled back, she could see long fangs within his mouth.

A vampire! No it couldn't be, there wasn't such things as vampires. Were there? She paused, well if she believed in ghosts, demons, other world and dolls that came alive, why couldn't there be vampires? But, oh god, a real vampire in her home. What did he want? To snack, well he had come knocking at the wrong house for that, she had already shown him that she was no ordinary mortal.

The vampire stood up straight, trying to hide his surprise. Heidi dropped her head to one side studying him. He was fascinating, she was spellbound. But then there was the fact her fire ball still hovered in the air further down that hall, had he done that? No, there was someone else there. She could see hands imprinted on the ball, impossible. Her own hand was burning because of it, yet someone had caught it, or something.

She ground her teeth, the pain was getting worse and the vampire or other being weren't attempting to explain themselves. So bravely she spun around walking down the hall, she could feel the vampire following her. He flicked on the kitchen lights as she entered the room. Heidi didn't turn around, she walked over to the sink, leaning on the bench and holding her burnt hand under the running water.

She glanced over watching him. He had looked down the hall then continued out into the living area, alone. The fire ball down the hall had disappeared. He smiled at her not being shy with showing what he was. Heidi continued to stare at him emotionless, her hand was aching but she didn't show it. He was not what she expected a vampire to look like. His features were strong, his hair dark brown, eyes silver and skin pale but she knew those two had changed with the being he was. What did he want and who was down the hall? She turned away, trying to act like she wasn't threatened when maybe for the first time she was.

"That's pretty strong powers for a mortal," he commented, slowly walking into the kitchen, she glared at him.

"I'm no ordinary mortal."

"No kidding."

"Cut the chit chat, who are you and what do you want?" she snapped.

"My name is Gabriel and I am here to help you."

She shook her head, how many times had she heard that before? 'I'm here to help you.' Everyone thought they were there to help her yet no one actually did, she was fine by herself. If she needed the help, she had Xane, she needed no one else. Still she was a little curious to how he knew about her and what he did know. And of course she was curious about vampires but curiosities weren't going to distract her.

"Listen to him Heidi, trust him. He possesses the name of an angel. He could really want to help us."

"Well as you can see Gabriel, I'm quite capable of looking after myself," she whispered, still not turning to him, her hand now playing with the water.

"I saw. This is quite a place you have here. Anyone else live with you?"

"No."

"Okay, like you said I'll cut the chit chat. I was a mortal man a few years ago and was killed then revived as a vampire. I know all about the other world and Xane and my allegiance lies with those who fight against him. He is very evil and has come through this world to kill four mortal women, to kill you. I'm here to watch over you and make sure he doesn't succeed."

"Like I said, I don't need your help, my war is not with Xane it's with you, now leave."

"What?! What do you mean? Hasn't Xane destroyed your family, your life, your . . ."

"No, he salvaged it," she hissed, turning around to the vampire.

Gabriel looked over his shoulder as the second person from the first hall stepped out. A woman. She was beautiful with long flowing silver-violet hair and deep topaz blue eyes. She was tall and her skin pale, she wore a long purple velvet dress, with a laced bodice and sleeves that flared. Heidi wasn't sure but she would assume her to be a witch, she was unlike her vampire friend.

Gabriel smiled at his friend, the two of them staring at her, she already hated them. But they were immortals, she wasn't going to get rid of them easily then something else caught her eyes, another being, slipping from the second hall, another vampire. This vampire was female and also tall and beautiful. She had slightly darker skin for a vampire but the silver eyes and sharp fangs. Her hair was long and black; she wore a long sensual red dress.

Heidi gulped, why so many, what were they going to do with her? She knew Xane could be bad, that was one of the reason she loved him. Yes, he had caused mayhem in this world but from what she knew about his world, he answered to someone else. Shouldn't they be after that immortal? He was a misfit like her but what had he done to gain so many enemies in his own world and enemies she would perceive to be the bad ones. For although they said they were fighting against him, they were still immortals, vampires and witches, she would have assumed it was they who were bad. After all, they were the ones who had come uninvited into her home. She turned off the tap, moving around the bench to stand in the middle of the living area with them, facing three immortals.

"We are not leaving, we have come here for a purpose and will not leave until it is fulfilled," the witch spoke, in a beautiful melody.

"Do what you wish. I suppose I can't force you to leave, so here is the deal. You don't talk to me, don't preach to me and the first hall is all mine, you don't enter it. I will come to get food but will not acknowledge you and when Xane returns, he will kill you."

The three immortals smiled, they didn't have to look at one another to all be thinking the same thing. Yes, she hated them, especially the witch who seemed the more superior one. At times Xane had hurt her but he had also been there to care for her, he was all she had. She saw his mortality, his love and she was promised to him. She wasn't going to let these immortals ruin her new purpose in life.

"We can live with the terms of the house, as for Xane, he won't be returning. Not while I'm here, if you don't believe me try to call him on his wicked charm," the witch answered.

Heidi sneered, she snatched a wet cloth, wrapping it around her hand and storming away into her hall. The nerve of them, why wouldn't everyone just leave her alone! She slammed the door to her room, sliding down the other side of it. She was sure that the immortals had meant what they said and were staying. Would Xane really not return while they were there? Heidi took a deep breath, letting her body rest into the door, feeling Olivia's effects take over her.

"Xane please come back to me," she whispered, stroking the necklace, it had been three months. He couldn't be gone much longer. "Xane!" she hissed, watching the shadows in the room, nothing changed.

She sighed, letting her body really sink into the door, her hands flopping to the floor beside her. Tears welled in her eyes but she bit her lip, not letting them slide down her cheeks. What was going on? All this was becoming so confusing and right now she really did want to have Olivia's trick and fall asleep, to let her body stay while she retreated to safety. But she wanted to wait for Xane.

She closed her eyes finally giving in, her head falling to her shoulder. Hopefully Xane would come back soon. Otherwise, she had to deal with these immortals on her own. Maybe she would have to escape from them, who knew the extent of their power or what they really wanted with her. Of course they had said but the truth was always danced around, and she was left to lie in the pieces of pain.

"*They're right, he's not coming back. I know who they are and although they may look like they can't be trusted, they can. They know of a prophecy to defeat Xane. They know of others he has manipulated. Did you really think he would make you his queen and be yours for eternity? Eternity is a long time Heidi, and you're not an immortal. Trust them, they'll bring a shadow of innocence back to your life.*"

"Shut up Olivia!"

*   *   *

Something was wrong with her power. It jolted her, her whole body shook with the vibrations, the tears flowing freely with the pain. Every time she moved, she seemed to be electrocuted, fire flickered in her hands that she couldn't control it. The skin burning, she could barely walk, barely scream out for help, although did she want them outside to help her?

The immortals had been living in her cabin for a month, sometimes she thought they weren't there but ever time she looked down the hall, one would be standing there, staring right back. Most of the time she would growl and go back in her room, at least they had listened to her order. But then there were other times when she needed food or to jump across the hall into the bathroom. When she did go out in the kitchen there would normally be one of them out there, still watching. She hated it.

She called Xane every time she thought of him but of course he never came. It had been four months now, he had said it wouldn't take him that long. She was angry with him and with all the doubt Olivia was putting in her mind, she was going crazy waiting. When he did show up, she wouldn't be so forthcoming, so trusting for he had abandoned her and left her with immortals from his world. Did he know they were there, did he care? He had promised to protect her.

In the back of her mind, she could hear Olivia giggling and playing with something. How could the spirit always find a way to smile? This life was miserable, she was always in pain, always becoming weaker when she should be getting stronger. She saw no reason to smile. Couldn't Olivia tell she was in pain, couldn't she feel something was wrong? Her body was fiercely jolting, she could barely reach the door. Her power was attacking her.

Her hand fell on the doorknob and she gasped, it was hot, the fire had touched the metal first. What was going on? With a quick lift of her leg, she knocked the door open her body falling into the floor. She lifted her head looking through her hair out to the kitchen. Sure enough, someone had moved to the end of the hall. The male vampire, Gabriel if she remembered correctly. His eyes widened and he stepped right up to the line she had drawn but did not cross it.

Heidi took in a deep breath trying to get herself from the floor. The only thing that helped her in a time like this was to have a shower. But she probably couldn't make it alone, should she give in and call for his help? For once she did, she was in favor of them and had to listen to what they wanted, had to let them into her mind. She couldn't let Olivia be right.

She climbed to her feet, slowly stepping towards the bathroom, another burst of fire escaped her body, causing her to scream and collapse back to the floor. The vampire remained at the end of the hall but she could see his body fidgeting, he wanted to help. His order was strong and he wouldn't move unless it changed, no she couldn't give in. Not for a man's help, where was the witch? However when she glanced at him, he did look worried.

Heidi pulled her knees beneath her again, trying to stand but the shocks wouldn't stop and she fell back against the wall, crying. She couldn't move, all her energy had been sucked up by the power and when she ate, Olivia make her sick. She couldn't keep anything down, couldn't sleep, for at night, Olivia made the invisible visitors come. She hated Olivia! The spirit should be happy, Xane wasn't returning. Why was she still punishing her? Another jolt hit her body and for a few seconds she couldn't see, oh god. Her head was thrown back against the wall and she was sure she could feel blood on her brow.

"Help me," she whispered, her fingers digging into the carpet. Her teeth clenched, trying to hold in the scream she wanted to release.

"I didn't hear you," the vampire spoke. Was he lying to make her pay or did he really not hear her? Heidi glanced back down the hall, he was leaning forward his head turned to the side, face tight with concentration, he hadn't heard.

"Please help me!" she cried as the fire formed in her hands again.

Before the words had left her mouth, her body was flying through the air. Gabriel had come down the hall so fast, all she had seen was a blur. She was rushed in his arms to the bathroom. Where the taps were turned on and she was placed down in the bottom of the shower. The water was cold and at first it shocked her, she hated the cold but then it was relieving. The jolting and the pain slowly stopped and her hands didn't hurt so much, she dropped her head back against the glass, looking to the vampire.

He was sitting on the edge of the bath looking around the bathroom, not at her. Why wouldn't he look at her? She was clothed, sure her clothing was a white nighty like usual and it was now see-through but he was a man. Shouldn't that please him? Unless he hated her and she was just a job he had to make sure survived.

She turned away ashamed, everyone who knew her hated her and in the real world she didn't exist. She ran her fingers through her knotted hair, letting her eyes dart over the tiles. She could still feel his eyes on her but until he spoke, she would not turn to him. Would not let him see through her confusion to the young human girl she was. Resting her palms on the base of the shower, she let the water calm her hands, her powers subsiding.

"I don't hate you," he whispered, now looking at her.

Heidi glanced back to him, had he read her mind? "It's best not to lie to me."

"I'm not."

"Then you must pity me and that's worse."

"I don't pity you. I'm naturally sensitive and sad things pain me, I'm sorry that I hadn't come sooner before Xane had a tighter hold on you.

I'm sorry that all this is happening to you and you have no one there, but I do not pity."

She glared at him, of course he pitied her, being sorry for someone's life was pity. "You're a fool."

He shrugged, looking back down to his feet. Heidi turned away, this was stupid, she didn't want him in here. She would rather the witch but then the witch was scary, perhaps she and the other vampire left. Was this man all there was in the house with her? She didn't like that. Where was Olivia? Shouldn't she be in her head lecturing her about something, the spirit was never there when she actually wanted to ask a question.

"What's your story?" she asked, twisting her wrists and wriggling her fingers, her hands were fine. Not even a scar, it always happened that way, she would feel the pain but see no evidence. Her head slumped to the side relaxing in the water, her eyes moving to him.

"I was born in Italy in a struggling community so when I was old enough, I joined the army. I traveled some of the world with a good friend of mine but then quit due to what I had seen and started a chefs course. I studied for two years before coming to Australia, Melbourne and getting a job on the army base as a cook. That's were I worked and I bought a classic old home to live in, it was run down but mine so I loved it.

"A few years later my friend called me up and said he also had got out of the army and was coming to Australia to visit with his wife. My place was big enough for them to stay so I said they could and was excited to have the company. They arrived and I met his wife. She was a beautiful Italian girl, with long dark hair, perfect olive skin and the most miraculous green eyes you had ever seen." He paused, staring at the roof, a smile crossing his lips. Heidi couldn't help but smile too, she was a little shocked he was sharing but it distracted her. Besides it was only fair, he knew all about her.

"Anyway, my friend Brenton started working on the army base also and I got to spend a lot of time with her in the day. She was really quiet and delicate, kind of like you, mysteriously beautiful. Brenton didn't seem quite right and she was very hesitant around me, it was stressful but I couldn't tell them to leave. One night I heard them having sex but it wasn't mutual, he was practically raping her." Gabriel paused, taking in another deep breath and wiping his eyes as if tears fell from them which they did not.

"By this time I had fallen in love with her. She had warmed to me and I found out pieces of her life, which wasn't a wonderful one. But then I found out the most vital piece, she wasn't Brenton's wife, she was his little sister. He had lied and he had been abusing her for years."

Heidi gasped, she stood up in the shower, turning off the water then wrapping a towel around her body. She stepped over to the bath, sitting beside him. Gabriel remained silent as she got herself comfortable. He reached out placing his hand on her knee but she didn't object. He was just steadying her. She was no longer threatened by him. He smiled, brushing a bit of her hair back before resting his head back against the tiles.

"What was her name?" she asked, wanting him to continue.

"Angelica. She told me stories of the supernatural and more of her life, being hunted by a demon, Xane. I don't know whether to believe her but how could I not? She begged me not to tell Brenton what I knew, for he would kill her, I stupidly remained silent. One night I met a vampire friend she had met a year ago and that's when I believed. The vampire was Sahna. She is also here and was also a mortal once. You should ask her about her story. She is the one who has started this quest."

"I didn't know her name."

"You didn't ask Heidi, don't judge before you know someone. Everything was starting to be okay, sure Brenton still lied and tried to take her but I believed and I would do anything to stop it. I had met Xane with Sahna but only briefly, otherwise I didn't know much about him. One night I went downstairs to find Angelica leaning into a fire she had made. She burnt her arms and was hysterical, she was yelling at someone within the flames. She went to hospital and I told them what Brenton was doing to her.

"Brenton become a fugitive and I bought an apartment in the city with my insurance money, after the house had burnt down for me and Angelica. Xane had healed her in the hospital with the deal that she kill Sahna but she couldn't. Anyway we managed to be happy for a while, Sahna become our friend and visited often and I planned to marry Angelica. Then her brother found us and killed me." Gabriel stopped again. He looked faint, could a vampire faint?

"Sahna found me and created me. I was taken to their world to grow and learn to survive. All the while Angelica was left in Brenton's hands until she managed to kill him. I know my destiny is not to be with her but it doesn't stop me from loving her. I'm have married Sahna now but

Angelica will always be my first love. Angelica story has ended and so the prophecy continues, with you."

"Poor Angelica," Heidi sighed, thinking over his story.

"Yes, my poor Angel. That is why we are here, hunting for the next one on Xane's list, in hope to save them and to tell them that they could kill him. Your next Heidi and I know you don't want to hear it because you love him but he will kill you . . ."

"I know he told me."

"He did?" Gabriel was shocked.

"He told me he had to kill me and wouldn't if I gave him a child. He would take care of me for the rest of my life."

"He told you this, this is his plan? You know he's lying don't you? You don't know the Xane I know, you haven't seen what I have."

Heidi shrugged. "Maybe you don't know the Xane I know."

She stood from the bath, holding the towel tighter around her body and walked out into the hall. She hadn't said it in a mean way, just simply with a warning that they had two different ideas about the demon and that whatever he said to her would not be repeated. She respected him for telling her and Xane already knew the story, he didn't need to hear Gabriel's version. Besides she needed some secrets of her own.

When she glanced at the end of the hall, she caught the female vampire, Sahna. The woman lent against the wall, watching her walk back into the room, their eyes held until they were out of sight. Heidi shut the door behind her, falling onto her bed. All the power had exhausted her. She needed rest and needed to think. One day she might take Gabriel's advice and ask Sahna what her story was, then maybe she would go to the true immortal witch and ask her too.

But that time wasn't now, she had already let one of them get too close. But in a way it wasn't really a bad thing, she did like Gabriel. He was honest; he hadn't held her down or tried to save her. He had placed her where she wanted to be and let her heal herself, the way she knew how. He had earned her respect for that. She closed her eyes. If Xane didn't hurry up, she might accept the immortals in her home and then what would the demon do? After all, it was his fault they stayed there and his fault she was allowing herself to warm to them.

*   *   *

She had run out into the kitchen in the middle of the night so they wouldn't see her. She quickly grabbed some food then ran back to her room, slamming the door behind her. Gabriel and Sahna had gone out hunting but the witch remained, sitting in the lounge room and reading, listening. Gabriel had told her that the witches name was Xanthe, but she had yet to speak with her. It had been two day since she had spoken to Gabriel but she still didn't want them here or to talk to the women.

Since she had let Gabriel up the hall to help her, he came up whenever he wanted, normally on the mark of every three hours to check on her. He would just smile, sometimes bring food but nothing much was exchanged before he left again. Heidi didn't mind because he didn't try to force her to talk or do anything. She had got used to them in the house and Olivia had started to die down a bit.

Heidi leapt onto her bed, throwing the packets of chips on her blanket. One good thing about having the immortals, there was always food in the fridge and cupboards. And always things she wanted to eat, though she never thanked Xanthe for it. She knew it was the witch, what did the vampires want with mortal food? They probably forgot that people needed to eat. She hopped into her bed, opening a packet of chips, eating while she grabbed her cross stitch. It kept her hands busy and when Olivia begun to annoy her all she had to do was stab herself with the needle and the spirit would go away.

"What are they doing here?" a voice hissed in the corner.

Heidi darted her eyes to Xane, sitting cross legged on the chair in the corner. He had his hands clasped, his face stern and eyes dancing with flames. Heidi looked back to her cross stitch, what was he doing here? She hadn't seen him for months, he couldn't expect to return and everything go back to normal. He had promised to protect her but where was he when they had come? Where was he when she was lying in the hall screaming? Where was he when Olivia kept making her pass out, so she grew weaker and when she just needed him by her side?

"Where have you been?" she muttered, concentrating on her work.

"Have you spoken to them? How did they find you?" he questioned again, growing enraged.

"Where were you?" she asked again, ignoring that he had spoken.

"Heidi, don't play with me."

"Xane don't patronize me!" she hissed, darting her eyes to him, he calmed.

"I was stuck in my world, I had to sort out some business for when you arrive, sorry I didn't mean to be so long."

"Well while you were gone, they came. I couldn't get them out but they don't come near me."

"What do they want?"

"Just to warn me about how evil you are and that you have killed other women, I was next. Don't worry, I didn't listen to them. On the other hand I have been calling you for a few months now, especially when they arrived."

He sat back in the chair, thinking for a few minutes before he rose, walking over to her and kissing her nose. Heidi smiled but she was hesitant, he hadn't answered her and she couldn't trust him anymore. He leant against her back still in thought. She knew he would stay now that they were here. Only because he wanted to listen to them and play his games, not because of her protection, her love was slipping away.

"I suppose I could wait and see what they want before I charge in there and kill them." He muttered, lying back on the bed, patting it beside him.

Heidi lay down beside him, placing her cross stitch on the bedside table and kicking the chips to the floor. She stared at the roof lost in her own thoughts, her own worry, no, she couldn't trust him. But she would humor him so she wouldn't be hurt. Maybe it was time to listen to the immortals or maybe it was time to listen to her own soul. Don't rely on anyone else and trust her own feelings for once, make her own decisions.

"I suppose you could."

Xane smiled. "I love you kitten."

She grinned, dipping her head down and gazing up at him, there was no reply.

CHAPTER SIXTEEN

He opened his stance then hit as hard as he could knocking the man before him to the ground. He smiled to himself, pacing around the large, open, tiled dome. The sweat poured off his body, his toned muscles heaving with his shortness of breath. He had beaten James! He had to be ready once he had beaten his trainer. And finally, for he had trained without a break for nine months straight, he was ready to leave here, ready to continue with his destiny.

James climbed to his feet brushing himself off and laughing, he was impressed. Drake laughed too, shaking his head, still out of breath from the long fight and slightly amazed he had won. Lachlan, another fellow hunter brought them both a bottle of water, Drake sculled the whole thing. He had been very impressed with himself in the last few months. He had managed to stay away from drinking, smoking and anything that would disadvantage him in anyway.

He nodded his thanks to Lachlan. He had met the fair haired man shortly after arriving at the hunter's headquarters. It had been the man that had come looking for him in the Adelaide bar. Not a ghost like Daniel had thought but someone who moved through crowds without being noticed. A true hunter. The man smiled, moving back over to the side of the room where he was on the computer corresponding with England. Drake threw the bottle in the bin, walking over to the cream leather lounges and falling into one.

He was ready, he wanted to leave now. He needed to find Heidi. James and Lachlan hadn't told him much on Heidi's whereabouts or what she was like. He knew they were waiting until he was ready to see her. But now he was ready and he had wasted time here, he needed to find her, then find Xane and avenge his family. Every night he thought of them, not all the good times they had had but of their deaths. Their heads without their bodies and then the demons torment, it was tearing out his heart.

But he had brought the samurai sword used to kill them with him. The sword was his chosen weapon to master and he had. Every time he had first looked at the sword, all he could see was his family's blood along the blade. Now when he looked at it, he saw a weapon not a decoration, he saw strength and if he wished, he saw the demons body skewered upon the end. Yes, this sword was the one that would take the demon's life.

"You're good. I think you're ready to go soon," James muttered, falling in the lounge beside him.

"You don't sound confident. I've worked so hard for you. I know all myths of every immortal. Hell, I've lost thirty kilos for you."

"Yes, you know of all immortals, you don't know of the mortals, I haven't told you their history."

"You will tell me, on the way there. How much do I really need to know? I'm ready for this," Drake pleaded.

"You are as ready as you'll ever be. Come lets do more research, more training and within the month, we will be with Heidi," James declared.

Drake nodded; he stood from the lounge, glancing to Lachlan before moving through the open room to his bed room. He let his body fall down on the bed. One month and he would see Heidi again; it had been nearly two years since he had seen her. He still had no idea why they were connected but it was clear they were. He hoped that there would be a little time with her before the demon returned, before the war begun.

He smiled, he was fighting a war. How did a simple counselor get stuck in an immortal war? Nevertheless, he was happy to be doing it, happy to prevent anyone else getting hurt from this demon, anyone else losing their family. He was more than ready to return to the world a new man, physically stronger and mentally. He was ready to fight and more than that, he was ready to win.

* * *

She sat on the floor, rocking back and forth talking to herself. Well, really answering the voices she heard in her head. She sat against the kitchen bench, trying to keep as quiet as possible but she knew they were listening. They were always listening. The three immortals sat in the lounge room, exchanging knowing glances but she chose to ignore them.

Xanthe was lying across one of the lounges reading. Every time Heidi saw her she was either reading, writing or painting. The witch still had yet to try and talk to her and be on her side but maybe that was her game. Maybe she waited for the helpless to run to her. Well she was not helpless and wouldn't be running to a witch anytime soon. Although she did have to admit when she passed through the lounge room while Xanthe wasn't there, she would sneak a peek at one of her paintings. They were beautiful, gothic pictures which she found desirably alluring. She wouldn't let Xanthe know that in a hurry though if asked.

Gabriel and Sahna were huddled up on the lounge watching a movie, obviously a favorite mortal pastime of theirs. The two of them were venturing out of the cabin more, leaving her mostly with the witch, who never left. However Gabriel never failed to come into her room at night and tuck her into bed then read her stories, like she was a child. She would gather herself up in the blankets and glare at him but really she didn't mind that much.

Sahna was still distant but she would catch the female vampire staring at her from time to time. Frustration and anger written in her face, the vampire didn't like her. So she had never attempted a conversation with her, neither the witch. Though she could tell Xanthe didn't hate her, she was just patient, unlike her company.

All up she was finding herself spending most of her time alone, as she wanted it. Sometimes in the night Xane would come to her only ever in his cat form. He would snuggle and purr around her body as she slept, she was even pulling away from him. No one could be trusted, especially the supernatural. Everyone here claimed to want to help her but they all had their own secrets for doing so, secrets she didn't know. Although she was guaranteed to know their secrets when it resulted with her being left in pain and alone after their mission was over. After all, they were only there until they got what they wanted.

The singing in her head started again, a language she couldn't understand but she sung the words nevertheless. Olivia was keeping distant but still she played her tormenting games. She had even added in the supernatural so when they came up the hall. Heidi didn't know if it was them or one of Olivia's games. Really she no longer cared, they all annoyed her at times and could never be trusted. So she spoke little to them and never about what they wanted to know.

Heidi stopped singing, leaning back against the bench, her head dropping to her shoulder and eyes stared at the witch. Xanthe was the most powerful, she wanted to know the extent of her powers then she wanted to take them. As the thought passed her mind, the witch lifted her head from her book, catching her eye. Heidi smiled, she would not turn away first. She held the witch's eyes until laughter from Gabriel broke their gaze. Both snapped their heads to the vampires, Gabriel was laughing at his own comment.

Before Xanthe looked back at her, Heidi stood from the floor, walking down the hall. She hid just around the corner, peering back into the lounge room to see the witch look back at the bench. Her eyes darkened then snapped to where Heidi hid around the corner. She giggled, skipping down the hall and into her bedroom. The witch was fun to play with, she took everything so seriously.

If a man didn't come into the cabin by the time she was sixteen, she was leaving, leaving all of them. She couldn't put up with this boredom or these games. She wanted to be free and she felt trapped, the best thing would be to leave. But she would give it a chance, wait until she was sixteen and if there was no reason for her to stay, she would go. She only had a month to wait until her sixteenth birthday, until it would have been two years since she had met Xane and her life had really changed.

She jumped from the doorway to her bed, throwing the covers over her head. She giggled. Olivia's laughter was becoming contagious. With that thought came another burst of laughter within her head. She couldn't help but to laugh along. Two years since she had lost every aspect of herself and at sixteen, she was smart enough to take on her own life, cunning enough. Her whole body shook with an unknown excitement, one month and she was free, unless something better came along . . .

*   *   *

He felt like he was going to be sick, not from a sickness but from nerves. He sat in the passenger side of the car, staring out at the dirt road that led them through the woods. James drove which made him nervous because he wasn't confident this was the right way, maybe James had forgotten. For who would live this far out in the woods? Heidi, that's who would live out here, he should trust James. The older man knew where she was and where to go, he was just nervous.

They had been driving for two hours since leaving the hunters headquarters. Traffic through the city had slowed them down which made his nerves worse. What if she wasn't there anymore? What if she was dead, injured or they were too late and Xane had forced her to side with him?

He knew Melinda was probably dead, no reports had returned of seeing the girl since she had entered the house. James had said she was pregnant and that Heidi wasn't happy, although she wouldn't have killed her own sister, would she? No, she loved Melinda, no matter how selfish the girl was. The reason James though she was dead was because his spies hadn't heard any baby cries, hadn't seen the girl. But then they hadn't see Heidi since she had entered too but Heidi hid. Melinda was too social to hide.

Here he was, thinking too much again, he was going to drive himself crazy if he kept this up. James reached over patting his back, a silent gesture that everything was going to be okay. There was no reason to worry. But he was starting to think, he had crossed the demon more than the older men. When Xane was involved there was always room to worry. Still he obeyed and took in a few deep breaths. His eyes watching the trees roll past.

The tree line finally ended and they pulled out into a clearing. In the center of the clearing was a large cabin. Drake's eyes widened, surely she couldn't live there? No one could live there. The cabin was old and parts of the roof had been burnt. All the glass from the windows had been smashed and the front door looked like it was jammed. Grass grew to the window ledges and the shutters had fallen off. The place was trashed, but what had he expected? Really when he thought about it, it was this.

James turned off the ignition, the two of them sat still in the car watching the house. Was James shocked too? Was this how he had left it? Drake was starting to think that Heidi wasn't there anymore, that no one was. Before he could say it to James, he watched shadows move through the dark windows. James had seen it too; he could feel the man's body tighten beside his. Why were they worried? It was probably just Heidi, or not.

"Are you ready? Whoever is inside knows we're here so we might as well go in," he whispered. Drake nodded, knowing James had thought of the same thing.

The two men hopped out of the car, slowly moving around to the boot. James popped it, pulling out a cross bow. Drake was going to yell that they didn't need weapons but he knew the possibility that they did was high. He reached into the boot pulling out the weapon he had mastered, his samurai sword. He smiled; he had a secret admiration for the sleek Kantana sword. He loved the way it felt in his hands, the way it drove through the air without a sound. He liked the honor and integrity of the samurai faith. And most of all, it was destined to kill the demon.

Taking in a deep breath, he followed James to the front door, was he really ready for this? Was he ready to walk through this rundown door and face a destroyed cabin? How could someone possibly live there? Thinking too much again, just breathe he told himself. They reached the door and James glanced back over his shoulder, with a look that asked was he ready. Drake slowly nodded, he wasn't going to be anymore ready than he was now.

James took a step back and kicked open the front door to a dark musty cabin. The two men stepped in. Drake took a few minutes before his eyes could adjust to the darkness. When they did, he saw someone sitting on the couch to the right side of the room. He lifted his sword from his side as James aimed the cross bow, who was it? All he could see was that it was a woman and she was too tall to be Heidi.

The woman slowly walked into the center of the living room. Drake kept his guard up but James lowered his. What was wrong with him? He didn't know this woman wasn't a threat. Everything about her screamed that they should keep their guard up. The woman was beautiful, she was tall and slim, clothed in a long red dress. Her hair was black and long, her eyes silver and her lips painted in a deep red. The woman smiled but her eyes were focused on James, she had barely looked his way.

"Sahna! Wow, I thought you were dead but you're, you're so beautiful. Does Antony know . . . ?"

"No," the woman interrupted James, for the first time, she glanced at Drake and smiled revealing two fangs, a vampire. A real vampire! Did James know she was a vampire, did he know who she was? "I was saved from a certain death," she hissed, with a shrug of her shoulders.

"Becoming a vampire is not a new lease on life."

"Says he who hasn't lost his."

Drake leant over to James, trying to shake the shocked man from his frozen state. "She is a vampire, run her through and let's get on with it," he whispered

"It's not that simple Drake," James replied.

"Exactly, it's not that simple," the vampire repeated, how had she heard him?

"Fine, you sort out the vampire. I'm finding Heidi," he muttered. Though he was feeling less confident of finding her alive, the vampire had probably killed her or Heidi had run when she saw the creature.

Drake held his sword firm, walking down the hall directly in front of him, an eye turned to the vampire. Would she try and kill him? No, she glanced at him but her attention remained on James. Vampires were nothing like he expected them to be. She was beautiful and calm, not the vicious creature he had imagined. God, why did the bad have to look so good? Still she was an immortal so why wasn't James killing her? When he returned if James hadn't run her through then he would. There was no place for immortals in this world. No matter how attractive or human like they were.

He walked slowly down the hall keeping his ears sharp and peering into each room he passed. This cabin was a whole lot bigger on the inside than it looked. It would have been beautiful if it was taken care of but it wasn't. There was no glass in any windows and every mirror he passed had been smashed. Sheets and curtains were lying on the floor and in some rooms it looked like fires had once burnt. There were six rooms and one bathroom up the first hall, all bedrooms were empty.

Drake turned around starting back down to the lounge room, when he passed the bathroom and heard water running. He paused, listening to make sure what he heard was right. Yes, there was definitely water running in the bathroom. He stepped to the door, slightly opening it. The door was slammed straight away on his face. Drake threw his body against the door, swinging it open with all his strength. He practically fell into the room but managed to keep his sword out before his body. Someone screamed.

The shower was running with the door closed. Standing in front of the closed door was a male. Tall and muscular, a vampire, another enchanted being. He leant against the door guarding whoever was inside, whoever had shrieked. Drake raised his sword, although it would do no damage to a vampire, he would die fighting. The male vampire made no move to attack him. He sneered looking him up and down but wouldn't move from the shower door.

Behind the door Drake could hear sobbing and his heart ached with each one, he hadn't seen her but he knew it was Heidi. What were two vampires doing here with her? Were they minding her while Xane was away or were they snacking on her? Had they hurt her? He so badly wanted to see her but nothing showed through the mist. His attention snapped back to the vampire. The expression on the immortals face showed him he wasn't going to get what he wanted.

"Who are you?" the vampire growled, arching his arms out behind him.

"Who are you and what are you doing with her? Let me see her!" Drake hissed.

The vampire smirked. "Why should I while you point a sword her way?"

Drake paused, in a way he was right. If the vampire was there to protect her why would he let someone in with a sword? What was he saying? Of course a vampire wasn't there to protect her. They killed, fed and left this world. There was no soul to them and definitely no heart. The only reason he would be looking after her was if he was ordered to. Nevertheless, Drake lowered his sword. It wouldn't kill the demon anyway.

"Smart move."

Drake glared at the immortal, he hoped James had killed the one out in the lounge room and would join him with a stake. "Let me see her," he ordered again, the vampire shook his head, his eyes glowing.

"Answer me first. Who are you and what is your business here? How do you know what I am?" the vampire questioned. Drake raised his eyebrow, didn't everyone know a vampire when they saw one? Probably not. He should answer the being, it wouldn't hurt and he was desperate to get to the sobbing girl in the shower. To scoop her up in his arms and make her pain go away, saving her in a way was saving the memories of his family.

"My name is Drake Commack and I am a hunter as you may have guessed. I have come to save her so let me see her." He found himself begging but he couldn't help it. What else was there to do?

"I have her locked in here not to hide her but to stop her from killing you. I don't think you know her and she will kill you before you have a chance to speak," the vampire warned.

"I don't think you know who I am," Drake hissed.

The vampire shrugged stepping aside, his arms folding over his chest. Drake stepped up to the shower door, glancing back over his shoulder. He was afraid of being attacked from behind although the vampire had sat on the side of the bath and made no move for him. What did he want? Shaking his head, he slowly opened the door. A burst of mist escaped into his face before the piercing scream echoed around the room. His hands snapped to his ears, his vision blurring, was that normal?

When the screaming stopped, Drake darted his eyes into the shower cell, gasping. In the middle of the water stream stood the most beautiful girl he had ever seen. He almost couldn't believe it was her. Heidi glared at him with dull large brown eyes, her skin was pale and she was extremely thin. She hadn't changed much in height but had filled out in her hips and breasts. Her hair was so long that it reached the small of her back and started to curl as it passed her shoulders.

She was breathtakingly beautiful. He would never have expected that the cute girl he counseled two years ago would turn out like this. She was still wearing a nighty, too small for her and white, which he could see through but a nighty nevertheless. There was a light scar on her right check and bruises over her body. Drake took a step back. She looked at him with such hate. This wasn't how he expected to unite with her.

The vampire knocked his shoulder, which caused Drake to duck around to him. As he did, Heidi let out another scream sending a fire ball straight at him. Luckily, the vampire had alerted him but that posed more questions. Why was the vampire saving him? And more so, how had Heidi shot fire at him? After the fire left her hands, her screams grew louder and there was a thump. He looked around to see her on the shower floor, rocking and talking to herself, oblivious to them now. What the hell was going on?

Her hands were burning, he could tell that. Shooting fire at him hurt her as much as it would have hurt him. Drake hit the vampire away, standing up straight. He moved towards her when the vampire placed his hand on his shoulder. He shook his head, warning him away but how could he leave her? She was in pain; something very bad had happened to her, he hated himself for not being there.

"Olivia stop tormenting me! He is dead! Let me be!" she screamed, to no one or no one he knew of.

"Heidi it's me, I'm not dead!" he cried, when the vampire stepped in front of him.

"She can't hear us now. Go out, your friend calls for you."

He didn't want to leave but there wasn't much he could do here, he had lost his touch, he couldn't save her now. He lifted his sword pointing it at the vampire with warning before leaving the room. He headed back down the hall into the lounge room, entering the room he saw James sitting on the lounge across from the vampire. Was he talking to her? Why wasn't he killing her? Everything he had been taught over these last nine months had been thrown out the window. He couldn't understand anything now. Drake walked over to them impatiently falling next to his friend. Down the hall he could hear the water turn off and a door slam shut.

"Sahna I love you but . . . but you are one of them now," James sighed, glancing at Drake and nodding before turning his attention back to the female.

"I am still me James. You are playing into what Xane wanted. He wanted you to hunt me like you were him. Don't you see that? Besides we want the same thing. Our quest is to save the last girl from the demon, we have failed on the first three but together we could succeed." She spoke, her voice strong and flowing, almost hypnotizing.

"What is she talking about?" Drake asked, directing his questions at his friend, not the vampire.

"You remember Antony don't you? Well this is his younger cousin Sahna. Sahna was one of us five or more years ago. One day we were attacked and Xane took her, we though she had been killed but as Sahna has just explained, he tried to have her killed. She was saved by another immortal that kept her soul within her body as Xane's minions turned her into a vampire. I had no idea until now," he answered.

"As you said, she is one of them now," Drake commented.

The vampire glared at him. "Not so. You see, I have seen the world you seek to fight and there is a war there, two sides, two stories. There is the good and the bad. Xane is bad and has set out into this world to make trouble. We are here to stop him as you want to. You want to kill him but can't for you don't know how. We know how but can't due to the laws of our world but if we work together, he will be vanquished and we never have to have our worlds crossed again."

"We can't trust you," Drake spat.

"As we can't trust you but it's a sacrifice we have to make to save Heidi."

"Why do you want to save her?" Drake questioned again, he could feel James growing tense beside him.

"Because he wants to kill her, therefore there is a reason for that and we will do what we can to help. He has hunted three other women we have known deeply and succeeded."

Drake snapped his head to James. "Is this true? What do you think?"

"I think we can trust her and yes, she's right. First there was Claudia an English woman, who he made his lover. He then hunted and killed her. Then there was Angelica an Italian woman, who was also hunted and killed, I didn't know her as well. Then the third was . . ." James paused.

"Varela an American woman, Xane hated her and she felt mutual. They fought but he being immortal eventually won. And now there is Heidi. If we don't help her, he will kill her too, she's already hunted by him," Sahna finished off.

"Right. I didn't know the third woman," James commented.

Drake nodded, it was all too hard to consume but not unbelievable. He glanced back to the vampire and could see she was sincere. If she wasn't lying then she was no threat and the hunters could benefit working with them. Still there was something he was still puzzled about, how was the other vampire involved? And why was he the one looking after Heidi not the female?

"When we came here Heidi banned us from entering her hall, the first one. As you can see there is a line at the start, we obeyed for a while before she had one of her episodes and really needed help. Gabriel was the only one here at the time and she allowed him to go down there and help her. She hates him but at least he is the one close enough to help when needed. Another woman lives with us, a witch, but she and myself are not allowed in that hall. Heidi is complicated and it is stressful trying to help someone who doesn't want it, someone who is insane," Sahna replied to his unsaid question.

"How did Gabriel come into this?" James asked.

"Gabriel was also a mortal. He and Angelica were engaged before he was killed by Angelica's brother. I saved him, which meant making him like me but we strive for the same thing." She glanced back to Drake. "He has to be down there, as you saw she would have killed you if you went down there alone. The shower is the only thing that stops the fire and burning." She explained.

"Who is Olivia?" he asked, reminiscing his meeting again with Heidi.

"We don't know. She talks to her all the time but none of us can find any reference in Heidi's life to an Olivia. Xanthe said she sees two spirits within Heidi and that maybe the second was once a human, Olivia. All I know is they contradict one another and aren't that accepting of each other choices."

"Can I go see her again?"

"We will all go down there soon, wait until Xanthe returns so we can go together and sort out our plan."

"Sounds good," James commented.

Drake placed his sword down by his feet, James was right, it did sound good. He couldn't believe there were good immortals but he would have to assume there was. After all, there was good and bad mortals. Maybe the immortals and the mortals weren't so different and they all did want the same thing; Xane's death.

Even Xane's own kind wanted him dead. What had he done in his world? And how powerful was he so that he couldn't be killed? Hopefully their friend wouldn't be long and they could all go see Heidi together, they had all come here on their own paths of fate and when paths join together they become highways. Xane had better beware for this highway was headed straight for him and to his destruction.

* * *

Gabriel lay her down on the bed then pulled the blankets high over her body, trying to stop her from shaking. She couldn't stop, her body was in pain and starting to go into one of its fits again, Gabriel knew that. He had taken her for a shower when the jolting started but this time it hadn't worked. Olivia still managed to break through and torment her, she had seen Drake there. He looked very different from what she remembered but it was still him. Why must Olivia do that to her?

Gabriel laid out a fresh nighty and underwear for her before heading to the door. He opened it but closed it again turning back to her. He moved back to the bed sitting beside her and running his fingers through her hair. Heidi turned away from him, why wouldn't he just leave her alone? She didn't want to be comforted by him. She wanted Xane and he couldn't come until the other immortals were meters away or they would sense him.

"You were screaming out the name Drake again, who is he Heidi? You said he was dead," Gabriel whispered.

"Leave me vampire."

"I don't want to play games, please tell me? Is he dead or did he seem dead? I know you see things that aren't there but tonight, Drake was there. He is a hunter and has come to kill me and Sahna. Couldn't you see he was really there?" he whispered.

"Drake was my school counselor, he tried to help me and Xane killed his family then him for it," she spat.

"Please remember, was he actually killed?"

"The news said . . . said he was critically injured and then we never heard anymore. I assumed he had, then when Xane attacked Layla he admitted to killing Drake."

"He is alive. Xane must have thought he wouldn't survive but he did. Get changed and I'll go get him, okay?" he said, standing from the bed.

She didn't answer, she didn't really believe him but hadn't the energy to complain. Gabriel left the room while Heidi climbed out of the bed now that her head wasn't spinning so much. She threw off the towel she had wrapped herself in after her shower before pulling on her underwear and nighty. She brushed her hands through her hair then jumped back into her bed, pulling the blanket high around her.

Drake couldn't really be here, could he? No Xane had killed him. She had replayed the images in her head over and over again. Drake was dead. But what if Gabriel wasn't lying, what if the image she had nearly killed was Drake? What would she do? Be happy, angry or ashamed for how she lived and that she was responsible for Melinda's death? Would he try to counsel her or also be changed? The image of him had certainly changed, he was stronger, handsome and grounded, not the sensitive man she remembered. The man who could be walked on and who never said no. No, the man she had seen tonight was the opposite, it couldn't be him.

A few moments later and Gabriel returned followed by Sahna. Heidi glared at them, now the female vampire could enter her hall. When would she have her privacy? Walking in behind the two vampires was the witch then the man she had seen months ago with the doctor. James, the man out of prison, what was he doing here? She hated him and would kill him as soon as she regained her strength. But then stepping in behind James was Drake, solid and as he was in her image, he was alive.

Heidi smirked. "Well isn't this a pretty picture, immortals and mortals all together. Don't tell me the war is already over and I missed it," she hissed, with a teasing smile. Xanthe and Sahna rolled their eyes. Gabriel gave her a knowing smirk. James glared at her. He probably wanted to kill her too but Drake. Drake smiled the brightest smile she had seen in a long time.

"Heidi we have come to talk to you about all of this, we wanted to tell you the whole story," Xanthe whispered.

"You know I don't want to hear it so get out!" she hissed back.

Xanthe grabbed Sahna's hand starting for the door. "Have your way now but in the morning you will listen," the witch warned, leaving, Sahna and Gabriel behind her.

"Just as I remembered," James snickered.

"Same to you pathetic old man," she spat back at James, who left.

Drake stood staring at her from the doorway. Heidi leant back against the pillows, watching him walk around the room before coming to sit on the bed. His eyes continue to drift around the room. Heidi took in a deep breath. He was here and as Gabriel had said, alive. She wanted to hug him but held herself back, she didn't know what he wanted and couldn't give in to soon. After all, she hadn't seen him in years. He was just her ex-counselor. Why would he come across the country to find her?

He turned and looked her, she stared back waiting for him to buckle first but he wasn't. This wasn't the Drake she remembered. Finally she couldn't contain herself and leapt out of bed, wrapping her arms around him, he smiled. His fingers ran through her hair and he kissed the top of her head. She could feel his body shaking, he was crying. He was so happy she had hugged him, she felt like crying also. She missed him so much. He was the last thing real she had left in her life and she wasn't going to let it slip away now.

"Oh Heidi, I though you were dead, I missed you." He whispered.

"I thought the same," she replied not letting him go as he didn't, his hold was so tight it was starting to hurt.

"I want to help you, please let me in this time. And the people out there only want to help too. Will you come talk to us in the morning?"

"Anything you want."

He smiled. "Thank you, now get some sleep, you look so tired," he whispered pulling her away and kissing her cheek.

She nodded, snuggling back down into the blanket and watched as he left the room. She couldn't contain her excitement, he was here and he cared for her. A few minutes after he left, the room darkened and the window slid open. Heidi held her breath and here was her darkness to destroy it all. Through the window jumped the cat which morphed into the panther then Xane. The demon sat beside her, curling his body around her and kissing her nose.

"I honestly thought he was dead, the man is tougher than I thought, never mind I'll kill him soon."

Panic shot through her body. "No!"

Xane's hold tightened on her shoulder, his eyes bursting into flames as he turned her face to his. Oh god, he was angry, she couldn't let on she cared for Drake or he would die, again. Before she could create a lie, Xane snarled, backhanding her across the face. Heidi let her body fall forwards on the bed, her head spinning again. She hadn't seen that coming. Why did he have to hit her? And worst she couldn't get angry, she couldn't fight back without risking her sanity.

"What do you mean, no?" he snapped.

Heidi pulled his arms away from her forcing a smile, her mind ticking, where was Olivia when she needed an idea? "I mean you can't kill him. You said you needed a mortal for me to seduce so you could possess him. Drake's perfect, he's strong and fertile, you can control him easily," she hissed, stroking her fingers through Xane's hair. Trying not to quiver as she did so, don't show pain or weakness she told herself.

Xane stared at the wall thinking before he smiled, grabbing her face and kissing her. Heidi let out the breath she had been holding, good he had bought it, he had no suspicion how she felt. All he knew was that she wanted to be queen so bad she would screw over anyone she knew. Well he was wrong. She hadn't trusted him since he had left her with the immortals from his world and wouldn't come when she called. Of course, since then he was always around, it felt like he was using her to get to them. Drake was the best thing for her right now.

"I hate that man but I hate the hunter more. You're right my wicked queen, Drake will be our puppet. You're weak kitten, rest and I'll return later tonight." He kissed the tip of her nose again before disappearing.

Heidi's smile died. "I'm afraid I've become the puppet," she whispered sadly to herself, before letting her body fall back to the bed into Olivia's deadly slumber.

*   *   *

She couldn't tell how much time had gone by. Really she couldn't tell if it was night or day. In the dark bedroom she was locked and tormented by her stepfather. No one came to question where she was. No one came to pay respects to her mother and the baby. There was only her hidden away and her stepfather who tore her soul everyday.

Her stepfather would go to work through the day and at night he would return. It was normally the only time she was allowed out so she could go to the bathroom, prepare his dinner before he would drag her back upstairs and have his way with her. She didn't even have a moment to herself, a single second alone out in the house. And within this room she had all the time to herself, which was driving her insane.

Sometimes it seemed she would even hear voices in her head, they would warn her of the devil and of gods. They would tell her to anger her stepfather so he would kill her and this pain would be over and sometimes they would tell her to run. Of course all she could do was listen. There was no way to run from him, he made sure of that. It seemed like he was always watching and waiting for her try and run so he could pounce and beat her.

Olivia curled her legs under her body sitting below the window, she wished she could look out it and entertain herself, by watching the people go by but her stepfather had taped it up, probably afraid someone would see her. He had every right to be afraid for the day he did let down his guard, she would run away. She would tell the world what he had done to her and her mother.

Her stepfather had left an hour ago. She couldn't tell if it was to go drinking with the other hunters at night or to work in the day. Really, she didn't care, as long as he was out and she didn't have to look at him. But then sometimes being with herself was worse. She slept and talked to herself, neither keeping her alive any longer. Soon the voices would get their wish and she would be dead, with no one ever knowing the truth.

Downstairs she heard the door open and someone come into the house. She sighed, her stepfather again and that meant it was night time. Olivia moved from beneath the window, sliding herself under the bed. Her stepfather knew that was where she hid but at least she would never voluntarily let him have her. She lay straight, listening to the footfall walk up the stairs. They weren't as heavy as normal. Maybe it wasn't her stepfather.

If not him then who could it be? No one else entered the house. The footsteps walked into her old room, why would someone go in there? Unless . . . unless it was Adrian coming back for her. Olivia remained under the bed, listening to be sure, trying to listen for the steps that sounded barely a step. After a few minutes the footfall turned, coming to the bedroom door, there was a soft knock on it.

She gasped, her body freezing beneath the bed. The person on the other side of the door knocked again but she couldn't bring herself to move. She was hoping that it was Adrian, she had a feeling that it could be but what if it was not? What if it was someone searching for her? Another hunter maybe, who was trying to take her out into the woods so her father could kill her? Pretty soon he would be getting bored with her.

"Olivia!" Adrian's voice hissed, through the door.

"Adrian," she whispered herself, still unable to bring herself to move.

There was a scrapping sound on the other side of the door before a big bang and the door was snapped into two pieces. Surely he hadn't done that, she had kicked at the door for hours. A boy couldn't snap it as if it were a stick. She looked from beneath the bed watching Adrian's feet walk around the room, moving cupboards and chairs to find her. Slowly, she climbed from beneath the bed causing him to turn around and stare at her. He didn't look a day older.

"You never came back for me. You left me with him and he killed my mother and the baby, he keeps me in his bed. Why didn't you come back for me? You promised!" she cried, watching his eyes run up and down her body before he stepped forward embracing her.

"I'm sorry, I got caught up in the war but I'm back now. Quick we have to leave before he returns for you."

"Who is winning the war?" she whispered, tilting her head to the side.

"Nobody wins war, there is only lose, now quick. You look like you're on the brink of death. You haven't been eating his food have you?" Adrian asked, pulling her back and taking her hand, Olivia remained still.

"Did you not love me?" she cried, he was growing frustrated.

"Of course I love you."

"Why are you in such a hurry?"

"Because he will return soon, I want you safe," he lied. She could tell he was lying, his eyes wouldn't look at her. They darted all around the room, searching for something she couldn't see.

"What is the real reason!" she screamed.

"I am not who you think I am. I only have a short time within this body before I become . . ." he stopped. He had already told her too much but that still didn't mean she understood him.

"What!" she gasped.

Adrian sighed, walking over and sitting on the bed, he patted the bed for her to sit beside him. As she did he began to change, grow taller and stronger, grow into a man. He looked like the devil the voices in her head warned her about. The enchanting man with skin as white as hers and hair as dark as the moonless night. He had lied to her! She thought he was her friend but he was the devil, playing with her life, giving her gifts so that she would stay in the hands of the ones that destroyed her life.

Olivia screamed. She pushed against the devil's chest, knocking him back onto the bed. He fell only because he was surprised and then she ran out the open door. Her first chance to escape and she had taken it. She ran down the stairs and out the front door, onto the street. It was night and there wasn't anyone around but she wouldn't care if there was. She would have run no matter who tried to stop her. Within the house she could hear the devil calling her name but that only pushed her more.

She was so ashamed. She had fallen in love with the devil. He had tricked her and she believed his boy form, she deserved all the punishment god had for her. She kept running across the street and into the woods where she had seen the gypsy stand so many times, disappearing beyond the first tree line. Where had that gypsy witch gone? She hadn't seen her in months. Olivia ran away from the world and into the woods where the darkness would protect her. It would provide the cover for her safety and the distance that her soul needed from the world.

* * *

He walked silently down the hall, one hand steadying his body along the wall and the other clenching his sword. He had lived in the cabin for a week and still the sword never left his hand. For if it did, his guard would have been down and that left him open for the supernatural to attack. He still couldn't trust them. Of course James trusted them but how could he? He didn't know them before they were immortals. All his training had told him to kill them. Not listen to their story first and only kill then if they hadn't previously been a mortal.

He didn't hate them, no. They were pleasant enough and good, that he could tell. But he didn't trust them. He hadn't seen the monsters they could become. The vampires would disappear every night and swear they only fed off animals or criminals. How could he relax with real vampires around? And then there was the witch, well she never left. She would hide behind her papers and observe, waiting for the right time to let him know who she really was. She was mysterious and beautiful, he was greatly attracted to her but his morals were stronger than the muscle between his legs.

He glanced back over his shoulder. No one was following him or watching, good. He was sneaking down the first hall to Heidi's room. The female vampire had ordered that he or James not enter Heidi's room alone. He wasn't sure if she thought they were going to steal the girl or make her snap. But he couldn't stay away any longer. He desired wrapping his arms around her small body and holding her, making everything okay. He didn't need a vampire to tell him when he could see a girl he knew before they all did.

He walked to the door, pausing for a few moments to glance around himself, still no one there. Without another moment of hesitation, or moment for them to find him, he opened the door, slipping into the dark room and closing it behind him. He switched on the lamp beside the bed, his dark eyes drifting over to the girl sleeping wrapped beneath her blankets. He smiled, approaching her. She looked so peaceful, so angelic. Completely the opposite from who she was. Drake slid onto the bed next to her, careful not to disturb her as he lay his arm over her.

She didn't wake, so he held her tighter, one arm resting under his head so he could stare into her face. He couldn't understand how she must be feeling. To be trapped here with all of them. At least he had a rough idea of what was going on but she, she knew nothing. All this was about her yet no one had bothered to explain why. No one had just held her and told her it was going to be okay. No one had given her any other alternative but to trust Xane.

It saddened him that they didn't see her as he did. They didn't see the sad, sacred girl, who used powers to guard her heart. The ones out there hated her because she wouldn't cooperate with them but how could they expect that when they hadn't given her the same respect? They had waltzed in here and taken over, never asking how she felt. They never tried to plead with the human inside of her. He couldn't understand how they had handled all this but what he did know was they had made it worse.

Or did it all come back to Xane? For without the demon, the immortals would have never come for her. Even though her life was never going to be a luxury, it could have been better than this. And there was also the fact that she had powers, how had she got them? The immortals couldn't tell him and Heidi had no idea. She was in pain because of then, hateful and a vengeful little girl with powers one should not possess. Which left him with another question, just how mortal was Heidi?

Beneath his arm the girl started to shake from a dream. Her head arched up and her eyes darting within her eyelids. Drake watched in amazement as her hair flicked from black to snow blonde, then again. What was happening? But before he could call for help it stopped, snow blonde again and fast asleep. He stared at her in shock. She had looked so different with long black hair. Reaching out, he ran his fingers down the side of her face, she was still perfect. It was like she didn't even know it was happening to her, how strange.

Drake lent down to kiss her upon the head when the door was opened. He glared over at the witch, she had followed him. How dare they do this to them! The witch stepped into the room, glancing first to him then to Heidi, her eyes remaining on the girl. No sympathy in her face, what did she know that he didn't?

Well since she didn't offer the information, he wasn't going to request it. As long as he was concerned, they were his enemy. The witch glanced back to him, her eyes now darting to the sword he held her way. He hadn't even realized he had raised the sword but was impressed his body had reacted to his thoughts.

"Can't I even say goodnight?" he spat, his sword still drawn.

"Of course you can. I was just looking for you because I was hoping we could speak. There are a few things I want to explain to you. If we are all going to work together, we will do it right, don't you think?"

Drake lowered the sword, drifting his eyes to the sleeping girl. "I'll be with you in a minute."

"I'll be waiting for you on the front porch. Oh and Drake I want to speak with you only, don't bring your hunter friend, he is in too deep to listen." With her last comment, she shut the door.

Drake stared after her, what had she meant by that? He would have thought anyone of them would speak to James before him. But he would go to her. He was now curious what she wanted to speak with him about, especially if James couldn't come. He had the slightest feeling that she didn't like James. Sahna was the only one who did and he wasn't sure how they felt about him.

He kissed Heidi's cheek before standing from the bed, knocking the cupboard door open with his sword. Drake spun around to close it when something inside caught his eye. He pulled out a doll, a beautiful doll with long black hair and a white dress, he gasped. It looked like Heidi when her hair had turned black. Well similar anyway, black hair, large eyes but the dolls were violet, no, darker. They were the same color as the necklace Heidi wore, what did it mean?

He quickly placed the doll back on the shelf. In the morning he would ask Heidi where she got it from. And try to explain to her that he thought it could be her. How strange it was, it was Heidi but not, then who could it be? He shook his head moving from the room, his thoughts drifting to the witch. She was waiting for him and maybe she could explain all of this. Maybe he could plead with her to give Heidi a chance and for her not to let the others treat the girl the way they did.

He shut the door behind him, walking past his room, where he threw in his sword. His guard was down. He moved through the lounge room, glancing at James who was asleep over the kitchen bench, a book resting over his head. Drake smirked, walking past him and out the front door. He caught a glimpse of the vampires heading into the woods, hunting. They confused him, two vampires both once mortals now in love. Beautiful in a way but it didn't change the fact that they were demons.

He glanced around the porch, the witch wasn't there, this wasn't right. Maybe he should have brought his sword after all. Her beauty deceived his heart, he couldn't trust her. Drake spun around ready to go back inside and get his sword when two hands grabbed his shoulders. He was spun around with inhuman force, his back thrown up against the cabin wall.

But before he could fight off whoever was attacking him, lips pressed against his, her lips. Her hands gripping at his chest, he lost all control. His hands grabbed the back of her head holding her lips to his, holding her body against him. He wanted her and obviously she wanted him. How could he have let himself lust after a witch, how could he want to be one with one of them?

CHAPTER SEVENTEEN

She could hear them all arguing and of course it was about her, hate or love her, they couldn't decide. They spoke of names she didn't know, women who were somehow in reference to her. She hated when they spoke the way they did. Sahna and James honored someone called Claudia, Gabriel praised the woman named Angelica and Xanthe respected a woman named Varela.

Always the same names, always the same people to defend them but there was no one to speak highly of her. No, she was the one no one believed in, the one they were angered that had been brought into this. For she wasn't as gifted as the other women. Well she hated them, she hated the way they spoke like they knew everything. Hated that they wished she was more than she was. And hated that her life didn't feel real, it felt like she was just born for what they wanted.

Well she was never going to be what they wanted, so why didn't they just leave? The only one she could count on was Drake. He also didn't understand what they spoke about but nevertheless he loved her. He knew she was made for more and deserved to be here. Even though when she didn't believe him, she loved him for thinking it. Not even Xane would stick around long enough to tell her that her life wasn't wasted.

In the lounge room the voices started yelling, mortals and immortals challenging each other for the alpha role. A male's voice rose above the rest and yelled something before a door was slammed in her hall. Heidi jumped with the bang, it had to be Drake. Drake was the only one allowed to stay in her hall, all the others slept in the second hall. With Drake's final words the voices in the lounge room stopped. She didn't want to know what the argument was about this time.

Heidi stood from the corner of her room, her eyes darting to the window where the black cat sat. She glared at it before leaving the room. Quietly tip-toeing down the hallway to Drake's room, she knocked on the door. When he didn't answer, she opened the door, glancing in. Drake lay on his bed, his head turned into the pillow and his body still. Was he crying? No, she couldn't bear to think of him as sad. He had been so strong in the two months he had been here.

She entered the room approaching the bed and sliding down onto it. If he needed his space, she would leave but his body posed no rejection so she pulled the blankets up over them and lay with her back pressed against his side. When he needed to talk to her she was there and if he only needed her presence, she was still there. Drake rolled onto his side, laying his arm over her body.

"What was it about this time?"

"Same old over heated argument, nothing to worry about."

"It didn't sound like nothing to worry about."

"I'm not worried, are you?" he said with a smirk, although she couldn't see it, she knew he was.

"No. Can I sleep here tonight? The voices stop when I'm with you."

"Of course Heidi. You know I love you don't you? I will always be here for you."

"You're a hunter now and I'm . . . I'm the victim. Your work will take you away and as James says, soon I'll be dead."

"Don't listen to James."

"Why? He's right isn't he? Everything they scream about out there is real." She cried.

Drake sighed. "Look. There's that cat in the window again. I wonder who it belongs to," he answered changing the subject.

Heidi raised her eyes to the window where the cat sat, its curious eyes watching them. This time she sighed, she was never going to get away from Xane and his watching eyes. All she wanted was a few moments to be with Drake, a few moments to be sane before Olivia came again. She rolled away from the window, staring into Drake's eyes. She knew Xane was waiting for her to sleep with him but she couldn't. She couldn't do that to Drake, he believed her, he was the only one who did.

"I should go back to my room."

"I though you were going to sleep here tonight?" Drake protested.

She shook her head getting out of the bed when Drake grabbed her arm, holding her wrist, his eyes pleading for her to stay. She was just about to give in when the door was opened and the witch stepped in. Xanthe smiled at them and when Drake's eyes fell on the witch he let her go. Heidi took a few steps back, watching the two of them smile at one another. Watching the two of them fall in love.

She sneered, so that's was how it was going to be. She was Drake's focus until a real woman stepped into the picture and he let her go. She meant nothing to them. Heidi stormed out of the room, pushing past the beautiful witch. Really why would Drake want her when he could have Xanthe? Drake called goodnight to her and when she was in the hall, his door was shut. She hissed, disgusting, she hated them all. It was a mistake to go to him, to want to trust in him. She had been right the first time. No one was there for her.

She walked into her room, slamming the door behind her and falling to her bed. Would no one ever love her? Would she never grow from the child into a woman? If only Olivia would allow her the strength to run away then she would, even to die, to be free of them. Maybe they were right and her life was pointless, an insane little sixteen year old left to die nameless in a cabin, no one would care, really she would save them all the trouble of worrying about her.

*　　*　　*

She sat in the corner of her room laying the doll in her lap. Her hand darting from and over the doll's face, making blood tears appear then disappear. She could do it all by herself now, no help from Xane needed. She could make the clothes change then smash the doll and have it pieced back together, no more then an hour later. She liked playing with the doll for it kept Olivia quiet for a short while. Olivia was afraid of EnDarla.

It was very early in the morning, she hadn't even looked out the window yet to see if the sun had risen. Sahna and Gabriel were most likely still out hunting but she couldn't sleep, not with all the dreams of Olivia's life. Why did the spirit always want to torment her? In a way they needed each other and they needed each other to be sane so they could survive.

Heidi dropped the doll watching it shatter into tiny pieces, kicking them under the bed. When she would look later, it would surely be put back together. Nothing stayed broken around here, nothing but her. She had even lately been keeping her distance from Drake, he was to busy with Xanthe to notice anyway. The witch had consumed all of his thoughts and emotions, stealing the only thing stable she had left in her life. Oh how she hated that witch.

But what did it matter? In four months she would be seventeen and as a seventeen year old, she would be able to run away from them. She was getting older and stronger, not a silly child anymore. Olivia had stopped making her so weak, maybe the spirit wished for the same thing, for them to escape. And escaping is what she was going to do. She would run from Xane and his sick plans. Run from the supernatural who tried to control her, waiting for a better moment. Run from the demon hunters who had no place being with her or judging her, just run.

"*We need to eat Heidi.*" Olivia whispered now that the doll was out of her hands. Heidi twisted her head to one side, her eyes running up and down the door. Yes, she was a bit hungry. She was glad Olivia was there to remind her to eat because most of the time she forgot. She guessed they had formed somewhat of a friendship.

"Yes, I am hungry," she replied.

"*Eat and then let us go for a walk through the woods, they can't stop us from leaving.*"

She shook her head. "No they can't. Can't make us do anything."

"*Not at all. So come eat and we'll go for a peaceful walk,*" Olivia pleaded.

"Maybe there will be something to burn," Heidi said with a smile.

She heard Olivia sigh. "*Not unless we see the devil.*"

Heidi laughed, she didn't know why but she always laughed when Olivia referred Xane as the devil. There was no devil and Xane was not it. Taking the spirits advice she climbed to her feet, walking out of the room and down the long hall. When she passed Drake's room she paused, pressing her ear to the door. Silence, he and Xanthe were most likely curled up together. One day she would be a woman also and they would want her. No longer a child but beautiful and when she was, no one would have her.

She walked out into the kitchen, looking in the cupboards to see what she would like to eat. She felt like a full meal, with roast meat and vegetables, it made her stomach gurgle thinking about it. But she couldn't cook and wouldn't ask anyone to make it for her. She would have to settle for something out of a packet or a microwave meal. Heidi leant up on the shelves, pulling down a packet of chips when the shelf she was leaning on gave way and she fell, all the food falling with it.

Someone burst out in laughter behind her. Heidi whipped her head to the demon hunter as he tried to control himself. It must be so funny to him that she couldn't look after herself. That she sat on the floor surrounded by cans of food and a tea towel across her head. She glared at James, hitting the towel off and standing to her feet. She stormed around to the other side of the counter, slamming her body down in the chair, hopeless.

"You do have to admit you were quite a sight," he said with a chuckle, walking into the kitchen and fixing the shelf. "You want me to make you something to eat? You haven't been out here in a week you know?"

Heidi huffed looking away from him, she was so hungry though. And a week had passed, she had lost track of time, when she ate, when she slept. Every now and then she would see the calendar and know that her next birthday was growing close. After all, she hadn't even known she had turned sixteen until Drake had arrived on her birthday and told her afterwards. But how had eight months already passed with Drake here? It only seemed like a few weeks, she even lost track of how often she saw Xane, she was sure it was becoming less.

She glanced back to James, who was stacking the shelf again. Oh god, she was so hungry and maybe he could make her a nice meal. She hated him and could tell he hated her but under the eyes of the supernatural he wouldn't dare speak his mind. She knew because he was always the one starting the fights. He was the one that doubted her the most. The others did too but he was the first to voice it. If he doubted her so much, why was he still here?

"Can you cook?" she asked, dipping her head to one side when she caught his gaze.

James smiled, it was the first time she had truly seen him smile. "Young lady, I can cook better than any restaurant in Melbourne," he joked.

She didn't smile, she hated him too much to relax and be amused. The smile snapped off his face and he stood from the floor leaning over the bench top, centimeters from her face. He stared into her eyes, holding her gaze, trying to intimated her but he wouldn't win. After a few moments, he turned away shaking his head, he moved over to the stove turning it on and waiting. She would make him speak first.

"What do you want then?" he spat, turning his back to her.

Heidi smiled, she had won. "A roast."

"A roast! It's five in the morning! How about a bacon and egg roll?" he exclaimed.

"No, I want a roast."

James spun around to her glaring for a few seconds before his face softened. "How about I make you bacon and eggs now then a roast dinner tonight, deal?"

"Whatever."

He shook his head, spinning back around to the hot pan. She was a little disappointed because she wanted a roast now and Olivia might not let her eat tonight. But she was tired and if she angered him too much he would walk away, leaving her with no hot food in her stomach. She lay down on the bench top, listening to a burst of laughter coming from Drake's room. She wanted to shoot a fire ball right through the wall now but she didn't, what would be the point?

The front door opened behind her, she glanced over her shoulder to see Sahna and Gabriel stroll in. Sahna lifted her eyebrow to James before continuing down the second hall, the sun would be rising soon. Gabriel paused in the living room, winking at James then smiling at her. Heidi turned away from him. Were they both congratulating James, did they think he had got through to her? No, she just wanted food and she would play nice until she got it.

"Do you want barbeque sauce on your roll?" James asked.

Heidi glanced up at the man, nodding before laying her head back on the bench. She was suddenly so tired, the smell of the food exhausting her body. James pushed a plate next to her. She sat up starting to eat the food, savoring every taste and the delicious warm feeling sliding down her throat. He was right about something, he was a good cook. James pushed a glass of orange juice in front of her, watching her eagerly drink it down. He smiled, leaning back against the sink.

"You know I was so excited to meet you. I thought that you would be stronger than the woman I loved but you're completely the opposite." He commented, waiting for a reply. Heidi slowed her eating, crossing her eyebrows together but not answering. She knew he was disappointed in her, they all were. She was kind of curious to whom the woman he loved was but she wouldn't ask.

"You're crazy, unreliable, selfish, oblivious, darkened, unsociable and not willing to listen or learn. I hate you! Because you are the way you are. Claudia has died in vein, they all have. Three beautiful innocent women have died and you are the one that has lived, it's not fair. Three souls hunted and destroyed, lives too sad to tell. I don't know why Xane hasn't done to you what he did to them. I don't know why you aren't paying for everything you have done. You don't deserve the help here or these people in your life, to be honest, you don't deserve life."

She pushed the empty plate away, glaring at him. She knew he felt this way but never thought he would have the guts to say it to her. But it was good in a way, it meant he had angered her just enough to kill him. And she would kill him now. She didn't know who this Claudia or the other woman was but it sounded like they deserved what they got. Although she did know of Angelica and she didn't deserve death. Maybe she deserved the same fate too but that was not for him to decide.

"Tell me how you really feel James!" She mocked, twisted her head to the other side, her hands clutched by her sides, they were already hurting.

"I hate you, I want you dead. So no one else wastes their time trying to help someone who doesn't want to be helped. You are the reason this demon will never die, people like you keep the gateway open for them to come through!" he hissed. He had walked across the kitchen, grabbing her by the shoulders and practically spitting his words into her face.

Heidi gave him the most evil smile she could but inside her heart fell. He was right. She knew he was right, everyone knew he was but what could she do about it? It didn't hurt any less hearing someone else say it and her emotions couldn't be controlled with Olivia crying in her mind. She could nearly make her cry but she wouldn't. No, show no weakness. No matter how right he was or how she felt, she wouldn't let him have the last laugh.

"So kill me James, or I will you," she hissed, sitting up on the stool and leaning her lips to his ear, she felt his body tighten. Why would he do that? She moved back staring into his eyes and caught the fear flash through his. Or was it something else?

He took a deep breath then grabbed her cheeks slamming his lips to hers, she glared at him. Her hands were burning, she pushed them to his chest making him gasp and pull away. Heidi smiled, crossing one leg over the other and twisting her hand through the air, little flickers of flames dancing on her palm. It hurt but soon he would leave her and she could cry in peace, cry with Olivia. Why was Olivia crying so hard anyway?

James suddenly smiled, taking a few steps away from her. "In that case, I've already won," he said with a sneer.

Heidi snapped her head to him, closing her palm and dropping it by her side. The flames disappeared from her hand but their flicker continued in her heart. What did he mean by that? Was he really going to try and kill her right now? Well, go ahead. When he tried she would be ready. She stood from the stool, sneering back at him and striding across the room. James leant against the doorframe to the second hall, smiling.

"*Heidi sit! Don't move, please, he is killing you!*" Olivia screamed.

"He hasn't killed me yet," Heidi hissed, causing James to cross his eyebrows together.

"*He has poisoned you. You're dying. This world has stronger poisons than those of mine. Why did you think he made you the food so willingly?*" the spirit cried.

Heidi froze, oh god, Olivia couldn't be right, could she? She darted her eyes back to James who was again smiling, yes, he had killed her. He had said he had but she misread his words, he had won. She couldn't let a demon hunter win but her body was buzzing, distracting her from her plan to kill him. Her heart was beating so fast that it could have burst but then it slowed, nearly stopping. Her body shook and her head felt light, what had he done to her?

Her knees buckled beneath her body and she fell to the floor. Sweat was pouring from her and she still tried to move to James, who was chuckling but she couldn't gain the strength. The bastard had killed her? Someone who prided themselves on being a good soul only hunting the bad had killed a mortal! But she should be happy, shouldn't she? After all, she did deserve this and she was bad with powers, she deserved to be hunted by him. She mightn't even be all that mortal. Her body heaved and she started to cough, blood.

"*Call for help! If it's the last thing we can do, is to call for help!*"

Olivia was right. Heidi drew in all the strength she had left and screamed her piercing scream. James suddenly looked panicked, he started to move across the room, when doors down the halls were thrown open. Heidi watched as Gabriel and Sahna ran from the second hall, their eyes fearful. Gabriel ran to her side, pulling her into his arms but she barely felt his hands on her body. Sahna started screaming, why was she so afraid? The vampire ran across the room to James, grabbing him around the neck and lifting his body from the floor.

"You fool! You have ruined everything, she had better survive James or I'll tear you apart myself!" she screamed.

"I did you all a favor, she is not one of them. She needs to die so we all can move on and forget!" James cried back truly fearful.

"You fool! You don't know the prophecy! We need her alive. Of course we're all disappointed with who she is compared to the strength we have seen but we still need her alive. Without her we can't kill Xane!"

"Sahna now is not the time, quick help me! She's fading away! Xanthe!" Gabriel yelled.

Heidi let her body fall into his arms, her eyes closing. She knew it! Knew they all hated her but she hadn't known why they had been using her. It was all about Xane; what had Sahna said? She could kill Xane; that was the only reason she was still alive, because they needed her. Did no one care about her? Did no one want her to be here and love her for her? No, not even Drake was here when she needed him.

Around her there was more yelling and more voices, she could hear Drake and Xanthe. She could hear crying and more screams. She felt her body rising into the air and being rushed somewhere but she no longer cared. She wanted to die now, stop the pain, stop the voices and her pitiful life. She wanted it all to end and she didn't care whether Xane lived, he wasn't the demon they all made him to be anyway.

Speaking of Xane where was he? When she was dying, he had promised that no one would hurt her. If she died so did his dream for having a child but then maybe it was for the best. After all she did deserve it. It was for the best. Everyone could go back to their lives and forget about her. She wouldn't have to live here knowing no one really cared for her, they were all using her. Heidi let her body disappear into a world she was glad to leave behind. She let her mind fade into darkness, into hell.

* * *

She was so beautiful, with her long silvery hair and bright violet eyes. She was filled with goodness and he felt enlightened when she was within his arms. Yes, he loved her, truly loved her. But hence the problem, she was a witch from another world and he was the mortal hunter from this one. There was no place for their love within this world but he couldn't tell his heart that. It beat faster as she lay in his arms, reading scripts he couldn't understand, her silence making her all the more alluring.

They lay on his bed relaxing in the early morning. He wasn't sure what time it was although it was still dark. He had woken no more than fifteen minutes ago and doubted Xanthe had even gone to sleep. The witch did need to sleep but not as much as mortals, on average she had four hours a night. While he needed much more, especially when he was stressed and he had been really stressed lately.

All he could think about was the girl down the hall and his feelings for her. Also Xanthe was on his mind all the time and occasionally his past family. He would never completely forget about them but they didn't make him feel the way he did now. Never had he felt such love, he had found new love with the witch and he really loved her, maybe more than he had Serena. But he beat himself up for falling for her. How could he already feel love again when his wife had only died two and half year ago? But he couldn't stop loving Xanthe, and then there was James who was stressing him the most.

Lecturing him about getting too close to Heidi, so he had pulled away and the snow blonde girl had stopped talking to him. James also disapproved of his relationship with the immortals. For he was closer to them than he had been any hunter, they accepted him and it felt like they were all connected. He was growing impatient with James, who in the last few days had been disappearing a lot.

Drake sighed, he couldn't understand why James was hesitant around the immortals. Couldn't he see they were like them? They all wanted the same thing, Xane dead. Besides Xanthe was the only true immortal, Sahna and Gabriel were both mortal once. Hell, Sahna even was a hunter along side of James years ago. James just couldn't handle not being in control and when he cried to the headquarters in England they told him to hold his tongue.

It was funny how a few months ago it was he that was hesitant and the hunter almost forcing him to be friends with them. Now that he was, it was wrong. How could someone change their mind so much? Whatever reasons James had for his behavior he didn't share, so Drake had followed what his heart and head said. He befriended the immortals, he believed their words of vengeance.

He had always seen James as the leader, which he was over the majority of the hunters. Aside from one other man, he was named Antony and he lived in the headquarters in England. He was the hunter's rightful leader. But Antony didn't want to be acknowledged as one so James had taken his place. He could decide whatever they would do until Antony would speak against him and James would cower.

Drake could tell James hated not having full control but it was probably for the best. Who knew what he would do if all the control lay within him? The man in England seemed more stable and more involved. Drake couldn't wait until he could meet him. Still he shouldn't be paying with the weight of everyone's stress.

Drake rolled onto his back, placing his hands behind his head and staring at the ceiling. In the kitchen he could hear someone cooking, they must have been hungry to be eating this early. He thought he heard people talking out there, he smiled. Yes, this was his family and he felt more fulfilled being here with them than he had anywhere else. They had all been brought here out of pain and together they grew stronger for the war ahead.

"Stop stressing Drake," Xanthe whispered, rolling up her parchment and placing it onto the floor.

"Can I ask you something?"

Xanthe raised her eyebrow. "Sure."

"Well if there is two vampires here how come they never try to attack us, never become wild."

Xanthe smiled. "Sahna and Gabriel train very hard not to want human blood but they can't stay away from it. The problem is because they do have a soul they feel the pain of their victims, they feel like killers. So they only attack those who they justify as deserving. As for others in this home, you and James have enlightened senses which turn them off and Heidi doesn't smell like a mortal. Don't get me wrong, they put on a good act but their needs are growing stronger. Like I said, this isn't for you to worry about; they won't hurt you or James. Worry is your curse, you know?"

"I can't help it, you know I worry. We haven't got forever and I'm having trouble getting through to her. She won't believe me when I say she's capable of far more," he answered.

Xanthe's face darkened. "I was talking about James, why must every conversation return to Heidi?"

Drake sighed. "Sorry, I don't know what it is about her that I can't seem to get her out of my head. I love you Xanthe."

Xanthe laughed. "I know you do Drake and I love you. I understand the spell cast on you by the girl but I find it hard to accept it when she is so unwilling to listen."

"She's just different. You can't expect everything to go the way you planned. You never know, she knows more about Xane than any of us and if he pushes her the wrong way, she'll turn and it will be all over."

Xanthe smirked. "It's not quite that simple but you're right, everyone is there own person, and this wasn't going to be easy."

"Nothing is easy."

Xanthe sat up on the bed, leaning over him smiling. Yes, he loved her more than she might be willing to know. The only problem was, when this was all over she would probably go back to her world and he would be left in the mortal world. But he couldn't think of that now, they had to save Heidi first and after decide their future.

He smiled, looking into the eyes of the witch and without any further hesitation, he grabbing the back of her head pulling her lips to his. Her body shifted over his as she kissed him passionately. While she kissed him, he undid the back of her dress, holding her naked body on him while she undressed him.

She was always so eager when it came to their lovemaking, he didn't even have time to pleasure her before she put him within her. Rocking back and forth on his hips, her face flushed and heated with ecstasy. He knew she loved him, but he sometimes wanted more then love, he wanted her in full, he wanted her spirit. Drake hunched up gripping the body on top of him, his climax again. She always brought him there too fast but at least he achieved it for her too. Xanthe rolled off his body laughing, her arms sliding across his chest, both catching their breaths.

"I love you Drake."

He was just about to reply when there was a piercing scream out in the lounge room. His body snapped up on the bed, his heart beating faster. Heidi. Something had happened out there, or she had killed someone. Oh no, he had to get out there. He leapt from the bed searching for his pants when Xanthe caught his arm, shaking her head.

"Gabriel will handle it, Drake. She is not always your responsibility. Now come back to bed, please," she pleaded.

He sighed, sliding into the bed beside her, his pants and shirt clutch in his hand. She moved over on the bed, resting her head on his shoulder and her hand stroking his chest but he barely felt her. All he could do was listen through the wall into the lounge room, listening to the thunder of footsteps then more screams, Heidi's? No, Sahna was screaming and then yelling at James and Gabriel. What the hell was going on out there?

This time both he and Xanthe snapped up in the bed when the witch's name was called. For a few seconds it seemed like his heart had stopped beating. Drake leapt from the bed, pulling on his pants and throwing his shirt to the ground. All Xanthe had to do was wave her finger over her body and she was fully clothed. The two of them ran from the room out into the living area, where they froze at the doorway.

James stood against the wall beside the door fighting Sahna, who was keeping him on his toes. The vampire was screaming at him, her teeth inches from his throat, she was crying while James looked dumbfounded. In the center of the floor was Gabriel who had fallen to his knees, his hands clutching Heidi. Drake gulped, running into the room Xanthe on his heels. Heidi lay in Gabriel's arms convulsing, blood streaming from her mouth and her eyes flickering only showing the whites.

Xanthe gasped, falling beside Gabriel, her hands on Heidi's arms. Drake felt like he was going to be sick, what had happened out here? Had James done this to her? "It's all over! We will never save them now, never save our world!" Gabriel screamed at Xanthe.

The witch rested her hand on his shoulder, tears filling her eyes. "She is different remember and she possesses Xane's power, she is strong. Drake, take her into the bathroom and throw her in the shower fill her mouth with water and try to make her throw up without drowning her. We will take care of the hunter," she ordered.

Drake didn't need to be told twice, he swung Heidi into his arms turning to the first hall when James started yelling at him. "Drake leave with me now, they are demons! Look how easily they have turned. Come with me Drake, you have got too personal. They will be rid of you soon. These are the creatures we kill!"

Drake spun around glancing at the three immortals descending on the hunter but he couldn't care. He was one of the immortals, not a hunter. At least he didn't kill innocent mortals, he would never hurt Heidi. Without humoring the older man with an answer, he continued running up the hall and into the bathroom. He started the shower, placing Heidi in the bottom of it. He hopped in behind her, holding her face in the water and breathing into her mouth when she lost all air.

He was struggling to keep her alive, he had been sitting on the shower floor for a few minutes now and she still hadn't thrown up. Her lips were becoming blue and her skin more pale then he had seen it. He tore off her blood stained nighty trying to give her more air but nothing was working. She couldn't die! He couldn't believe James had done this to her. What had he given her?

Tears were falling from his eyes as he held her dead weight against him. After a few minutes, Gabriel ran into the bathroom turning the taps on stronger and hopping in the shower. He counted to three and the two of them lifted Heidi up so that her face was against the shower head. Gabriel counted to three and they brought her down, Drake breathing into her mouth, bringing up a little water but nothing that brought her back. They counted again, taking her up and then down to breath, it was exhausting but he wouldn't give up.

When they held her up for the seventh time, Drake was starting to feel dizzy, his eyes darting around the room. He could see the sun coming up through the window and soon Gabriel would have to retreat. And then there was that cat sitting on the bathroom floor, that cat was always walking around here, mostly in Heidi's room. He wondered who it belonged to? They brought her down and he breathed into her mouth, finally a gasp of air was taken further and her body hunched over.

"Throw her onto her stomach!" Gabriel yelled.

Drake did just that, he threw her over on his lap pulling her hair from her back. Without warning Gabriel hit her back, she started to cough and be sick as Xanthe had instructed. He glanced back to the vampire, he was breathing heavily. Gabriel winked at him before stepping out of the shower. His shin was starting to burn and decay off his body and he looked like he could pass out. The sun was getting higher. Gabriel stripped off his wet clothes and ran from the room, hiding in the darkened second hall where Sahna was hopefully already safe.

Heidi coughed again, still trying to gasp for air. Drake spun her around, holding her on his lap, his arms wrapping around her. She was struggling to breathe but she seemed fine, well she would be fine. Drake kissed her head, holding her arms tightly. He was trying so hard not to admire her in this state. Trying hard not to adore her soft perfect skin or to look at her breasts and think how sexy she was in her white panties. He couldn't think of any of those things. His love for her was pure not sexual, but she was so beautiful.

He looked away, feeling her body breathing against his bare chest, she was alive. He felt like bursting into tears, he was so happy but at the same time so angry. He probably might kill James if he saw him again. How dare he try to kill her but how had he done it? Heidi hated James and there was no way he would have got close enough to do anything. Something in the room moved and Drake glanced up to Xanthe leaning against the doorframe, she smiled.

"She's okay, I think" he whispered, placing another kiss on Heidi's head.

Xanthe nodded. "Good, James has gone and he is not allowed to return, we will deal with the hunters later. He said he snuck drugs into her food, so if she's back now, she should stay here."

Drugs! God what was that man thinking? They nearly killed her and where did he get the drugs from? But instead of yelling what was on his mind he calmed, smiling back at his lover. "Good. Can you get me a towel, what should I do with her?"

"Let's get her into bed."

Xanthe grabbed a towel, coming into the room and helping him wrap it around Heidi. Drake carried her to her room, laying her on the bed still wrapped in the towel. He lay down beside her, holding her tight and watching her chest rise with its breaths. He was scared to leave her and wanted to be there when she woke. She must have been so scared, thinking no one was there for her. Knowing how they all felt and dying in front of them. He kissed her soft cheek, pulling the blanket over her body.

"She will be alright Drake," Xanthe whispered, from the door way.

"I want to stay and be sure, I love her." he whispered.

Xanthe sighed. "Don't confuse love with lust Drake. There is a strong difference and you must never want her. The minute your love changes for her, you have left yourself open for Xane and torture. You can't be with her."

"I don't love her the way I love you."

The witch slowly nodded but she didn't believe him. Drake looked back to Heidi holding her hand tighter. He saw the black cat jump on the bed curling by his foot. Did it know something was wrong with her? Drake glanced back at Xanthe who was watching him intently. She had no reason to be worried, he would never love Heidi the way he loved her. Heidi was a child and he knew what had happened to her, he couldn't do the same thing, he just cared so very, very much for her.

"Where do you suppose this cat has come from?" he asked, changing the subject.

Xanthe crossed her eyebrows together. "What cat?"

"The black one on the bed, it's always following Heidi around the house and every time I come in here it's on the window. It looks healthy, can't be a stray but it has no collar."

"There is no cat Drake," Xanthe slowly, whispered worried.

"Can't you see it? It's right on the bed next to Heidi . . ."

Before he had finished his sentence, Xanthe ran into the room waving her hand around Heidi, the cat jumped under her arm and out the window. The witch froze, glancing at Heidi then to him. "That's not a cat. That was Xane. He has been here all along, he has heard us. We have been waiting to protect her from him and here he is in her head. We have to leave!"

"What, I can't leave her!" he said shaking. The cat had disappeared, not jumped anywhere just vanished, they were in trouble.

"We won't. She'll rest here and be fine. Come with me and we'll get the car ready then take her away from here. Quick Drake, trust me."

"I do."

He leant over kissing Heidi's head before jumping from the bed and running out the door, they would leave at dusk. He had to get everything ready, had to help Xanthe hide her scrolls. He was unsure why but he had to do it. It would be okay if they left with her, everything would work out fine but right now they had to go.

Xane had been here all along, who knows what he had done to her, what he had said. And now this, she had nearly been killed, tears fell from his eyes. He had come here to save her and got distracted. Now the demon had its claws in her soul, there was no going back.

*   *   *

They had left her alone, her body was still heaving and she could barely concentrate on anything but at least she was alone. She could feel that she was going to die, nothing felt right within her but she wouldn't go without her revenge. He had tried to kill her! He thought he was better than her and for that, before she left this world, she would make him pay. Her eyes snapped open and she looked around the hazy room, but her weary eyes wouldn't stop her. Nothing was going to stop her.

She waited a few minutes to make sure no one would return before pulling herself out of bed. She was only in a towel and her underwear but she didn't care, clothes were not important now. Heidi climbed on her bed, trying to steady her shaky legs as she opened the small window. Using all her energy, she pulled her body through the window, blocking out the pain and the feeling that she might die on the spot.

She fell to the ground, her towel getting stuck in the hinges but she didn't dwell on it. She climbed from the ground, feeling dizzy but breaking into a run to focus the thoughts of death from her mind. She ran down the path she had over two years ago when she was running from the cabin after Layla's death. She turned the direction of the doctor's cabin, not really knowing why, but it made sense. If James had gone anywhere, it would have been to Doctor Dylan's. He was still close enough to keep an eye on them, to know if she died, but far enough that the immortals didn't care.

She did hope that the doctor wasn't there, she didn't want to kill him right now but if he was to witness James' death, then he had to go too. Heidi smiled to herself, yes, it was perfect. She would strike fear in his heart before he dies and once he had left this earth then she would let herself go. James wouldn't know that he had succeeded and she would leave satisfied, perfect.

She hurried through the woodlands, slowing as she stepped into the clearing of the doctor's cabin. Her smile grew wider, the doctor's car was not in the clearing. It would mean she didn't have to kill him. Heidi stepped out into the clearing, slowly approaching the door and knocking on it. It was only a few seconds before James opened it, staring at her in shock. His eyes lingering on her body before he spun around grabbing a long black jacket from the back of a chair and throwing it at her.

"Thought you'd be on your way in the ground by now," he commented, leaning against the doorframe, his eyes unmoving from her. Was that fear she saw in them?

Heidi grinned. "Assumptions are a curse. Besides you should know me well enough that I wouldn't go before you did," she hissed.

James smiled. "I should have expected nothing else but you to turn up on my door step with my death wish."

Heidi glared at him, pulling the jacket on and doing it up, she took her eyes off him but knew he wasn't going anywhere. She didn't have to be beside him to kill him. When she looked back to him, her focus disappeared for a few seconds but she hid it well. James had his head bowed, staring at the ground, her eyes glanced to his hand trembling against the doorframe. His fear and sadness wouldn't change her mind, he had tried to kill her and for that he would die.

"Since I'm in half a good mood you may decide how you're going to die."

"You can do whatever you please just hear me out first. I didn't want to kill you but you must understand I have no choice. You're the thing keeping the demon within this world and I have seen so many lives destroyed because of him. I half wanted to kill you because you weren't who I wanted to help and because the demon loves you. I would be paying him back for what he has taken from me. I wanted to stop Drake from getting in so deep. I was trying to save you both. It was selfish and I'm sorry."

Heidi glared at him, she didn't care what he had to say, nothing would change the fact that he tried to kill her. She clenched her hand by her side, harboring all her anger then drawing it out. She wouldn't shoot a simple fire ball at him. She would burn him from the inside out. She would kill him the way she had the men that attacked her in the night. She took a few steps back, still glaring at him, watching as his throat tightened and his hand rested on his head.

"Wait! I have one request from you. One question, please give me the dignity of answering it before you take my life."

Heidi sighed, dropping her head to one side and placing her hands on her hips. He didn't deserve one last request but she was curious what he would ask for. "What do you want to know?" she spat.

"Why have you sided with Xane? What has he offered you that would make you destroy the world that you were born to?" he asked, releasing the breath he had been holding. What kind of question was that? She wanted to scream but she sighed, twisting her head to the other side, tapping one foot upon the ground.

"Fine, I'll humor you. You're going to die anyway. I am drawn to his power, which he gave me and because he was the only one who cared for me. Who loved me when no one else did. And you're wrong, I'm not his to control, I am there for there is no better offer. He offers me more power, to be queen of his world and once there I will be an immortal. What you don't understand is I hate this world, it has done me no favors."

"I don't know Xane as a generous man. Why would he do this for you, what does he want in return?"

She swung her head again, flicking her tongue on the roof of her mouth and darting her eyes up and down his body. "I answered your question, now . . . well you know what comes next."

"Wait. Just humor me one more time, please. You have to give him something in return, what?" he pleaded, stepping from the house. Heidi smiled. Okay, she would tell him and relish the shock in his face as he died.

"He wants a child and if I give him one, I'll be rewarded with everything I want," she said grinning.

But James didn't give her the reaction she was craving. He crossed his eyebrow together, tightening his lips before stepping down onto the grass, circling her. Heidi remained still, she would not be intimidated by him. She crossed her arms over her chest, staring straight ahead as he came to stand before her again, staring. Why wasn't he shocked? Why wasn't he so scared that something like that could happen? She wanted him to be afraid so she could return to the cabin and die herself, satisfied. No one would kill her without paying for it. It wasn't fair, he spoilt all her fun.

"Why would he want that? Why can't he have that anytime?"

"He can't physically have me, so I have to become close with a mortal man and he will take over his body and plant his seed and . . ."

"That's not true." James crossed his brow again, shaking his head. He was standing right in front of her now. This wasn't going according to plan. "That's why you're keeping Drake there, you need Drake! This is not right, he's tricking you. He doesn't need Drake."

"And how would you know?"

"Because he already conceived two children from a mortal woman five years ago. Two daughters and you know what he did after they were born? Killed them, tormented her then killed her. The only reason he needs Drake is to kill him in the process and torment you or new rules have been put in play after he killed his first two children. After all, who knows how many children he has."

"You lie!" she hissed.

"Fine, I'm lying. One, I have no reason to because you'll kill me anyway and two, you're a fool, you need to see the truth."

"Don't kill him Heidi, he's one of the good guys."

"Maybe he wants a son." She continued her conversation ignoring Olivia's silent pleas. He is a hunter! She screamed back within her mind. Wasn't it you who told me all hunters of any sort are evil?

"*Kill him!*"

"Or maybe you're not so different from the other women and he wants you dead. Maybe you're just a game to him and more fun because he doesn't have to chase you. He probably laughs every time you turn your back because you love him. Really Heidi, as if he would make you his queen, as if a mortal could rule over immortals. You have played exactly into his hands. At least the other women had some fight . . . oh, oh fuck! No, you can't kill me now! Don't you see I'm the only one who knows! Nooo!"

Heidi stepped back grinning but this time her heart did not feel it. James fell to the ground at her feet. Burning from the inside out, although she was not satisfied. She should have never told him her plans. Never let him speak for he had ruined her mood and now she would die unsatisfied. Even with James screaming and gargling at her feet, his arms raised to her, she did not feel better. The old stupid man was right.

And as much as she didn't want to believe that Xane already had children, he had lived for thousands of years. What made her think that she was anything special? Heidi growled, throwing down her hand and releasing her power from James, he was dead but hadn't completely disappeared. She didn't care. Leave him for the doctor to find or the intruders in her house as a warning. But still she hadn't enjoyed it, he had ruined everything. Xane had two daughter's, everything he had told her was a lie. She couldn't trust anyone.

She turned, running from the cabin, running back to the only place that had been a home to her, so she could die. James was dead and she had thought that it would fulfill her in some way before she died. But it didn't, it made her curious, afraid and angered, she was going to die without knowing the truth. No one had told her the truth all her life and now she was trapped within a demons hold when all he had done was play with her. She was so angry but to let him see that he would kill her and she wouldn't be able to find out what her life had really been about. Hell, she was dying now!

She hurried through the woods back to Layla's cabin and around to her window. A smile resting on her lips, it was funny she still thought of this as Layla's cabin nearly two years after her death. Well it was and always will be.

Out the front of the house she heard the witch arguing with Drake but that was good. It was a distraction so she could drop the trench coat and climb back through the window. She dragged her body over to the bedroom door, peering out to make sure no one was coming before collapsing into the bed. Yes, now it was time to die, she was unfulfilled but she always would be, she needed to die, this world did not deserve her.

She lay straight on the bed, closing her eyes when Xane appeared beside her in his human form. She didn't have to open her eyes to know it was him. She turned her head away from him, waiting for him to make some lie as to why he wasn't there when she was nearly killed, there for her when she was dying or there now. Of course he remained silent, playing his games, much like herself. How could she have ever liked him?

"*Because you are like him, you deserve one another!*" Olivia cried, bitterly and afraid. Was the spirit upset she had killed James? She had ordered her to do so or was she afraid Xane may be her weakness again? Well not anymore, she didn't need anyone, besides it would all be over soon.

"How are you feeling?" he asked.

Heidi snapped her eyes open, screwing up her nose. "How do you think I am? I'm dying all because of you!" she spat.

"Heidi I didn't . . ."

"Don't! You lie, you always lie. This is what you want. For me to die and you wipe your hands of the responsibility. I hate you! Now at least leave me alone to die in peace."

"We had a plan, what has changed your mind?"

"I had a plan! You had another and now everything is ruined."

Xane crossed his eyebrows together; he sat on the bed beside her his hands running down her arms. "I love you, our plan hasn't changed . . ."

"You already have children Xane! You had two daughters and you killed them! You slept with the mother yourself and then killed her!"

He froze, at first he looked angry because she knew, which only told her she was right. Then he looked to the ground saddened. His hand still held her wrist but she removed it from her mind, lying back down on the bed, she was growing weak and soon she would die. At least she could die without him getting what he wanted, without him winning. Xane sighed, looking back at her, leaning down and kissing her upon the nose. Heidi remained still, she was no fool.

"I don't know who told you this but they're not completely right. Yes I had two daughters to a mortal woman. I loved them but my destiny was always to kill her. Our daughters were not well, being from mortal and immortal they were dying and I took them to my world in hope to save them, I couldn't. Their mother was a bitch, you have to understand that she had death coming her way.

When others from my world, mainly Xanthe, found out about my desire for a family she had the gods bring in new rulings which prevented me from bedding with a mortal. I love you and still have the same desires but this time I know my children would not die, you are strong and possess powers which provides them with a stronger chance. And although I can't bed with you, I can do it through someone else. For every rule my world places, I can find a way to defy it."

"Did you love her?"

"No."

"Lying," she declared, closing her eyes.

Xane sighed. "Yes, at first I loved her a little, I have loved all three souls I have killed in one way or another but by the end I hate them. I love none of them like I love you. You can't understand how I feel about you," he pleaded.

Heidi looked away from him, she wanted to believe him. His story was convincing but she was tired of him. Tired of lies, other worlds, witches, demons, she was tired. Besides she was dying, what did all this matter anyway? She would never give him a child, never become queen and really she didn't want to. She wanted to go back to the day she met him and kill herself before any of this happened. She wanted this life to never have happened, people would never had to be in pain due to her. She wanted to die with some peace, for the first time in her life she wanted peace.

"I do love you Heidi," he whispered.

"I hate you. I hate everyone and everything, take back your doll and whatever else you have given me then get out of my life," she hissed.

"Heidi I . . ."

"Can't you see I'm dying Xane? Fuck off and leave me alone!"

The demon bowed his head, taking in a deep breath. He stood from the bed moving to the cupboard, glancing in at the doll but leaving it. He lent over on the bed, kissing the tip of her nose and straightening the hair around her face. She closed her eyes, dropping her head to one side, feeling her heart start to slow. Xane sat on the other side of her, holding her hand, his other stroking her face.

Every few minutes he would lean down and kiss her again, whispering loving things in her ear but she was drifting from him. Drifting into the darkness, she felt his kiss one last time and disappear. She was dead. And he had stayed with her until she had died, he did love her.

*   *   *

She opened her eyes, glancing through a doorway in a stone kingdom. Heidi crossed her eyebrows together, where was she? She had expected in death to be trapped in her world, not another. Taking in a deep breath, she turned around surprised to see nothing but darkness. Angrily she spun back to the stone doorway, her head tilting to one side as she peered through.

Inside the stone encased room she saw a beautiful child playing, the girl had long black hair and cream skin. When she took a step into the doorway, the child turned to her, bright blue eyes staring straight into her soul. Who was she? The girl smiled, waving her over to the collection of dolls at her feet. Heidi shook her head. She didn't know who she was or where she was. She wouldn't go play with a six year old girl.

"Come play!" the girl called, stepping towards her.

Then out of nowhere ran another child, a smaller girl, probably four. They were obviously sisters though the younger one had dark eyes and waving brown hair. The second girl ran to her sister and they laughed, falling onto the ground. It was beautiful, two sisters who loved one another yet to be faced with the hardship of the world. Heidi smiled, she wanted to step into the room and be lathered in their love but she didn't belong here. This was not her family and it was never her and Melinda.

The older girl squealed, getting up and running around the room, the younger girl chasing her. They ran around one another before the eldest tripped over one of the dolls smashing her head into the wall, Heidi gasped. The girl started crying as did the younger one who disappeared. Disappeared! How had the girl disappeared? She had a feeling she wasn't in her world anymore. The eldest one quickly calmed and snapped to her feet, her sister reappeared, they embraced.

Heidi ducked around the corner, she wasn't sure whether she should be still watching but she couldn't turn away. There was something about the girls that was so familiar. The two sat down once more playing with the beautiful dolls, much like her doll. Heidi took in a deep breath, she could feel her senses growing lighter, could feel her body drifting through death. She took one last look in the room, letting her eyes drift past the girls to something sliding across the far wall, a being.

A man, dark and demon like, perched in the corner of the room watching the children play. Jagged teeth shone within the moonlight as did its red eyes. Heidi gasped, it couldn't be him could it? Why would Xane be here? She wanted to run into the room and throw her body across the girls but her feet wouldn't allow her to move. Her vision blurred and the room before her disappeared, replaced by the ocean of her world.

Heidi spun around herself, where had she been? In another world of her mind or had her spirit drifted elsewhere? She stopped, turning when she saw EnDarla standing against the waters edge, her long black hair flying out behind her and her violet eyes staring at the two peaks. Heidi stepped by her side, taking her gaze.

"I died!" she whispered.

EnDarla smiled. "It is a good thing; death can be a blessing rather than a curse."

"I was left unsatisfied. I wanted to be a queen, wanted to be loved and now I want a child, a daughter."

"Why are you telling me this?"

"Because I wanted Xane's child and I thought since you were from the same world you should know. You should stop him from making that deal with others when he can't commit. But I was told he already had two daughters and he killed them. Now he has let me die, what was the point of my life?

EnDarla smirked, shaking her head and laughing on the inside. Heidi raised her eyebrow. What did this woman want with her anyway? "I'm in a calm mood today so I'll make you a deal."

"I'm listening."

"How much do you want a child?"

"A lot now, after I saw those two beautiful children playing, powerful children, I want one. I want someone to love me and share my secrets with."

EnDarla stared at her for a few moments her face expressionless; she was about to yell, about to lecture her with something before she smiled. "So go back, you're not dead yet or this world wouldn't exist. Go back and fulfill your life. I challenge you to try and be queen of my world, I challenge you to birth a princess. If you shall succeed the child must be raised within my kingdom and worship me. Do we have a deal?"

"I know nothing about you."

"That's all the fun of it, isn't it?"

Heidi shrugged, looking from EnDarla to the peaks. "What's in it for you?"

"Children are rare in my world given that we are mostly immortal. To have a child worship you brings more power than that of an adult. I want what I always have—power and I'll allow you to fight for your pathetic mortal life at the chance I might have more."

"But . . ."

"Go before I change my mind."

* * *

Drake had grabbed all the blankets he needed and already had the car running outside. Xanthe was waiting in the driver's seat while he ran back inside to get the sick girl from the room. Sahna and Gabriel had run out into the woods, searching for Xane, keeping the demon distracted while he and Xanthe got Heidi out of there.

Gabriel knew of an empty apartment in Melbourne city where they could run too. James had left and maybe he was right and Drake had become one of them. But Drake didn't want to be a hunter if it meant being so black and white. If it meant not saving the innocent soul inside a being, regardless of whom they might seem.

He ran down the hall to the lonely bedroom where Heidi lay, pale and barely breathing. In fact he didn't think she was breathing. Drake ran into the room, pulling the small body into his arms. Definitely not breathing, she was dead! No! They had saved her, how could she be dead again? He dropped her back on the bed, leaning her head back, he pressed his lips to hers, breathing. Trying to bring life back to her body, pumping her chest then breathing, nothing seemed to work.

Xanthe was waiting in the car and she was a witch, she could save Heidi. Quickly Drake wrapped the blanket around Heidi's body, throwing her over his shoulder and running from the room. There was no time to grab any of her things, besides he didn't want any of the tainted stuff to come with them. He ran out of the house, throwing Heidi in the back seat of the car.

"What happened? She is supposed to be getting better!" Xanthe exclaimed.

"I know. I don't know what happened! I ran into the room and she was like this!" he cried, running his hands through his hair.

"Never mind, we will heal her again, get in the back and start CPR, I'll drive."

Drake did as he was told, hopping into the back with Heidi. He pulled the girls head onto his lap and pressed his lips to hers, breathing for her again, trying to restart her heart. It seemed like hours he was trying when really it was a few minutes, but that was long enough before Heidi took a deep breath. Her eyes wide with fear and her body arching back as she swung her arms around trying to find where she was.

"Shhh Heidi, its okay, your with us now, your okay," he whispered, pulling her up against his chest and kissing her cheek.

"I don't want to be back here. Why did you save me?" she cried.

He didn't know how to answer her, she was still gasping for air and her eyes darting around like crazy. Oh god, he hoped she was okay, she had already died twice today they didn't need to go for a third time. Why did she want to die? Had she done it to herself the second time, did she want it that bad?

Drake leant down and pressed his lips to her cheek when Heidi turned her head and pressed her lips to his. She moved her lips over his, her hands reaching up to his face. She dragged her nails down the side, stinging him. He gasped, pulling away, but she didn't seem to notice, she fainted in his arms, alive but empty. Drake snapped his eyes to the rearview mirror, catching Xanthe's dart away. He hadn't kissed her, she had kissed him but he had liked it.

"Xanthe I didn't . . ."

"I know. It doesn't matter anyway. She is alive and that is what's important," she replied.

"About what went on in there, I don't wish anything upon her but why are you all so desperate that she is alive?"

Xanthe was silent for a few moments, her eyes focused on the road as they drove through the woods, heading to the city. "I haven't told you everything. You know how I briefly told you the story of three other girls Xane has hunted? Well there's more to it then just being randomly picked. He hunts these four souls through every life, finds them normally around sixteen, tortures them and will kill them before they are twenty. Every life it's the same, some less personal than others. Sometimes he kills them as infants should he find them, but either way they never live past twenty.

"This has been the curse since the time of the patron gods, since the pharaohs and way before Christ. We don't know how the curse started but I have an idea. Anyway it's always the four women and this time, he has made himself known in the mortal world more than any other. He has become personal and another first, he had got one of the women pregnant, he is stronger and they are stronger. He has been detected by hunters and killed endlessly. Normally it is only the destined souls he kills but in the last few years, it has been anyone. He doesn't care anymore.

"He is getting sloppy but more ruthless. When Sahna was killed she was naturally angered and sort to find some way to kill him. She discovered the prophecy and now we know how to kill him. You see, the only time theses four women have walked the earth at the same time was when their souls were first created, until now."

"I don't see what this has to do with Heidi," he commented, listening as hard as he could and trying to understand.

Xanthe smiled at him through the rearview mirror. "The prophecy states that shall the four souls walk the earth at the same time they have the power to kill him. They have to come to our world and be blessed under our laws and then with the sword of Helios, their souls will work as one and they can kill him.

"The sword of Helios was created by the forefather god Apollo and within its blade is a poison for the gods, their demons. Immortals have tried to use it against the gods but so far the sword's poison has remained rumored. Yet, no mortal has tried the blade, no mortal with powers from the ancient gods. That is what the four souls are. So should the legend be true, the four souls have that power within their souls to use the blade against Xane."

"That maybe so, why are you telling me this when there is nothing we can do to make this happen?"

"What do you mean?"

"They may have finally all walked the earth at the same time but the other three women are dead."

"Oh yes, that's the other thing. They're not dead. We only told James that because he would try and break them out. He has no idea what is at stake here or what we are finally so close to doing. The hunters think they're dead and so does Xane. We locked them in a place together, far away, where Xane couldn't detect them. He can't feel them and assumes they're dead but we need the last one, and then we can take them to our world and stop the war. For their souls and for the followers of Helios in our world."

Drake paused, could she be telling him the truth? Were there really women out there who had been through the same thing as Heidi? And for one to bare his children? Is that what he had tried with his girl? "Are we taking Heidi to them now?"

"No, not yet she's not old enough."

"Old enough? What do you mean?"

"They're in prison."

"Prison? Is that the safe place and what happened for them to get in prison?"

"It's a long story. But that's the only place Xane can't detect them and they can't leave or run away. They don't know of the prophecy or each other. Except Varela, I think. Their lives were leading them there anyway. We just gave them a little push for their protection."

"What? And I suppose you want Heidi in there with them? Do you know what happens in prisons? I counseled people from prisons! I don't see how . . ."

"Drake, you haven't been there, it was the only way and yes Heidi has to get there. We have to wait until she's eighteen for it's a high security prison. Remember Drake she has probably already done worse than the three in there."

A high security prison! He wanted to yell again in objection but sealed his lips. Xanthe didn't need to take blame for this. It was all Xane's fault this was happening. But at least if he followed their plans, the demon would one day be killed. He had to let fate guide them. After all, should Heidi be surrounded by other people she would have already been to prison and there would be no hope of getting her out, this way she could be saved. Yes, he had to go along with their plans, he had to save her.

"Okay, I understand, I'll do anything I can to help you and your world," he whispered, he didn't completely agree but there was nothing else to do.

Xanthe smiled. "Thank you Drake, I don't deserve you."

Drake smiled back. "No I don't deserve you. I love you."

"I love you too, and Drake, Heidi will be okay through all this, I promise."

CHAPTER EIGHTEEN

"Truth or dare?"

She sat on the gravel of her world, flicking her fingers through the oil ocean. Although her world had never become normal again she had found some peace within its darkness. Her eyes rose to Xane who sat on the shore beside her. It was the second time he had revealed to her that he could go to her world, the first when he had saved her after she was pulled into the fire by Olivia. Olivia, where was the spirit?

He smiled down at her, his eyes darkened but not out of hatred. He was watching her, always watching, but today she didn't mind. This world was her escape and she had some control over what happened here. Perhaps Xane did too for the minute he had appeared, EnDarla had vanished.

Heidi dropped her head to the side stretching her arms back and sighing. All the while Xane smiled at her, waiting for her answer. What was it she would choose today? The silly little game had somewhat bound her, by no laws just by her morals and the enchantment it held. Truth or dare—to act or react?

"Truth," she answered. She would always chose to act over speak, especially the truth. However today she was somewhat distracted and calm, she chose truth to see the surprise in his eyes.

He smiled, knowing what she would choose. "Tell me where they have taken you."

"Melbourne, to an apartment in the city. Only Xanthe and Drake are with me."

He grinned slowly nodding his head. "Perfect."

Heidi dropped her head to the other side, biting her lower lip. Now it was his turn before the smile could slide from his lips she spoke. "Truth or dare?"

His smile grew wider. "Truth." Damn it, she had hoped for dare.

"Will you kill me?"

He snapped his head back. It was probably the last thing he had expected to come from her lips. Really, she hadn't even thought about what she would ask. She just had closed her eyes and let the first question float through her mind. Although, she would like to know the answer. If he had killed the other girls he had followed and if he had been sent to kill her would he one day follow through with that?

"Yes."

She knew that he would answer honestly, she just hadn't known if she was ready to hear it. However as the word passed his lips she found no surprise in it. He had told her months ago that it was his mission to kill her, that fate would forbid him to do nothing else. Even when he had retracted his words she had known that it would happen, known the immortal stories. Kill her he might have to but she would not let him, not yet.

"Truth or dare?" he quickly asked, darting his eyes away so she couldn't read him.

"Dare"

He smiled, she was becoming predictable to him, never would she open her soul and say truth for the truth of her own mind was too much to face. "I dare you to try and kill them."

She remained looking away, choosing not to show him any emotion but she could feel his eyes upon her. One day she probably would try and kill them, just not any time soon. Slowly she looked back into his fiery eyes and nodded causing the biggest smile to slide across his lips. But it was no longer he she was thinking about, it was the last time she was here. With EnDarla, the challenge her doll had set. Another goal formed in her mind as she leant forward, pressing her nose against Xane's and sliding into his arms.

"Truth or dare Xane?"

He laughed. "Okay dare."

"The plan we created together, your promise?"

"Yes?"

"Keep it."

As his brows crossed in confusion she smiled, leaning forwards and kissing him on the nose before closing her eyes and throwing her head back laughing. Laughter she had heard from both he and her doll, laughter that rattled the soul much like her scream. She let her body float, taking her back to reality, back to the immortals that she would one day have to kill.

*   *   *

She sat on the lounge, watching the pictures on the television screen roll by even though she barely paid any attention to it. Her mind was drifting as it always did. Drifting to her world and this time she was able to control it. Her eyes open and the eye of her mind closed, a distance as she battled the darkness of her world. She could feel her body jolting but now could even control it. She knew when it was time to throw her hand under the water to stop the flames, she knew how everything worked.

She had been living in the Melbourne apartment for two months, with Drake and Xanthe. They had saved her again when she had died and taken her away from the cabin. At first she was angered but now realized the change had been good. It silenced Olivia for a while and there was something about the haunting apartment she loved. Really it didn't look haunting now but it had when she first arrived.

When she had arrived, the apartment had been destroyed. Sahna had taken ownership of it but wouldn't go there herself, nor Gabriel. Of course it looked normal from the outside but inside, walls had been crashed through. In the only bedroom, the bed had been turned over and there were chains on the bed poles. There had been blood everywhere and not a thing remained a whole object. Lounges had been torn apart and thrown over yet there wasn't any evidence to the type of people who had lived here.

Within two days Drake and Xanthe had fixed and tided everything up. They had bought new furniture and even sealed off half the large lounge room to make a second bedroom for her. Sahna and Gabriel still would not return but that was probably for the best, nor had she seen Xane. Aside from weird visions of him in her world, he hadn't approached her in this one. She knew he would find her again, Xanthe had said as long as she was living Xane would always find her, but for now, she was alone.

Of course Drake and Xanthe were there but they were acting like love sick teenagers and hiding in the bedroom. Or going for walks to have dinner and enjoy one another's company, she never went with them. When she was around them, they made her feel like a child and Xanthe was still distant from her but that was okay, she hated the witch. She could tolerate her but hated her. Xanthe was skeptical when Drake spent time with her or when he refused to leave. Heidi smiled, Drake was as much hers as he was the witches and Xanthe hated it.

She was growing closer with Drake, every day she grew older. She loved him in so many different ways as she was sure he felt about her. She barely spoke to the witch or the female vampire but would occasionally talk to Gabriel when he called to see how they were doing. The vampires had never found Xane. They had stayed in the cabin searching through everything. When one night while they were hunting the cabin was burnt to the ground, she knew it was Xane. After all, he had burnt her house down.

She had been sad that the cabin wasn't there to run back to, but that part of her life was over and it was time for a stronger one to begin. When Xanthe and Drake weren't home, she went hunting around the apartment to discover who had lived there, discover why the vampires wouldn't return. Gabriel wouldn't tell her anything only he lived there when he was mortal and had bought the place. She guessed through things Xanthe had let loose that Gabriel had also died there.

The only time the vampire had said any more was when she had found a beautiful ring. It was white gold with an emerald in the middle and a crest of diamonds on the sides. She had asked him if he knew about it and he had admitted to buying it. Heidi had guessed that this was where the woman he loved had lived and the ring was hers. It made her respect the vampire more for everything he had told her wasn't just to get close and figure her out, it was the truth. He had said she could keep the ring and she had promised only until she saw him again then he could have it back.

Green was not her color and she didn't wear a lot of jewelry only the necklace Xane had given her. She didn't even have her ears pierced. But it was beautiful and she did wear it on her middle finger, she would protect it for him. She doubted he would ever ask for it back but as long as he knew he could.

She jolted again and felt the tingling rushing down her arms towards her hands. Sighing, Heidi moved from the lounge into the kitchen where she held her hands under the water, calming her body. She heard Drake and Xanthe return from lunch, the witch walked into the lounge room. Glancing at her over the sink, before spinning on her heels and walking to the bedroom.

Drake came in moving behind her and hugging her back, Heidi rested her head against his chest waiting for him to speak but he didn't. He had so much going on in his head but she wasn't the one to hear his thoughts anymore, he knew things she didn't. Things Xanthe wanted to hide from her but she would make Drake crack soon, she always won in the end. He kissed her cheek then moved into the lounge room falling in front of the television.

She glanced over her shoulder, feeling her forbidden feelings growing stronger. He was so strong now, so centered and attractive, her body yearned for him to want her but it was wrong and he would never want a girl when he had the beautiful powerful witch. Heidi shut off the water, moving through the lounge room and into her room. She fell on the bed, pulling the blankets high over her head to block out the light.

Olivia was making her tired again, she slept more than any normal person did and when she was awake, she had excess energy. She couldn't fight the spirit when she made her sleep or sick, Olivia was always afraid that food was poisoned no matter how many times she would scream at her that it wasn't.

Nevertheless she didn't mind all the sleep, it made her days shorter and the world easier to face. Heidi closed her eyes, leaving her body in the hands of a nineteenth century spirit while her soul vacated to her world. Time to clean up the aftermath of the storm, clean within the silent eye before the second burst hit.

* * *

She ran through the woods, tree branches cutting her arms and slicing open her legs but she could not stop. Behind her she could hear the thunder of the dogs searching the woods for any intruders. Behind the dogs were the hunters, to gloat when the kill was over. But she had outsmarted the dogs several times before and she could do it again. She just had to get to the stream, roll in the mud and climb the trees. The dogs couldn't find her then.

She hurried down the hill to the stream where she dropped into the mud. Her ribs ached with the movement but nothing would stop her from being free. She would do whatever she had to, to remain this way. After she was covered in the mud, she climbed the nearest tallest tree, laying across the branches, watching the ground for the dogs. Of course her stepfather would be the one leading the pack. He always had since she had escaped but she wouldn't give him the satisfaction of seeing her defeated.

He had taken everything from her, ruined her life and if it was the last thing she did, she would kill him. Kill all the hunters for what they stood for, kill all of them for what they had accepted and done. They were weak. If they were really as strong as they believed, they would be fighting in the war, fighting for their people, but they weren't good enough, they were weak.

The dogs grew closer, Olivia adjusted herself in the tree, relaxing and staying as still as possible. The dogs ran past, leaving her unnoticed and a few minutes after, the hunters stepped out next to the stream. Puffing and panting, exhausted, they glanced around the stream, their rifles in their hands before continuing after the dogs. They were gone, after a few more minutes she couldn't even hear them.

Olivia smiled, draping her body over the thick branches, getting ready to sleep, to gain more energy. She had survived another day. She had fooled them for another few hours. Every day that passed they grew less determined, they were starting to think that she had left or already died but no, she was waiting to kill them. She would not die until every one of them was dead. She smiled. Yes, once all of them were dead, she would be truly free.

*   *   *

He stood in the center of the lounge room after the two women had gone to bed. He had pushed aside the lounge and anything else which would get in his way while he trained. Leaving him with plenty of room to move about and keep up his strength. He loved this time at night, where he would be alone to practice, the only thing he found useful from the hunters. Where he would think, harbor his anger and prepare for the war that was about to come. Though things were good now, he knew it was only the calm before the storm and when the storm came, he wanted to be ready.

He took his stances, stretching then thrusting out his leg followed by his sword. Flip the blade through his fingers without cutting himself and thrusting it back through the air. His focus on the patience of his stance then the discipline of his movements, he was getting good at this. He stretched out and sliced the sword through the air. Then brought it back to guard his body and out with all the strength he could dominant. Then again, thrusting, stepping back and forth, in the dance of death until he was exhausted.

He slid the sword under the lounge, walking into the kitchen panting. His body was drenched in sweat. He paced back and forth trying to catch his breath before taking a long drink of water. The drink was refreshing. It even made him consider going back into the lounge room and training some more. But that would be desperate, he had done enough for tonight, it was just as bad to overdo it then not doing it at all.

"I should stay out here more if that's the performance I would see." Xanthe spoke from the lounge room doorway.

Drake glanced over to the beautiful woman and smiled, he didn't realize she was watching and didn't mind that she had been. "Next time I'll give you a little more of a show," he teased.

Xanthe grinned, she walked into the room, wrapping her arms around his waist and resting her head on his chest. "I can't wait until tomorrow. How about you bring that sword of yours into the room now," she whispered.

He couldn't stop the smile spreading across his lips. He kissed the top of her head. Before she could speak, he scooped her up into his arms, she giggled, throwing her long hair back. He walked behind the lounge, kicking his toe under, sliding the sword out, then quickly hitting the hilt which snapped it up in the air. He caught the blade without cutting himself, handing it to his lover. He had practiced getting the sword from beneath the lounge many times but not with someone in his arms before. Xanthe laughed, holding the sword out in the direction of the bedroom.

In the bedroom, he dropped Xanthe onto the bed, crawling over her. She was laughing and when she did, her eyes sparkled. Some of the furniture lifted in the room, spinning around them. Drake laughed, kissing her and tearing open her shirt as she was trying to do to him. How he wished he was powerful like her, how he wished he could return to her world and be with her forever.

She managed to get his pants to his knees but he had already got her in her underwear. The two of them were laughing rolling over one another, with their belongings spinning faster and faster around them. Xanthe rolled him over onto his back straddling his waist when everything suddenly fell from the air. The witch snapped her head to their door. Drake followed her gaze, disappointed their fun had been interrupted.

At the door stood Heidi, she was dressed in a long purple night gown that was longer then her feet. Her head was twisted to one side and eyes wide as she stared back at them. One of her hands crept up the doorframe and the other slid on to her hip, she didn't look happy nor was she sad. Drake cleared his throat, grabbing Xanthe by the waist and putting her by his side. Xanthe quickly pulled the sheet over her body, leaning her head on his shoulder.

"What can I do for you girl?" he asked, in his usual manner trying not to change his tone because of Xanthe.

"I can't clear my head," she whispered, darting her eyes to the floor.

Drake sighed, when Heidi spoke like that, she was warning him that she couldn't control the voices in her head, couldn't control her powers and if she wasn't calmed then it all would get the best of her. He glanced at Xanthe who shook her head, he knew she didn't want the interruption but looking after Heidi was what had brought them together. He glanced back to the snow blonde girl at the door, surprised to see that it looked like she was crying.

"Try to go to sleep," Xanthe muttered.

Heidi snapped her eyes to the witch. "I tried, I can't."

Drake quickly pulled his pants on when he felt Xanthe's hand on his arm. "Drake she is fine, please let her go, stay with me," she whispered in his ear.

"I need you," Heidi whispered from the doorway, her eyes on Xanthe not on him.

He darted his eyes between them, both women he loved. Women who, with time, would not be in his life, who did he choose? If he chose Heidi, Xanthe would be disappointed but know he would be back with her in the morning and in some way understand. If he chose Xanthe, Heidi would hate him and every day they were already pulling apart. The logical choice was to choose Heidi, for choosing her meant he would still have both of them. He looked back at Xanthe who bowed her head slowly nodding, Drake smiled. He loved her for understanding.

"Come on, I'll take you back to bed," he whispered.

Heidi smiled, turning around and starting back to her room, Drake climbed from the bed doing up his pants and pulling on a shirt. Xanthe grabbed his wrist once Heidi had left the room, "Careful, sleep safely and I love you."

"I love you too, good night."

He left the room, walking out into the lounge room then to where Heidi was sitting on her bed. He stepped into the small room having the door slam behind him. Had she done that? No, she couldn't move objects, could she? He sat down on the bed, pulling her into his arms and pulling the blanket over them. He kissed her cheek but he had to stop at that, for if he dared he may place kisses all over her body. She rested her head back into her chest, her eyes closed and small body curled into a ball.

"The voices stop when your arms are around me," she whispered.

"If that were the case I'd never let go," he whispered, knowing that she would have a witty comment to snap back. Probably even throw him out of her room and not talk to anyone for a week. That was normally the case when he let down his guard and showed her his feelings.

"Then don't," she whispered.

Her breaths slowed and her body fell still, she was asleep. Drake wrapped his arms tighter around her. He couldn't believe she hadn't got mad, no insanity, no games just simply open to be loved. He sat up on the bed, rolling her over to look into her face. She was growing more and more beautiful, still wickedly childlike but with a soul holding power greater than a witch. It wouldn't be much longer before he wouldn't even be able to hide his desires from Xanthe.

"I love you Heidi," he whispered.

He slowly bent down while she was asleep and pressed his lips to hers. Quickly moving back afterwards but she did not wake so he cupped her face, kissing her again. Trying to remember to hold back, trying to not love her for the woman she was. He had to force himself to see her as a child or he would say something she shouldn't hear. Besides, he loved Xanthe. Could one truly love two women at the same time? He sighed, for at least one more year, she could be his. He knew about the prophecy and knew about the other women but for now there was no one but them.

* * *

She lay in bed listening to Xanthe and Drake arguing in the kitchen. She couldn't hear what it was about but didn't have to guess that it was about her. She pulled the blankets over her head for the morning sun through the window was bright and she needed to escape this argument, needed to sleep her seventeenth birthday away. She snapped the blankets back, yes, that was right. She was seventeen today, three years had passed since the supernatural had invaded her life.

She was seventeen, she wasn't a kid anymore. She was a woman, a woman who still acted like a child. She would never grow up living in this environment, her teenage years were almost over and she had never got to experience them. And soon she would become a woman, she was sure she would not experience that either. It seemed like everything moved around her, the world outside changed however she didn't know. She was trapped in an imaginary world where her body aged but her mind didn't.

She sighed, listening to Xanthe yelling something and the front door slam, she was gone. Heidi climbed out of bed, wrapping her cream robe around her body. Xanthe had bought her all sorts of clothes and girly things when they had got here then burnt all her nighties.

At first she had been really upset but now enjoyed the more grown up clothes and the fresh feeling they left as they sat upon her skin. She never put on the jewelry or wore the rings and then there was the makeup, which she didn't even know how to use. She barely ever did her hair, unless Xanthe came into the room and did it for her. Even then she would tear it straight out before the witch had reached the door.

She stepped from the bedroom, glancing around the living area to find Drake, he wasn't there. Had he left with Xanthe? She walked out into the front hall leaning her head towards the bathroom, no sound. Her eyes then darted to the shut bedroom door, to his bedroom. She walked towards the door, tapping lightly.

"Xanthe not now, my day is as planned so either join me on my terms or I'll see you tonight," he spat. She had never heard Drake sound so cold.

"It's Heidi," she whispered. She could feel Olivia waking up in her head, feel the spirit stirring, she hadn't felt her for a while. At least Olivia didn't torment her as much. But today she could feel a fire within her mind, please don't let anything go wrong today, she silently begged.

She opened the door, leaning against the frame. Drake smiled at her, patting the bed beside him. She wasted no time in coming to his side and leaning her head against his shoulder. It was so different from where they had come. She wouldn't even talk to him let alone touch him, now here they were, sitting side by side. Each had lost everything they once had. Now all that was left was each other and she didn't want to let it go. Without thinking about it, she lent up kissing his cheek. Drake smiled, wrapping his arm around her, laughing.

"Look at us," he whispered.

"I was just thinking that," she answered.

Drake looked down to her, his smile widening. "I think this is the first time we've ever been on the same level, we have to celebrate."

"What did you have in mind?"

"Well I was thinking maybe we will get you out of this house, against Xanthe wishes, but who cares. We'll go to a movie, shopping, dinner or whatever you want. It's your birthday, you choose. What is the one thing you want, really want?"

Heidi bowed her head, pulling away from him, what did she want? She didn't care about the outside world, she didn't know it. She didn't care for food for Olivia was ready to make her sick anyway. She didn't want to die, didn't want anything but this all to stop, she wanted peace. Nothing but peace, no memories, no pain, just happiness in the end. But before all that she wanted to experience love, wanted someone to love her in return, wanted to be a woman before she died. And maybe as she had once dreamt, she wanted a daughter. But how could she explain that to Drake?

"What's wrong girl? Come on tell me what's on your mind, please, there must be something."

She took in a deep breath before turning and looking at him. "I want love. I want to experience a good side to love. I want to end the memories I have of men. I want to be a woman," she whispered, feeling immediately foolish. How could he understand that?

He looked shocked. She should have known he wouldn't understand, why had she told him the only sane thing within her? "You are a woman. You're beautiful, smart and brave. Why can't you see what I can? Is there anything else you want to do today?"

She shook her head, looking away, he really didn't understand. She couldn't even stand to be in the same room with him anymore. Without so much as an answer, she stood from the bed moving to the door. She would rather hide in her room then be patronized, no one understood her. She was stupid for thinking they ever could. She should listen to Olivia more by hiding in her room and sleeping. Dream her birthday away, for along with it would go any fantasies or expectations.

"I love you," he whispered.

Heidi opened the door keeping her back to him. He always said he loved her but he could never love her like he did Xanthe. "I love you too," she replied heartlessly.

"No. I really love you and if you wouldn't hate my afterwards, I would have thrown you on this bed a thousand times before and had you."

She spun around to him, what had he said? Drake sat on the bed shaking, his eyes glassy and his lip trembling. He wasn't lying, why hadn't he ever told her this before, why had she not noticed? Because love was always the furthest thing from her mind, how could anyone ever love her? She took a few steps closer to him. All she wanted was one kiss, one demonstration of love, would he allow that or more so, would Xanthe?

"What?!"

"I said I love you. I guess I always have and if being a woman is really what you want. You have me" he whispered, his face flushed.

"I couldn't, what about Xanthe?"

"Xanthe understands me, come here and look in my eyes, if you can tell me what you really want, without fear or hesitation. I'll do what you please. But if you can't, we are going out to lunch and that's the last this is ever spoken about, deal?"

Heidi nodded, walking back to the bed and standing in front of Drake, did she really want this? Was it Drake she wanted? A little bit, if she was honest with herself, but she didn't expect him to really allow this. Would he or was he calling her bluff? For the thing was, she wanted it and he was the only one she trusted to hold her. She looked into Drake's eyes staring for a few minutes. He smiled, placing his arms around her waist. She couldn't do it, not with him. She respected him to much and his relationship with Xanthe could be over. But as she stared deep to his eyes, she knew she loved him.

"I see hesitation," he whispered.

Heidi sighed, glancing to the floor. He was right she wasn't ready and it would be best if they just go to lunch. The outside world might distract her anyway. But why wasn't he rising from the bed and pulling her out the door? Did some part of him want this too? "Where do you want to take me to lunch?" she whispered.

Drake didn't answer, his hands ran up her back and before she could step away, he grabbed the back of her head, pressing his lips to hers. She froze, he was kissing her, really kissing her. He pulled her closer, kissing her and his hands running down her body, she didn't pull away. She leant into him, her fingers moving through his hair, she felt suddenly so hot. Drake threw her down on the bed beside him climbing over her, she felt a flutter of fear rise through her heart but she didn't betray it.

She lay back on the bed, trying to convince herself this was right, when it felt so wrong. In her head Olivia was giggling and trying to taunt her with the pain of sex but she wouldn't listen. She was still trying to comprehend that Drake was actually leaning over her, like she had seen him and Xanthe do so many times. She lay back, watching Drake strip off his shirt, her eyes widening as his abs flexed. Would she really dare to touch him? Drake leant down, pressing his lips to hers again, his hand running up her leg and trying to pull off her panties. It was all happening so fast?

After her underwear was off, he pulled up her dress and undid his own pants. It seemed his hands were everywhere at once, on her face, on her body and tearing off their clothes. She could barely keep up, all she could do was cancel the fear that was rising, this wasn't right. She couldn't do this to Drake or was it Drake doing this to her? She couldn't tell anymore. Drake lay her back for a minute, slowing down and pulling the pillows beneath her head.

"I want you. Do you want me?" he asked. His body on top of hers and his face so close.

"Yes," she whispered, breathless.

Drake smiled, he kissed her again then she felt his hardness between her legs, she gasped as he moved within her. She ground her teeth holding onto him as close as she could. Oh god they were having sex! He moved over her harder and faster, she dug her head into his chest, it hurt! Rape hurt and willingly having sex hurt, why were people so obsessed with this? She clung onto Drake hoping it would finish soon and she could just curl beside him. Drake started moving harder and faster, his hands grabbing her arms and holding them above her head, her wrists hurt.

"Drake stop, you're hurting me, please stop!" she cried.

He didn't stop. Heidi heard Olivia scream within her mind but she wouldn't let that panic her. She struggled against Drake and when he still didn't move, she dug her nails into his back. He growled, snapping his head up to her. Heidi screamed. Drake's eyes were completely black, his face twisted and his teeth jagged. Where was Drake? What had happened to him? She could barely think for Olivia was getting louder or was it she who was making all the noise.

"Get off me! Get off me!" she screamed.

"But why? This is what you wanted isn't it? To produce my child, to use the vessel and you did so well kitten. I nearly believed you myself." Xane's voice answered her.

She screamed again. "No, no this is not what I wanted. What have you done to Drake? Get away from me!"

Drake's face darkened and he pulled away from her. Heidi quickly tried scrambling away when hands grabbed the back of her head, slamming her face into the wall. Olivia screamed and she cried but there was nothing she could do. She fell from the bed to the floor. The world closing with darkness, the last thing she saw was the demon stepping out of Drake's body to have her. He had lied.

*   *   *

Someone was screaming, someone crying and a battle, she could hear them all. She kept her eyes closed, listening to the fight continue in the room. She didn't want to open them, didn't want to know who was losing. There were fingers running through her hair, delicate fingers, she didn't know who they belonged to, all she knew was that the person who was brushing her hair was afraid. What had happened?

"We have to get out of here, run straight through the door and don't look back. Don't watch him die. No mortal can win against an immortal."

"Oh god!" she cried, rolling over and clutching her stomach.

"Heidi? Heidi sweetheart open your eyes, come on dear I need to see that you're alright," Xanthe whispered in her ear.

She opened her eyes glancing up to the witch who had her wrapped in her arms. She moved closer to her, her nails digging into the woman's dress, Xanthe made no move to push away. She seemed to hold her just as tight, keeping her head against her breasts. Heidi knew she was trying to avoid her glancing at the fight behind her, the fight she could hear between Drake and Xane. Olivia was right, no mortal can win against an immortal though she couldn't run away. This was all her fault.

A part of her wanted to glance back and see what was happening but she knew that Xanthe would turn her head away. Besides she felt faint as it was, her body ached and she was sure she could feel the stickiness of blood over her leg. Still Drake was no match for Xane and if she didn't do something, the last person she cared about would die. What could she do? Drake probably didn't want to see her right now, how awful he must feel.

"*Run away! Get away from the demon, he has broken his promise to us,*" Olivia screamed again.

"Let me be," Heidi cried pressing her body against Xanthe's. The witch held her tight, why didn't she hate her? She had tried to take her lover away, they had slept together. She should hate her.

"*He promised he would never hurt you, this is the last time Heidi. Give back his gifts, his magic and run!*"

Heidi slowly raised her head, staring a few minutes at Xanthe before slowly turning. The witch didn't try and stop her but she did hold her hand, comforting her. The two men fought within the room, of course Xane was winning. He was in his demon form and leaning over the defeated slumped body of Drake. The hunter had collapsed against the drawers, he had cuts all over his body and his eyes were blood shot.

Oh god Xane was going to kill him! No matter how strong Drake was he couldn't keep fighting. Especially when his mind was focused elsewhere, when he was filled with panic and resentment. Where was his drive and discipline? He had been worn down from the hunter way now, all that was left was reality. A mere mortal trying to kill a powerful demon; impossible. Not even the witch he loved could help him, no one could.

And Olivia was right again, she couldn't go to Drake and she couldn't side with Xane any longer. He had disappointed her for the last time, he had promised never to hurt her. Then he had let others hurt her and when there was no one else to play with her, he hurt her himself. She should have known Xane was never really gone, he was waiting until she would do as he planned, let someone in and then he would take over. She was dying again and no one was going to help her this time. He didn't love her, probably never had.

She moved away from Xanthe, sliding back against the head of the bed, pulling the blankets around her shaking body. Why wasn't the witch helping her lover? Drake was going to die and he wouldn't have even affected Xane, the demon thought this was fun. But when she looked into his face, he wasn't happy, he was frustrated and scared. This was all too confusing, everything was confusing. Some birthday this was, her birthdays were curses, the best thing to do was escape.

She closed her eyes, forcing her soul away from this world and into her own. She stood on the gravel beach, her eyes darting around the stormy earth, around the mini tornados hovering over the field of thorns. There was something different. The caves were no longer open mouths to hell, they had been sealed over. Two even had trees attempting to grow on them. She stared at them, how beautiful it was to see some beauty she had created in this world still existed.

"You can't be here," someone spoke behind her.

Heidi turned around, dropping her head to one side and flicking her tongue followed by a smile, Olivia. It was strange to see the spirit whole and to see her looking real without trying to kill her. Olivia sat down on the gravel in a long white gown, her hair beautifully styled on her head tied with flowers. Heidi sat down also noticing she had on a long black gown and her hair waved in the breeze, they were so different but could look so alike.

"And why not? This is my world not yours Olivia. Why are you here? To convince me to run away again? Well I don't care, I'm staying here. I can't return and see Drake die, I can't face Xane. I can't run like you did, there are no woods to shelter me."

"I know," the spirit sighed, glancing around at the thundering storm above them. She raised her hand and the clouds started to dissipate. Heidi smiled in amazement, for the first time in a long while she could see the beautiful blue sky. "If we do our own thing the world falls apart, if we work together we can fix it. Don't you see Heidi, we are two parts of the same soul and our joint decision will resolve. You are the tormented being and I am your shadow of innocence."

Heidi dropped her head to the other side, staring at the spirit. She could be right, after all she had been right about most things and she was tired of all this. Tired of Xane's games, tired of sharing Drake's love and worrying about his death. Tired of the supernatural trying to guide her life and tired of . . . of everything."

"So let's end it, take hold of our own destiny and end it," Olivia whispered, her eyes gleaming.

Heidi smiled, flicking her tongue on the roof of her mouth again. "Yes, then no one can bother, no more fighting over something that isn't there."

"It will all be over, no memories, peace."

"Peace," Heidi repeated.

"Return and take hold of your own destiny."

Heidi grinned, snapping her head back to the spirit. Yes, take hold of her destiny. No one would be in her life when she didn't want them there, the spirits smile faded. Before she could move, Heidi jumped from the ground snapping her fingers and causing the spirit to rise from the ground. She laughed, spinning her wrist round and round before flicking her hand so that the spirit screamed and disappeared. Olivia was gone, gone back to her own time. No one would be in her life if they weren't welcome.

"Time to take hold," Heidi laughed, closing her eyes and reopening back in Drake's room in the Melbourne apartment.

Drake had risen to his feet, fighting Xane who blocked every strike. Xanthe was over against the wall, holding Drake's sword waiting for the right time to give it back to him. Though Drake didn't seem to need it, he seemed to be enjoying hitting the demon with his fists. Heidi lent back, no longer feeling any pain and most of all, she couldn't feel Olivia. She had won. She was free and taking control of her own destiny, her own death. She glanced back around the room, everyone was distracted. Good, this was her chance.

When no one had glanced her way in few minutes and everyone was still alive, Heidi stood on the bed. With one quick movement she jumped off the bed and ran as fast as she could to the window, before anyone could react she jumped through it. The glass shattered around her body but she didn't care. She would soon be dead and all this confusion would be over.

But Drake and Xane had reacted faster than she had expected. Drake ran to the window sweeping his arms down to grab her but missed. Xane copied but it wasn't his arms that dove for her, it was his wings and they missed. Missed her body but caught hold of her neck, dragging their claws through the back of her neck, sliding through her shoulders and neck. He yelled as Drake and Xanthe screamed, but she felt nothing, nothing but a rush of air. Nothing but freedom and finally her peace of mind, her own destiny.

* * *

He dropped his body onto the lounge, sighing. He hated it when they fought but there was only one thing they shared completely differed opinions on and that was Heidi. The fast becoming woman in the room next to the lounge room was seventeen today. That meant there was one more year before they had to find a way to put her in prison then release them all. But Xanthe clashed with Heidi and she wanted to send Heidi in there now, while Xane wasn't around to kill her first.

He knew Xanthe had a point when she said that Heidi could be so angered and bad that if she was caught even at seventeen, she would be tried as an adult and put with the other three but what if it didn't work? After all Heidi killed without getting caught and she wasn't going to go to prison willingly. Besides one more year would guarantee she went with the others and he wasn't ready to loose Heidi yet. Xanthe knew that which was why she was even more angered.

He wasn't ready to have Heidi out of his life for when she went to prison and they freed the other women, his journey was over. Xanthe and the two vampires would take the women to their world where they would fight the war, where they would end Xane's rein and he would be stuck here. Never to see Heidi again, never to be apart of the war. He was only involved in the lead up then left here, but there wasn't anything left for him here now. He wasn't ready for it to end yet. He wanted to keep Heidi just a little longer, he understood the risk but this was the only selfish thing he asked. And he wanted to keep Xanthe with him, was love so selfish?

He glanced back to the witch who had bowed her head over the sink. What was running through her head? Did she understand his reasons for why he did what he did? He could tell she was trying to calm herself, as was he. He didn't want to fight with her, he loved her. Drake stood from the lounge walking into the kitchen where he wrapped his arms around her. To his surprise she pushed him away, spinning around to glare at him, he didn't want this. If it meant that much to her, he would do what she wanted just to make her happy, could he really do that?

"What are you going to do today then? What are you going to do for another year with her Drake? She only grows stronger and more beautiful, the curse will soon be at hand and mortals won't be able to keep away from her. We can't keep her locked in here for another year but to let her out means Xane will find her."

"I don't want her like that, you know that Xanthe. I was thinking about taking her for a day out, she's been stuck in one place for too long."

"No. She leaves here without my presence around her and Xane will find her, this time he won't be so lenient and she will die."

"It's her birthday, she needs some happiness. I'll order take out then give her a day to remember. Come on we don't have to do this," he said grabbing her hands and forcing her to look at him. "Stay with us and see the girl I see."

"I need to go for a walk. Do what you want with her just don't leave the apartment and Drake, don't be so trusting of her."

Xanthe stormed out of the lounge room and into the front hall. Drake followed her just as angered. "Don't lecture me witch, you should trust her a little more. You put so much faith into her soul yet you hate her so much, how can you hate her and expect her to save your world?" he spat.

Xanthe slammed the door, not even bothering with a reply. He was right and this time he had won their argument. He turned, heading into their room and slamming the door behind him to make a point to the still aware witch. He was her lover not some company she could order about and most of all, he was mortal. In ways he may be weaker than her but that didn't mean her values were any stronger than his.

He flopped onto the bed, staring at the roof and trying to calm down. Soon he would go wake up Heidi and give her a wonderful birthday. He would go against the witch's orders and take her out for the day. Really, he would do anything she wanted to see a smile on her face. It had been so long since he had seen her smile, even an evil grin. This apartment was surrounded by unhappiness, it wasn't fair. He wanted so badly for her to smile, for her to feel her age and enjoy life. He wanted the same for himself. Xanthe made him happy but it would all soon end and he couldn't escape that. He sat up just about to go out when there was a knock on his door, he sighed, falling back down.

"Xanthe not now, my day is as planned so either join me on my terms or I'll see you tonight!" he spat. He was not willing to go for another round of fighting but he would have loved the witch to join them, to see what he did.

"It's Heidi," the timid voice replied.

Heidi! What was she doing awake? Oh no, she hadn't heard him and Xanthe fighting had she? Before he could tell her to come in, the door opened. She lent against the frame like she always did, glancing around the room then to him. Oh god, she was more beautiful every time he looked at her. He felt it as Xanthe had warned, love as well as lust. Her large eyes seemed to stare through him and her long snow blonde hair that flowed passed her waist was hypnotizing. She looked like a ghost standing there in her black night gown, hair flowing and skin appearing more pale.

He quickly smiled so he didn't worry her, patting the bed beside him. With no hesitation, she stepped into the room sitting against him, her head on his shoulder, perfect. Her body was so small but so soft, pure. He couldn't believe she was thirteen when he first had met her, shy and fearful, always hiding so she didn't get hurt. Now a beautiful seventeen year old, still the same girl but instead of hiding she spoke her thoughts and had a power so strong no one could harm her or go unharmed.

They both had come so far and in strange ways, their lives swept around one another's. He could never get her out of his head when he was away from her and according to Gabriel, she was the same. She was always accusing a spirit named Olivia of producing his image, it never was there, but that meant she was thinking about him. The voices in her head seemed to be less recurring when he was around. He never quite knew what went on in there. He didn't know if she was happy or sad, or content, she seemed lost in a world she couldn't understand.

"Look at us," he whispered, half to himself and half to her. He wished she would speak with him; tell him what she saw, what she felt. What Xane meant to her. All he ever got was silence, not a hateful silence he received as her counselor but desire not to worry him with her thoughts.

"I was just thinking that," she replied, still staring straight ahead. He smiled, she had never admitted to thinking anything to anyone else, never admitting to being human.

"I think this is the first time we've ever been on the same level. We have to celebrate," he declared.

"What did you have in mind?"

Why did she always sound so tired? She slept so much. Why did it always sound like she no longer cared? "Well I was thinking, maybe, we will get you out of this house, against Xanthe's wishes, but who cares. We'll go to a movie, shopping, dinner or whatever you want. It's your birthday, you choose. What is the one thing you want, really want?" he asked, dying to do anything to see her smile.

Heidi bowed her head, pulling away from him. She was so serious, what was going on in that head? Her lips were pursed and she stared at the floor lost in thought. A sudden flicker went through his mind where he saw himself kissing those full lips, he shook the thought away. Now was not the time to let his feelings grow stronger, just because she wasn't verbally attacking him.

He sighed, she had gone into one of her trances, there was no getting her back now and of all days to do this. But when he glanced at her again, he swore he saw a twinkle of tears in her eyes. Perhaps there was something alive in her and maybe he could bring it to the surface.

"What's wrong girl? Come on tell me what's on your mind, please, there must be something."

Taking in a deep breath, she slowly spoke to him. "I want love. I want to experience a good side of love. I want to end the memories I have of men. I want to be a woman."

He froze, had she really said what he thought she had? Did she really feel like that? The only thing she wanted was love but that was the one thing he couldn't give her. Not that he didn't love her for oh god, did he love her, but because he couldn't prove it to her. He couldn't fulfill her, couldn't hold her in his arms or kiss her, no matter how much he wanted to. She was not his to take and besides that couldn't be what she really wanted. Once upon a time she would have killed anyone that touched her.

Maybe that was it. Like she had said, she had only experienced bad things with love. She had never had someone love her, someone want to be inside of her, not out of desire, but because they wanted to be so close to her. It calmed him in a way because he had thought Xane had already taken her, maybe he didn't have that strong a hold on her after all. Her head was filled with everything bad, nothing good. He had to make her feel better, there was no way he would have sex with her but he could try to convince her she was beautiful and that there may be one day when another man would feel the same. How could people not love her?

"You are a woman. You're beautiful, smart and brave. Why can't you see what I can? Is there anything else you want to do today?"

She shook her head, standing from the bed and heading for the door, nothing. All she wanted was for someone to love her, to let her know and to do one thing that most other girls her age did. Did she want it from him? She couldn't love him, could she? Drake bowed his head, if he took her and she became upset, he would never forgive himself but what if she wanted it? Would he do it? What about Xanthe?

Xanthe, he loved as much as Heidi, however in two different ways, both lustful and love of the heart, yet he was committed to one and the other he couldn't be free with. Xanthe he loved with all his soul, he wanted nothing more than to have the powerful woman in his live but they were equals. While Heidi was different, yes he loved her, cared for her but she would never be his and while he was infatuated with her, he would never be free.

Xanthe had warned him over and over again, she loved him and he might loose her. What the hell! He was loosing her anyway and their priority was Heidi. The girl was about to walk through that door and when she did her soul would become more distant. He had to do it for them, he did love her, Xanthe would understand. It was a matter of did Heidi love him enough not to kill him?

"I love you," he whispered, just as she opened the door.

She kept her back to him. "I love you too." She didn't believe him, didn't understand what he was trying to tell her, she had said it so heartlessly.

"No. I really love you and if you wouldn't hate me afterwards I would have thrown you on this bed and had you a thousand times before." He couldn't believe he had just said that to her, he hadn't been thinking. But maybe that was it, he had spoken what was truly on his mind and now that she knew, what was she going to do to him?

"What!?" she asked, spinning around. He was shaking but when he looked in her face, he didn't see anger, only confusion.

"I said I love you. I guess I always have and if being a woman is really what you want, without fear or hesitation. I'll do what you please. But if you can't, we are going out for lunch and that's the last this is ever spoken about, deal?"

She nodded, slowly approaching the bed and coming to stand in front of him. What did he do? He slowly raised his arms, wrapping them around her waist. Her body was so tiny compared to Xanthe's, so soft. It felt strange to touch her knowing what he wanted to do to her and that it could be possible. He waited to see if she moved away before he made another move.

She made no move to run away but she didn't make a move to kiss him either. He felt his heart sink, slightly surprised by his disappointment. Was he really upset that she didn't kiss him? Not because she would want him but because he wouldn't get to kiss her back, wouldn't get to pull her body into his and feel those soft breasts against his chest.

"I see hesitation," he whispered, giving her the chance to pull away.

She sighed, darting her eyes to the floor, it was over before it had even begun. He should have been happy, should have been overjoyed for Xanthe but he wasn't. He still wanted to kiss her, wanted her to want him.

"Where do you want to go for lunch?" she whispered.

Was she trying to get out of this? The look on her face told him otherwise, she looked disappointed too. Then it occurred to him that she wouldn't naturally make the first move. One, she didn't know how to and two, she had been searching him to see if he really wanted her. Well he did and he would sort things out with Xanthe later. Heidi was here right now and he wouldn't let her slip away in the night, he couldn't lose her.

He ran his hands up her back and behind her head, pulling her face to his, pressing his lips against hers. He kissed her as hard and passionately as he could and he felt her body fall into his. Her hands ran though his hair as she let his mouth guide hers. Even if he wanted to stop, he couldn't. All his passion was coming out, all the love and all the lust he had been warned about. But how could he have stayed away? She was so perfect, so in need of love. He threw her backwards on the bed, climbing over her, she looked a little confused but not afraid.

He took off his shirt still kissing her, his body slowly leaning down over hers so he could reach beneath the silk dress and pull off her panties. He tried not to go too fast but his body shook, he wanted her. He then ran his hands back up her legs, cherishing every part of her soft skin. He took off his own pants.

He kissed her again and again, his hands sliding all over her. No matter how many times he tried to slow it down, he couldn't. He wanted her, wanted to be inside of her. He wanted to touch every part of her. He was trembling so badly but managed to slow, pulling a pillow under her head to make her more comfortable.

"I want you. Do you want me?" he whispered, feeling like a teenager.

Her eyes were wide and her lips open, she was so beautiful he nearly couldn't wait for a reply. "Yes," she finally whispered.

He smiled, with her permission he pushed himself within her. A small gasp escaped her lips. Was she not expecting him to really have her? But oh how he wanted her. He kissed her again and moved himself over her, his hands flying around her body, he was going too fast but he couldn't help himself. He had to slow it down for he might scare her, but it was good. It was so good and she was so precious, pressing her head into his chest and holding onto him, he loved her.

Something moved in the shadows of the window, his eyes caught it briefly but he couldn't dwell on it. Not even if it was Xanthe, the witch would understand. If she didn't, she should have never left him home alone with Heidi. She had known this would happen, she had warned him about it enough. He moved faster, his passion growing stronger, his heart fluttering.

The darkness in the corner of his eye was moving closer. What the hell was it? He couldn't focus on it, no, look at what he really wanted, look at her. As he stared at her, she started to fade from his eyes. His stomach heaved, he was going to be sick, he felt faint and most of all, he felt exhilarating strength. His body moved faster and he heard her screams. What was happening? All he could see was blackness, all he could hear were cries. He couldn't even fell his body move.

"*She is mine!*"

*   *   *

"Drake! Drake! Oh no. Get off her Xane! You want to fight, then fight me!" he heard Xanthe scream.

"And what would be the fun in that when I can fight you any time?" he heard another voice answer, the voice in his head. The voice he hadn't heard in so many years. The demon!

"You can't do this! What do you want with her? She's a child, she's weaker than the other three."

"Oh you're so wrong. Just because she doesn't jump when told, does not mean she is weaker. As you know she is the powerful one this time, she is the strongest my dear witch."

"You've always had a weakness for her, its sick."

Drake stirred, he could feel hands on his face, his head laying on someone's lap, Xanthe. He opened his eyes, glancing to the witch. She flashed him a quick smile before resuming her face of anger. Drake glanced to where she was looking, to Xane. What had happened? Xane stood on the other side of the room, his arms folded across his chest and fiery eyes glaring at Xanthe. Behind him on the floor lay Heidi, all he could see were naked legs, a mass of snow blonde hair and blood. Oh god, had he killed her? What had happened!

He tried to rise but his body ached, Xanthe rested her hands on his shoulders placing a kiss on his cheek. She knew what had happened but she didn't hate him, he knew she would understand. Only the problem was he didn't quite know if he could forgive himself for what had happened. Slowly he sat up, his only thought was getting to Heidi but when he moved for her, Xane lent down and struck him, sending him to the other side of the room. Xanthe snapped to her feet to block the second blow but the demon grabbed her arm, throwing her behind him.

That action worked in their favor for Xanthe grabbed Heidi. He was surprised that she had. He almost believed that Xanthe truly hated Heidi and if Xane gave her the reason, Heidi would die, she wouldn't move to save her. But she had and she had pulled the girl onto the bed, wrapping a towel around her body, rocking her against her body. What a wonderful woman he loved, a woman that could look after a girl her lover had just slept with but that didn't matter anymore. What mattered was Xane was here and was going to kill them all if he didn't do something.

He bent his backwards and used the energy to snap to his feet, his hand snapped to his side, no sword. His sword was out in the lounge room again, he had no weapon. But it wouldn't stop him, his bare hands would do. He would do whatever he could to kill the man although it was impossible, he wouldn't back down.

Growling, he charged at the demon and hit him over the head with his fists. The demon was knocked backwards more with surprise than with force. He shook his head then smiled. Yes, he wanted this fight, he had got what he came here to get now he would end it with a fight. The demon smiled, cracking his fists and striking out at Drake. Drake ducked his first attack but Xane was quicker than he anticipated and was knocked back down with the second.

Xanthe gasped, which drove him harder to get up and fight for them. Xanthe was immortal and would never die but this bastard would make her life miserable if he didn't fight. He jumped to his feet charging again, the demon met his force, the two of them battling, fist to fist and block against block. Their strength was equaled or was Xane just toying with him?

As the thought passed his mind, the demon smiled, hitting his fist up and smashing Drake in the jaw. Drake flew through the air and fell against the chest of drawers, his head spinning. He couldn't focus his eyes, nor could he select any sounds for a few seconds before he heard the echo of laughter. How was he going to win this? He was already exhausted, this couldn't be it.

"Oh god!" came a gasp from the bed.

"Heidi? Heidi sweetheart open your eyes, come on dear. I need to see that you're alright," Xanthe cried.

Drake managed to snap his eyes to the bed, to where Heidi was huddled up against Xanthe. A sight he thought he would never see. Xanthe stroked her hair, holding her tight, her eyes catching Drake's. She was in bad shape. He didn't need to see her face to see that this was not going to end well. He had heard the pain in her cry, could hear the desperation in her breaths. She didn't know what had happened. But he didn't have to guess twice that Xane had used him to hurt her. That Xane had raped and beaten her.

It was all his fault! He should have known this would happen. After all Xanthe did and he had been too stubborn to listen. Now he was paying for his arrogance. One of the women he loved was laying half dead upon the lap of the other he adored. Could Xanthe ever really forgive him for this? He had ruined everything for himself, Heidi and the prophecy. His selfishness had put them all at risk and he still wasn't in the clear. He was still facing the demon and there was no sign that Heidi would live through this one.

He glanced back to Xanthe, who kept kissing Heidi's head and trying to wrap some clothes around her body. He could see the body beneath the sheets shaking. He could hear her soft moans, he wasn't able to watch it. Heidi cried another thing under her breath, she was crying and clutching Xanthe. Drake snapped his eyes back to Xane. The demon was also frozen, staring at her before glancing to him, letting him know if he made a move he would hit him down.

Suddenly Heidi pushed Xanthe away, sitting up and turning around to them, he gulped and he heard Xane gasp. Blood stained her hair and body, even through the sheets they could see she was torn up. Her eyes were black, nothing else but blackness and coming from her eyes were tears of blood. Her lips were white as her face and the light scar on her cheek had reopened. She didn't seem to notice that she was in pain.

Drake growled, why did the demon look so shocked? He had done this to her! He had torn her apart so that she now looked like a ghost child, something out of a horror film! He felt like he was going to be sick but more than that, he was angry. The fury raged through his veins, he had promised to destroy Xane. Warned him that it was personal and now it was more than personal. He snapped to his feet, charging again at the demon and this time hitting him, hitting him over and over again. Not even giving him the chance to defend himself or fight back.

In the corner of his eyes, he watched Heidi crawl back against the bed head, holding the sheet around her body, clutching it against her heart. She dropped her head to the side and her breathing slowed, she was vacant. Xanthe tried to wake her, was even yelling and shaking her but nothing woke her. While he was distracted, Xane hit him again. He was hideous in his demon form, maybe he would have better luck if he was a man. But still mortal form didn't change that this was what he was inside, a sick creature that fantasized in tearing poor innocent girls apart. But as he fought back, Xane seemed equally distracted. Why was the demon so shocked with Heidi's appearance?

"It's personal!" Drake hissed.

Xane smiled. "Yes it is," he laughed.

The demon threw his arm back, creating a fire ball in his hand. Drake glanced at his hand. Oh no, he was going to die! If he was hit with one of those, he wouldn't be able to fight it off. Xanthe screamed, diving from the bed between them. Xane growled vanishing the fire ball. He ran to the witch, the two of them striking one another and flying back against the opposite walls. When Xanthe was down, Drake made his move running for the demon, getting knocked back again but he would not give up.

He knew Xane could not kill Xanthe and she could not kill him. There was no worry of them fighting for they probably wouldn't bother, but he, he could fight. He ran again, hitting at the demon's head but kicking his leg so that he fell and on his way down he slammed his head down into his knee. He glanced back at Xanthe who was fine, leaning against the door. Then to Heidi who had come back, her empty eyes darting between them, could she see through that blackness?

Xane rose to his feet and grabbed his shoulder throwing him backwards into the floor. Drake shook his head, looking at Xanthe who screamed his name, pointing. The demon grabbed him by the shoulder pulling him up but that wasn't what Xanthe was screaming at, it was Heidi. The two glanced at the girl who had stood on the bed, naked, her body covered in blood. Her long hair sticking to her body and those blood stained eyes staring right through them.

Before they could do anything, she jumped to the floor, running. He had never seen her move so fast. She ran towards the window and jumped, kicking her legs out smashing through the glass. Xanthe screamed again, he even thought he heard a cry from Xane.

Drake hit Xane in the face running to the window, he threw his arms out, glass sliding into his torso but he couldn't care. He swept his arms down missing her, the demon reached out too and missed. Then his wings dove after her, why was he trying to save her? Hadn't this day been all to kill her?

His wings also missed other than the claws. Was it on purpose or did he forget about the claws? For Drake sure hadn't. The claws grabbed hold of her back but weren't strong enough to hold her. Heidi kept falling and the claws sliced through her shoulders and neck. Blood sprayed everywhere and her eyes rolled backwards, she fell. Xane disappeared and Drake didn't wait to watch her hit the ground, he ran from the room. He only had boxers on but that wasn't on his mind.

He ran out of the apartment and down the six flights of stairs to the car park, Xanthe on his heels. It was the middle of the day but luckily for them no one was home during the day. Everyone was at work and the car park was hidden from view of the street. He ran out onto the cement, stopping in his tracks, Xane was already down there. He was leaning over Heidi's body. Heidi was still alive, barely but still gasping, staring straight up with those black eyes. Xanthe grabbed his shoulder.

"Stop, he will kill you out of anger, he won't her. She's already dead," Xanthe whispered.

Drake took a few steps forward, listening to what the demon had to say to his girl. "I'm sorry, my kitten. It wasn't meant to end like this, I . . . I"

"You promised you would never hurt me, your promise is broken."

With one broken arm, Heidi moved it from the ground snatching the necklace from her neck. She dropped it into his hand. Her breathing slowing as did the gasps coming from her neck. Xane bent his head over her, was he crying? The demon rolled his fingers around the treasured necklace. Drake took another step forward, he would kill him now. But Xanthe held him back again, shaking her head and watching, was she sad? Why did she care if the demon cried? What did she know that she hadn't told him?

Xane shook his head, reaching his hands over Heidi, forming a glow over her body. This time Xanthe pushed past him, standing before Xane. "No, Xane you can't. Every time you use the healing powers of a witch, a witch will die. She is dead, this is what you wanted, let it be. You can't kill one of our kind," she warned.

"Let us hope it is you then," he muttered. He raised his hands over her body creating a glow around her, Drake held Xanthe's hand. He didn't understand this. He wasn't sure what he had to do. "I can only heal her from the fall. Everything I have done will still be here."

"She will still die. You may fix her bones but you have sliced her throat, broken her spirit and torn her body apart. You have killed a witch for nothing!" she screamed.

Xane turned to her, smiling at the two of them, blowing a kiss to Heidi then he disappeared. Xanthe growled, running to Heidi and feeling her pulse before running towards the apartment building.

"Wait! What is happening? What do I do?" Drake cried.

"Stay with her, she is alive, for now. I'm going upstairs to call an ambulance then Sahna and Gabriel. You stay with her, if it's anyone she needs, it's you."

Drake watched Xanthe run off. He turned back to Heidi in shock. There was a flicker of light within her heart. Maybe doctors could help her, maybe they could keep her alive. Everything would be alright, he had to tell himself this or else all hope would be lost. Everything they had worked for would be destroyed and most of all Xane would still live. He was even more confused about the demon now that he had watched him.

Why had Xane healed her? And the necklace, he knew the tales of the other three and the evil charms from James. They had tried everything to get rid of those necklaces except for the most obvious thing, give it back. He was scared and amazed. His eyes drifted over Heidi. Xanthe was wrong, he wasn't the best thing for her right now. He hated himself for what had happened and was sure she would hate him too.

He ran over to the tiny body slammed in the car park, wrapping his arms under it and lifting her onto his lap. He kissed her check and as he did the blood disappeared from her eyes. He smiled, holding her close, maybe for the last time but if that was so, he would never let her go. He glanced back up to the smashed window, waiting for the ambulance, waiting for hope.

CHAPTER NINETEEN

All she could hear was the slow and constant sound of beeping, it grew faster and louder. Her breathing was hard and her body tight. She snapped open her eyes. Hospital, she was in hospital again, she knew one when she saw one. How had she got there? She was supposed to be dead, that was how Olivia and herself had planned it, dead. Olivia, where was Olivia, she couldn't feel her presence. She had to get out of here, had to die. She had hurt Xane by handing back his gift and now she could end her own pain.

She glanced to the machine by her side keeping her alive. There were seven tubs from it to her. She looked away, no one else was in the room; good she was alone, she thought. Now it was time to die. But she couldn't move. She was strapped to the bed and the machines. Heidi sighed, relaxing back into the pillows. It hurt to move right now anyway. As soon as they let her free, she would jump out of the window, again.

Xane wouldn't return for her any time soon, he thought she was dead. Besides it would only be another fight, this time between him and her, she hated him. He had ruined everything, he had promised never to hurt her and he had. He had hurt her and those she loved, speaking of Xanthe and Drake, where were they? Where they okay? Had Xane tried to kill them after her or had they run away? She needed Drake here, needed to tell him it was okay. It wasn't his fault it was hers, she needed him. And she didn't care if Xanthe was there too.

Her eyes snapped back to the hospital window, it was dark. Was it the night of her birthday or another, she no longer knew. She was so tired, she needed to sleep but as she rested her head against the pillows, someone knocked on the door. She glanced over to Gabriel. When had he come? Gabriel entered the room closing the door behind him. He smiled slowly walking to her side and sitting down, his hand wrapping around hers.

"Hello sweetheart, heard there was a full on fight. Sorry I missed it," he joked.

She smiled and then tried to ask where everyone else was but nothing came out, Gabriel's smile faded.

"It's okay sweetheart, don't try to talk, rest. Xane has gone. Drake needed some good stitches. He's fine, pretty strong for a mortal. Xanthe is good, a little afraid for your wellbeing but good. It's been two weeks since the incident, Sahna and I are here in the night and Xanthe and Drake through the day. We are all here to help you. I know you feel pretty shit at the moment but I promise you'll get better, Xanthe will help you," he whispered.

Heidi shook her head, it wasn't going to be okay. She couldn't forget her life. It would never be okay. She looked down at her body, she could barely see anything through all the bandages and sheets. But something did catch her attention, the emerald ring. She moved her fingers flicking it off her finger and catching it in her palm, glancing to Gabriel. He stared at the ring, his eyes flashed with tears, mortality. However he didn't move to take the ring, he still couldn't deal with it.

Gabriel lent forward placing a kiss on her head and rose from the chair. "You can keep it sweetheart." He grabbed the ring from her palm slipping it back on her finger, quickly.

She shook her head, it wasn't hers, it was his or more so, Angelica's.

"I'll cut you a deal. Keep it unless you find its rightful owner, okay? Now I'll go find a nurse and be back soon, rest," he said leaving.

Heidi shook her head, her brow crossed, wasn't the rightful owner dead? Isn't this what it was all about? That Xane killed three important souls and somehow the fourth was her. They had all come to her to save her life and fight Xane. Why did she always feel like she didn't know the whole story?

The door swung closed behind Gabriel. Heidi tried to take a deep breath but it hurt her throat, everything hurt. Why weren't the drugs they were pumping into her stopping the pain? She was so angry, felt so betrayed. She slowly raised her hand, aiming it at the window, focusing all her anger but nothing happened, no fire, no power, no voices. She was an average mortal, nothing more. She was alone, completely alone and nothing anyone did could save her from that. Not even Xane, oh how she hated him now. If there was a way for her to destroy him like he had her life, she would.

*   *   *

She was dying, she had been dying for a long time now. But no matter how hard she tried to survive, she couldn't through the winter without shelter. She had to do the worst thing she could and go home, death no longer scared her. The hunters could do what they wished with her just as long as she got to see her mother's possessions one last time. To touch things that belonged to her and feel love before death dragged her away.

She walked through the woods, her arms wrapping around her body as the snow fell. It was sad to her that people killed one another in wars, that there was so much hate when mother nature could take care of every one of them should she choose. She was far more lethal than any riffle. Olivia sighed, but mother nature wasn't enough to rely on for dealing with her stepfather.

She moved the tree branches from her face. Already she couldn't feel her fingers or her feet. The coldness had already reached her heart. The only thing warm within her was the rage of retribution. Silent vows that they would die before she did. All hunters of every kind, those who hunted for food, those for women, demons and those who hunted war, they all had to die. This world didn't need them and their twisted ideas of justice.

As she got closer to the village, she broke into a run, running through the last tree line and into the clearing. Across the road she could see her house, her run-down home. It was so different since she had left it seven months ago. However she couldn't think of that at this moment, she had to concentrate on getting inside and to her room. Taking in a deep breath, Olivia dashed across the road and into her home. She slammed the door behind her; silence.

Her stepfather was out, she could tell that already or he would be on top of her in a flash. But where was he and why had he destroyed her home? She walked upstairs to her room, slowly opening the door and peering in at the way she had left it. Only one thing had changed, there was a man sitting on her bed. Olivia stepped into the room closing the door behind her. It was he, the boy that had changed into a man in an instant. The devil, what was he doing here? Slowly, she approached the bed, sitting down beside him.

"Why are you here?" she asked, staring out the window as he was.

"Waiting for you to return," he whispered.

"Why?"

"We're friends remember?"

"Were friends, besides I'm not here to stay only to get my vengeance."

He turned to her smiling, fiery eyes staring into hers, who was he? Olivia dropped her head to the side, waiting for him to answer her, waiting for him to instruct her otherwise or try to hurt her as every other man would. But he did neither of these, he smiled then jumped down to the floor, kneeling in front of her. His large strong hands wrapping around hers. He kissed her thin hands, without taking his eyes from her, not so much as a blink.

"What is your vengeance?" he asked softly. Yes, he was the devil but she had never expected the devils curse to be so alluring.

Olivia smiled, dropping her head towards him. "To rid the world of the hunters."

His smile widened. "So if death is what your peace is, let me help you. I can create a veil of darkness for you to hide your wrath under."

Olivia lent forward wrapping her arms around his neck, he was her friend. "Together we are stronger than the hunters and they will receive their justice." If trusting the devil was the only way to get what she wanted, then so be it.

* * *

He was exhausted, he had been sitting with her for forty hours and no matter how much anyone tried to convince him to go home he wouldn't. He couldn't leave her, if she woke again, he needed to be there. It had been nearly two days since she had woken for the first time in two weeks but after she fell back asleep, that was it. They hadn't got so much as a peep out of her. Although the monitor was steady, her breathing struggled but her heart was strong.

It was night, soon Sahna and Gabriel would be here, trying to get him to leave. Maybe tonight he would. Not because he wanted too but because Xanthe was asleep on his lap. She was so tired, she also couldn't leave Heidi. She didn't trust the doctors to keep her alive. The doctors couldn't tell them if she was going to be alright. Gabriel had said when Heidi had awoken, she couldn't speak but the doctors argued with that. Of course he believed the vampire. He knew she probably would never talk again, no medicine could fix what Xane had done.

They had come so close to the end, so close to having Heidi with the other women and the war truly beginning. He didn't care if Heidi and Xanthe left him now, he wanted the demon dead. Xanthe had promised to return for him after but who knew how long the war could last, it had already been going for ten years. He had promised to wait for her, and he would, he would wait for her until the day he died. That's how love was. You were willing to sacrifice your life for the one who would love you in return.

He licked his lips, his mouth was so dry, he needed water. Drake glanced down to Xanthe who was still asleep on his lap. Very carefully he lifted her head and sat her up in the chair before standing. Behind him, she stood, he knew as soon as he moved her, she would wake. He glanced over his shoulder smiling, when he saw her stretch out her arms and yawn.

"I'm going to get some water, do you want some too?" he asked her.

"Yes thank you, I'll come with you. Heidi will be fine for a few minutes, besides Sahna and Gabriel will be here soon."

He nodded, linking his arm through hers and walking out of the room. They watched as a nurse entered the room after them, another round of observation. They turned down the hall, heading to the elevators where it would take them down to the cafeteria. While he was down there he might as well get some food too, he had barely eaten in two days. He held Xanthe's hand as they traveled down the elevator, she pressed her body against his, staring up into his eyes. It was getting harder to let go of her every day.

They sat down in the cafeteria with a sandwich between them and two bottles of water. But once they sat down neither moved for their drinks or food, they watched the people around them. Mothers holding their children with fear that they might die, should they let go. Father's lecturing their sons, parents in tears, children in tears, teenagers harboring guilt and then them.

A couple, one a witch and the other a hunter, two people who had seen more than anyone in this world could understand. They didn't belong here. And even when Xanthe returned to her own world, he knew too much to be apart of this one.

"What did you mean when you warned Xane of healing Heidi?" he asked, he couldn't look at her, didn't want to see the disappointment in her eyes for they hadn't spoken of the day.

Xanthe sighed. "Only witches and the gods have the power to heal and should a strong demon, such as Xane choose to heal, he has to drain the power of a witch to do it. It's not that I wasn't going to heal her myself but by Xane doing it, he drew all the power from a witch, including her immortality and she dies. If I was to heal her, I would weaken but in time gain back strength. I would have healed her Drake."

"I know. Speaking about the day I just want to say . . ."

"Don't, it doesn't matter now, what has been done is done. I knew it would happen as much as my heart didn't want to believe it, I knew it would. It wasn't your fault, just greater powers at hand. I love you Drake. You may have had her body and heart for a short while but you will always have my soul and soon her path would take her to a greater destiny."

"I love you," he whispered, glancing down at his watch. "We should head back soon. Sahna and Gabriel will be wondering what we have done with ourselves."

Xanthe grabbed his hand, the two of them rising from the table and heading back upstairs to Heidi's room. Yes, he had decided tonight he would go home and while Heidi was looked after, he would have the witch. Love her until there was no more love to offer. He could feel she wanted him. They walked down the hall, Xanthe slowing when they came to Heidi's door, the door was opened. No nurse ever left it open, neither did they.

They looked into the room to see Heidi sitting up in the bed, awake, her eyes staring straight ahead. They were black again, with blood tears slowly descending down her cheeks, her lips trembled. She was in a trance. Drake rushed into the room, running to the bed and grabbing her in his arms, she was so cold and the beeping had stopped. How could she be sitting up like that but dead? Who had turned off the machines, she was dying, shouldn't an alarm be set off for the nurses?

Xanthe hurried into the room and around to the other side of the bed where the plug was, she turned it back on. The hospital room's door slammed behind them, Drake and Xanthe whipped around to Xane. The demon was in his mortal form, leaning against the back of the door, smiling at them. Drake felt every hair on his body stand on end, every slice of energy returned ready for action. He was a little shocked to see the demon though. He had thought that last time had been it for a while. Even the supernatural living with him, were convinced of this.

"Get out of here! You've done enough Xane, she is practically, dead are you happy?" Xanthe yelled, lunging her body over Heidi's. She placed her hands on Heidi's head and the girl fell back down in the bed, her eyes close, she was asleep again.

"Yes, I am, this has been kind of fun but there just one more thing Xanthe, do you know what it is? I'll tell you, while you play in this world, who protects your people? Who is their savior?" he laughed.

"My people are strong. You cannot destroy our hope."

"Maybe not I, but EnDarla can."

Xanthe gasped, her eyes darting back and forth. Xane burst out into another fit of laughter. He lent forward knocking Drake out of the road as he grabbed Xanthe around the neck. "There is a prophecy and it is nearly completed, enjoy your final days on this earth Xane for soon it will come to an end," the witch spat.

Xane glared at her dropping her body to the floor. "Yes I heard rumors of a prophecy but what does it matter, nothing like that could be true. Besides when I find the vampire who started it, she will pay for the confusion. I offer you a trade, Heidi's life for your people. I will return within twenty-four hours. If she is dead then your people are released if not, I will kill her anyway and one by one the land of the light will perish in your name. As for Sahna, there is no way for you to save her."

Drake glared at him, how could he be so heartless? How could he do this to them? He glanced at Xanthe who was staring at Heidi. She wasn't considering it, was she? If a few of her people had to die for them to destroy Xane then it was a sacrifice she had to make. The demon suddenly laughed again, moving for the door when Drake flexed his arms charging after him.

"Drake no!" Xanthe cried. He paused as Xane left the room before turning to his lover.

"Your not . . ."

"Of course not. There is no other way for him to die without her alive. I have to go back and sort it out though, very soon anyway. Don't go after him, Sahna and Gabriel will be fine, Sahna is strong."

He shook his head. "Not this time Xanthe. I can't let him get away this time."

Before she could cry out again, he ran from the room. He heard her scream behind him, a cry of fear and sadness but it wouldn't stop him. He charged passed the nurses and doctors, his eyes focused on the demon briskly walking through the hospital unnoticed. He followed him out onto the quiet night street, where he ran up behind him ready to hit. Before he could, Xane whipped around knocking him down first, nothing would stop him today.

Xane then continued on, focused on something at the end of the street, he saw who it was, Sahna. The two vampires walked side by side before Sahna caught sight of Xane, her hands rising to Gabriel's arm. Drake climbed to his feet, running as fast as he could after the demon. Gabriel pushed Sahna and she broke into a run. He stood between her and the demon but when Xane passed him, he threw the vampire aside like he was nothing. He was only focused on Sahna, Drake kept running, he didn't know how he would save her but he would try.

"You can't kill me! Not someone from Decsendra!" Sahna screamed.

"I don't care for laws anymore!"

Drake ran harder. He could hear Xanthe on the street, screaming for him to stop. She was running for Gabriel. Sahna didn't turn back again but Xane had slowed, he burst into his demon form, hissing as a ball of flames emerged from his hand. He threw one at the vampire, missing her and then a second. Drake didn't stop, he ran past the demon, kicking him in the back of his knees and knocking him down. Then without stopping, he ran for the vampire, to cover her from the flames around her.

Sahna was screaming trying to move away from the flames, they wouldn't kill her but would burn her. Drake ripped off his shirt throwing it on the flames and jumping until they were out. The vampire smiled at him, running towards his arms when she froze, her mouth open in a silent scream, Drake snapped his head over his shoulder. Xane had risen again and aimed two bursts of power for the vampire. They were too close for her to escape them, Sahna screamed, Xanthe screamed and he jumped.

Drake threw himself in front of the vampire, kicking her down and then was hit in the back with such a force that he was thrown several meters away. He glanced back at the vampire. She was lying on the ground crying, down the road Gabriel was running for her and Xanthe to him. Xane was laughing walking to him. He passed the vampire without a flinch and grabbed him by the hair, lifting him to stare into those fiery pits of hell. Drake felt his body convulsing but other than that he felt no pain.

"That will do," Xane laughed, dropping him then disappearing in a burst of lightning.

Drake coughed, trying to say something witty back but nothing came to mind and he couldn't get the words out. He glanced up as Xanthe dropped to his side crying, she kissed his cheeks, her fingers digging into his arms. He smiled, lifting his hand to brush her hair from her face, she was so beautiful, his love, his life.

She was the only image he wanted in his head, he closed his eyes. He needed to rest and all he saw behind the darkness of his eyelids was her. The powerful witch who fought for a greater good, then behind her a shadow, the shadow of innocence—Heidi.

*   *   *

She opened her eyes to the beautiful land of her world. It had changed, all the darkness had left, leaving its original state, leaving the world she had created. Crystal blue seas that met a perfect sky, fluffy heart shaped clouds that gave way for the golden sun to kiss the sparkling sand. Beside the sand were the field of flowers, full and the color of rainbows that lapped to the mountains. Yes, the strong, safe mountains in the distance, covered in pine trees that pointed towards the sky.

She smiled, walking along the beach, it was beautiful, this was her safe beautiful land and she never wanted to leave it. It had become the land she loved once more, it was no longer tainted with evil. Did that mean the evil was no longer within her or she just found a way to push past it? Heidi smiled, she didn't care what the reason was, she was back and she was safe.

Slowly, she walked from the sand to the field, she walked across the flowers, being careful if some thorns decided to hide within them, nothing. It was safe, everything was perfect. She walked the trail up to the base of the mountains. They were so much taller from where she stood than on the beach. When she glanced back to the beach, she couldn't even see it. But it didn't matter, she needed to find where the opening was, when there had been caves.

She ran her hand along the trees moving through them, her mind darting to Olivia, and the visions she received from the spirit. When something sparkling on the ground caught her eyes. She stepped to the little diamond, staring down at it but would not pick it up. She looked up further and there was another diamond, then another. She followed the path until they came to a stop in front of an old burnt tree. A tree unlike all the others, then at the base of the tree was her doll, was EnDarla.

Heidi glared at the doll, this world wasn't at peace, it was still tainted. Everything she touched remained ruined. She picked up the doll running her hands down its face to make it cry, when it didn't she slammed the head in the rock at her foot. The face shattered, blood stained the rock, Heidi smiled, throwing the doll away. She wouldn't be bothered by it again, this world had been her safe place and she would fight to keep it that way.

She closed her eyes reopening them in the hospital room, alone. She glanced out the window, night time. Shouldn't Sahna and Gabriel be here? Oh how badly she wanted to see Drake but she couldn't control the sleep the doctors kept her in and without the tubes she wouldn't live.

Outside of her room she could hear a fluster of voices, yells and then her door was thrown open with Sahna and Xanthe coming in. Sahna threw herself against the door, holding off the nurses, while Xanthe stepped up to her bed, the witch had been crying. Her hands trembled and tears stained her face, the vampire also looked fearful. What was going on? What had happened? She was scared, she wanted Drake.

"Drake is dead!" Xanthe answered, her unspoken thought.

Heidi stared at her to see if she was teasing or lying, she wasn't. She tried to not cry, tried to object but nothing would come out, her whole body shook. Sahna locked the door, moving away from it and grabbing Heidi's hand as Xanthe grabbed her other. Now it looked like the witch was going to crumble too, Heidi bowed her head. This couldn't be happening, not Drake. She couldn't loose him again, she never got to say sorry, never got to make it better. Oh god, not Drake!

"Xane killed him," Sahna continued, for Xanthe who was having trouble controlling her breathing.

"I have to tell you something Heidi." Xanthe interrupted, sitting beside her on the bed. Outside the door there was yelling and people trying to get in but the two immortals didn't seem to notice. "There is one way for Xane to die. There are four souls he hunts and each life, before the age of twenty, he kills then. But if the four souls walked the earth at the same time and band together, they would be strong enough to kill him. That time is now. We have trapped the other three women in prison here.

You have probably already heard us talk about them. We need you to go to them and then we can free all of you and take you back to Desendra.

"I will heal you from the pain Xane has caused, but you must get in jail. I know you have killed before but then you had powers and there is no way to prove it. You must do it again, kill in front of the police and, if you must, kill some of them too. Do anything to get with the other women and we will save you within a week. I know you somewhat love Xane but you must understand . . ."

Heidi hissed, shaking her head, trying to tell the witch that she understood and hated the demon. Xanthe smiled, nodding her head, she seemed so weak. She pushed Heidi back on the bed, leaning over her body and creating a bright light which sat on her chest. Heidi closed her eyes, feeling her body rising, feeling the tubes being ripped out and her body growing stronger. Her neck tightened but she could again breathe, all her skin seemed to tighten. The witch was healing her! She would have never thought she would live to have the witch heal her.

Once Xanthe had healed her, she fell from the bed to the floor, Sahna rushed to Xanthe, cradling her in her arms. She pulled a sword from her sash placing it on the bed, it was Drake's. His prized sword that Xane had destroyed his family with, the sword the hunter had planned for Xane. Heidi ran her fingers along the blade. She would honor him by using it to fulfill her destiny. She would do as Xanthe asked for him, she would help destroy Xane.

Besides, she belonged in prison and had she not met them, she would already be there. But she never thought that the other women were alive also, that the immortals had lied to the hunters. No wonder they panicked so much when James had tried to kill her. If her life is lost then so was all hope for them. A few weeks ago she would have found this amusing and even played with her life to panic them. But now, this was a fact to kill Xane and killing him was something she desperately wanted to do.

Then there were the other women. As much as she hated being surrounded by people, she would have to try her best to get along with them. Then something Gabriel had said came back to her. He had asked her to give the ring back to his love, now she understood. She understood all of the confusion and for his kindness, she would pass on the ring to its rightful owner. She would lead the other women through another world. In a way it would be good to met people like her, she was no longer alone.

"Who are you going to kill?" Sahna whispered, staring at her. It was one of the first times she had spoken with the vampire.

"Hunters," she replied, twisting her head to one side as her hand run up the blade.

"The demon hunters?"

"Yes, they abandoned Drake, they never wanted to help me like the other women, they tried to kill me. They are just as bad as the demons they hunt," she answered. She wasn't sure if it was Olivia speaking through her or the way she really felt. Olivia was gone. It was all her, the hunters had to pay, they never helped and if they did, it was only for their own gain. She had to make them aware that they were just as evil, and then once their spirits were destroyed, she would kill them.

"I know where their headquarters are in Melbourne. I will take you to them if you promise to spare one hunter, should he be in Australia."

Heidi snapped her head to Sahna. "You want me to kill them, why? You were one of them."

"Not these hunters. I was around in a different time, a time when the hunter had a soul. As you said they don't help the ones that need it, they are selfish with power but one is good hearted. His name is Tony, he is my cousin. Should he have known of you, this would have never happened, trust me on this."

"I'll do as you wish. Take me to the headquarters."

Sahna handed her a small piece of paper, she pulled the unconscious witch from her lap and stood up, holding out her hand. Heidi placed her hand in Sahna's and before she could contemplate what was going on, the vampire jumped out of the window. Really practically flew from the window then dashed across the surface, dragging her behind her. They dashed across the land so fast that mortal eyes couldn't see. Until they reached the outskirts of Melbourne, until they stood in front of a dome shaped mansion. Heidi took a few steps back trying to catch her breath, she felt dizzy but strong. Xanthe had healed her well.

"They are inside," Sahna whispered, looking over her shoulder, she wanted to get back to Xanthe.

"Okay. Go back to Xanthe and say thank you for me, then call the police. Tell them of murders out here and when they come I'll put up a show," she said with a smirk.

The vampire smiled, it was the first time they had ever got along and when she looked into Sahna's eyes she saw the regret, saw the guilt for not believing. But it didn't matter now. How was anyone supposed to believe in her when she hadn't herself but now she did. Now she could see what they saw, see what Drake did. She took a deep breath, holding the sword in front of her body, flicking her tongue on the roof of her mouth. The men inside deserved this.

"Tony, right?"

"Right. Good luck Heidi, we'll see one another soon."

The vampire dashed away before Heidi could mutter that she had a feeling they would never see one another again. She twisted her head to each side cracking her neck, before walking up the path. When she looked down at herself, she realized she was still in the hospital gown. Quickly she tore it apart, tying some of the white material around her breasts and some around her waist as a short jagged skirt. She smiled, it looked good, felt good for the moment and it was a good thing she had underwear on.

She took a few more steps to the front door. She wasn't sure how she was going to do this. Did they know about her? Know what had happened with James? How would she kill them? She wasn't as strong as a man and she didn't have her powers to back her up. She was just a mortal, as mortal as they were. She smiled, yes, they were all mortals and although she didn't have powers, she was strong and slightly evil. She could match everything they threw her way. And with that thought, she stepped to the door knocking, holding the sword behind her back.

The door was opened to a tall man with green eyes and long dark hair, he raised his eyebrow at her. His finger wrapped around the knife in his belt. She could peer past him into a large room, filled with weapons, technology and men, lots of men training. So this was where Drake had been, this was where they had trained him to die. She sneered but remembered she needed to catch them off guard, take advantage of her childlike looks and use it to her power. She pursed her lips and looked up to the strong man with sad eyes.

"Sorry sir but my name is Heidi and I was nearly killed by a demon. A man named Drake said I could find help here," she whimpered.

The man's eyes widened, he opened the door to let her through. All the men in the building stopped to look at her, some with curiosity, some with lust. She smiled sweetly, following the man who had answered the door over to some chairs. They would have been nearly fifteen men in the dome and four up on the balconies. The man who had answered the door walked to another and they all stood together, talking for a few minutes before another approached her.

"Why didn't Drake bring you himself?" the man asked.

"He was killed. If you can't help me then I should leave. I'm so scared," she cried.

With that comment, she had nearly twelve jump to her feet, all trying to calm her down. All offering comments to make her feel better, some speaking of the other women, some sad about Drake and one walked away. She glanced over the other men to the darker one, striding across the floor. He would have been in his early thirties, he was not that tall but a handsome man. With olive skin and dark eyes, she would guess him to be Indian. He watched her as he walked away, his head held low. He ran up the stairs and disappeared into a room.

Heidi snapped her eyes back to the men in front of her. "So who are you? What is this place?" she cried.

"We are demon hunters. We can help you as you can us, tell us what you know."

"Demon hunters? You hunt demons and you couldn't think of a better name to call yourselves?" she almost laughed and blew her cover, but it was pathetic if you thought about it. "Okay, well let me see, I know that not one of you helped Drake. I know that not one of you helped me and I know that this world doesn't need hunters as it doesn't need the immortals." She sneered, but the men were stupidly slow, they had no idea what was coming.

Heidi leapt to her feet, swinging the sword from behind her back and slicing off eleven heads. One of them got away. He ran through the dome to the stairs but she was faster, she ran up behind him, stabbing him through the back. She continued up the stairs, every man she came across, she demanded his name then ran him through. She ran into each room, destroy all the hunters had created. Then there was one room left, the room the Indian man had hid in, Heidi opened the door. The man sat on the bed, hugging a four year old boy in his arms. She pointed the sword to his neck.

"What is your name?" she demanded.

The child was crying but she was not weakened, she glared down the blade at the man. "My name is Tony," he answered.

She pulled the sword from his neck and pointed it at the child's. "Who is this?"

"This is Nathan, my son. Please spare him, if you have to kill me do it, I probably deserve to die with all I have failed to do but he, he knows nothing of this," the man begged. Heidi smiled, she could see why Sahna wanted to save him. He was strangely a good hunter, he wasn't one of them and she would stick to her word.

She lent down to his ear. "By thankful your blood runs through an immortal for she has saved you today," she whispered.

The man bowed his head, tears welling in his eyes. "Give Sahna my thanks," he whispered.

"How about you do it. I'm going to prison to save this pathetic world and another."

He looked to her, his eyes darting over her face. "Who are you?"

"I'm the fourth. Ruby, emerald, sapphire and me, the amethyst" she laughed, she didn't expect him to understand but it was funny to her.

"They are alive?"

"Yes, and they need me so we can fulfill our destiny, hah, I am a part of something bigger than this pitiful life," she said to herself.

The man smiled the brightest smile she had seen on a human face, "Good luck."

She dropped her head to one side, winking, then she ran from the room. Outside she could hear sirens. Good, Sahna had done as she asked. She glanced back up to the room. At least there was someone to speak of her, someone that knew. And truth be told, she kind of liked him, wished they could have met earlier. But never mind, all she wanted to do was destroy Xane, to shock him and run him through. She wanted to make him feel guilt and think twice before ever betraying her again.

The doors to the mansion were thrown open, seven cops ran in and she lent over the balcony laughing. She raised the sword in the air and licked it before the police. Some cringed and some grew more angered. They looked around the room, shocked that a small girl could have done such a thing and before they questioned whether she had. She jumped from the second story, landing swiftly on her feet and ran to them. Slicing Drake's sword through their bodies, it wasn't hard to kill them. They had never helped her and in her eyes, police were hunters too.

They screamed and she screamed her rage, swinging the sword with such skill she never thought she could possess. She ran towards them, running as many officers though as she could before one sounded the shot. Not that of a gun, but a taser, her body jolted and she was thrown to the ground, she smiled. It would be over soon, she would be free and in the company of those who were like her. It was now that her life truly began and this time, she would go into it with such strength no weapon could match.

CHAPTER TWENTY

She was in so much pain, she could barely move. She hunched over in the middle of the isolation cell, crying. She thought that she would never stop crying. The door opened and closed but she didn't look up, she didn't have to to know who it was. The doctor. She hadn't seen him in over two years yet here he was rushing to her side, trying to find what was hurting her so much. She wondered what he was thinking, what he knew. She wondered if he knew about Melinda or James.

She had been in prison for a week and everyday was filled with beatings and rape. She couldn't take it, so a few hours ago when the guards came close enough, she grabbed one of their tasers. She shocked each one of the six me then stabbed them to death with a fork. Although a crime like that was not unnoticed here, she was caught, beaten and thrown in isolation. She couldn't bear to be here, why had she come? What had possessed her to trust the immortals and send herself into hell when she could still be free. Free? She had never really known what freedom was.

Xanthe had probably been lying to her just so she could get rid of her. Making up some lie about prophecy and curses so that she got what she deserved. Maybe this was what she deserved. Though it didn't feel like anyone deserved this, no matter how bad they were. All bad people had hidden reasons why the hate grew within them. She had been tried as an adult and sent straight to the high security prison which she had aimed for, but now she was scared. She couldn't live with this abuse, this was not fair. Xanthe said she would be here by now to save her, she was stupid for believing.

Dr Dylan brushed her hair, looking over her body and fixing what he could but he couldn't help her. No one could help her now. He wrapped his arms around her, trying not to cry himself. He didn't want this for her, she could tell that. He must have been so shocked when he saw her here, nevertheless he wanted to help.

"Oh Heidi, oh poor sweet Heidi. It will all get better I promise sweetheart, please trust me, talk to me," he pleaded.

She cried harder. She couldn't contain all the years of pain anymore, all the grief. She screamed, so hard the walls seemed to shake around them. Dr Dylan threw his body over hers trying to calm her for he knew the guards wouldn't be away for long and they were very excited by her, especially since she had killed their fellow mates. They wanted to make her pay and what was disturbing, they enjoyed it. They should be behind these bars also.

She continued to scream, slamming her fist into the cement floor, crying out her pain. The doctor behind her didn't move from her side, he lent over her as if to protect her. He kissed her long hair and ran his fingers down her arms, he cried for her. But none of this would stop her, nothing would stop her. She had found a hell worse than being victim to Xane.

*   *   *

The scream rang through the long caged halls. It was the most painful scream she had ever heard. Even after all she had seen and heard it was the most painful scream. It made all the hairs on her body stand on end. It made her body shake with its harsh vibrations. Her body snapped up on the wooden plank bed, her topaz eyes darting out into the prison hall. Who was screaming? The cries were coming from the isolation cells. Her heart fell, the cries sounded like they were from a young girl but that was impossible, wasn't it?

A thunder of footsteps pounded from the other direction, probably the guards. She glared out as they passed, she hated them. She was lucky if she went a day without one of them trying to rape her or harm her. She wanted them to die and if she could, she would have done it herself. She threw her long golden blonde hair over her shoulder, waiting for the screaming to end, it didn't.

Pulling her knees to her chest, she huddled into the corner of the cell. She couldn't wait for this all to be over. Her life and this pain. She had been in prison for nearly four long years. All memories of her life on the outside were fading. Every day she woke up to looking at the cell walls, every night she fell asleep thinking about the cell.

When she had been caught, she had thought this wasn't real, after all nothing in her life had been. She had thought that somehow she would get out or die, but it was worse. She lived in here, seeing nothing but criminals and the guards that were worse than the people they kept captive. Of course she would die here but it wouldn't be for years. The only reason why she wasn't dead now was for some hope her daughters were in the outside world.

The last of the guards passed, all heading for isolation and then the doctor heading away from isolation. He stopped in front of her cell, his face shining with sweat and his hands shaking. She had seen him a number of times but never spoke to him. Why was he looking at her like that? The doctor moved up to her cell resting against the bars, his lips quivering. What was going on?

She stared at him but she didn't dare speak to him, never had. He waited half wanting to talk to her and half listening to the screams down the hall, then the yells. The guards were trying to shut the woman up but it sounded like she was putting up quite a fight. The doctor smiled secretly to himself, nodding as if he were about to burst into laughter. She crossed her eyebrows together curious.

"How are you feeling Claudia?" he suddenly asked, focusing on her again.

She remained silent, although she wanted to know what was going on, she wouldn't trust him to speak. The doctor's smile only grew wider as he nodded again, what was his deal?

"It will all get better soon, I promise."

With his strange remark, he turned and continued running down the hall. Claudia shook her long hair, well if that wasn't the strangest thing she had seen in here, she thought to herself. Why would he promise such a thing? She pulled the grey blanket over her legs holding herself tighter, hoping the screams would stop soon.

They were starting to hurt her, all her bones were aching. Claudia sighed, resting her head back against the wall, her fingers moving over the ruby necklace around her neck, her heart becoming numb again to her previous life. She let her mind drift over the doctors words. 'It will all get better soon,' she smiled, if only he was right.

*   *   *

Someone was screaming and they had been for a good few minutes, longer than she ever could. A few minutes after the shrill screams had started, a force of guards ran in the direction of the isolation room, she pitied the woman inside. She only knew too well what they could get away with doing in isolation. But the screams didn't stop. Then came a growl and yells from the men as they struggled to contain the one inside.

She had climbed out of her bed, hurrying to the bars and peering out but of course she could see nothing. She could hear footsteps coming her way, footsteps of one person and as he came into view, she saw the doctor. She had met him a few times but still didn't know his name. Most of the time he had helped her, she had been unconscious, due to the guards. Her emerald eyes stared at him, her fingers nervously playing with the ends of her long dark brown hair.

To her surprise, the doctor slowed as he came to her cell, his eyes staring in at her. She pursed her lips, waiting for him to mention the screams. It looked like he wanted to but as his mouth opened, there was a loud crunch echoing down the hall and the prison fell silent. She hoped they hadn't killed the woman, god knows it happened one too many times. She took a few steps away from the bars as the doctor took one closer.

"What happened? Who was screaming?" she asked, for some reason she didn't really feel threatened by him.

"A young woman was brought in for homicide. She's only seventeen and hasn't quite understood her consequences," he replied.

"Seventeen? Should she be in a juvenile center?"

"Not when you have done what she has. She was tried as an adult and now she has to pay but she'll be alright, I'll make sure of it."

She almost laughed crazily. "Are you kidding? It just sounded like they killed her."

"They haven't. She's a strong one. Go back to sleep, Angelica, everything will be alright. I have to get into the west wing," he said, looking back down the hall, his face crossed with sadness.

"The only reason you have hope is because you haven't been stuck in here for three years," she hissed, moving back to the bed.

The doctor snapped his eyes back to her, looking her up and down. "No, I have hope because I believe in hope. I believe the right will always work its way around. I promise you this, you'll see," he whispered, turning down the hall.

Angelica smirked, she didn't understand what he was talking about but it was amusing because he had no idea of the world she knew. And what was the funniest, it was like he was almost talking as if he knew she was innocent, well pretty much innocent. She let her body fall down on the bed. In two hours they would be woken up for breakfast but she couldn't go back to sleep now. Although the screaming had stopped, it was still ringing in her ears and she couldn't stop her mind from thinking, from starting to believe again.

* * *

Silence, she hated the silence. It meant that something was wrong and if it was on her end, it was most likely in the east wing. What could be going on? She sat back against the wall on the floor. Her hands running down her pregnant stomach, soon her baby would be born and she still didn't know how she was even pregnant.

It was nearly eight years ago when she lost her first child and had the surgery that would prevent her from ever having another baby. Yet here she was, in prison for two and half years and pregnant. The guards were scared to come near her because they all thought one of them had done it but she knew otherwise.

She could remember the dream like it was yesterday, she could remember the witch leaning over her body in the height of a storm. She remembered her whispering comforting words as she injected her with the sperm of her dead lover and magic. Magic to support and nurture an egg, creating a baby, spells to help it grow without a womb. She had been so happy but before she could speak to Xanthe, she was gone. No answers, only fading memories.

Though now that eight months had passed, she was scared for no one could have a baby in prison and her little treasure would be taken away from her. Her reminder of Leith would be placed in the arms of stranger and her child would grow to hate her because she was in prison. They wouldn't know of the pain, sacrifices or the love she had. It wouldn't know of the world she had seen, only the sheltered one it would be raised in. All of that saddened her but she had to fight, for as long as her baby was alive she would get it back.

She could hear women wolf whistling down the hall, someone was coming down it. She remained on the ground, waiting to see who passed, waiting for something else to think about. The doctor stopped in front of her cell, out of breath and his face reddened. He scrambled with his keys to unlock her door. What was he doing here? She wasn't due for a check up until tomorrow evening.

Dr Dylan undid the lock, hurrying into her cell. He ran to her on the floor, his hands first running along her belly before grabbing her hands. She gulped, what was he going to tell her? That the prophecy had been ruined? One of the girls had been killed or that something was going to happen to her baby? Dr Dylan took a few minutes to catch his breath, minutes that seemed like hours to her. His hands were shaking in hers and his eyes darted over her, she couldn't wait any longer.

"Dylan, what happened? Is it the baby?"

"Oh no Varela, your baby is fine. It's about the last woman. They found her. She's here in the east wing, probably unconscious now but nevertheless here. Tell me what to do and I will summon your witch for you all, so that she may set you free. I can always get you out of here if she doesn't come."

Varela smiled, her heart beating faster. She was here, finally, it took them long enough but finally all four souls walked the earth at the same time, all four souls will meet. Xane had better be wary because he was their first target. She could barely contain her excitement, freedom was so close. Maybe she would be out before she had her baby and could keep him with her.

"That's perfect. Don't worry about Xanthe, she'll be watching. What is she like? Do any of the others know?"

"Claudia and Angelica don't know, Heidi does. But there's a problem, Heidi is different, she is strong and powerful but uncooperative. She doesn't hate Xane the way you women do. Well from what I remember anyway. She will be hard to work with," he said nervously.

"I'm sure she's not that bad, I will help her," Varela answered.

"I'm not sure. She really has powers. I watched her shoot a cat with a fire ball from her hand. I heard her scream her pain, she was calling them from him. And when she was caught, she was in the demon hunter headquarters, she had killed them all, Varela. Everyone that had been there for you three girls, everyone that had lost just as much to this demon has been killed by her hand."

"Powers!" she was fascinated but now wasn't the time to think of that. She had been through too much and come too far to let the prophecy fade now. "You said she is strong. There is a reason she is the way she is. All of us are different and have opposite qualities, together we are unstoppable.

No matter how unlikely she may be, she is one of us and this is her fight too. Don't worry Dylan, I'll help her."

Dylan smiled squeezing her hand. He lent forward and kissed her check. "You have such strength Varela. I will do anything I can to help."

"Thank you."

He left and she let her body fall back against the wall once more, a smile on her lips. Now she had something different to think about, something exciting to anticipate. Everything was falling into place. Everything was now in Xanthe's hands. It would probably take her a few days to comprehend that she was going to be free. After she killed Xane she would come back and reward Dylan for everything he had done, for believing her.

Her baby kicked harder against her hands. "Hush little one. It will all be over soon. I will fight for our freedom and this generation has the chance to succeed. Hush now, it won't be long."

$$* \quad * \quad *$$

He was shaking with the vibrations of the magic running through his now immortal veins. Everything had changed and after it all, he was as he had thought, made for something more. He stood on the hill, overlooking the Melbourne high security prison, the prison Heidi had been sent to. She was only seventeen but with what she had done, she had been tried as an adult. Which worked out well for them and the prophecy. After all they nearly didn't even get her in there, but of all things, she had gone willingly.

The forth soul was now trapped with the other three women. He couldn't wait to get them out and met them. He knew most of their stories for Xanthe had told him, but to meet them and put faces to names, he couldn't wait. He also couldn't wait to go back to Xanthe's world and see it for what it was. To take the women there and play an important part of the war. He couldn't wait to see Xane defeated and see the shock on the demon's face when he sees that he is now one of them.

Drake smiled down at the prison, slowly turning around to his team, to his lover. Xanthe stood to the side also watching the prison, her eyes darting between it and the moon. To his left was Gabriel who looked more anxious than he did, the vampire lurked on a tree stump his muscles flexing. The vampire wanted a fight. Behind Gabriel stood Sahna who was pacing back and forth, cracking her neck and shaking her arms as if to shake away all the nerves, yes they were ready.

"When do we go and how?" Gabriel asked, directing the question at Xanthe.

Xanthe looked at Drake first before answering. "When the moon is high, very soon Gabriel. The plan is that no mortal is harmed unless harming the chosen ones. No mortal is to escape for this is their justice and no one is to know what we can do. Be discreet with your powers, each go to the woman you best know. Sahna to Claudia, Gabriel to Angelica, me to Varela and Drake for Heidi. They know and trust us so we can get them out faster. Once out, take them to the ocean, there I will build the portal and our new world will begin," she announced proudly.

"And you're sure Xane will not feel their presence before we get them there?" Sahna asked, twisting her fingers back, she was worried.

"Keep faith Sahna, our sense united will block theirs long enough to get to Desendra."

"Can we snack on anyone who deserves it?" Gabriel asked, with a smile. Sahna glanced back at her husband, smiling.

His questions sent shivers up Drake's spine. How could he be so open about feeding upon a mortal? But then they only fed on those who deserved to meet their justice anyway. He was glad he was not one of them, a vampire wouldn't suit him. He was glad that Xanthe had got to him first, that Xanthe loved him and made him a warlock. He still had no idea what being a warlock meant, or what he could do. But as soon as his lover was alone, she would teach him and he would make the powerful witch his wife.

"You don't have to get permission to eat Gabriel," the witch muttered.

"The moon has moved Xanthe," Sahna said, interrupting their silent thoughts. The four of them looked up to the moon that had shifted directly above the earth.

"Bless us Delitra," Xanthe whispered, starting down the hill.

Drake smiled, he had no idea who Delitra was but was fascinated. There was so much he didn't know, so much he would soon find out. He turned, being joined by Sahna and Gabriel, getting ready for the fight ahead.

Something suddenly blew hot air from behind them, the four turned around to the black portal. Xanthe screamed something but he couldn't hear her. The portal was too strong and before either of them could run from its power, they were sucked in. Sucked away from the mortal world, away from the prophecy and away from saving the women.

* * *

She was dead. He should be happy but he wasn't, he felt empty. He had made sure of the last woman's death and now he was rewarded with a hundred years of rest before one soul would be reborn and resurface again. It was a great achievement, it had been fun, so why did he feel so bad? Why did he hate himself so much? He could go back home, he could forget this world for a little while . . . he didn't even get to say goodbye and see them go.

He had one last desire before he returned to his world, he wanted to go to the highest peak in Melbourne and think of the girls, his girls. He wanted to make peace with who he had become before returning, after all they had all died in Melbourne, coincidence, maybe.

Maybe it was because each time they were reborn, they were smarter and stronger. Technologies had changed and they could track him easier and then there were the hunters always trying to find him, they were like an annoying fly. But he would kill them all soon enough, besides all their work had ended with no success.

Still, every time got harder to kill them and this time was the hardest yet. At one point they had come so close together but he had still won. They had all died, the first three a few months from each other then the last, his beloved Heidi three years later.

He materialized upon the hill, staring out over the ocean. The sea did make him feel calmer but only for a little while, for soon he would be home and his world was in a war. All thanks to Xanthe, who had started it years ago, if he ever saw her, she would pay. He would also make her pay for creating two immortals when it was forbidden, she would pay.

"Bless us Delitra."

He almost laughed. It was if thinking about her actually put her voice in his head. But wait, that was Xanthe's voice, he could suddenly sense her and the other hybrid pests. Xane smiled to himself, he walked around the side of the hill to one that looked down on a prison of some sort. So this was where they hid? He stepped behind a hill spying on the two vampires, the witch and Drake . . . fuck! She had made Drake too. He hated that man.

They were descending down the hill. He wasn't going to let them get away with this. If he was going back to his world then so were they, he wouldn't let Xanthe create an army of hybrids. He flicked his hand, creating a large portal behind them, his power excels nearly all of theirs, maybe just above Xanthe's he was stronger. The portal grew, grabbing hold of the immortals and pulled them to it.

Xane laughed, watching as Sahna was thrown through first, then Gabriel and Drake. As the portal caught hold of Xanthe, he stepped from behind the tree glaring at her. Her eyes widened with fear as she was ripped away. He clicked his fingers, snapping the portal shut then sealing it for good. He sealed all links to this world for a hundred years and with his order, he was materialized back to Desendra, back to his kingdom.

He stepped up to the open window of his stone kingdom. It was the time of the darkness, his time. The lava in the river bubbled and the dark sky was filled with shrieking griffins and harpy's, his guards. Xane spun around, his wings flying from his back and veiling him from the heated air as he walked down the winding stairs to his bedroom. Laughter and screams echoed the halls, none of which fazed him, it was time to rest. He had won this battle. Soon he would win the war of his world then begin the new creation. Xane smiled, this story had ended and soon his would begin.

EPILOGUE

She couldn't stay here any longer. Everyone she had ever known had betrayed her. Her mother, the hunters and now the devil she thought had been on her side. But he had lead her stepfather to her, he had whispered in his ear alerting the pathetic man to her presence in the house. They had a plan together and he had selfishly betrayed it, even the devil had to pay for his wrongs.

Though the devil was already dead, he could not be harmed nor killed so her only choice was to run away, again. Run from this life, run from the memories and run to a certain death. The devil had played his games and told her stepfather about her whereabouts, so then came the hunters. She found herself fleeing for her life in the darkness. Running with the truth flickering in her heart, that she was not going to survive this. They had won.

Strings of pain shot down her legs, causing her knees to become weak, forcing her to the ground. Her small body hit the ground, rolling over on the thick green grass. She closed her eyes, trying to hide the flood of tears. Rolling over on the grass, she tried to force away the pain, for her legs to again feel alive. No hope. Her life was over and she had to accept it, her only savior in her life had been Adrian and he had turned into the devil.

Her blonde wild hair fell over her pale face as she struggled. Her hands clutched at her stomach. She tried to call out but there was a dry lump in her throat, preventing any sound to escape her lips. Straightening her arms out, Olivia arched her back, peering around the clearing in the woods. The woods she had spent the last eight months of her life in before going home for a short while to be sent out here once more.

The pounding of hunting boots echoed through the forest floor, the sound of tall strong bodies brushing through the shrubs, cutting their way to their prey. Men's voices were bouncing off the tall evergreen, while villagers ran through the woods, hunting . . . hunting her. Oh she hated them, she had known this day would come, but knowing didn't make this fate any easier.

The hunters called death threats behind her. Her blood ran cold, her heart racing with fear striking her mind her soul. She could not run, could not move, she was left for the dead. What was happening? Her body screamed at her mind, tears flowing down her face, growing weaker with every passing second.

She gathered what strength she did have left to roll underneath the bushes, not far from her feet. Pulling the cover of the bushes over her head, she hid behind them. Inserting her fingers through the branches to created a hole which she could peer from waiting, watching.

The hunters were coming, she could still hear them calling and she knew this time that they would find her. This time she wanted them to find her. She couldn't live in this world anymore, couldn't bare the memories of her life or the betrayal from her friend. But really, what more had she expected from the devil? The hunters yelled more things her way, more curses. Her stepfather was probably enjoying every moment, after all this is what he had planned for.

The least she could do was scare them, give them exactly what they wanted. She could vacate her mind and visit her world one last time while letting her body move on its own. She had done it many times before but never willingly. Best to let it happen now then feel what they would do to her. Better not to see their shocked faces when they looked on the body of a possessed child. If only they knew it wasn't her, if they knew what her stepfather had done to her and her mother, would they still follow his command?

Unconscious of her actions, she rose to her feet, heading back into the center of the clearing. Her body moving as her mind fell blank but she remained standing. Her legs apart in an attack posture, her long white night gown shredded and falling around her ankles. Her dark eyes were wild, staring at the path she had come down not that long ago. Her snow blonde hair was wildly flapping in the breeze, whipping around her small body. "In the clearing!" a hunter directed. She smiled, good, they had found her.

Several cries echoed as the pounding of hunting boots pressed down the path, weapons rattling in their strong hands. Olivia twisted her head to one side, running one hand down her small body. She flicked her tongue over her teeth. In seconds the hunters burst into the clearing, knives and spears gripped tightly in their hands. The group of men, were at first taken aback by the sight of her, standing in the clearing, a crazed look about her.

Olivia listened to their curses and heard her voice answer them but swore she hadn't moved her lips. The hate in their eyes hurt her, how could they hate her so much? She was paying for something she had never done. She didn't do anything her stepfather had said she did, but now she would. Now she would fight and take a life. Now she would act the insane little girl he had called her for years.

The group cried out, rushing at her, their weapons held out in front of them. She remained where she was as the men drew closer. One man ran his spear past her, the blade clipping her arm. Another threw his knife embedding into her upper chest, next to her shoulder blade. Her body jolted with the impact. But she would not fall, they would not win, they were the enemy, not her.

The men smiled at her, blood trickling down her naked body, she smiled back, her head arching back. She flicked her tongue, causing a clicking sound on the roof of her mouth. Some of the hunters stopped, fear ripping through their eyes at the unholy sight. More of the hunting party turned, running back to the safety of their village.

Her stepfather threw his spear at her, his spear sliding past her head. The handle knocking her to the ground, her eyes starting to flicker back. The darkness that had settled in moments before had now ceased. The events played in front of her, coming to sight.

She stared down at her body in shock, she was naked, wounded and puzzled. How had this happened? Great amounts of pain flooded in, causing her to hunch to her side. She was already weakened by the poison but this was unbearable. She glanced over at the bushes, wondering how she had ended up in the clearing . . . the clearing that was holding the hunters.

She screamed, trying to cover her body with her hand, where was her night gown? The men were now smiling, their weapons once again raised as they crept in on her. Her stepfather leading them, she glared at him. How could he? Why were they doing this? Questions rolled through her crazy mind as she tried to scramble to the bushes. Tried to escape her unfairly written fate.

Someone grabbed her arm, pulling her from sight. She turned to her rescuer, a handsome man. He stood over her, handing her his long black cloak. His skin was as pale as hers. His hair as black as the cloak that had covered his toned body. He stood tall over her wounded body, a thin smile on his lips as his dark eyes twinkled with wonder. There was something about him, something familiar. Could it be the devil in a slightly different form?

The enchanting man scooped her up in his arms, running from the clearing to a small stream. Where he mopped the blood from her body, she watched his face as he cleaned her up. Why was he helping her when he had caused all this? His strong hands were soft and caring against her burning skin. She could see by his reaction that she was going to die.

"Farewell until next time, my sweet," he whispered. He lent forward taking the amethyst necklace from her neck, then he was gone.

Closing her eyes for what seemed like a few minutes. She was shocked to find that when she reopened them the devil was gone, replaced by the small group of hunters. Was it all a dream? What was going on in her head? All the voices and memories were driving her insane. The men were smiling as one by one they lent down by her small body. Each of the hunters took turns with having their way with her. She tried to scream, tried to fight but each time she moved some part of her body was sliced.

She glared up as her stepfather moved on top of her, his green eyes laughing into hers. Olivia winked, she would show them. She would show them what the devil looked like. Snapping her arm up, she flexed her fingers snatching the knife beside her, swinging it across his neck. He fell from her body dead.

One of the other men picked her up, slapping her to the ground once more, though she no longer felt any pain from her torn body. She darted her hands up at them in rage and gasped when every weapon from the ground shuddered then shot back into the bodies of their owners. Satisfied she closed her golden-brown eyes once more. She fell deeper and deeper into what seemed like a sleep. "*Farewell until next time.*"